Collector's Library

Collector's Library

BEST SHORT STORIES OF W. SOMERSET MAUGHAM

BEST SHORT STORIES OF W. SOMERSET MAUGHAM

Introduced by
NED HALLEY

Collector's Library

This edition published in 2011 by
Collector's Library
an imprint of CRW Publishing Limited
69 Gloucester Crescent, London NW1 7EG

ISBN 978 1 907360 34 3

Typeset in Great Britain by Antony Gray
Printed and bound in China by Imago

1

Contents

Introduction

Somerset Maugham's short stories are among the most accessible in all English literature. They are wonderfully easy to read. Maugham addresses the reader with a candour entirely his own. He is matter-of-fact in his depiction of character, direct in his handling of narrative. He does not play tricks or contrive surprise outcomes. But his people and his plots are nonetheless powerfully compelling. The lack of embellishment heightens both tension and credibility.

No other writer comes close to Maugham in this respect. How did he do it? A great part of the secret has to be his own life, which was long and extremely eventful. He harvested the experiences of his travels and acquaintanceships, his triumphs and his sorrows, with ruthless determination. Even though he was arguably the most celebrated, and certainly the best paid, writer of his day, he did not consider himself a serious creative force. 'I have small power of imagination,' he confessed, 'but an acute power of observation.'

William Somerset Maugham, always known in his circle as Willie, was born in Paris on 24 January 1874. His father, Robert Ormond Maugham, belonged to a family with a long pedigree in the legal profession and was the lawyer for the British Embassy. William was a late baby whose three elder brothers had already been sent away to English boarding schools, so his early upbringing was in effect that of an only child. But the happy years were ended by the death of his adored, artistic and socially accomplished mother Edith from tuberculosis, aged just forty-one, a week after the boy's eighth birthday. Two years later, his father succumbed to cancer.

Willie, who knew little of England and had French as his first language, was sent to live at the home of his late father's younger brother, Henry Maugham, the Vicar of Whitstable on the Kent coast. Henry Maugham and his German-born wife Sophie were childless, but seem not to have welcomed their new charge with any enthusiasm. The boy was promptly sent, as a boarder, to the King's School in Canterbury, just a few miles distant.

By his own account, Willie had a wretched time of it. He was below average height and to begin with spoke rather broken English. He was mocked on both accounts. He seems to have won little sympathy from his uncle, whose Christian calling did not inhibit his glacial snobbery and detachment. Sophie, downtrodden, ailing and homesick, proved no substitute for Willie's mourned mother (whose photograph he kept by his bed from this time and for all of his life) and he developed a disabling stammer which he never entirely shook off.

But such melancholic childhoods can translate into lives of energy and creativity. Willie endured the school until 1889, and after his sixteenth birthday in January of the following year refused to return. Abetted by Sophie, he was allowed to continue his education in Germany, at the esteemed and cosmopolitan university of Heidelberg, where he studied the German language and its literature, and found love.

His inamorato was John Ellingham Brooks, a

Cambridge-educated lawyer, talented musician, impecunious aesthete and conspicuous homosexual. Ten years older than Maugham, he introduced him not only to the love that dares not speak its name, but to the philosophical writings of figures such as Dutch theologian Spinoza and German pessimist Schopenhauer. Above all, Brooks encouraged his protégé to write. Maugham needed no second asking, and within the year had completed his first book, a biography of the German composer Giacomo Meyerbeer (1791–1864), a pioneer of grand opera whose reputation had been maliciously ruined by a jealous Richard Wagner.

Maugham and Brooks were to remain long-term friends, but after just a year at Heidelberg, the aspiring young writer was recalled to England. His uncle was anxious he should find a profession, but conceded Willie might not be as suited to the law as so many other Maughams had proved (one brother, later Viscount Maugham, rose to the Lord Chancellorship) and was content when, after a very short dalliance with accountancy, Willie enrolled at St Thomas's Hospital in Lambeth as a medical student. It is a testament to his forbearance and intellect that he stayed the five-year course. All along, in tandem with his medical studies, he observed and noted the character and circumstances of the patients, many in desperate straits, in his care. In 1897, he qualified as a doctor and published his first novel, *Liza of Lambeth*, a gritty tragedy of working-class lives and loves in the impoverished London borough. It drew unreservedly on the author's own experiences.

The book amply illustrated the powers of observation and ear for dialogue that were to be Maugham's hallmarks, and it sold strongly following favourable reviews. The handsome young doctor, writing with stark and spare realism – and plenty of drama – on themes of adultery and domestic violence set against the background of Queen Victoria's golden jubilee, became as famous overnight as he might very well have anticipated.

He quit medicine for ever, and set off for Seville in Spain to begin the writer's life he had so long imagined for himself. As a member of a homosexual milieu, he considered the Continent a far safer place for him. He was well aware that Oscar Wilde, sensationally convicted for sodomy in a British court two years earlier, had fled to France. But unlike Wilde, who died in miserable exile in 1900, Maugham was at liberty to come and go between his own home in London and those he subsequently rented in Spain, on Capri in southern Italy, and on the French Riviera. He wrote assiduously through the years leading up to the First World War, producing ten novels, at least as many plays, and a growing canon of short stories. He needed patience, because it was not until the sudden success of a 1907 play, *Lady Frederick*, that he repeated the éclat of *Liza of Lambeth*. Within a year, he had three more plays – all previously rejected by London managements – running in the West End. This is what made him famous as a writer in every genre. He suddenly became a major figure in literary and social circles.

Maugham is now largely forgotten as a playwright, but his novel of 1915, *Of Human Bondage*, immortalised him as a writer of fiction. This great work, with its title borrowed from the proposal in Spinoza's *Ethics* that we can escape enslavement to our passions by actively confronting them, is a closely autobiographical saga but also a touchingly philosophical tale. It established both Maugham's worldwide reputation and his technique of writing from life, basing characters and incidents on barely disguised episodes from his own experiences.

At the time he was completing *Of Human Bondage*, Maugham was serving with the Red Cross in France. At forty, he was past the age to enlist for armed service in the First World War and had volunteered as an ambulance driver. It was in France he met Gerald Haxton, the American adventurer who became his secretary and lover for the next thirty years. It was also in 1915 that two more extraordinary chapters in Maugham's life opened.

One was his recruitment by British Intelligence as a spy, first against German interests in Europe, and later, in 1917, against the Bolsheviks in Russia. The second was the birth of Maugham's only child, Liza, whom he had fathered with the socialite Syrie Wellcome, daughter of Irish philanthropist Dr Thomas Barnardo and wife of American pharmaceutical millionaire Henry Wellcome, who consequently divorced her. Maugham married Syrie in 1917. It was his only marriage, an incendiary one that ended in a bitter divorce a decade later, but by no means his only relationship with a woman. Maugham was sexually promiscuous, but equivocal about his orientation. 'Three quarters normal, one quarter queer,' he would quip, then concede that he might have it the wrong way round. He wrote endlessly, even racily, about heterosexual love but never at all about homosexual love.

In 1916, between espionage missions, Maugham

embarked on his first great journey across the world, with Haxton, to the South Seas to research the life of the painter Paul Gauguin, who had died in 1903. The resulting novel, *The Moon and Sixpence*, was another major success, and the pattern of Maugham's travels was now established. Through the 1920s and 1930s he and Haxton made frequent tours across Asia and the Pacific, which proved to be the cradle for the extraordinary series of short stories that populate these peak years of Maugham's output.

This period, of economic depression and political turmoil in the Western world and the decline of the British Empire in the East, handed Maugham the opportunity to observe the last years of a way of life that might otherwise have faded even more completely from memory than it has. Maugham did write popular travel books, but it is in the medium of the short story that he gives such poignant life to the people he encountered along the way: Malayan planters and South Sea missionaries, officious residents and dedicated doctors, the stateless refugees and the lonely, voracious women.

It is beyond doubt that the author drew many of these characters straight from life. Maugham, already fe fited as a writer around the world, could count on an enthusiastic welcome in even the most remote outposts of the Empire, and while he remained shy and taciturn in spite of his fame he was not above exploiting the attractive and genial Haxton, always on hand, when it came to gleaning local anecdotes, gossip and scandalous rumour in expatriate communities wherever they went.

Journalists who followed in Maugham's wake were able eagerly to report the outrage that some of the writer's hosts had felt when coming across their own incautious revelations in his tales. A number of his interlocutors (Maugham occasionally failed even to change names) were so unmistakable they took legal action, and further printings had to be judiciously edited. But the author nevertheless took a pride in being a good listener, notwithstanding his indiscretion. In *The Book-Bag* (page 129 of this edition) the writer–narrator is complimented by Featherstone, his host in Malaya, on his talent for drawing people out: 'I have an inkling that the fact of your being a writer attracts their confidence. They feel that what they tell you will excite your interest in an impersonal way that makes it easier for them to discharge their souls.'

The enduring freshness of the stories no doubt owes much to the authenticity of dialogue and incident. The simplicity of the language – Maugham never claimed to have a vast vocabulary – also contributes, and while many of the stories are specific to their locations and periods, he has a peculiar knack of making the most foreign of places and people, and their predicaments, familiar and somehow recognisable. It is surprising how few words in the stories are unfamiliar even today. It's worth mentioning in connection with the stories in this edition that FMS stands for the Federated Malay States; in colonial Malaya (now Malaysia) it was common for expats to use the initials in much the same way the British abroad have always referred to the UK rather than Britain. Another oddity is the drink, gin pahit, which crops up in several of the stories. Malay for 'bitter gin', this popular potion of colonial times had alleged medicinal properties and comprised three parts gin to one of Angostura bitters. It must have been bitter indeed. Another regularly mentioned drink, the stengah, from the Malay for 'half', was a half-measure of whisky with soda. Barang means belongings or luggage, a malacca is a walking stick and white ducks are the components of a linen suit.

Besides his simplicity of language, Maugham deserves credit too for his distinctive linearity. He wrote his stories, by his own admission, on the classical principle of knowing the ending to begin with and unwinding the narrative inexorably to the foregone conclusion. There are no red herrings. Our intelligence is not insulted, and however frightful the cruelties of action or intention, we are never made to feel uncomfortably shocked. Maugham is non-judgemental, as is perhaps fitting for a man with his predilections. He is a camera, not a critic.

Maugham never made much claim to literary distinction, although he was clearly affected by the indifference of the haughtier literary critics of his day. 'I have never pretended to be anything but a storyteller,' he mused in later life. 'It has amused me to tell stories and I have told a great many. It is a misfortune for me that the telling of a story just for the sake of the story is not an activity that is in favour with the intelligentsia.'

He did have his champions. George Orwell described him as 'the modern writer who has influenced me most', and his highly original spy stories of 1928 under the title *Ashenden*, based of course on his own espionage experiences, were adapted for a training manual by MI6 and were acknowledged by Ian Fleming as a key inspiration for his James Bond novels. Raymond Chandler wrote of the Ashenden series: 'There are no other spy stories, none at all.'

Maugham would have been little endeared to his detractors by his epic success both in book sales and movie treatments. He is said to be the second-most-adapted author (after Arthur Conan Doyle) for English-language films. *Rain* (page 321 of this edition), which first appeared in the 1923 collection *The Trembling Leaf*, was filmed three times between 1928 and 1953 under the titles *Sadie Thompson*, *Miss Sadie Thompson* and *Rain*, with, successively, Gloria Swanson, Joan Crawford and Rita Hayworth in the title role. Sadie's depiction by Maugham as 'plump, and in a coarse fashion pretty', with fat calves that bulged over the tops of her boots in no way deterred Hollywood directors from casting the most beautiful actresses to portray her.

Another much-adapted story is *The Letter* (page 21 of this edition), which was also produced as a play, then filmed in 1929 with Jeanne Eagels in the role of Leslie Crosbie, and again in 1940 with Bette Davis. There have been two British television adaptations since, starring Eileen Atkins in 1969 and Lee Remick in 1982.

The Second World War took Maugham to Hollywood, where he had great success as an adaptive scriptwriter and equal success on the social circuit. He did much to engender US support for Britain's war effort, and worked covertly for British Intelligence, just as in the 1914–18 conflict. But Maugham had in effect left Britain in 1927, following his divorce from Syrie, which attracted unwelcome attention to his homosexuality – still a criminal practice. He bought a grand house, the Villa Mauresque, at St Jean Cap Ferrat on the Côte d'Azur. It was his home, and a place of legendary hospitality to a glittering circle of guests, for the rest of his life, barring the forced exile from 1940 when France surrendered to Germany and Mussolini's army occupied the Riviera. Maugham escaped on the last coal-ship to leave before the troops arrived. The beautiful villa was successively looted of its wine, art and furnishings by the Italians and Germans, then wrecked by the Allies, who managed to leave behind them an unexploded shell, in Maugham's bedroom.

In 1946, the villa restored, Maugham returned. But he was now without Haxton, who had died during the war. The grand old man of letters, now in his seventies, took up with a former lover/secretary, Alan Searle, and resumed both his worldwide travels and the salon life at Cap Ferrat. His last years were soured by bitter legal disputes over his wealth. Searle persuaded the writer to adopt him as a son and to disown his daughter Liza. Maugham declared in a memoir that she had not been fathered by him. This cruelty lost him many friends and admirers. Rebecca West called it 'a characteristically reptilian statement'.

Liza, now married to John Hope, Lord Glendevon, mother to four children and an intimate of the Royal Family, was saddened by this turn of events. She had the adoption annulled in a French court, aware her father had been suffering from dementia. Maugham, and Searle, admitted defeat but father and daughter were never reconciled. He died on 15 December 1965, aged ninety-one. Lady Glendevon lived into old age until 1998. An obituarist in the *Independent* wrote of her as 'the only child of William Somerset Maugham, perhaps the century's grumpiest writer . . . '

It seems an infelicitous memorial to an immortal craftsman, a man who, although born a Victorian, had a career so prolific and so prolonged – well into the television age – that he turned into one of the first great celebrity writers. He is cursed with being remembered for his undoubted personal foibles. In time, he will surely be forgiven. It was his own wish that he should be remembered as a storyteller. The enduring appeal of these little compact masterpieces ensures his wish will for ever be fulfilled.

BIOGRAPHY

William Somerset Maugham was born at the British Embassy in Paris in 1874 into a family of lawyers. Orphaned at ten and exiled to an indifferent uncle and hated boarding school in Kent, he escaped briefly to Heidelberg University where he discovered literature, love and his urge to write. Under pressure to find a profession, he qualified as a doctor in London, exploiting his medical experiences not to practice but to pen a sensational novel, *Liza of Lambeth*, that launched his career. There followed a long and extraordinary life in which Maugham produced many hit plays and bestselling novels, took lovers of both sexes, spied in two world wars for Britain, travelled the world and became enormously rich. Along the way, based entirely on his own acquaintances and adventures, he compiled the greatest collection of short stories ever written. He lived his last forty years in an extravagant art-filled villa on the Riviera and died in 1965, aged ninety-one.

FURTHER READING

Brown, Ivor, *W. S. Maugham*, International Profiles, 1970

Calder, R. L., *W. S. Maugham and the Quest for Freedom*, Heinemann, 1972

Hastings, Selina, *The Secret Lives of Somerset Maugham*, Random House, 2010

Kanin, G., *Remembering Mr Maugham*, Scribner, 2000

Maugham, Robin, *Conversations with Willie: Recollections of W. Somerset Maugham*, Simon & Schuster, 1978

Maugham, Robin, *Somerset and all the Maughams*, Heinemann, 1966

Maugham, W. Somerset, *Of Human Bondage*, Penguin, 1969

Menard, Wilmon, *The Two Worlds of Somerset Maugham*, Sherbourne Press, 1965

Meyers, Jeffrey, *Somerset Maugham*, Jonathan Cape, 1980

Morgan, Ted, *Maugham: A Biography*, Touchstone, 1984

BEST SHORT STORIES OF
W. SOMERSET MAUGHAM

The Letter

Outside on the quay the sun beat fiercely. A stream of motors, lorries and buses, private cars and hirelings, sped up and down the crowded thoroughfare, and every chauffeur blew his horn; rickshaws threaded their nimble paths amid the throng, and the panting coolies found breath to yell at one another; coolies, carrying heavy bales, sidled along at their quick jog-trot and shouted to the passers-by to make way; itinerant vendors proclaimed their wares. Singapore is the meeting place of a hundred peoples; and men of all colours, black Tamils, yellow Chinks, brown Malays, Armenians, Jews and Bengalis, called to one another in raucous tones. But inside the office of Messrs Ripley, Joyce & Naylor it was pleasantly cool; it was dark after the dusty glitter of the street and agreeably quiet after its unceasing din. Mr Joyce sat in his private room, at the table, with an electric fan turned full on him. He was leaning back, his elbows on the arms of the chair, with the tips of the outstretched fingers of one hand resting neatly against the tips of the outstretched fingers of the other. His gaze rested on the battered volumes of the Law Reports which stood on a long shelf in front of him. On the top of a cupboard were square boxes of japanned tin on which were painted the names of various clients.

There was a knock at the door.

'Come in.'

A Chinese clerk, very neat in his white ducks, opened it.

'Mr Crosbie is here, sir.'

He spoke beautiful English, accenting each word with precision, and Mr Joyce had often wondered at the extent of his vocabulary. Ong Chi Seng was a Cantonese, and he had studied law at Gray's Inn. He was spending a year or two with Messrs Ripley, Joyce & Naylor in order to prepare himself for practice on his own account. He was industrious, obliging, and of exemplary character.

'Show him in,' said Mr Joyce.

He rose to shake hands with his visitor and asked him to sit down. The light fell on him as he did so. The face of Mr Joyce remained in shadow. He was by nature a silent man, and now he looked at Robert Crosbie for quite a minute without speaking. Crosbie was a big fellow well over six feet high, with broad shoulders, and muscular. He was a rubber-planter, hard with the constant exercise of walking over the estate and with the tennis which was his relaxation when the day's work was over. He was deeply sunburned. His hairy hands, his feet in clumsy boots, were enormous, and Mr Joyce found himself thinking that a blow of that great fist would easily kill the fragile Tamil. But there was no fierceness in his blue eyes: they were confiding and gentle; and his face, with its big, undistinguished features, was open, frank and honest. But at this moment it bore a look of deep distress. It was drawn and haggard.

'You look as though you hadn't had much sleep the last night or two,' said Mr Joyce.

'I haven't.'

Mr Joyce noticed now the old felt hat, with its broad double brim, which Crosbie had placed on the table; and then his eyes travelled to the khaki shorts he wore, showing his red hairy thighs, the tennis shirt open at the neck, without a tie, and the dirty khaki jacket with the ends of the sleeves turned up. He looked as though he had just come in from a long tramp among the rubber trees.

Mr Joyce gave a slight frown. 'You must pull yourself together, you know. You must keep your head.'

'Oh, I'm all right.'

'Have you seen your wife today?'

'No, I'm to see her this afternoon. You know, it is a damned shame that they should have arrested her.'

'I think they had to do that,' Mr Joyce answered in his level, soft tone.

'I should have thought they'd have let her out on bail.'

'It's a very serious charge.'

'It is damnable. She did what any decent woman would do in her place. Only, nine women out of ten wouldn't have the pluck. Leslie's the best woman in the world. She wouldn't hurt a fly. Why, hang it all, man, I've been married to her for twelve years, do you think I don't know her? God, if I'd got hold of the man I'd have wrung his neck. I'd have killed him without a moment's hesitation. So would you.'

'My dear fellow, everybody's on your side. No one has a good word to say for Hammond. We're going to get her off. I don't suppose either the assessors or the judge will go into court without having already made up their minds to bring in a verdict of not guilty.'

'The whole thing's a farce,' said Crosbie violently. 'She ought never to have been arrested in the first place, and then it's terrible, after all the poor girl's gone through, to subject her to the ordeal of a trial.

There's not a soul I've met since I've been in Singapore, man or woman, who hasn't told me that Leslie was absolutely justified. I think it's awful to keep her in prison all these weeks.'

'The law is the law. After all, she confesses that she killed the man. It is terrible, and I'm dreadfully sorry both for you and for her.'

'I don't matter a hang,' interrupted Crosbie.

'But the fact remains that murder has been committed, and in a civilised community a trial is inevitable.'

'Is it murder to exterminate noxious vermin? She shot him as she would have shot a mad dog.'

Mr Joyce leaned back again in his chair and once more placed the tips of his ten fingers together. The little construction he formed looked like the skeleton of a roof. He was silent for a moment.

'I should be wanting in my duty as your legal adviser,' he said at last, in an even voice, looking at his client with his cool, brown eyes, 'if I did not tell you that there is one point which causes me just a little anxiety. If your wife had only shot Hammond once, the whole thing would be absolutely plain sailing. Unfortunately she fired six times.'

'Her explanation is perfectly simple. In the circumstances anyone would have done the same.'

'I dare say,' said Mr Joyce, 'and of course I think the explanation is very reasonable. But it's no good closing our eyes to the facts. It's always a good plan to put yourself in another man's place, and I can't deny that if I were prosecuting for the Crown that's the point on which I should centre my inquiry.'

'My dear fellow, that's perfectly idiotic.'

Mr Joyce shot a sharp glance at Robert Crosbie.

The shadow of a smile hovered over his shapely lips. Crosbie was a good fellow, but he could hardly be described as intelligent.

'I dare say it's of no importance,' answered the lawyer, 'I just thought it was a point worth mentioning. You haven't got very long to wait now, and when it's all over I recommend you go off somewhere with your wife on a trip and forget all about it. Even though we are almost dead certain to get an acquittal, a trial of that sort is anxious work and you'll both want a rest.'

For the first time Crosbie smiled, and his smile strangely changed his face. You forgot the uncouthness and saw only the goodness of his soul.

'I think I shall want it more than Leslie. She's borne up wonderfully. By God, there's a plucky little woman for you.'

'Yes, I've been very much struck by her self-control,' said the lawyer. 'I should never have guessed that she was capable of such determination.'

His duties as her counsel had made it necessary for him to have a good many interviews with Mrs Crosbie since her arrest. Though things had been made as easy as could be for her, the fact remained that she was in jail, awaiting her trial for murder, and it would not have been surprising if her nerves had failed her. She appeared to bear her ordeal with composure. She read a great deal, took such exercise as was possible, and by favour of the authorities worked at the pillow lace which had always formed the entertainment of her long hours of leisure. When Mr Joyce saw her she was neatly dressed in cool, fresh, simple frocks, her hair was carefully arranged, and her nails were manicured. Her manner was collected. She was able even to jest upon the little inconveniences of her position. There was something casual about the way in which she spoke of the tragedy, which suggested to Mr Joyce that only her good breeding prevented her from finding something a trifle ludicrous in a situation which was eminently serious. It surprised him, for he had never thought that she had a sense of humour.

He had known her off and on for a good many years. When she paid visits to Singapore she generally came to dine with his wife and himself, and once or twice she had passed a weekend with them at their bungalow by the sea. His wife had spent a fortnight with her on the estate and had met Geoffrey Hammond several times. The two couples had been on friendly, if not on intimate, terms, and it was on this account that Robert Crosbie had rushed over to Singapore immediately after the catastrophe and begged Mr Joyce to take charge personally of his unhappy wife's defence.

The story she told him the first time he saw her she had never varied in the smallest detail. She told it as coolly then, a few hours after the tragedy, as she told it now. She told it connectedly, in a level, even voice, and her only sign of confusion was when a slight colour came into her cheeks as she described one or two of its incidents. She was the last woman to whom one would have expected such a thing to happen. She was in her early thirties, a fragile creature, neither short nor tall, and graceful rather than pretty. Her wrists and ankles were very delicate, but she was extremely thin and you could see the bones of her hands through the white skin, and the veins were large and blue. Her face was colourless, slightly sallow, and her lips were pale. You did not notice the colour of her eyes. She had a great deal of light-brown hair and it had a slight natural wave; it was the sort of hair that with a little touching-up would have been very pretty, but you could not imagine that Mrs Crosbie would think of resorting to any such device. She was a quiet, pleasant, unassuming woman. Her manner was engaging and if she was not very popular it was because she suffered from a certain shyness. This was comprehensible enough, for the planter's life is lonely, and in her own house, with people she knew, she was in her quiet way charming. Mrs Joyce after her fortnight's stay had told her husband that Leslie was a very agreeable hostess. There was more in her, she said, than people thought; and when you came to know her you were surprised how much she had read and how entertaining she could be.

She was the last woman in the world to commit murder.

Mr Joyce dismissed Robert Crosbie with such reassuring words as he could find and, once more alone in his office, turned over the pages of the brief. But it was a mechanical action, for all its details were familiar to him. The case was the sensation of the day, and it was discussed in all the clubs, at all the dinner tables, up and down the Peninsula from Singapore to Penang. The facts that Mrs Crosbie gave were simple. Her husband had gone to Singapore on business and she was alone for the night. She dined by herself, late, at a quarter to nine, and after dinner sat in the sitting-room working at her lace. It opened on to the verandah. There was no one in the bungalow, for the servants had retired to their own quarters at the back of the compound. She was surprised to hear a step on the gravel path in the garden, a booted step which suggested a white man rather than a native, for she had not heard a motor drive up and she could not imagine who could be coming to see her at that time of night. Someone ascended the few stairs that led up to the bungalow, walked across the verandah, and appeared at the door of the room in which she sat. At the first moment she did not recognise the visitor. She sat with a shaded lamp and he stood with his back to the darkness.

'May I come in?' he said.

She did not even recognise the voice.

'Who is it?' she asked.

She worked with spectacles, and she took them off as she spoke.

'Geoff Hammond.'

'Of course. Come in and have a drink.'

She rose and shook hands with him cordially. She was a little surprised to see him, for though he was a neighbour neither she nor Robert had been lately on very intimate terms with him, and she had not seen him for some weeks. He was the manager of a rubber estate nearly eight miles from theirs and she wondered why he had chosen this late hour to come and see them.

'Robert's away,' she said. 'He had to go to Singapore for the night.'

Perhaps he thought his visit called for some explanation, for he said

'I'm sorry. I felt rather lonely tonight, so I thought I'd just come along and see how you were getting on.'

'How on earth did you come? I never heard a car.'

'I left it down the road. I thought you might both be in bed and asleep.'

This was natural enough. The planter gets up at

dawn in order to take the roll-call of the workers, and soon after dinner he is glad to go to bed. Hammond's car was in point of fact found next day a quarter of a mile from the bungalow.

Since Robert was away there was no whisky and soda in the room. Leslie did not call the boy, since he was probably asleep, but fetched it herself. Her guest mixed himself a drink and filled his pipe.

Geoff Hammond had a host of friends in the colony. He was at this time in his late thirties, but he had come out as a lad. He had been one of the first to volunteer on the outbreak of war, and had done very well. A wound in the knee caused him to be invalided out of the army after two years, but he returned to the Federated Malay States with a DSO and an MC. He was one of the best billiard players in the colony. He had been a beautiful dancer and a fine tennis player, but though he was able no longer to dance, and his tennis, with a stiff knee, was not so good as it had been, he had the gift of popularity and was universally liked. He was a tall, good-looking fellow, with attractive blue eyes and a fine head of black, curling hair. Old stagers said his only fault was that he was too fond of the girls, and after the catastrophe they shook their heads and vowed that they had always known this would get him into trouble.

He began now to talk to Leslie about local affairs, the forthcoming races in Singapore, the price of rubber and his chances of killing a tiger which had been lately seen in the neighbourhood. She was anxious to finish by a certain date the piece of lace on which she was working, for she wanted to send it home for her mother's birthday, and so put on her spectacles again and drew towards her chair the little table on which stood the pillow.

'I wish you wouldn't wear those great horn-spectacles,' he said. 'I don't know why a pretty woman should do her best to look plain.'

She was a trifle taken aback at this remark. He had never used that tone with her before. She thought the best thing was to make light of it.

'I have no pretensions to being a raving beauty, you know, and, if you ask me point blank, I'm bound to tell you that I don't care two pins if you think me plain or not.'

'I don't think you're plain. I think you're awfully pretty.'

'Sweet of you,' she answered ironically. 'But in that case I can only think you half-witted.'

He chuckled. But he rose from his chair and sat down in another by her side.

'You're not going to have the face to deny that you have the prettiest hands in the world,' he said.

He made a gesture as though to take one of them. She gave him a little tap.

'Don't be an idiot. Sit down where you were before and talk sensibly, or else I shall send you home.'

He did not move.

'Don't you know that I'm awfully in love with you?' he said.

She remained quite cool.

'I don't. I don't believe it for a minute, and even if it were true I don't want you to say it.'

She was the more surprised at what he was saying, since during the seven years she had known him he had never paid her any particular attention. When he came back from the war they had seen a good deal of one another, and once when he was ill Robert had gone over and brought him back to their bungalow in his car. He had stayed with them then for a fortnight. But their interests were dissimilar and the acquaintance had never ripened into friendship. For the last two or three years they had seen little of him. Now and then he came over to play tennis, now and then they met him at some planter's who was giving a party, but it often happened that they did not set eyes on him for a month at a time.

Now he took another whisky and soda. Leslie wondered if he had been drinking before. There was something odd about him, and it made her a trifle uneasy. She watched him help himself with disapproval.

'I wouldn't drink any more if I were you,' she said, good-humouredly still.

He emptied his glass and put it down.

'Do you think I'm talking to you like this because I'm drunk?' he asked abruptly.

'That is the most obvious explanation, isn't it?'

'Well, it's a lie. I've loved you ever since I first knew you. I've held my tongue as long as I could, and now it's got to come out. I love you, I love you, I love you.'

She rose and carefully put aside the pillow.

'Good-night,' she said.

'I'm not going now.'

At last she began to lose her temper.

'But, you poor fool, don't you know that I've never loved anyone but Robert, and even if I didn't love Robert you're the last man I should fall for.'

'What do I care? Robert's away.'

'If you don't go this minute I shall call the boys and have you thrown out.'

'They're out of earshot.'

She was very angry now. She made a movement as though to go on to the verandah from which the house-boy would certainly hear her, but he seized her arm.

'Let me go,' she cried furiously.

'Not much. I've got you now.'

She opened her mouth and called, 'Boy, boy,' but with a quick gesture he put his hand over it. Then before she knew what he was about he had taken her in his arms and was kissing her passionately. She struggled, turning her lips away from his burning mouth.

'No, no, no,' she cried. 'Leave me alone. I won't.'

She grew confused about what happened then. All that had been said before she remembered accurately, but now his words assailed her ears through a mist of horror and fear. He seemed to plead for her love. He broke into violent protestations of passion. And all the time he held her in his tempestuous embrace. She was helpless, for he was a strong, powerful man, and her arms were pinioned to her sides; her struggles were unavailing and she felt herself growing weaker; she was afraid she would faint, and his hot breath on her face made her feel desperately sick. He kissed her mouth, her eyes, her cheeks, her hair. The pressure of his arms was killing her. He lifted her off her feet. She tried to kick him, but he only held her more closely. He was carrying her now. He wasn't speaking any more, but she knew that his face was pale and his eyes hot with desire. He was taking her into the bedroom. He was no longer a civilised man, but a savage. And as he ran he stumbled against a table which was in the way. His stiff knee made him a little awkward on his feet, and with the burden of the woman in his arms he fell. In a moment she had snatched herself away from him. She ran round the sofa. He was up in a flash and flung himself towards her. There was a revolver on the desk. She was not a nervous woman, but Robert was to be away for the night and she had meant to take it into her room when she went to bed. That was why it happened to be there. She was frantic with terror now. She did not know what she was doing. She heard a report. She saw Hammond stagger. He gave a cry. He said something, she didn't know what. He lurched out of the room on to the verandah. She was in a frenzy now, she was beside herself, she followed him out, yes, that was it, she must have followed him out, though she remembered nothing of it, she followed firing automatically shot after shot till the six chambers were empty. Hammond fell down on the floor of the verandah. He crumpled into a bloody heap.

When the boys, startled by the reports, rushed up, they found her standing over Hammond with the revolver still in her hand, and Hammond lifeless. She looked at them for a moment without speaking. They stood in a frightened, huddled bunch. She let the revolver fall from her hand and without a word turned and went into the sitting-room. They watched her go into her bedroom and turn the key in the lock. They dared not touch the dead body, but looked at it with terrified eyes, talking excitedly to one another in undertones. Then the head-boy collected himself; he had been with them for many years, he was Chinese and a level-headed fellow. Robert had gone into Singapore on his motorcycle and the car stood in the garage. He told the seis to get it out; they must go at once to the Assistant District Officer and tell him what had happened. He picked up the revolver and put it in his pocket. The ADO, a man called Withers, lived on the outskirts of the nearest town, which was about thirty-five miles away. It took them an hour and a half to reach him. Everyone was asleep, and they had to rouse the boys. Presently Withers came out and they told him their errand. The head-boy showed him the revolver in proof of what he said. The ADO went into his room to dress, sent for his car, and in a little while was following them back along the deserted road. The dawn was just breaking as he reached the Crosbies' bungalow. He ran up the steps of the verandah, and stopped short as he saw Hammond's body lying where he had fallen. He touched the face. It was quite cold.

'Where's mem?' he asked the head-boy.

The Chinese pointed to the bedroom. Withers went to the door and knocked. There was no answer. He knocked again.

'Mrs Crosbie,' he called.

'Who is it?'

'Withers.'

There was another pause. Then the door was unlocked and slowly opened. Leslie stood before him. She had not been to bed and wore the tea-gown in which she had dined. She stood and looked silently at the ADO.

'Your house-boy fetched me,' he said. 'Hammond. What have you done?'

'He tried to rape me and I shot him.'

'My God! I say, you'd better come out here. You must tell me exactly what happened.'

'Not now. I can't. You must give me time. Send for my husband.'

Withers was a young man, and he did not know

exactly what to do in an emergency which was so out of the run of his duties. Leslie refused to say anything till at last Robert arrived. Then she told the two men the story, from which since then, though she had repeated it over and over again, she had never in the slightest degree diverged.

The point to which Mr Joyce recurred was the shooting. As a lawyer he was bothered that Leslie had fired not once but six times, and the examination of the dead man showed that four of the shots had been fired close to the body. One might almost have thought that when the man fell she stood over him and emptied the contents of the revolver into him. She confessed that her memory, so accurate for all that had preceded, failed her here. Her mind was blank. It pointed to an uncontrollable fury; but uncontrollable fury was the last thing you would have expected from this quiet and demure woman. Mr Joyce had known her a good many years, and had always thought her an unemotional person; during the weeks that had passed since the tragedy her composure had been amazing.

Mr Joyce shrugged his shoulders.

'The fact is, I suppose,' he reflected, 'that you can never tell what hidden possibilities of savagery there are in the most respectable of women.'

There was a knock at the door.

'Come in.'

The Chinese clerk entered and closed the door behind him. He closed it gently, with deliberation, but decidedly, and advanced to the table at which Mr Joyce was sitting.

'May I trouble you, sir, for a few words' private conversation?' he said.

The elaborate accuracy with which the clerk expressed himself always faintly amused Mr Joyce, and now he smiled.

'It's no trouble, Chi Seng,' he replied.

'The matter on which I desire to speak to you, sir, is delicate and confidential.'

'Fire away.'

Mr Joyce met his clerk's shrewd eyes. As usual Ong Chi Seng was dressed in the height of local fashion. He wore very shiny patent-leather shoes and gay silk socks. In his black tie was a pearl and ruby pin, and on the fourth finger of his left hand a diamond ring. From the pocket of his neat white coat protruded a gold fountain pen and a gold pencil. He wore a gold wristwatch, and on the bridge of his nose invisible pince-nez. He gave a little cough.

'The matter has to do with the case *R.* v. *Crosbie*, sir.'

'Yes?'

'A circumstance has come to my knowledge, sir, which seems to me to put a different complexion on it.'

'What circumstance?'

'It has come to my knowledge, sir, that there is a letter in existence from the defendant to the unfortunate victim of the tragedy.'

'I shouldn't be at all surprised. In the course of the last seven years I have no doubt that Mrs Crosbie often had occasion to write to Mr Hammond.'

Mr Joyce had a high opinion of his clerk's intelligence and his words were designed to conceal his thoughts.

'That is very probable, sir. Mrs Crosbie must have communicated with the deceased frequently, to invite him to dine with her for example, or to propose a tennis game. That was my first thought when the matter was brought to my notice. This letter, however, was written on the day of the late Mr Hammond's death.'

Mr Joyce did not flicker an eyelash. He continued to look at Ong Chi Seng with the smile of faint amusement with which he generally talked to him.

'Who has told you this?'

'The circumstances were brought to my knowledge, sir, by a fliend of mine.'

Mr Joyce knew better than to insist.

'You will no doubt recall, sir, that Mrs Crosbie has stated that until the fatal night she had had no communication with the deceased for several weeks.'

'Have you got the letter?'

'No, sir.'

'What are its contents?'

'My fliend gave me a copy. Would you like to peruse it, sir?'

'I should.'

Ong Chi Seng took from an inside pocket a bulky wallet. It was filled with papers, Singapore dollar notes and cigarette cards. From the confusion he presently extracted a half sheet of thin notepaper and placed it before Mr Joyce. The letter read as follows:

R. will be away for the night. I absolutely must see you. I shall expect you at eleven. I am desperate and if you don't come I won't answer for the consequences. Don't drive up. – L.

It was written in the flowing hand which the Chinese

were taught at the foreign schools. The writing, so lacking in character, was oddly incongruous with the ominous words

'What makes you think that this note was written by Mrs Crosbie?'

'I have every confidence in the veracity of my informant, sir,' replied Ong Chi Seng. 'And the matter can very easily be put to the proof. Mrs Crosbie will no doubt be able to tell you at once whether she wrote such a letter or not.'

Since the beginning of the conversation Mr Joyce had not taken his eyes off the respectful countenance of his clerk. He wondered now if he discerned in it a faint expression of mockery.

'It is inconceivable that Mrs Crosbie should have written such a letter,' said Mr Joyce.

'If that is your opinion, sir, the matter is of course ended. My fliend spoke to me on the subject only because he thought, as I was in your office, you might like to know of the existence of this letter before a communication was made to the Deputy Public Prosecutor.'

'Who has the original?' asked Mr Joyce sharply.

Ong Chi Seng made no sign that he perceived in this question and its manner a change of attitude.

'You will remember, sir, no doubt, that after the death of Mr Hammond it was discovered that he had had relations with a Chinese woman. The letter is at present in her possession.'

That was one of the things which had turned public opinion most vehemently against Hammond. It came to be known that for several months he had had a Chinese woman living in his house.

For a moment neither of them spoke. Indeed

everything had been said and each understood the other perfectly.

'I'm obliged to you, Chi Seng. I will give the matter my consideration.'

'Very good, sir. Do you wish me to make a communication to that effect to my fliend?'

'I dare say it would be as well if you kept in touch with him,' Mr Joyce answered with gravity.

'Yes, sir.'

The clerk noiselessly left the room, shutting the door again with deliberation, and left Mr Joyce to his reflections. He stared at the copy, in its neat, impersonal writing, of Leslie's letter. Vague suspicions troubled him. They were so disconcerting that he made an effort to put them out of his mind. There must be a simple explanation of the letter, and Leslie without doubt could give it at once, but, by heaven, an explanation was needed. He rose from his chair, put the letter in his pocket, and took his topi. When he went out Ong Chi Seng was busily writing at his desk.

'I'm going out for a few minutes, Chi Seng,' he said.

'Mr George Reed is coming by appointment at twelve o'clock, sir. Where shall I say you've gone?'

Mr Joyce gave him a thin smile.

'You can say that you haven't the least idea.'

But he knew perfectly well that Ong Chi Seng was aware that he was going to the jail. Though the crime had been committed in Belanda and the trial was to take place at Belanda Bharu, since there was in the jail there no convenience for the detention of a white woman Mrs Crosbie had been brought to Singapore.

When she was led into the room in which he

waited she held out her thin, distinguished hand, and gave him a pleasant smile. She was as ever neatly and simply dressed and her abundant, pale hair was arranged with care.

'I wasn't expecting to see you this morning,' she said graciously.

She might have been in her own house, and Mr Joyce almost expected to hear her call the boy and tell him to bring the visitor a gin pahit.

'How are you?' he asked.

'I'm in the best of health, thank you.' A flicker of amusement flashed across her eyes. 'This is a wonderful place for a rest cure.'

The attendant withdrew and they were left alone.

'Do sit down,' said Leslie.

He took a chair. He did not quite know how to begin. She was so cool that it seemed almost impossible to say to her the thing he had come to say. Though she was not pretty there was something agreeable in her appearance. She had elegance, but it was the elegance of good breeding in which there was nothing of the artifice of society. You had only to look at her to know what sort of people she had and what kind of surroundings she had lived in. Her fragility gave her a singular refinement. It was impossible to associate her with the vaguest idea of grossness.

'I'm looking forward to seeing Robert this afternoon,' she said, in her good-humoured, easy voice. (It was a pleasure to hear her speak, her voice and her accent were so distinctive of her class.) 'Poor dear, it's been a great trial to his nerves. I'm thankful it'll all be over in a few days.'

'It's only five days now.'

'I know. Each morning when I awake I say to

myself, "one less".' She smiled then. 'Just as I used to do at school when the holidays were coming.'

'By the way, am I right in thinking that you had no communication whatever with Hammond for several weeks before the catastrophe?'

'I'm quite positive of that. The last time we met was at a tennis-party at the MacFarrens'. I don't think I said more than two words to him. They have two courts, you know, and we didn't happen to be in the same sets.'

'And you haven't written to him?'

'Oh, no.'

'Are you quite sure of that?'

'Oh, quite,' she answered, with a little smile. 'There was nothing I should write to him for except to ask him to dine or to play tennis, and I hadn't done either for months.'

'At one time you'd been on fairly intimate terms with him. How did it happen that you had stopped asking him to anything?'

Mrs Crosbie shrugged her thin shoulders.

'One gets tired of people. We hadn't anything very much in common. Of course, when he was ill Robert and I did everything we could for him, but the last year or two he'd been quite well, and he was very popular. He had a good many calls on his time, and there didn't seem to be any need to shower invitations upon him.'

'Are you quite certain that was all?'

Mrs Crosbie hesitated for a moment.

'Well, I may just as well tell you. It had come to our ears that he was living with a Chinese woman, and Robert said he wouldn't have him in the house. I had seen her myself.'

Mr Joyce was sitting in a straight-backed armchair, resting his chin on his hand, and his eyes were fixed on Leslie. Was it his fancy that as she made this remark her black pupils were filled on a sudden, for the fraction of a second, with a dull red light? The effect was startling. Mr Joyce shifted in his chair. He placed the tips of his ten fingers together. He spoke very slowly, choosing his words.

'I think I should tell you that there is in existence a letter in your handwriting to Geoff Hammond.'

He watched her closely. She made no movement, nor did her face change colour, but she took a noticeable time to reply.

'In the past I've often sent him little notes to ask him to something or other, or to get me something when I knew he was going to Singapore.'

'This letter asks him to come and see you because Robert was going to Singapore.'

'That's impossible. I never did anything of the kind.'

'You'd better read it for yourself.'

He took it out of his pocket and handed it to her. She gave it a glance and with a smile of scorn handed it back to him.

'That's not my handwriting.'

'I know, it's said to be an exact copy of the original.'

She read the words now, and as she read a horrible change came over her. Her colourless face grew dreadful to look at. It turned green. The flesh seemed on a sudden to fall away and her skin was tightly stretched over the bones. Her lips receded, showing her teeth, so that she had the appearance of making a grimace. She stared at Mr Joyce with eyes that started from their sockets. He was looking now at a gibbering death's head.

'What does it mean?' she whispered.

Her mouth was so dry that she could utter no more than a hoarse sound. It was no longer a human voice.

'That is for you to say,' he answered.

'I didn't write it. I swear I didn't write it.'

'Be very careful what you say. If the original is in your handwriting it would be useless to deny it.'

'It would be a forgery.'

'It would be difficult to prove that. It would be easy to prove that it was genuine.'

A shiver passed through her lean body. But great beads of sweat stood on her forehead. She took a handkerchief from her bag and wiped the palms of her hands. She glanced at the letter again and gave Mr Joyce a sidelong look.

'It's not dated. If I had written it and forgotten all about it, it might have been written years ago. If you'll give me time, I'll try and remember the circumstances.'

'I noticed there was no date. If this letter were in the hands of the prosecution they would cross-examine the boys. They would soon find out whether someone took a letter to Hammond on the day of his death.'

Mrs Crosbie clasped her hands violently and swayed in her chair so that he thought she would faint.

'I swear to you that I didn't write that letter.'

Mr Joyce was silent for a little while. He took his eyes from her distraught face, and looked down on the floor. He was reflecting.

'In these circumstances we need not go into the matter further,' he said slowly, at last breaking the silence. 'If the possessor of this letter sees fit to place it in the hands of the prosecution you will be prepared.'

His words suggested that he had nothing more to say to her, but he made no movement of departure. He waited. To himself he seemed to wait a very long time. He did not look at Leslie, but he was conscious that she sat very still. She made no sound.

At last it was he who spoke. 'If you have nothing more to say to me I think I'll be getting back to my office.'

'What would anyone who read the letter be inclined to think that it meant?' she asked then.

'He'd know that you had told a deliberate lie,' answered Mr Joyce sharply.

'When?'

'You have stated definitely that you had had no communication with Hammond for at least three months.'

'The whole thing has been a terrible shock to me. The events of that dreadful night have been a nightmare. It's not very strange if one detail has escaped my memory.'

'It would be very unfortunate, when your memory has reproduced so exactly every particular of your interview with Hammond, that you should have forgotten so important a point as that he came to see you in the bungalow on the night of his death at your express desire.'

'I hadn't forgotten. After what happened I was afraid to mention it. I thought you'd none of you believe my story if I admitted that he'd come at my invitation. I dare say it was stupid of me; but I lost my head, and after I'd said once that I'd had no communication with Hammond I was obliged to stick to it.'

By now Leslie had recovered her admirable

composure, and she met Mr Joyce's appraising glance with candour. Her gentleness was very disarming.

'You will be required to explain, then, *why* you asked Hammond to come and see you when Robert was away for the night.'

She turned her eyes full on the lawyer. He had been mistaken in thinking them insignificant, they were rather fine eyes, and unless he was mistaken they were bright now with tears. Her voice had a little break in it.

'It was a surprise I was preparing for Robert. His birthday is next month. I knew he wanted a new gun and you know I'm dreadfully stupid about sporting things. I wanted to talk to Geoff about it. I thought I'd get him to order it for me.'

'Perhaps the terms of the letter are not very clear to your recollection. Will you have another look at it?'

'No, I don't want to,' she said quickly.

'Does it seem to you the sort of letter a woman would write to a somewhat distant acquaintance because she wanted to consult him about buying a gun?'

'I dare say it's rather extravagant and emotional. I do express myself like that, you know. I'm quite prepared to admit it's very silly.' She smiled. 'And after all, Geoff Hammond wasn't quite a distant acquaintance. When he was ill I'd nursed him like a mother. I asked him to come when Robert was away, because Robert wouldn't have him in the house.'

Mr Joyce was tired of sitting so long in the same position. He rose and walked once or twice up and down the room, choosing the words he proposed to say; then he leaned over the back of the chair in which he had been sitting. He spoke slowly in a tone of deep gravity.

'Mrs Crosbie, I want to talk to you very, very seriously. This case was comparatively plain sailing. There was only one point which seemed to me to require explanation: as far as I could judge, you had fired no less than four shots into Hammond when he was lying on the ground. It was hard to accept the possibility that a delicate, frightened and habitually self-controlled woman, of gentle nurture and refined instincts, should have surrendered to an absolutely uncontrolled frenzy. But of course it was admissible. Although Geoffrey Hammond was much liked and on the whole thought highly of, I was prepared to prove that he was the sort of man who might be guilty of the crime which in justification of your act you accused him of. The fact, which was discovered after his death, that he had been living with a Chinese woman gave us something very definite to go upon. That robbed him of any sympathy which might have been felt for him. We made up our minds to make use of the odium which such a connection cast upon him in the minds of all respectable people. I told your husband this morning that I was certain of an acquittal, and I wasn't just telling him that to give him heart. I do not believe the assessors would have left the court.'

They looked into one another's eyes. Mrs Crosbie was strangely still. She was like a little bird paralysed by the fascination of a snake. He went on in the same quiet tones.

'But this letter has thrown an entirely different complexion on the case. I am your legal adviser, I shall represent you in court. I take your story as you tell it me, and I shall conduct your defence according to its terms. It may be that I believe your statements, and it may be that I doubt them. The duty of counsel is to persuade the court that the evidence placed before it is not such as to justify it in bringing in a verdict of guilty, and any private opinion he may have of the guilt or innocence of his client is entirely beside the point.'

He was astonished to see in Leslie's eyes the flicker of a smile. Piqued, he went on somewhat dryly.

'You're not going to deny that Hammond came to your house at your urgent, and I may even say, hysterical, invitation?'

Mrs Crosbie, hesitating for an instant, seemed to consider.

'They can prove that the letter was taken to his bungalow by one of the house-boys. He rode over on his bicycle.'

'You mustn't expect other people to be stupider than you. The letter will put them on the track of suspicions which have entered nobody's head. I will not tell you what I personally thought when I saw the copy. I do not wish you to tell me anything but what is needed to save your neck.'

Mrs Crosbie gave a shrill cry. She sprang to her feet, white with terror.

'You don't think they'd hang me?'

'If they came to the conclusion that you hadn't killed Hammond in self-defence, it would be the duty of the assessors to bring in a verdict of guilty. The charge is murder. It would be the duty of the judge to sentence you to death.'

'But what can they prove?' she gasped.

'I don't know what they can prove. You know. I don't want to know. But if their suspicions are aroused, if they begin to make enquiries, if the natives are questioned – what is it that can be discovered?'

She crumpled up suddenly. She fell on the floor before he could catch her. She had fainted. He looked round the room for water, but there was none there, and he did not want to be disturbed. He stretched her out on the floor and kneeling beside her waited for her to recover. When she opened her eyes he was disconcerted by the ghastly fear that he saw in them.

'Keep quite still,' he said. 'You'll be better in a moment.'

'You won't let them hang me,' she whispered.

She began to cry, hysterically, while in undertones he sought to quieten her.

'For goodness' sake, pull yourself together,' he said.

'Give me a minute.'

Her courage was amazing. He could see the effort she made to regain her self-control, and soon she was once more calm.

'Let me get up now.'

He gave her his hand and helped her to her feet. Taking her arm, he led her to the chair. She sat down wearily.

'Don't talk to me for a minute or two,' she said.

'Very well.'

When at last she spoke it was to say something which he did not expect. She gave a little sigh.

'I'm afraid I've made rather a mess of things,' she said.

He did not answer, and once more there was a silence.

'Isn't it possible to get hold of the letter?' she said at last.

'I do not think anything would have been said to

me about it if the person in whose possession it is was not prepared to sell it.'

'Who's got it?'

'The Chinese woman who was living in Hammond's house.'

A spot of colour flickered for an instant on Leslie's cheekbones.

'Does she want an awful lot for it?'

'I imagine that she has a very shrewd idea of its value. I doubt if it would be possible to get hold of it except for a very large sum.'

'Are you going to let me be hanged?'

'Do you think it's so simple as all that to secure possession of an unwelcome piece of evidence? It's no different from suborning a witness. You have no right to make any such suggestion to me.'

'Then what is going to happen to me?'

'Justice must take its course.'

She grew very pale. A little shudder passed through her body.

'I put myself in your hands. Of course I have no right to ask you to do anything that isn't proper.'

Mr Joyce had not bargained for the little break in her voice which her habitual self-restraint made quite intolerably moving. She looked at him with humble eyes and he thought that if he rejected their appeal they would haunt him for the rest of his life. After all, nothing could bring poor Hammond back to life again. He wondered what really was the explanation of that letter. It was not fair to conclude from it that she had killed Hammond without provocation. He had lived in the East a long time and his sense of professional honour was not perhaps so acute as it had been twenty years before. He stared at the floor.

He made up his mind to do something which he knew was unjustifiable, but it stuck in his throat and he felt dully resentful towards Leslie. It embarrassed him a little to speak.

'I don't know exactly what your husband's circumstances are?'

Flushing a rosy red, she shot a swift glance at him.

'He has a good many tin shares and a small share in two or three rubber estates. I suppose he could raise money.'

'He would have to be told what it was for.'

She was silent for a moment. She seemed to think.

'He's in love with me still. He would make any sacrifice to save me. Is there any need for him to see the letter?'

Mr Joyce frowned a little, and, quick to notice, she went on.

'Robert is an old friend of yours. I'm not asking you to do anything for me, I'm asking you to save a rather simple, kind man who never did you any harm from all the pain that's possible.'

Mr Joyce did not reply. He rose to go and Mrs Crosbie, with the grace that was natural to her, held out her hand. She was shaken by the scene, and her look was haggard, but she made a brave attempt to speed him with courtesy.

'It's so good of you to take all this trouble for me. I can't begin to tell you how grateful I am.'

Mr Joyce returned to his office. He sat in his own room, quite still, attempting to do no work, and pondered. His imagination brought him many strange ideas. He shuddered a little. At last there was the discreet knock on the door which he was expecting. Ong Chi Seng came in.

'I was just going out to have my tiffin, sir,' he said.

'All right.'

'I didn't know if there was anything you wanted before I went, sir.'

'I don't think so. Did you make another appointment for Mr Reed?'

'Yes, sir. He will come at three o'clock.'

'Good.'

Ong Chi Seng turned away, walked to the door, and put his long slim fingers on the handle. Then, as though on an afterthought, he turned back.

'Is there anything you wish me to say to my fliend, sir?' Although Ong Chi Seng spoke English so admirably he had still a difficulty with the letter r, and he pronounced the word 'fliend'.

'What friend?'

'About the letter Mrs Crosbie wrote to Hammond deceased, sir.'

'Oh! I'd forgotten about that. I mentioned it to Mrs Crosbie and she denies having written anything of the sort. It's evidently a forgery.'

Mr Joyce took the copy from his pocket and handed it to Ong Chi Seng. Ong Chi Seng ignored the gesture.

'In that case, sir, I suppose there would be no objection if my fliend delivered the letter to the Deputy Public Prosecutor.'

'None. But I don't quite see what good that would do your friend.'

'My fliend, sir, thought it was his duty in the interests of justice.'

'I am the last man in the world to interfere with any one who wishes to do his duty, Chi Seng.'

The eyes of the lawyer and of the Chinese clerk

met. Not the shadow of a smile hovered on the lips of either, but they understood each other perfectly.

'I quite understand, sir,' said Ong Chi Seng, 'but from my study of the case *R.* v. *Crosbie* I am of the opinion that the production of such a letter would be damaging to our client.'

'I have always had a very high opinion of your legal acumen, Chi Seng.'

'It has occurred to me, sir, that if I could persuade my fliend to induce the Chinese woman who has the letter to deliver it into our hands it would save a great deal of trouble.'

Mr Joyce idly drew faces on his blotting-paper.

'I suppose your friend is a businessman. In what circumstances do you think he would be induced to part with the letter?'

'He has not got the letter. The Chinese woman has the letter. He is only a relation of the Chinese woman. She is an ignorant woman; she did not know the value of the letter till my fliend told her.'

'What value did he put on it?'

'Ten thousand dollars, sir.'

'Good God! Where on earth do you suppose Mrs Crosbie can get ten thousand dollars! I tell you the letter's a forgery.'

He looked up at Ong Chi Seng as he spoke. The clerk was unmoved by the outburst. He stood at the side of the desk, civil, cool and observant.

'Mr Crosbie owns an eighth share of the Betong Rubber Estate and a sixth share of the Selantan River Rubber Estate. I have a fliend who will lend him the money on the security of his properties.'

'You have a large circle of acquaintance, Chi Seng.'

'Yes, sir.'

'Well, you can tell them to go to hell. I would never advise Mr Crosbie to give a penny more than five thousand for a letter that can be very easily explained.'

'The Chinese woman does not want to sell the letter, sir. My fliend took a long time to persuade her. It is useless to offer her less than the sum mentioned.'

Mr Joyce looked at Ong Chi Seng for at least three minutes. The clerk bore the searching scrutiny without embarrassment. He stood in a respectful attitude with downcast eyes. Mr Joyce knew his man. Clever fellow, Chi Seng, he thought, I wonder how much he's going to get out of it.

'Ten thousand dollars is a very large sum.'

'Mr Crosbie will certainly pay it rather than see his wife hanged, sir.'

Again Mr Joyce paused. What more did Chi Seng know than he had said? He must be pretty sure of his ground if he was obviously so unwilling to bargain. That sum had been fixed because whoever it was that was managing the affair knew it was the largest amount that Robert Crosbie could raise.

'Where is the Chinese woman now?' asked Mr Joyce.

'She is staying at the house of my fliend, sir.'

'Will she come here?'

'I think it more better if you go to her, sir. I can take you to the house tonight and she will give you the letter. She is a very ignorant woman, sir, and she does not understand cheques.'

'I wasn't thinking of giving her a cheque. I will bring banknotes with me.'

'It would only be waste of valuable time to bring less than ten thousand dollars, sir.'

'I quite understand.'

'I will go and tell my fliend after I have had my tiffin, sir.'

'Very good. You'd better meet me outside the club at ten o'clock tonight.'

'With pleasure, sir,' said Ong Chi Seng.

He gave Mr Joyce a little bow and left the room. Mr Joyce went out to have luncheon too. He went to the club and here, as he had expected, he saw Robert Crosbie. He was sitting at a crowded table, and as he passed him, looking for a place, Mr Joyce touched him on the shoulder.

'I'd like a word or two with you before you go,' he said.

'Right you are. Let me know when you're ready.'

Mr Joyce had made up his mind how to tackle him. He played a rubber of bridge after luncheon in order to allow time for the club to empty itself. He did not want on this particular matter to see Crosbie in his office. Presently Crosbie came into the card-room and looked on till the game was finished. The other players went off on their various affairs, and the two were left alone.

'A rather unfortunate thing has happened, old man,' said Mr Joyce, in a tone which he sought to render as casual as possible. 'It appears that your wife sent a letter to Hammond asking him to come to the bungalow on the night he was killed.'

'But that's impossible,' cried Crosbie. 'She's always stated that she had had no communication with Hammond. I know from my own knowledge that she hadn't set eyes on him for a couple of months.'

'The fact remains that the letter exists. It's in the possession of the Chinese woman Hammond was living with. Your wife meant to give you a present on your birthday, and she wanted Hammond to help her to get it. In the emotional excitement that she suffered from after the tragedy, she forgot all about it, and having once denied having any communication with Hammond, she was afraid to say that she had made a mistake. It was of course very unfortunate, but I dare say it was not unnatural.'

Crosbie did not speak. His large, red face bore an expression of complete bewilderment, and Mr Joyce was at once relieved and exasperated by his lack of comprehension. He was a stupid man, and Mr Joyce had no patience with stupidity. But his distress since the catastrophe had touched a soft spot in the lawyer's heart; and Mrs Crosbie had struck the right note when she asked him to help her, not for her sake, but for her husband's.

'I need not tell you that it would be very awkward if this letter found its way into the hands of the prosecution. Your wife has lied, and she would be asked to explain the lie. It alters things a little if Hammond did not intrude, an unwanted guest, but came to your house by invitation. It would be easy to arouse in the assessors a certain indecision of mind.'

Mr Joyce hesitated. He was face to face now with his decision. If it had been a time for humour, he could have smiled at the reflection that he was taking so grave a step, and that the man for whom he was taking it had not the smallest conception of its gravity. If he gave the matter a thought, he probably imagined that what Mr Joyce was doing was what any lawyer did in the ordinary run of business.

'My dear Robert, you are not only my client, but my friend. I think we must get hold of that letter. It'll cost a good deal of money. Except for that I should have preferred to say nothing to you about it.'

'How much?'

'Ten thousand dollars.'

'That's a devil of a lot. With the slump and one thing and another it'll take just about all I've got.'

'Can you get it at once?'

'I suppose so. Old Charlie Meadows will let me have it on my tin shares and on those two estates I'm interested in.'

'Then will you?'

'Is it absolutely necessary?'

'If you want your wife to be acquitted.'

Crosbie grew very red. His mouth sagged strangely.

'But . . .' He could not find words, his face now was purple. 'But I don't understand. She can explain. You don't mean to say they'd find her guilty? They couldn't hang her for putting a noxious vermin out of the way.'

'Of course they wouldn't hang her. They might only find her guilty of manslaughter. She'd probably get off with two or three years.'

Crosbie started to his feet and his red face was distraught with horror.

'Three years.'

Then something seemed to dawn in that slow intelligence of his. His mind was darkness across which shot suddenly a flash of lightning, and though the succeeding darkness was as profound, there remained the memory of something not seen but perhaps just descried. Mr Joyce saw that Crosbie's big red hands, coarse and hard with all the odd jobs he had set them to, trembled.

'What was the present she wanted to make me?'

'She says she wanted to give you a new gun.'

Once more that great red face flushed a deeper red.

'When have you got to have the money ready?'

There was something odd in his voice now. It sounded as though he spoke with invisible hands clutching at his throat.

'At ten o'clock tonight. I thought you could bring it to my office at about six.'

'Is the woman coming to you?'

'No, I'm going to her.'

'I'll bring the money. I'll come with you.'

Mr Joyce looked at him sharply.

'Do you think there's any need for you to do that? I think it would be better if you left me to deal with this matter by myself.'

'It's my money, isn't it? I'm going to come.'

Mr Joyce shrugged his shoulders. They rose and shook hands. Mr Joyce looked at him curiously.

At ten o'clock they met in the empty club.

'Everything all right?' asked Mr Joyce.

'Yes. I've got the money in my pocket.'

'Let's go then.'

They walked down the steps. Mr Joyce's car was waiting for them in the square, silent at that hour, and as they came to it Ong Chi Seng stepped out of the shadow of a house. He took his seat beside the driver and gave him a direction. They drove past the Hôtel de l'Europe and turned up by the Sailors' Home to get into Victoria Street. Here the Chinese shops were open still, idlers lounged about, and in the roadway rickshaws and motor cars and gharries gave a busy air to the scene. Suddenly their car stopped and Chi Seng turned round.

'I think it more better if we walk here, sir,' he said.

They got out and he went on. They followed a step or two behind. Then he asked them to stop.

'You wait here, sir. I go in and speak to my fliend.'

He went into a shop, open to the street, where three or four Chinese were standing behind the counter. It was one of those strange shops where nothing was on view and you wondered what it was they sold there. They saw him address a stout man in a duck suit with a large gold chain across his breast and the man shot a quick glance out into the night. He gave Chi Seng a key and Chi Seng came out. He beckoned to the two men waiting and slid into a doorway at the side of the shop. They followed him and found themselves at the foot of a flight of stairs.

'If you wait a minute I will light a match,' he said, always resourceful. 'You come upstairs, please.'

He held a Japanese match in front of them, but it scarcely dispelled the darkness and they groped their way up behind him. On the first floor he unlocked a door and going in lit a gas-jet.

'Come in, please,' he said.

It was a small square room, with one window, and the only furniture consisted of two low Chinese beds covered with matting. In one corner was a large chest, with an elaborate lock, and on this stood a shabby tray with an opium pipe on it and a lamp. There was in the room the faint, acrid scent of the drug. They sat down and Ong Chi Seng offered them cigarettes. In a moment the door was opened by the fat Chinaman whom they had seen behind the counter. He bade them good-evening in very good English and sat down by the side of his fellow-countryman.

'The Chinese woman is just coming,' said Chi Seng.

A boy from the shop brought in a tray with a teapot and cups and the Chinaman offered them a cup of tea. Crosbie refused. The Chinese talked to one another in undertones, but Crosbie and Mr Joyce were silent. At last there was the sound of a voice outside; someone was calling in a low tone and the Chinaman went to the door. He opened it, spoke a few words, and ushered a woman in. Mr Joyce looked at her. He had heard much about her since Hammond's death, but he had never seen her. She was a stoutish person, not very young, with a broad, phlegmatic face. She was powdered and rouged and her eyebrows were a thin black line, but she gave you the impression of a woman of character. She wore a pale blue jacket and a white skirt, her costume was not quite European nor quite Chinese, but on her feet were little Chinese silk slippers. She wore heavy gold chains round her neck, gold bangles on her wrists, gold ear-rings and elaborate gold pins in her black hair. She walked in slowly, with the air of a woman sure of herself, but with a certain heaviness of tread, and sat down on the bed beside Ong Chi Seng. He said something to her and nodding she gave an incurious glance at the two white men.

'Has she got the letter?' asked Mr Joyce.

'Yes, sir.'

Crosbie said nothing, but produced a roll of five-hundred-dollar notes. He counted out twenty and handed them to Chi Seng.

'Will you see if that is correct?'

The clerk counted them and gave them to the fat Chinaman.

'Quite correct, sir.'

The Chinaman counted them once more and put

them in his pocket. He spoke again to the woman and she drew from her bosom a letter. She gave it to Chi Seng who cast his eyes over it.

'This is the right document, sir,' he said, and was about to give it to Mr Joyce when Crosbie took it from him.

'Let me look at it,' he said.

Mr Joyce watched him read and then held out his hand for it.

'You'd better let me have it.'

Crosbie folded it up deliberately and put it in his pocket.

'No, I'm going to keep it myself. It's cost me enough money.'

Mr Joyce made no rejoinder. The three Chinese watched the little passage, but what they thought about it, or whether they thought, it was impossible to tell from their impassive countenances. Mr Joyce rose to his feet.

'Do you want me any more tonight, sir?' said Ong Chi Seng.

'No.' He knew that the clerk wished to stay behind in order to get his agreed share of the money, and he turned to Crosbie. 'Are you ready?'

Crosbie did not answer, but stood up. The Chinaman went to the door and opened it for them. Chi Seng found a bit of candle and lit it in order to light them down, and the two Chinese accompanied them to the street. They left the woman sitting quietly on the bed smoking a cigarette. When they reached the street the Chinese left them and went once more upstairs.

'What are you going to do with that letter?' asked Mr Joyce.

'Keep it.'

They walked to where the car was waiting for them and here Mr Joyce offered his friend a lift. Crosbie shook his head.

'I'm going to walk.' He hesitated a little and shuffled his feet. 'I went to Singapore on the night of Hammond's death partly to buy a new gun that a man I knew wanted to dispose of. Good-night.'

He disappeared quickly into the darkness.

Mr Joyce was quite right about the trial. The assessors went into court fully determined to acquit Mrs Crosbie. She gave evidence on her own behalf. She told her story simply and with straightforwardness. The Director of Public Prosecutions was a kindly man and it was plain that he took no great pleasure in his task. He asked the necessary questions in a deprecating manner. His speech for the prosecution might really have been a speech for the defence, and the assessors took less than five minutes to consider their popular verdict. It was impossible to prevent the great outburst of applause with which it was received by the crowd that packed the courthouse. The judge congratulated Mrs Crosbie and she was a free woman.

No one had expressed a more violent disapprobation of Hammond's behaviour than Mrs Joyce; she was a woman loyal to her friends and she had insisted on the Crosbies staying with her after the trial – for she in common with everyone else had no doubt of the result – till they could make arrangements to go away. It was out of the question for poor, dear, brave Leslie to return to the bungalow at which the horrible catastrophe had taken place. The trial was over by half-past twelve and when they reached the Joyces' house a grand luncheon was awaiting them. Cocktails were ready, Mrs Joyce's million-dollar cocktail was celebrated through all the Malay States, and Mrs Joyce drank Leslie's health. She was a talkative, vivacious woman, and now she was in the highest spirits. It was fortunate, for the rest of them were silent. She did not wonder; her husband never had much to say, and the other two were naturally exhausted from the long strain to which they had been subjected. During luncheon she carried on a bright and spirited monologue. Then coffee was served.

'Now, children,' she said in her gay, bustling fashion, 'you must have a rest and after tea I shall take you both for a drive to the sea.'

Mr Joyce, who lunched at home only by exception, had of course to go back to his office.

'I'm afraid I can't do that, Mrs Joyce,' said Crosbie. 'I've got to get back to the estate at once.'

'Not today?' she cried.

'Yes, now. I've neglected it for too long and I have urgent business. But I shall be very grateful if you will keep Leslie until we have decided what to do.'

Mrs Joyce was about to expostulate, but her husband prevented her.

'If he must go, he must, and there's an end of it.'

There was something in the lawyer's tone which made her look at him quickly. She held her tongue and there was a moment's silence.

Then Crosbie spoke again. 'If you'll forgive me, I'll start at once so that I can get there before dark.' He rose from the table. 'Will you come and see me off, Leslie?'

'Of course.'

They went out of the dining-room together.

'I think that's rather inconsiderate of him,' said Mrs Joyce. 'He must know that Leslie wants to be with him just now.'

'I'm sure he wouldn't go if it wasn't absolutely necessary.'

'Well, I'll just see that Leslie's room is ready for her. She wants a complete rest, of course, and then amusement.'

Mrs Joyce left the room and Joyce sat down again. In a short time he heard Crosbie start the engine of his motorcycle and then noisily scrunch over the gravel of the garden path. He got up and went into the drawing-room. Mrs Crosbie was standing in the middle of it, looking into space, and in her hand was an open letter. He recognised it. She gave him a glance as he came in and he saw that she was deathly pale.

'He knows,' she whispered.

Mr Joyce went up to her and took the letter from her hand. He lit a match and set the paper afire. She watched it burn. When he could hold it no longer he dropped it on the tiled floor and they both looked at the paper curl and blacken. Then he trod it into ashes with his foot.

'What does he know?'

She gave him a long, long stare and into her eyes came a strange look. Was it contempt or despair? Mr Joyce could not tell.

'He knows that Geoff was my lover.'

Mr Joyce made no movement and uttered no sound.

'He'd been my lover for years. He became my lover almost immediately after he came back from the war. We knew how careful we must be. When we became lovers I pretended I was tired of him, and he seldom came to the house when Robert was there. I used to drive out to a place we knew and he met me, two or three times a week, and when Robert went to Singapore he used to come to the bungalow late, when the boys had gone for the night. We saw one another constantly, all the time, and not a soul had the smallest suspicion of it. And then lately, a year ago, he began to change. I didn't know what was the matter. I couldn't believe that he didn't care for me any more. He always denied it. I was frantic. I made scenes. Sometimes I thought he hated me. Oh, if you knew what agonies I endured. I passed through hell. I knew he didn't want me any more and I wouldn't let him go. Misery! Misery! I loved him. I'd given him everything. He was all my life. And then I heard he was living with a Chinese woman. I couldn't believe it. I wouldn't believe it. At last I saw her, I saw her with my own eyes, walking in the village, with her gold bracelets and her necklaces, an old, fat, Chinese woman. She was older than I was. Horrible! They all knew in the kampong that she was his mistress. And when I passed her, she looked at me and I knew that she knew I was his mistress too. I sent for him. I told him I must see him. You've read the letter. I was mad to write it. I didn't know what I was doing. I didn't care. I hadn't seen him for ten days. It was a lifetime. And when last we'd parted he took me in his arms and kissed me and told me not to worry. And he went straight from my arms to hers.'

She had been speaking in a low voice, vehemently, and now she stopped and wrung her hands.

'That damned letter. We'd always been so careful. He always tore up any word I wrote to him the moment he'd read it. How was I to know he'd leave that one? He came and I told him I knew about the Chinawoman. He denied it. He said it was only scandal. I was beside myself. I don't know what I said to him. Oh, I hated him then. I tore him limb from limb. I said everything I could to wound him. I insulted him. I could have spat in his face. And at last he turned on me. He told me he was sick and tired of me and never wanted to see me again. He said I bored him to death. And then he acknowledged that it was true about the Chinawoman. He said he'd known her for years, before the war, and she was the only woman who really meant anything to him, and the rest was just pastime. And he said he was glad I knew, and now at last I'd leave him alone. And then I don't know what happened, I was beside myself, I saw red. I seized the revolver and I fired. He gave a cry and I saw I'd hit him. He staggered and rushed for the verandah. I ran after him and fired again. He fell, and then I stood over him and I fired and fired till the revolver went click, click, and I knew there were no more cartridges.'

At last she stopped, panting. Her face was no longer human, it was distorted with cruelty and rage and pain. You would never have thought that this quiet, refined woman was capable of such a fiendish passion. Mr Joyce took a step backwards. He was absolutely aghast at the sight of her. It was not a face, it was a gibbering, hideous mask. Then they heard a voice calling from another room, a loud, friendly, cheerful voice. It was Mrs Joyce.

'Come along, Leslie darling, your room's ready. You must be dropping with sleep.'

Mrs Crosbie's features gradually composed themselves. Those passions, so clearly delineated, were smoothed away as with your hand you would smooth a crumpled paper, and in a minute the face was cool and calm and unlined. She was a trifle pale, but her lips broke into a pleasant, affable smile. She was once more the well-bred and even distinguished woman.

'I'm coming, Dorothy dear. I'm sorry to give you so much trouble.'

The Verger

There had been a christening that afternoon at St Peter's, Neville Square, and Albert Edward Foreman still wore his verger's gown. He kept his new one, its folds as full and stiff as though it were made not of alpaca but of perennial bronze, for funerals and weddings (St Peter's, Neville Square, was a church much favoured by the fashionable for these ceremonies) and now he wore only his second-best. He wore it with complacence, for it was the dignified symbol of his office, and without it (when he took it off to go home) he had the disconcerting sensation of being somewhat insufficiently clad. He took pains with it; he pressed it and ironed it himself. During the sixteen years he had been verger of this church he had had a succession of such gowns, but he had never been able to throw them away when they were worn out and the complete series, neatly wrapped up in brown paper, lay in the bottom drawers of the wardrobe in his bedroom.

The verger busied himself quietly, replacing the painted wooden cover on the marble font, taking away a chair that had been brought for an infirm old lady, and waited for the vicar to have finished in the vestry so that he could tidy up in there and go home. Presently he saw him walk across the chancel, genuflect in front of the high altar and come down the aisle; but he still wore his cassock.

'What's he 'anging about for?' the verger said to himself. 'Don't 'e know I want my tea?'

The vicar had been but recently appointed, a red-faced energetic man in his early forties, and Albert Edward still regretted his predecessor, a clergyman of the old school who preached leisurely sermons in a silvery voice and dined out a great deal with his more aristocratic parishioners. He liked things in church to be just so, but he never fussed; he was not like this new man who wanted to have his finger in every pie. But Albert Edward was tolerant. St Peter's was in a very good neighbourhood and the parishioners were a very nice class of people. The new vicar had come from the East End and he couldn't be expected to fall in all at once with the discreet ways of his fashionable congregation.

'All this 'ustle,' said Albert Edward. 'But give 'im time, he'll learn.'

When the vicar had walked down the aisle so far that he could address the verger without raising his voice more than was becoming in a place of worship he stopped.

'Foreman, will you come into the vestry for a minute. I have something to say to you.'

'Very good, sir.'

The vicar waited for him to come up and they walked up the church together.

'A very nice christening, I thought, sir. Funny 'ow the baby stopped cryin' the moment you took him.'

'I've noticed they very often do,' said the vicar, with a little smile. 'After all I've had a good deal of practice with them.'

It was a source of subdued pride to him that he could nearly always quiet a whimpering infant by the manner in which he held it and he was not unconscious of the amused admiration with which mothers and nurses watched him settle the baby in the crook of his surpliced arm. The verger knew that it pleased him to be complimented on his talent.

The vicar preceded Albert Edward into the vestry. Albert Edward was a trifle surprised to find the two churchwardens there. He had not seen them come in. They gave him pleasant nods.

'Good-afternoon, my lord. Good-afternoon, sir,' he said to one after the other.

They were elderly men, both of them, and they had been churchwardens almost as long as Albert Edward had been verger. They were sitting now at a handsome refectory table that the old vicar had brought many years before from Italy and the vicar sat down in the vacant chair between them. Albert Edward faced them, the table between him and them, and wondered with slight uneasiness what was the matter. He remembered still the occasion on which the organist had got into trouble and the bother they had all had to hush things up. In a church like St Peter's, Neville Square, they couldn't afford a scandal. On the vicar's red face was a look of resolute benignity, but the others bore an expression that was slightly troubled.

'He's been naggin' them, he 'as,' said the verger to himself. 'He's jockeyed them into doin' something, but they don't 'alf like it. That's what it is, you mark my words.'

But his thoughts did not appear on Albert Edward's cleancut and distinguished features. He stood in a respectful but not obsequious attitude. He had been in service before he was appointed to his ecclesiastical office, but only in very good houses, and his deportment was irreproachable. Starting as a pageboy in the household of a merchant-prince, he had risen by due degrees from the position of fourth to first footman, for a year he had been single-handed butler to a widowed peeress and, till the vacancy occurred at St Peter's, butler with two men under him in the house of a retired ambassador. He was tall, spare, grave and dignified. He looked, if not like a duke, at least like an actor of the old school who specialised in dukes' parts. He had tact, firmness and self-assurance. His character was unimpeachable.

The vicar began briskly.

'Foreman, we've got something rather unpleasant to say to you. You've been here a great many years and I think his lordship and the general agree with me that you've fulfilled the duties of your office to the satisfaction of everybody concerned.'

The two churchwardens nodded.

'But a most extraordinary circumstance came to my knowledge the other day and I felt it my duty to impart it to the churchwardens. I discovered to my astonishment that you could neither read nor write.'

The verger's face betrayed no sign of embarrassment. 'The last vicar knew that, sir,' he replied. 'He said it didn't make no difference. He always said there was a great deal too much education in the world for 'is taste.'

'It's the most amazing thing I ever heard,' cried the general. 'Do you mean to say that you've been verger of this church for sixteen years and never learned to read or write?'

'I went into service when I was twelve, sir. The cook in the first place tried to teach me once, but I didn't seem to 'ave the knack for it, and then what with one thing and another I never seemed to 'ave the time. I've never really found the want of it. I think a lot of these young fellows waste a rare lot of time readin' when they might be doin' something useful.'

'But don't you want to know the news?' said the other churchwarden. 'Don't you ever want to write a letter?'

'No, me lord, I seem to manage very well without. And of late years now they've all these pictures in the papers I get to know what's goin' on pretty well. Me wife's quite a scholar and if I want to write a letter she writes it for me. It's not as if I was a bettin' man.'

The two churchwardens gave the vicar a troubled glance and then looked down at the table.

'Well, Foreman, I've talked the matter over with these gentlemen and they quite agree with me that the situation is impossible. At a church like St Peter's, Neville Square, we cannot have a verger who can neither read nor write.'

Albert Edward's thin, sallow face reddened and he moved uneasily on his feet, but he made no reply.

'Understand me, Foreman, I have no complaint to make against you. You do your work quite satisfactorily; I have the highest opinion both of your character and of your capacity; but we haven't the right to take the risk of some accident that might happen owing to your lamentable ignorance. It's a matter of prudence as well as of principle.'

'But couldn't you learn, Foreman?' asked the general.

'No, sir, I'm afraid I couldn't, not now. You see, I'm not as young as I was and if I couldn't seem able to get the letters in me 'ead when I was a nipper I don't think there's much chance of it now.'

'We don't want to be harsh with you, Foreman,' said the vicar. 'But the churchwardens and I have quite made up our minds. We'll give you three months and if at the end of that time you cannot read and write I'm afraid you'll have to go.'

Albert Edward had never liked the new vicar. He'd said from the beginning that they'd made a mistake when they gave him St Peter's. He wasn't the type of man they wanted with a classy congregation like that. And now he straightened himself a little. He knew his value and he wasn't going to allow himself to be put upon.

'I'm very sorry, sir, I'm afraid it's no good. I'm too old a dog to learn new tricks. I've lived a good many years without knowin' 'ow to read and write, and without wishin' to praise myself – self-praise is no recommendation – I don't mind sayin' I've done my duty in that state of life in which it 'as pleased a merciful providence to place me, and if I *could* learn now I don't know as I'd want to.'

'In that case, Foreman, I'm afraid you must go.'

'Yes, sir, I quite understand. I shall be 'appy to 'and in my resignation as soon as you've found somebody to take my place.'

But when Albert Edward with his usual politeness had closed the church door behind the vicar and the two churchwardens he could not sustain the air of unruffled dignity with which he had borne the blow inflicted upon him and his lips quivered. He walked slowly back to the vestry and hung up on its proper peg his verger's gown. He sighed as he thought of all the grand funerals and smart weddings he had seen. He tidied everything up, put on his coat, and hat in hand walked down the aisle. He locked the church door behind him. He strolled across the square, but deep in his sad thoughts he did not take the street that led him home, where a nice strong cup of tea awaited him; he took the wrong turning. He walked slowly along. His heart was heavy. He did not know what he should do with himself. He did not fancy the notion of going back to domestic service; after being his own master for so many years – for the vicar and churchwardens could say what they liked, it was he that had run St Peter's, Neville Square – he could scarcely demean himself by accepting a situation. He had saved a tidy sum, but not enough to live on without doing something, and life seemed to cost more every year. He had never thought to be troubled with such questions. The vergers of St Peter's, like the popes of Rome, were there for life. He had often thought of the pleasant reference the vicar would make in his sermon at evensong the first Sunday after his death to the long and faithful service and the exemplary character of their late verger, Albert Edward Foreman. He sighed deeply. Albert Edward was a non-smoker and a total abstainer, but with a certain latitude; that is to say he liked a glass of beer with his dinner and when he was tired he enjoyed a cigarette. It occurred to him now that one would comfort him and since he did not carry them he looked about him for a shop where he could buy a packet of Gold Flakes. He did not at once see one and walked on a little. It was a long street, with all sorts of shops in it, but there was not a single one where you could buy cigarettes.

'That's strange,' said Albert Edward.

To make sure, he walked right up the street again. No, there was no doubt about it. He stopped and looked reflectively up and down.

'I can't be the only man as walks along this street and wants a fag,' he said. 'I shouldn't wonder but what a fellow might do very well with a little shop here. Tobacco and sweets, you know.'

He gave a sudden start.

'That's an idea,' he said. 'Strange 'ow things come to you when you least expect it.'

He turned, walked home, and had his tea.

'You're very silent this afternoon, Albert,' his wife remarked.

'I'm thinkin',' he said.

He considered the matter from every point of view and next day he went along the street and by good luck found a little shop to let that looked as though it would exactly suit him. Twenty-four hours later he had taken it and when a month after that he left St Peter's, Neville Square, for ever, Albert Edward Foreman set up in business as a tobacconist and newsagent. His wife said it was a dreadful come-down after being verger of St Peter's, but he answered that you had to move with the times, the church wasn't what it was, and 'enceforward he was going to render unto Caesar what was Caesar's. Albert Edward did very well. He did so well that in a year or so it struck him that he might take a second shop and put a manager in. He looked for another long street that hadn't got a tobacconist in it and when he found it, and a shop to let, took it and stocked it. This was a success too. Then it occurred to him that if he could run two he could run half a dozen, so he began walking about London, and whenever he found a long street that had no tobacconist and a shop to let he took it. In the course of ten years he had acquired no less than ten shops and he was making money hand over fist. He went round to all of them himself every Monday, collected the week's takings and took them to the bank.

One morning when he was there paying in a bundle of notes and a heavy bag of silver the cashier told him that the manager would like to see him. He was shown into an office and the manager shook hands with him.

'Mr Foreman, I wanted to have a talk to you about the money you've got on deposit with us. D'you know exactly how much it is?'

'Not within a pound or two, sir; but I've got a pretty rough idea.'

'Apart from what you paid in this morning it's a little over thirty thousand pounds. That's a very large sum to have on deposit and I should have thought you'd do better to invest it.'

'I wouldn't want to take no risk, sir. I know it's safe in the bank.'

'You needn't have the least anxiety. We'll make you out a list of absolutely gilt-edged securities. They'll bring you in a better rate of interest than we can possibly afford to give you.'

A troubled look settled on Mr Foreman's distinguished face. 'I've never 'ad anything to do with stocks and shares and I'd 'ave to leave it all in your 'ands,' he said.

The manager smiled. 'We'll do everything. All you'll have to do next time you come in is just to sign the transfers.'

'I could do that all right,' said Albert uncertainly. 'But 'ow should I know what I was signin'?'

'I suppose you can read,' said the manager a trifle sharply.

Mr Foreman gave him a disarming smile.

'Well, sir, that's just it. I can't. I know it sounds funny-like, but there it is, I can't read or write, only me name, an' I only learnt to do that when I went into business.'

The manager was so surprised that he jumped up from his chair.

'That's the most extraordinary thing I ever heard.'

'You see, it's like this, sir, I never 'ad the opportunity until it was too late and then some'ow I wouldn't. I got obstinate-like.'

The manager stared at him as though he were a prehistoric monster.

'And do you mean to say that you've built up this important business and amassed a fortune of thirty thousand pounds without being able to read or write? Good God, man, what would you be now if you had been able to?'

'I can tell you that, sir,' said Mr Foreman, a little smile on his still aristocratic features. 'I'd be verger of St Peter's, Neville Square.'

The Vessel of Wrath

There are few books in the world that contain more meat than the *Sailing Directions* published by the Hydrographic Department by order of the Lords Commissioners of the Admiralty. They are handsome volumes, bound (very flimsily) in cloth of different colours, and the most expensive of them is cheap. For four shillings you can buy the 'Yangtse Kiang Pilot', 'containing a description of, and sailing directions for, the Yangtse Kiang from the Wusung River to the highest navigable point, including the Han Kiang, the Kialing Kiang and the Min Kiang'; and for three shillings you can get 'Part III of the Eastern Archipelago Pilot', 'comprising the NE end of the Celebes, Molucca and Gilolo passages, Banda and Arafura Seas, and North, West and South-West coasts of New Guinea'. But it is not very safe to do so if you are a creature of settled habits that you have no wish to disturb or if you have an occupation that holds you fast to one place. These businesslike books take you upon enchanted journeys of the spirit; and their matter-of-fact style, the admirable order, the concision with which the material is set before you, the stern sense of the practical that informs every line, cannot dim the poetry that, like the spice-laden breeze that assails your senses with a more than material languor when you approach some of those magic islands of the Eastern seas, blows with so sweet a fragrance through the printed pages. They tell you the anchorages and the landing places, what supplies you can get at each spot, and where you can get water; they tell you the lights and buoys, tides, winds and weather that you will find there. They give you brief information about the population and the trade. And it is strange when you think how sedately it is all set down, with no words wasted, that so much else is given you besides. What? Well, mystery and beauty, romance and the glamour of the unknown. It is no common book that offers you, casually turning its pages, such a paragraph as this:

> Supplies. A few jungle fowl are preserved, the island is also the resort of vast numbers of sea birds. Turtle are found in the lagoon, as well as quantities of various fish, including grey mullet, shark and dog-fish; the seine cannot be used with any effect; but there is a fish which may be taken on a rod. A small store of tinned provisions and spirits is kept in a hut for the relief of shipwrecked persons. Good water may be obtained from a well near the landing place.

Can the imagination want more material than this to go on a journey through time and space?

In the volume from which I have copied this passage, the compilers with the same restraint have described the Alas Islands. They are composed of a group or chain of islands, 'for the most part low and wooded, extending about seventy-five miles east and west, and forty miles north and south'. The information about them, you are told, is very slight; there are channels between the different groups, and several vessels have passed through them, but the passages have not been thoroughly explored, and the positions of many of the dangers not yet determined; it is therefore advisable to avoid them. The population of the group is estimated at about eight thousand, of whom two hundred are Chinese and four hundred Mohammedans. The rest are heathen. The principal island is called Baru, it is surrounded by a reef, and here lives a Dutch Controleur. His white house with its red roof on the top of a little hill is the most prominent object that the vessels of the Royal Netherlands Steam Packet Company see when every other month on their way up to Macassar and every four weeks on their way down to Merauke in Dutch New Guinea they touch at the island.

At a certain moment of the world's history the Controleur was Mynheer Evert Gruyter and he ruled the people who inhabited the Alas Islands with firmness tempered by a keen sense of the ridiculous. He had thought it a very good joke to be placed at the age of twenty-seven in a position of such consequence and at thirty he was still amused by it. There was no cable communication between his islands and Batavia, and the mail arrived after so long a delay that even if he asked advice, by the time he received it, it was useless, and so he equably did what he thought best and trusted to his good fortune to keep out of trouble with the authorities. He was very short, not more than five feet four in height, and extremely fat; he was of a florid complexion. For coolness's sake he kept his head shaved and his face was hairless. It was round and red. His eyebrows were so fair that you hardly saw them; and he had little twinkling blue eyes. He knew that he had no dignity, but for the sake of his position made up for it by dressing very dapperly. He never went to his office, nor sat in court, nor walked abroad but in spotless white. His stengah-shifter, with its bright brass buttons, fitted him very tightly and displayed the shocking fact that, young though he was, he had a round and protruding belly. His good-humoured face shone with sweat and he constantly fanned himself with a palm-leaf fan.

But in his house Mr Gruyter preferred to wear nothing but a sarong and then with his white podgy little body he looked like a fat funny boy of sixteen. He was an early riser and his breakfast was always ready for him at six. It never varied. It consisted of a slice of papaya, three cold fried eggs, Edam cheese, sliced thin, and a cup of black coffee. When he had eaten it, he smoked a large Dutch cigar, read the papers if he had not read them through and through already, and then dressed to go down to his office.

One morning while he was thus occupied his head-boy came into his bedroom and told him that Tuan Jones wanted to know if he could see him. Mr Gruyter was standing in front of a looking-glass. He had his trousers on and was admiring his smooth chest. He arched his back in order to throw it out and throw in his belly and with a good deal of satisfaction gave his breast three or four resounding slaps. It was a manly chest. When the boy brought the message he looked at his own eyes in the mirror and exchanged a slightly ironic smile with them. He asked himself what the devil his visitor could want. Evert Gruyter spoke English, Dutch and Malay with equal facility, but he thought in Dutch. He liked to do this. It seemed to him a pleasantly ribald language.

'Ask the tuan to wait and say I shall come directly.' He put on his tunic, over his naked body, buttoned it up, and strutted into the sitting-room. The Reverend Owen Jones got up.

'Good-morning, Mr Jones,' said the Controleur.

'Have you come in to have a peg with me before I start my day's work?'

Mr Jones did not smile.

'I've come to see you upon a very distressing matter, Mr Gruyter,' he answered.

The Controleur was not disconcerted by his visitor's gravity nor depressed by his words. His little blue eyes beamed amiably.

'Sit down, my dear fellow, and have a cigar.'

Mr Gruyter knew quite well that the Reverend Owen Jones neither drank nor smoked, but it tickled something prankish in his nature to offer him a drink and a smoke whenever they met. Mr Jones shook his head.

Mr Jones was in charge of the Baptist Mission on the Alas Islands. His headquarters were at Baru, the largest of them, with the greatest population, but he had meeting-houses under the care of native helpers in several other islands of the group. He was a tall, thin melancholy man, with a long face, sallow and drawn, of about forty. His brown hair was already white on the temples and it receded from the forehead. This gave him a look of somewhat vacuous intellectuality. Mr Gruyter both disliked and respected him. He disliked him because he was narrow-minded and dogmatic. Himself a cheerful pagan who liked the good things of the flesh and was determined to get as many of them as his circumstances permitted, he had no patience with a man who disapproved of them all. He thought the customs of the country suited its inhabitants and had no patience with the missionary's energetic efforts to destroy a way of life that for centuries had worked very well. He respected him because he was honest, zealous and good. Mr Jones, an Australian of Welsh descent, was the only qualified doctor in the group and it was a comfort to know that if you fell ill you need not rely only on a Chinese practitioner, and none knew better than the Controleur how useful to all Mr Jones's skill had been and with what charity he had given it. On the occasion of an epidemic of influenza, the missionary had done the work of ten men, and no storm short of a typhoon could prevent him from crossing to one island or another if his help was needed.

He lived with his sister in a little white house about half a mile from the village, and when the Controleur first arrived, he came on board to meet him and begged him to stay till he could get his own house in order. The Controleur had accepted and soon saw for himself with what simplicity the couple lived. It was more than he could stand. Tea at three sparse meals a day and when he lit his cigar Mr Jones politely but firmly asked him to be good enough not to smoke since both his sister and he strongly disapproved of it. In twenty-four hours Mr Gruyter moved into his own house. He fled, with panic in his heart, as though from a plague-stricken city. The Controleur was fond of a joke and he liked to laugh; to be with a man who took your nonsense in deadly earnest and never even smiled at your best story was more than flesh and blood could stand. The Reverend Owen Jones was a worthy man, but as a companion he was impossible. His sister was worse. Neither had a sense of humour, but whereas the missionary was of a melancholy turn, doing his duty so conscientiously, with the obvious conviction that everything in the world was hopeless, Miss Jones was resolutely cheerful. She grimly looked on the bright side of things. With the ferocity of an avenging angel she sought out the good in her fellow men. Miss Jones taught in the mission school and helped her brother in his medical work. When he did operations she gave the anaesthetic and was matron, dresser and nurse of the tiny hospital which on his own initiative Mr Jones had added to the mission. But the Controleur was an obstinate little fellow and he never lost his capacity of extracting amusement from the Reverend Owen's dour struggle with the infirmities of human nature, and Miss Jones's ruthless optimism. He had to get his fun where he could. The Dutch boats came in three times in two months for a few hours and then he could have a good old crack with the captain and chief engineer, and once in a blue moon a pearling lugger came in from Thursday Island or Port Darwin and for two or three days he had a grand time. They were rough fellows, the pearlers, for the most part, but they were full of guts, and they had plenty of liquor on board, and good stories to tell, and the Controleur had them up to his house and gave them a fine dinner and the party was only counted a success if they were all too drunk to get back on the lugger again that night. But besides the missionary the only white man who lived on Baru was Ginger Ted, and he, of course, was a disgrace to civilisation. There was not a single thing to be said in his favour. He cast discredit on the white race. All the same, but for Ginger Ted the Controleur sometimes thought he would find life on the island of Baru almost more than he could bear.

Oddly enough it was on account of this scamp that Mr Jones, when he should have been instructing the pagan young in the mysteries of the Baptist faith, was paying Mr Gruyter this early visit.

'Sit down, Mr Jones,' said the Controleur. 'What can I do for you?'

'Well, I've come to see you about the man they call Ginger Ted. What are you going to do now?'

'Why, what's happened?'

'Haven't you heard? I thought the sergeant would have told you.'

'I don't encourage the members of my staff to come to my private house unless the matter is urgent,' said the Controleur rather grandly. 'I am unlike you, Mr Jones, I only work in order to have leisure and I like to enjoy my leisure without disturbance.'

But Mr Jones did not care much for small talk and he was not interested in general reflections.

'There was a disgraceful row in one of the Chinese shops last night. Ginger Ted wrecked the place and half killed a Chinaman.'

'Drunk again, I suppose,' said the Controleur placidly.

'Naturally. When is he anything else? They sent for the police and he assaulted the sergeant. They had to have six men to get him to the gaol.'

'He's a hefty fellow,' said the Controleur.

'I suppose you'll send him to Macassar.'

Evert Gruyter returned the missionary's outraged look with a merry twinkle. He was no fool and he knew already what Mr Jones was up to. It gave him considerable amusement to tease him a little.

'Fortunately my powers are wide enough to enable me to deal with the situation myself,' he answered.

'You have power to deport anyone you like, Mr Gruyter, and I'm sure it would save a lot of trouble if you got rid of the man altogether.'

'I have the power of course, but I am sure

you would be the last person to wish me to use it arbitrarily.'

'Mr Gruyter, the man's presence here is a public scandal. He's never sober from morning till night; it's notorious that he has relations with one native woman after another.'

'That is an interesting point, Mr Jones. I had always heard that alcoholic excess, though it stimulated sexual desire, prevented its gratification. What you tell me about Ginger Ted does not seem to bear out this theory.'

The missionary flushed a dull red.

'These are physiological matters which at the moment I have no wish to go into,' he said, frigidly. 'The behaviour of this man does incalculable damage to the prestige of the white race, and his example seriously hampers the efforts that are made in other quarters to induce the people of these islands to lead a less vicious life. He's an out and out bad lot.'

'Pardon my asking, but have you made any attempts to reform him?'

'When he first drifted here I did my best to get in touch with him. He repelled all my advances. When there was that first trouble I went to him and talked to him straight from the shoulder. He swore at me.'

'No one has a greater appreciation than I of the excellent work that you and other missionaries do on these islands, but are you sure that you always exercise your calling with all the tact possible?'

The Controleur was rather pleased with this phrase. It was extremely courteous and yet contained a reproof that he thought worth administering. The missionary looked at him gravely. His sad brown eyes were full of sincerity.

'Did Jesus exercise tact when he took a whip and drove the money-changers from the temple? No, Mr Gruyter. Tact is the subterfuge the lax avail themselves of to avoid doing their duty.'

Mr Jones's remark made the Controleur feel suddenly that he wanted a bottle of beer. The missionary leaned forward earnestly.

'Mr Gruyter, you know this man's transgressions just as well as I do. It's unnecessary for me to remind you of them. There are no excuses for him. Now he really has overstepped the limit. You'll never have a better chance than this. I beg you to use the power you have and turn him out once and for all.'

The Controleur's eyes twinkled more brightly than ever. He was having a lot of fun. He reflected that human beings were much more amusing when you did not feel called upon in dealing with them to allot praise or blame.

'But Mr Jones, do I understand you right? Are you asking me to give you an assurance to deport this man before I've heard the evidence against him and listened to his defence?'

'I don't know what his defence can be.'

The Controleur rose from his chair and really he managed to get quite a little dignity into his five feet four inches.

'I am here to administer justice according to the laws of the Dutch government. Permit me to tell you that I am exceedingly surprised that you should attempt to influence me in my judicial functions.'

The missionary was a trifle flustered. It had never occurred to him that this little whipper-snapper of a boy, ten years younger than himself, would dream of adopting such an attitude. He opened his mouth to explain and apologise, but the Controleur raised a podgy little hand.

'It is time for me to go to my office, Mr Jones. I wish you good-morning.'

The missionary, taken aback, bowed and without another word walked out of the room. He would have been surprised to see what the Controleur did when his back was turned. A broad grin broke on his lips and he put his thumb to his nose and cocked a snook at the Reverend Owen Jones.

A few minutes later he went down to his office. His head clerk, who was a Dutch half-caste, gave him his version of the previous night's row. It agreed pretty well with Mr Jones's. The court was sitting that day.

'Will you take Ginger Ted first, sir?' asked the clerk.

'I see no reason to do that. There are two or three cases held over from the last sitting. I will take him in his proper order.'

'I thought perhaps as he was a white man you would like to see him privately, sir.'

'The majesty of the law knows no difference between white and coloured, my friend,' said Mr Gruyter, somewhat pompously.

The court was a big square room with wooden benches on which, crowded together, sat natives of all kinds – Polynesians, Bugis, Chinese, Malays – and they all rose when a door was opened and a sergeant announced the arrival of the Controleur. He entered with his clerk and took his place on a little dais at a table of varnished pitch pine. Behind him was a large engraving of Queen Wilhelmina. He dispatched half a dozen cases and then Ginger Ted was brought in. He stood in the dock, handcuffed, with a warder on either side of him. The Controleur looked at him with a grave face, but he could not keep the amusement out of his eyes.

Ginger Ted was suffering from a hangover. He swayed a little as he stood and his eyes were vacant. He was a man still young, thirty perhaps, of somewhat over the middle height, rather fat, with a bloated red face and a shock of curly red hair. He had not come out of the tussle unscathed. He had a black eye and his mouth was cut and swollen. He wore khaki shorts, very dirty and ragged, and his singlet had been almost torn off his back. A great rent showed the thick mat of red hair with which his chest was covered, but showed also the astonishing whiteness of his skin. The Controleur looked at the charge sheet. He called the evidence. When he had heard it, when he had seen the Chinaman whose head Ginger Ted had broken with a bottle, when he had heard the agitated story of the sergeant who had been knocked flat when he tried to arrest him, when he had listened to the talk of the havoc wrought by Ginger Ted who in his drunken fury had smashed everything he could lay hands on, he turned and addressed the accused in English.

'Well, Ginger, what have you got to say for yourself?'

'I was blind. I don't remember a thing about it. If they say I half killed 'im I suppose I did. I'll pay the damage if they'll give me time.'

'You will, Ginger,' said the Controleur, 'but it's me who'll give you time.'

He looked at Ginger Ted for a minute in silence. He was an unappetising object. A man who had gone completely to pieces. He was horrible. It made you shudder to look at him and if Mr Jones had not been so officious, at that moment the Controleur would certainly have ordered him to be deported.

'You've been a trouble ever since you came to the islands, Ginger. You're a disgrace. You're incorrigibly idle. You've been picked up in the street dead drunk time and time again. You've kicked up row after row. You're hopeless. I told you the last time you were brought here that if you were arrested again I should deal with you severely. You've gone the limit this time and you're for it. I sentence you to six months' hard labour.'

'Me?'

'You.'

'By God, I'll kill you when I come out.'

He burst into a string of oaths both filthy and blasphemous. Mr Gruyter listened scornfully. You can swear much better in Dutch than in English and there was nothing that Ginger Ted said that he could not have effectively capped.

'Be quiet,' he ordered. 'You make me tired.'

The Controleur repeated his sentence in Malay and the prisoner was led struggling away.

Mr Gruyter sat down to tiffin in high good humour. It was astonishing how amusing life could be if you exercised a little ingenuity. There were people in Amsterdam, and even in Batavia and Surabaya, who looked upon his island home as a place of exile. They little knew how agreeable it was and what fun he could extract from unpromising material. They asked him whether he did not miss the club and the races and the cinema, the dances that were held once a week at the casino and the society of Dutch ladies. Not at all. He liked comfort. The substantial furniture of the room in which he sat had a satisfying solidity.

He liked reading French novels of a frivolous nature and he appreciated the sensation of reading one after the other without the uneasiness occasioned by the thought that he was wasting his time. It seemed to him a great luxury to waste time. When his young man's fancy turned to thoughts of love his head-boy brought to the house a little dark-skinned bright-eyed creature in a sarong. He took care to form no connection of a permanent nature. He thought that change kept the heart young. He enjoyed freedom and was not weighed down by a sense of responsibility. He did not mind the heat. It made a sluice over with cold water half a dozen times a day a pleasure that had almost an aesthetic quality. He played the piano. He wrote letters to his friends in Holland. He felt no need for the conversation of intellectual persons. He liked a good laugh, but he could get that out of a fool just as well as out of a professor of philosophy. He had a notion that he was a very wise little man.

Like all good Dutchmen in the Far East he began his lunch with a small glass of Hollands gin. It has a musty acrid flavour, and the taste for it must be acquired, but Mr Gruyter preferred it to any cocktail. When he drank it he felt besides that he was upholding the traditions of his race. Then he had *rystafel.* He had it every day. He heaped a soup plate high with rice, and then, his three boys waiting on him, helped himself to the curry that one handed him, to the fried egg that another brought, and to the condiment presented by the third. Then each one brought another dish, of bacon, or bananas, or pickled fish, and presently his plate was piled high in a huge pyramid. He stirred it all together and began to eat.

He ate slowly and with relish. He drank a bottle of beer.

He did not think while he was eating. His attention was applied to the mass in front of him and he consumed it with a happy concentration. It never palled on him. And when he had emptied the great plate it was a compensation to think that next day he would have *rystafel* again. He grew tired of it as little as the rest of us grow tired of bread. He finished his beer and lit his cigar. The boy brought him a cup of coffee. He leaned back in his chair then and allowed himself the luxury of reflection.

It tickled him to have sentenced Ginger Ted to the richly deserved punishment of six months' hard labour, and he smiled when he thought of him working on the roads with the other prisoners. It would have been silly to deport from the island the one man with whom he could occasionally have a heart-to-heart talk, and besides, the satisfaction it would have given the missionary would have been bad for that gentleman's character. Ginger Ted was a scamp and a scallywag, but the Controleur had a kindly feeling for him. They had drunk many a bottle of beer in one another's company, and when the pearl fishers from Port Darwin came in and they all made a night of it, they had got gloriously tight together. The Controleur liked the reckless way in which Ginger Ted squandered the priceless treasure of life.

Ginger Ted had wandered in one day on the ship that was going up from Merauke to Macassar. The captain did not know how he had found his way there, but he had travelled steerage with the natives, and he stopped off at the Alas Islands because he liked the look of them. Mr Gruyter had a suspicion that their attraction consisted perhaps in their being under the Dutch flag and so out of British jurisdiction. But his papers were in order, so there was no reason why he should not stay. He said that he was buying pearl-shell for an Australian firm, but it soon appeared that his commercial undertakings were not serious. Drink, indeed, took up so much of his time that he had little left over for other pursuits. He was in receipt of two pounds a week, paid monthly, which came regularly to him from England. The Controleur guessed that this sum was paid only so long as he kept well away from the persons who sent it. It was anyway too small to permit him any liberty of movement. Ginger Ted was reticent. The Controleur discovered that he was an Englishman, this he learnt from his passport, which described him as Edward Wilson, and that he had been in Australia. But why he had left England and what he had done in Australia he had no notion. Nor could he ever quite tell to what class Ginger Ted belonged. When you saw him in a filthy singlet and a pair of ragged trousers, a battered topi on his head, with the pearl fishers and heard his conversation, coarse, obscene and illiterate, you thought he must be a sailor before the mast who had deserted his ship, or a labourer, but when you saw his handwriting you were surprised to find that it was that of a man not without at least some education, and on occasion when you got him alone, if he had had a few drinks but was not yet drunk, he would talk of matters that neither a sailor nor a labourer would have been likely to know anything about. The Controleur had a certain sensitiveness and he realised that Ginger Ted did not speak to him as an inferior to a superior but as an equal. Most of his remittance was mortgaged before he received it, and the Chinamen to whom he owed money were standing at his elbow when the monthly letter was delivered to him, but with what was left he proceeded to get drunk. It was then that he made trouble, for when drunk he grew violent and was then likely to commit acts that brought him into the hands of the police. Hitherto Mr Gruyter had contented himself with keeping him in gaol till he was sober and giving him a talking to. When he was out of money he cadged what drink he could from anyone who would give it him. Rum, brandy, arak, it was all the same to him. Two or three times Mr Gruyter had got him work on plantations run by Chinese in one or other of the islands, but he could not stick to it, and in a few weeks was back again at Baru on the beach. It was a miracle how he kept body and soul together. He had, of course, a way with him. He picked up the various dialects spoken on the islands, and knew how to make the natives laugh. They despised him, but they respected his physical strength, and they liked his company. He was as a result never at a loss for a meal or a mat to sleep on. The strange thing was, and it was this that chiefly outraged the Reverend Owen Jones, that he could do anything he liked with a woman. The Controleur could not imagine what it was they saw in him. He was casual with them and rather brutal. He took what they gave him, but seemed incapable of gratitude. He used them for his pleasure and then flung them indifferently away. Once or twice this had got him into trouble, and Mr Gruyter had had to sentence an angry father for sticking a knife in Ginger

Ted's back one night, and a Chinese woman had sought to poison herself by swallowing opium because he had deserted her. Once Mr Jones came to the Controleur in a great state because the beachcomber had seduced one of his converts. The Controleur agreed that it was very deplorable, but could only advise Mr Jones to keep a sharp eye on these young persons. The Controleur liked it less when he discovered that a girl whom he fancied a good deal himself and had been seeing for several weeks had all the time been according her favours also to Ginger Ted. When he thought of this particular incident he smiled again at the thought of Ginger Ted doing six months' hard labour. It is seldom in this life that in the process of doing your bounden duty you can get back at a fellow who has played you a dirty trick.

A few days later Mr Gruyter was taking a walk, partly for exercise and partly to see that some job he wanted done was being duly proceeded with, when he passed a gang of prisoners working under the charge of a warder. Among them he saw Ginger Ted. He wore the prison sarong, a dingy tunic called in Malay a *baju*, and his own battered topi. They were repairing the road, and Ginger Ted was wielding a heavy pick. The way was narrow and the Controleur saw that he must pass within a foot of him. He remembered his threats. He knew that Ginger Ted was a man of violent passion and the language he had used in the dock made it plain that he had not seen what a good joke it was of the Controleur's to sentence him to six months' hard labour. If Ginger Ted suddenly attacked him with the pick, nothing on God's earth could save him. It was true that the warder would immediately shoot him down, but meanwhile the Controleur's head would be bashed in. It was with a funny little feeling in the pit of his stomach that Mr Gruyter walked through the gang of prisoners. They were working in pairs a few feet from one another. He set his mind on neither hastening his pace nor slackening it. As he passed Ginger Ted, the man swung his pick into the ground and looked up at the Controleur and as he caught his eye winked. The Controleur checked the smile that rose to his lips and with official dignity strode on. But that wink, so lusciously full of sardonic humour, filled him with satisfaction. If he had been the Caliph of Baghdad instead of a junior official in the Dutch Civil Service, he would forthwith have released Ginger Ted, sent slaves to bathe and perfume him, and having clothed him in a golden robe entertained him to a sumptuous repast.

Ginger Ted was an exemplary prisoner and in a month or two the Controleur, having occasion to send a gang to do some work on one of the outlying islands, included him in it. There was no gaol there, so the ten fellows he sent, under the charge of a warder, were billeted on the natives and after their day's work lived like free men. The job was sufficient to take up the rest of Ginger Ted's sentence.

The Controleur saw him before he left. 'Look here, Ginger,' he said to him, 'here's ten guilder for you so that you can buy yourself tobacco when you're gone.'

'Couldn't you make it a bit more? There's eight pounds a month coming in regularly.'

'I think that's enough. I'll keep the letters that come for you, and when you get back you'll have a tidy sum. You'll have enough to take you anywhere you want to go.'

'I'm very comfortable here,' said Ginger Ted.

'Well, the day you come back, clean yourself up and come over to my house. We'll have a bottle of beer together.'

'That'll be fine. I guess I'll be ready for a good crack then.'

Now chance steps in. The island to which Ginger Ted had been sent was called Maputiti, and like all the rest of them it was rocky, heavily wooded and surrounded by a reef. There was a village among coconuts on the seashore opposite the opening of the reef and another village on a brackish lake in the middle of the island. Some of the inhabitants of this village had been converted to Christianity. Communication with Baru was effected by a launch that touched at the various islands at irregular intervals. It carried passengers and produce. But the villagers were seafaring folk, and if they had to communicate urgently with Baru, they manned a prahu and sailed the fifty miles or so that separated them from it. It happened that when Ginger Ted's sentence had but another fortnight to run the Christian headman of the village on the lake was taken suddenly ill. The native remedies availed him nothing and he writhed in agony. Messengers were sent to Baru imploring the missionary's help; but as ill luck would have it Mr Jones was suffering at the moment from an attack of malaria. He was in bed and unable to move. He talked the matter over with his sister.

'It sounds like acute appendicitis,' he told her.

'You can't go, Owen,' she said.

'I can't let the man die.'

Mr Jones had a temperature of a hundred and four. His head was aching like mad. He had been delirious at night. His eyes were shining strangely and his sister felt that he was holding on to his wits by a sheer effort of will.

'You couldn't operate in the state you're in.'

'No, I couldn't. Then Hassan must go.'

Hassan was the dispenser.

'You couldn't trust Hassan. He'd never dare to do an operation on his own responsibility. And they'd never let him. I'll go. Hassan can stay here and look after you.'

'You can't remove an appendix!'

'Why not? I've seen you do it. I've done lots of minor operations.'

Mr Jones felt he didn't quite understand what she was saying.

'Is the launch in?'

'No, it's gone to one of the islands. But I can go in the prahu the men came in.'

'You? I wasn't thinking of you. You can't go.'

'I'm going, Owen.'

'Going where?' he said.

She saw that his mind was wandering already. She put her hand soothingly on his dry forehead. She gave him a dose of medicine. He muttered something and she realised that he did not know where he was. Of course she was anxious about him, but she knew that his illness was not dangerous, and she could leave him safely to the mission boy who was helping her nurse him and to the native dispenser. She slipped out of the room. She put her toilet things, a night-dress, and a change of clothes into a bag. A little chest with surgical instruments, bandages and antiseptic dressings was kept always ready. She gave them to the two natives who had come over from Maputiti, and telling the dispenser what she was going to do, gave him instructions to inform her brother when he was able to listen. Above all he was not to be anxious about her. She put on her topi and sallied forth. The mission was about half a mile from the village. She walked quickly. At the end of the jetty the prahu was waiting. Six men manned it. She took her place in the stern and they set off with a rapid stroke. Within the reef the sea was calm, but when they crossed the bar they came upon a long swell. But this was not the first journey of the sort Miss Jones had taken and she was confident in the seaworthiness of the boat she was in. It was noon and the sun beat down from a sultry sky. The only thing that harassed her was that they could not arrive before dark, and if she found it necessary to operate at once she could count only on the light of hurricane lamps.

Miss Jones was a woman of hard on forty. Nothing in her appearance would have prepared you for such determination as she had just shown. She had an odd drooping gracefulness, which suggested that she might be swayed by every breeze; it was almost an affectation; and it made the strength of character which you soon discovered in her seem positively monstrous. She was flat-chested, tall and extremely thin. She had a long sallow face and she was much afflicted with prickly heat. Her lank brown hair was drawn back straight from her forehead. She had rather small eyes, grey in colour, and because they were somewhat too close they gave her face a shrewish look. Her nose was long and thin and a trifle red. She suffered a good deal from indigestion. But this infirmity availed nothing against her ruthless determination to look upon the bright side of things. Firmly persuaded that the world was evil and men unspeakably vicious, she extracted any little piece of decency she could find in them with the modest pride with which a conjurer extracts a rabbit from a hat. She was quick, resourceful and competent.

When she arrived on the island she saw that there was not a moment to lose if she was to save the headman's life. Under the greatest difficulties, showing a native how to give the anaesthetic, she operated, and for the next three days nursed the patient with anxious assiduity. Everything went very well and she realised that her brother could not have made a better job of it. She waited long enough to take out the stitches and then prepared to go home. She could flatter herself that she had not wasted her time. She had given medical attention to such as needed it, she had strengthened the small Christian community in its faith, admonished such as were lax and cast the good seed in places where it might be hoped under divine providence to take root.

The launch, coming from one of the other islands, put in somewhat late in the afternoon, but it was full moon and they expected to reach Baru before midnight. They brought her things down to the wharf and the people who were seeing her off stood about repeating their thanks. Quite a little crowd collected. The launch was loaded with sacks of copra, but Miss Jones was used to its strong smell and it did not incommode her. She made herself as comfortable a place to sit in as she could, and waiting for the launch to start, chatted with her grateful flock. She was the only passenger. Suddenly a group of natives emerged from the trees that embowered the little village on the lagoon and she saw that among them was a white man. He wore a prison sarong and a *baju.* He had long red hair. She at once recognised Ginger Ted. A policeman was with him. They shook hands and Ginger Ted shook hands with the villagers who accompanied him. They bore bundles of fruit and a jar which Miss Jones guessed contained native spirit, and these they put in the launch. She discovered to her surprise that Ginger Ted was coming with her. His term was up and instructions had arrived that he was to be returned to Baru in the launch. He gave her a glance, but did not nod – indeed Miss Jones turned away her head – and stepped in. The mechanic started his engine and in a moment they were jug-jugging through the channel in the lagoon. Ginger Ted clambered on to a pile of sacks and lit a cigarette.

Miss Jones ignored him. Of course she knew him very well. Her heart sank when she thought that he was going to be once more in Baru, creating a scandal and drinking, a peril to the women and a thorn in the flesh of all decent people. She knew the steps her brother had taken to have him deported and she had no patience with the Controleur, who would not see a duty that stared him so plainly in the face. When they had crossed the bar and were in the open sea Ginger Ted took the stopper out of the jar of arak and putting his mouth to it took a long pull. Then he handed the jar to the two mechanics who formed the crew. One was a middle-aged man and the other a youth.

'I do not wish you to drink anything while we are on the journey,' said Miss Jones sternly to the elder one.

He smiled at her and drank.

'A little arak can do no one any harm,' he answered. He passed the jar to his companion, who drank also.

'If you drink again I shall complain to the Controleur,' said Miss Jones.

The elder man said something she could not understand, but which she suspected was very rude, and passed the jar back to Ginger Ted. They went along for an hour or more. The sea was like glass and the sun set radiantly. It set behind one of the islands and for a few minutes changed it into a mystic city of the skies. Miss Jones turned round to watch it and her heart was filled with gratitude for the beauty of the world.

'And only man is vile,' she quoted to herself.

They went due east. In the distance was a little island which she knew they passed close by. It was uninhabited. A rocky islet thickly grown with virgin forest. The boatman lit his lamps. The night fell and immediately the sky was thick with stars. The moon had not yet risen. Suddenly there was a slight jar and the launch began to vibrate strangely. The engine rattled. The head mechanic, calling to his mate to take the helm, crept under the housing. They seemed to be going more slowly. The engine stopped. She asked the youth what was the matter, but he did not know. Ginger Ted got down from the top of the copra sacks and slipped under the housing. When he reappeared she would have liked to ask him what had happened, but her dignity prevented her. She sat still and occupied herself with her thoughts. There was a long swell and the launch rolled slightly. The mechanic emerged once more into view and started the engine. Though it rattled like mad they began to move. The launch vibrated from stem to stern. They went very slowly. Evidently something was amiss, but Miss Jones was exasperated rather than alarmed.

The launch was supposed to do six knots, but now it was just crawling along; at that rate they would not get into Baru till long, long after midnight. The mechanic, still busy under the housing, shouted out something to the man at the helm. They spoke in Bugi, of which Miss Jones knew very little. But after a while she noticed that they had changed their course and seemed to be heading for the little uninhabited island a good deal to the lee of which they should have passed.

'Where are we going?' she asked the helmsman with sudden misgiving.

He pointed to the islet. She got up and went to the housing and called to the man to come out.

'You're not going there? Why? What's the matter?'

'I can't get to Baru,' he said.

'But you must. I insist. I order you to go to Baru.'

The man shrugged his shoulders. He turned his back on her and slipped once more under the housing. Then Ginger Ted addressed her.

'One of the blades of the propeller has broken off. He thinks he can get as far as that island. We shall have to stay the night there and he'll put on a new propeller in the morning when the tide's out.'

'I can't spend the night on an uninhabited island with three men,' she cried.

'A lot of women would jump at it.'

'I insist on going to Baru. Whatever happens we must get there tonight.'

'Don't get excited, old girl. We've got to beach the boat to put a new propeller on, and we shall be all right on the island.'

'How dare you speak to me like that! I think you're very insolent.'

'You'll be OK. We've got plenty of grub and we'll have a snack when we land. You have a drop of arak and you'll feel like a house on fire.'

'You're an impertinent man. If you don't go to Baru I'll have you all put in prison.'

'We're not going to Baru. We can't. We're going to that island and if you don't like it you can get out and swim.'

'Oh, you'll pay for this.'

'Shut up, you old cow,' said Ginger Ted.

Miss Jones gave a gasp of anger. But she controlled herself. Even out there, in the middle of the ocean, she had too much dignity to bandy words with that vile wretch. The launch, the engine rattling horribly, crawled on. It was pitch dark now, and she could no longer see the island they were making for. Miss Jones, deeply incensed, sat with lips tight shut and a frown on her brow; she was not used to being crossed. Then the moon rose and she could see the bulk of Ginger Ted sprawling on the top of the piled sacks of copra. The glimmer of his cigarette was strangely sinister. Now the island was vaguely outlined against the sky. They reached it and the boatman ran the launch on to the beach. Suddenly Miss Jones gave a gasp. The truth had dawned on her and her anger changed to fear. Her heart beat violently. She shook in every limb. She felt dreadfully faint. She saw it all. Was the broken propeller a put-up job or was it an accident? She could not be certain; anyhow, she knew that Ginger Ted would seize the opportunity. Ginger Ted would rape her. She knew his character. He was mad about women. That was what he had done, practically, to the girl at the mission, such a good little thing she was and an excellent sempstress; they would have prosecuted him for that and he would have been sentenced to years of imprisonment only very unfortunately the innocent child had gone back to him several times and indeed had only complained of his ill usage when he left her for somebody else. They had gone to the Controleur about it, but he had refused to take any steps, saying in that coarse way of his that even if what the girl said was true, it didn't look very much as though it had been an altogether unpleasant experience. Ginger Ted was a scoundrel. And she was a white woman. What chance was there that he would spare her? None. She knew men. But she must pull herself together. She must keep her wits about her. She must have courage. She was determined to sell her virtue dearly, and if he killed her – well, she would rather die than yield. And if she died she would rest in the arms of Jesus. For a moment a great light blinded her eyes and she saw the mansions of her Heavenly Father. They were a grand and sumptuous mixture of a picture palace and a railway station. The mechanics and Ginger Ted jumped out of the launch and, waist deep in water, gathered round the broken propeller. She took advantage of their preoccupation to get her case of surgical instruments out of the box. She took out the four scalpels it contained and secreted them in her clothing. If Ginger Ted touched her she would not hesitate to plunge a scalpel into his heart.

'Now then, miss, you'd better get out,' said Ginger Ted. 'You'll be better off on the beach than in the boat.'

She thought so too. At least there she would have freedom of action. Without a word she clambered over the copra sacks. He offered her his hand.

'I don't want your help,' she said coldly.

'You can go to hell,' he answered.

It was a little difficult to get out of the boat without showing her legs, but by the exercise of considerable ingenuity she managed it.

'Damned lucky we've got something to eat. We'll make a fire and then you'd better have a snack and a nip of arak.'

'I want nothing. I only want to be left alone.'

'It won't hurt me if you go hungry.'

She did not answer. She walked, with head erect, along the beach. She held the largest scalpel in her closed fist. The moon allowed her to see where she was going. She looked for a place to hide. The thick forest came down to the very edge of the beach; but, afraid of its darkness (after all, she was but a woman), she dared not plunge into its depth. She did not know what animals lurked there or what dangerous snakes. Besides, her instinct told her that it was better to keep those three had men in sight; then if they came towards her she would be prepared. Presently she found a little hollow. She looked round. They seemed to be occupied with their own affairs and they could not see her. She slipped in. There was a rock between them and her so that she was hidden from them and yet could watch them. She saw them go to and from the boat carrying things. She saw them build a fire. It lit them luridly and she saw them sit around it and eat, and she saw the jar of arak passed from one to the other. They were all going to get drunk. What would happen to her then? It might be that she could cope with Ginger Ted, though his strength terrified her, but against three she would be powerless. A mad idea came to her to go to Ginger Ted and fall on her knees before him and beg him to spare her. He must have some spark of decent feeling in him and she had always been so convinced that there was good even in the worst of men. He must have had a mother. Perhaps he had a sister. Ah, but how could you appeal to a man blinded with lust and drunk with arak? She began to feel terribly weak. She was afraid she was going to cry. That would never do. She needed all her self-control. She bit her lip. She watched them, like a tiger watching his prey; no, not like that, like a lamb watching three hungry wolves. She saw them put more wood on the fire and Ginger Ted, in his sarong, silhouetted by the flames. Perhaps after he had had his will of her he would pass her on to the others. How could she go back to her brother when such a thing had happened to her? Of course he would be sympathetic, but would he ever feel quite the same to her again? It would break his heart. And perhaps he would think that she ought to have resisted more. For his sake perhaps it would be better if she said nothing about it; naturally the men would say nothing. It would mean twenty years in prison for them. But then supposing she had a baby. Miss Jones instinctively clenched her hands with horror and nearly cut herself with the scalpel. Of course it would only infuriate them if she resisted.

'What shall I do?' she cried. 'What have I done to deserve this?'

She flung herself down on her knees and prayed to God to save her. She prayed long and earnestly. She reminded God that she was a virgin and just mentioned, in case it had slipped the divine memory, how much St Paul had valued that excellent state. And then she peeped round the rock again. The three men appeared to be smoking and the fire was dying down. Now was the time that Ginger Ted's lewd thoughts might be expected to turn to the woman who was at his mercy. She smothered a cry, for suddenly he got up and walked in her direction. She felt all her muscles grow taut, and though her heart was beating furiously she clenched the scalpel firmly in her hand. But it was for another purpose that Ginger Ted had got up. Miss Jones blushed and looked away. He strolled slowly back to the others and sitting down again raised the jar of arak to his lips. Miss Jones, crouching behind the rock, watched with straining eyes. The conversation round the fire grew less and presently she divined, rather than saw, that the two natives wrapped themselves in blankets and composed themselves to slumber. She understood. This was the moment Ginger Ted had been waiting for. When they were fast asleep he would get up cautiously and, without a sound, in order not to wake the others, creep stealthily towards her. Was it that he was unwilling to share her with them or did he know that his deed was so dastardly that he did not wish them to know of it? After all, he was a white man and she was a white women. He could not have sunk so low as to allow her to suffer the violence of natives. But his plan, which was so obvious to her, had given her an idea; when she saw him coming she would scream, she would scream so loudly that it would wake the two mechanics. She remembered now that the elder, though he had only one eye, had a kind face. But Ginger Ted did not move. She was feeling terribly tired. She began to fear that she would not have the strength now to resist him. She had gone through too much. She closed her eyes for a minute.

When she opened them it was broad daylight. She must have fallen asleep and, so shattered was she by emotion, have slept till long after dawn. It gave her quite a turn. She sought to rise, but something caught at her legs. She looked and found that she was covered with two empty copra sacks. Someone had come in the night and put them over her. Ginger Ted. She gave a little scream. The horrible thought flashed through her mind that he had outraged her in her sleep. No. It was impossible. And yet he had had her at his mercy. Defenceless. And he had spared her. She blushed furiously. She raised herself to her feet, feeling a little stiff, and arranged her disordered dress. The scalpel had fallen from her hand and she picked it up. She took the two copra sacks and emerged from her hiding-place. She walked towards the boat. It was floating in the shallow water of the lagoon.

'Come on, Miss Jones,' said Ginger Ted. 'We've finished. I was just going to wake you up.'

She could not look at him, but she felt herself as red as a turkey cock.

'Have a banana?' he said.

Without a word she took it. She was very hungry, and ate it with relish.

'Step on this rock and you'll be able to get in without wetting your feet.'

Miss Jones felt as though she could sink into the ground with shame, but she did as he told her. He took hold of her arm – good heavens, his hand was like an iron vice, never, never could she have struggled with him – and helped her into the launch. The mechanic started the engine and they slid out of the lagoon. In three hours they were at Baru.

That evening, having been officially released, Ginger Ted went to the Controleur's house. He wore no longer the prison uniform, but the ragged singlet and the khaki shorts in which he had been arrested. He had had his hair cut and it fitted his head now like a little curly red cap. He was thinner. He had lost his bloated flabbiness and looked younger and better. Mr Gruyter, a friendly grin on his round face, shook hands with him and asked him to sit down. The boy brought two bottles of beer.

'I'm glad to see you hadn't forgotten my invitation, Ginger,' said the Controleur.

'Not likely. I've been looking forward to this for six months.'

'Here's luck, Ginger Ted.'

'Same to you, Controleur.'

They emptied their glasses and the Controleur clapped his hands. The boy brought two more bottles.

'Well, you don't bear me any malice for the sentence I gave you, I hope.'

'No bloody fear. I was mad for a minute, but I got over it. I didn't have half a bad time, you know. Nice lot of girls on that island, Controleur. You ought to give 'em a look over one of these days.'

'You're a bad lot, Ginger.'

'Terrible.'

'Good beer, isn't it?'

'Fine.'

'Let's have some more.'

Ginger Ted's remittance had been arriving every month and the Controleur now had fifty pounds for him. When the damage he had done to the Chinaman's shop was paid for there would still be over thirty.

'That's quite a lot of money, Ginger. You ought to do something useful with it.'

'I mean to,' answered Ginger. 'Spend it.'

The Controleur sighed.

'Well, that's what money's for, I guess.'

The Controleur gave his guest the news. Not much had happened during the last six months. Time on the Alas Islands did not matter very much and the rest of the world did not matter at all.

'Any wars anywhere?' asked Ginger Ted.

'No. Not that I've noticed. Harry Jervis found a pretty big pearl. He says he's going to ask a thousand quid for it.'

'I hope he gets it.'

'And Charlie McCormack's married.'

'He always was a bit soft.'

Suddenly the boy appeared and said Mr Jones wished to know if he might come in. Before the Controleur could give an answer Mr Jones walked in.

'I won't detain you long,' he said. 'I've been trying to get hold of this good man all day and when I heard he was here I thought you wouldn't mind my coming.'

'How is Miss Jones?' asked the Controleur politely. 'None the worse for her night in the open, I trust.'

'She's naturally a bit shaken. She had a temperature and I've insisted on her going to bed, but I don't think it's serious.'

The two men had got up on the missionary's entrance, and now the missionary went up to Ginger Ted and held out his hand.

'I want to thank you. You did a great and noble thing. My sister is right, one should always look for the good in their fellow men; I am afraid I misjudged you in the past: I beg your pardon.'

He spoke very solemnly. Ginger Ted looked at him with amazement. He had not been able to prevent the missionary taking his hand. He still held it.

'What the hell are you talking about?'

'You had my sister at your mercy and you spared her. I thought you were all evil and I am ashamed. She was defenceless. She was in your power. You had pity on her. I thank you from the bottom of my heart. Neither my sister nor I will ever forget. God bless and guard you always.'

Mr Jones's voice shook a little and he turned his head away. He released Ginger Ted's hand and strode quickly to the door. Ginger Ted watched him with a blank face.

'What the blazes does he mean?' he asked.

The Controleur laughed. He tried to control himself, but the more he did the more he laughed. He shook and you saw the folds of his fat belly ripple under the sarong. He leaned back in his long chair and rolled from side to side. He did not laugh only with his face, he laughed with his whole body, and even the muscles of his podgy legs shook with mirth. He held his aching ribs. Ginger Ted looked at him frowning, and because he did not understand what the joke was he grew angry. He seized one of the empty beer bottles by the neck.

'If you don't stop laughing, I'll break your blood head open,' he said.

The Controleur mopped his face. He swallowed a mouthful of beer. He sighed and groaned because his sides were hurting him.

'He's thanking you for having respected the virtue of Miss Jones,' he spluttered at last.

'Me?' cried Ginger Ted.

The thought took quite a long time to travel through his head, but when at last he got it, he flew into a violent rage. There flowed from his mouth such a stream of blasphemous obscenities as would have startled a marine.

'That old cow,' he finished. 'What does he take me for?'

'You have the reputation of being rather hot stuff with the girls, Ginger,' giggled the little Controleur.

'I wouldn't touch her with the fag end of a barge-pole. It never entered my head. The nerve. I'll wring his blasted neck. Look here, give me my money, I'm going to get drunk.'

'I don't blame you,' said the Controleur.

'That old cow,' repeated Ginger Ted. 'That old cow.'

He was shocked and outraged. The suggestion really shattered his sense of decency.

The Controleur had the money at hand and having got Ginger Ted to sign the necessary papers gave it to him.

'Go and get drunk, Ginger Ted,' he said, 'but I warn you, if you get into mischief it'll be twelve months next time.'

'I shan't get into mischief,' said Ginger Ted sombrely. He was suffering from a sense of injury. 'It's an insult,' he shouted at the Controleur. 'That's what it is, it's a bloody insult.'

He lurched out of the house, and as he went he muttered to himself: 'Dirty swine, dirty swine.' Ginger Ted remained drunk for a week. Mr Jones went to see the Controleur again.

'I'm very sorry to hear that poor fellow has taken up his evil course again,' he said. 'My sister and I are dreadfully disappointed. I'm afraid it wasn't very wise to give him so much money at once.'

'It was his own money. I had no right to keep it back.'

'Not a legal right, perhaps, but surely a moral right.'

He told the Controleur the story of that fearful night on the island. With her feminine instinct, Miss Jones had realised that the man, inflamed with lust, was determined to take advantage of her, and, resolved to defend herself to the last, had armed herself with a scalpel. He told the Controleur how she had prayed and wept and how she had hidden herself. Her agony was indescribable, and she knew that she could never have survived the shame. She rocked to and fro and every moment she thought he was coming. And there was no help anywhere and at last she had fallen asleep; she was tired out, poor thing, she had undergone more than any human being could stand, and then when she awoke she found that he had covered her with copra sacks. He had found her asleep, and surely it was her innocence, her very helplessness that had moved him, he hadn't the heart to touch her; he covered her gently with two copra sacks and crept silently away.

'It shows you that deep down in him there is something sterling. My sister feels it's our duty to save him. We must do something for him.'

'Well, in your place I wouldn't try till he's got through all his money,' said the Controleur, 'and then if he's not in gaol you can do what you like.'

But Ginger Ted didn't want to be saved. About a fortnight after his release from prison he was sitting on a stool outside a Chinaman's shop looking vacantly down the street when he saw Miss Jones coming along. He stared at her for a minute and once more amazement seized him. He muttered to himself and there can be little doubt that his mutterings were disrespectful. But then he noticed that Miss Jones had seen him and he quickly turned his head away; he was conscious, notwithstanding, that she was looking at him. She was walking briskly, but she sensibly diminished her pace as she approached him. He thought she was going to stop and speak to him. He got up quickly and went into the shop. He did not venture to come out for at least five minutes. Half an hour later Mr Jones himself came along and he went straight up to Ginger Ted with outstretched hand.

'How do you do, Mr Edward? My sister told me I should find you here.'

Ginger Ted gave him a surly look and did not take the proffered hand. He made no answer.

'We'd be so very glad if you'd come to dinner with us next Sunday. My sister's a capital cook and she'll make you a real Australian dinner.'

'Go to hell,' said Ginger Ted.

'That's not very gracious,' said the missionary, but with a little laugh to show that he was not affronted. 'You go and see the Controleur from time to time, why shouldn't you come and see us? It's pleasant to talk to white people now and then. Won't you let bygones be bygones? I can assure you of a very cordial welcome.'

'I haven't got clothes fit to go out in,' said Ginger Ted sulkily.

'Oh, never mind about that. Come as you are.'

'I won't.'

'Why not? You must have a reason.'

Ginger Ted was a blunt man. He had no hesitation

in saying what we should all like to when we receive unwelcome invitations.

'I don't want to.'

'I'm sorry. My sister will be very disappointed.'

Mr Jones, determined to show that he was not in the least offended, gave him a breezy nod and walked on. Forty-eight hours later there mysteriously arrived at the house in which Ginger Ted lodged a parcel containing a suit of ducks, a tennis shirt, a pair of socks and some shoes. He was unaccustomed to receiving presents and next time he saw the Controleur asked him if it was he who had sent the things.

'Not on your life,' replied the Controleur. 'I'm perfectly indifferent to the state of your wardrobe.'

'Well, then, who the hell can have?'

'Search me.'

It was necessary from time to time for Miss Jones to see Mr Gruyter on business and shortly after this she came to see him one morning in his office. She was a capable woman and though she generally wanted him to do something he had no mind to, she did not waste his time. He was a little surprised then to discover that she had come on a very trivial errand. When he told her that he could not take cognisance of the matter in question, she did not as was her habit try to convince him, but accepted his refusal as definite. She got up to go and then as though it were an afterthought said: 'Oh, Mr Gruyter, my brother is very anxious that we should have the man they call Ginger Ted to supper with us and I've written him a little note inviting him for the day after tomorrow. I think he's rather shy, and I wonder if you'd come with him.'

'That's very kind of you.'

'My brother feels that we ought to do something for the poor fellow.'

'A woman's influence and all that sort of thing,' said the Controleur demurely.

'Will you persuade him to come? I'm sure he will if you make a point of it, and when he knows the way he'll come again. It seems such a pity to let a young man like that go to pieces altogether.'

The Controleur looked up at her. She was several inches taller than he. He thought her very unattractive. She reminded him strangely of wet linen hung on a clothes-line to dry. His eyes twinkled, but he kept a straight face.

'I'll do my best,' he said.

'How old is he?' she asked.

'According to his passport he's thirty-one.'

'And what is his real name?'

'Wilson.'

'Edward Wilson,' she said softly.

'It's astonishing that after the life he's led he should be so strong,' murmured the Controleur. 'He has the strength of an ox.'

'Those red-headed men sometimes are very powerful,' said Miss Jones, but spoke as though she were choking.

'Quite so,' said the Controleur.

Then for no obvious reason Miss Jones blushed. She hurriedly said goodbye to the Controleur and left his office.

'*Godverdomme!*' said the Controleur.

He knew now who had sent Ginger Ted the new clothes.

He met him during the course of the day and asked him whether he had heard from Miss Jones. Ginger

Ted took a crumpled ball of paper out of his pocket and gave it to him. It was the invitation. It ran as follows:

> DEAR MR WILSON – My brother and I would be so very glad if you would come and have supper with us next Thursday at 7.30. The Controleur has kindly promised to come. We have some new records from Australia which I am sure you will like. I am afraid I was not very nice to you last time we met, but I did not know you so well then, and I am big enough to admit it when I have committed an error. I hope you will forgive me and let me be your friend.
>
> Yours sincerely,
>
> MARTHA JONES

The Controleur noticed that she addressed him as Mr Wilson and referred to his own promise to go, so that when she told him she had already invited Ginger Ted she had a little anticipated the truth.

'What are you going to do?'

'I'm not going, if that's what you mean. Damned nerve.'

'You must answer the letter.'

'Well, I won't.'

'Now look here, Ginger, you put on those new clothes and you come as a favour to me. I've got to go, and damn it all, you can't leave me in the lurch. It won't hurt you just once.'

Ginger Ted looked at the Controleur suspiciously, but his face was serious and his manner sincere; he could not guess that within him the Dutchman bubbled with laughter.

'What the devil do they want me for?'

'I don't know. The pleasure of your society, I suppose.'

'Will there by any booze?'

'No, but come up to my house at seven, and we'll have a tiddly before we go.'

'Oh, all right,' said Ginger Ted sulkily.

The Controleur rubbed his little fat hands with joy. He was expecting a great deal of amusement from the party. But when Thursday came and seven o'clock Ginger Ted was dead drunk and Mr Gruyter had to go alone. He told the missionary and his sister the plain truth. Mr Jones shook his head.

'I'm afraid it's no good, Martha, the man's hopeless.'

For a moment Miss Jones was silent and the Controleur saw two tears trickle down her long thin nose. She bit her lip.

'No one is hopeless. Everyone has some good in him. I shall pray for him every night. It would be wicked to doubt the power of God.'

Perhaps Miss Jones was right in this, but the divine providence took a very funny way of effecting its ends. Ginger Ted began to drink more heavily than ever. He was so troublesome that even Mr Gruyter lost patience with him. He made up his mind that he could not have the fellow on the islands any more and resolved to deport him on the next boat that touched at Baru. Then a man died under mysterious circumstances after having been for a trip to one of the islands and the Controleur learnt that there had been several deaths on the same island. He sent the Chinese who was the official doctor of the group to look into the matter, and very soon received intelligence that the deaths were due to cholera. Two more took place at Baru and the certainty was forced upon him that there was an epidemic.

The Controleur cursed freely. He cursed in Dutch, he cursed in English and he cursed in Malay. Then he drank a bottle of beer and smoked a cigar. After that he took thought. He knew the Chinese doctor would be useless. He was a nervous little man from Java and the natives would refuse to obey his orders. The Controleur was efficient and knew pretty well what must be done, but he could not do everything single-handed. He did not like Mr Jones, but just then he was thankful that he was at hand, and he sent for him at once. In ten minutes Mr Jones was in the office. He was accompanied by his sister.

'You know what I want to see you about, Mr Jones,' he said abruptly.

'Yes. I've been expecting a message from you. That is why my sister has come with me. We are ready to put all our resources at your disposal. I need not tell you that my sister is as competent as a man.'

'I know. I shall be very glad of her assistance.'

They set to without further delay to discuss the steps that must be taken. Hospital huts would have to be erected and quarantine stations. The inhabitants of the various villages on the islands must be forced to take proper precautions. In a good many cases the infected villages drew their water from the same well as the uninfected, and in each case this difficulty would have to be dealt with according to circumstances. It was necessary to send round people to give orders and make sure that they were carried out. Negligence must be ruthlessly punished. The worst of it was that the natives would not obey other natives, and orders given by native policemen, themselves unconvinced of their efficacy, would certainly be disregarded. It was advisable for Mr Jones to stay at Baru where the population was largest and his medical attention most wanted; and what with the official duties that forced him to keep in touch with his headquarters, it was impossible for Mr Gruyter to visit all the other islands himself. Miss Jones must go; but the natives of some of the outlying islands were wild and treacherous; the Controleur had had a good deal of trouble with them. He did not like the idea of exposing her to danger.

'I'm not afraid,' she said.

'I dare say. But if you have your throat cut I shall get into trouble, and besides, we're so short-handed I don't want to risk losing your help.'

'Then let Mr Wilson come with me. He knows the natives better than anyone and can speak all their dialects.'

'Ginger Ted?' The Controleur stared at her. 'He's just getting over an attack of DTs.'

'I know,' she answered.

'You know a great deal, Miss Jones.'

Even though the moment was so serious Mr Gruyter could not but smile. He gave her a sharp look, but she met it coolly.

'There's nothing like responsibility for bringing out what there is in a man, and I think something like this may be the making of him.'

'Do you think it would be wise to trust yourself for days at a time to a man of such infamous character?' said the missionary.

'I put my trust in God,' she answered gravely.

'Do you think he'd be any use?' asked the Controleur. 'You know what he is.'

'I'm convinced of it.' Then she blushed. 'After all, no one knows better than I that he's capable of self-control.'

The Controleur bit his lip.

'Let's send for him.'

He gave a message to the sergeant and in a few minutes Ginger Ted stood before them. He looked ill. He had evidently been much shaken by his recent attack and his nerves were all to pieces. He was in rags and he had not shaved for a week. No one could have looked more disreputable.

'Look here, Ginger,' said the Controleur, 'it's about this cholera business. We've got to force the natives to take precautions and we want you to help us.'

'Why the hell should I?'

'No reason at all. Except philanthropy.'

'Nothing doing, Controleur. I'm not a philanthropist.'

'That settles that. That was all. You can go.'

But as Ginger Ted turned to the door Miss Jones stopped him.

'It was my suggestion, Mr Wilson. You see, they want me to go to Labobo and Sakunchi, and the natives there are so funny I was afraid to go alone. I thought if you came I should be safer.'

He gave her a look of extreme distaste.

'What do you suppose I care if they cut your throat?'

Miss Jones looked at him and her eyes filled with tears. She began to cry. He stood and watched her stupidly.

'There's no reason why you should.' She pulled herself together and dried her eyes. 'I'm being silly. I shall be all right. I'll go alone.'

'It's damned foolishness for a woman to go to Labobo.'

She gave him a little smile.

'I dare say it is, but you see, it's my job and I can't help myself. I'm sorry if I offended you by asking you. You must forget about it. I dare say it wasn't quite fair to ask you to take such a risk.'

For quite a minute Ginger Ted stood and looked at her. He shifted from one foot to the other. His surly face seemed to grow black.

'Oh, hell, have it your own way,' he said at last. 'I'll come with you. When d'you want to start?'

They set out next day, with drugs and disinfectants, in the government launch. Mr Gruyter as soon as he had put the necessary work in order was to start off in a prahu in the other direction. For four months the epidemic raged. Though everything possible was done to localise it, one island after another was attacked. The Controleur was busy from morning to night. He had no sooner got back to Baru from one or other of the islands to do what was necessary there than he had to set off again. He distributed food and medicine. He cheered the terrified people. He supervised everything. He worked like a dog. He saw nothing of Ginger Ted, but he heard from Mr Jones that the experiment was working out beyond all hopes. The scamp was behaving himself. He had a way with the natives; and by cajolery, firmness and on occasion the use of his fist, managed to make them take the steps necessary for their own safety. Miss Jones could congratulate herself on the success of the scheme. But the Controleur was too tired to be amused. When the epidemic had run its course he rejoiced because out of a population of eight thousand only six hundred had died.

Finally he was able to give the district a clean bill of health.

One evening he was sitting in his sarong on the verandah of his house and was reading a French novel with the happy consciousness that once more he could take things easy. His head-boy came in and told him that Ginger Ted wished to see him. He got up from his chair and shouted to him to come in. Company was just what he wanted. It had crossed the Controleur's mind that it would be pleasant to get drunk that night, but it is dull to get drunk alone, and he had regretfully put the thought aside. And heaven had sent Ginger Ted in the nick of time. By God, they would make a night of it. After four months they deserved a bit of fun. Ginger Ted entered. He was wearing a clean suit of white ducks. He was shaved. He looked another man.

'Why, Ginger, you look as if you'd been spending a month at a health resort instead of nursing a pack of natives dying of cholera. And look at your clothes. Have you just stepped out of a band-box?'

Ginger Ted smiled rather sheepishly. The head-boy brought two bottles of beer and poured them out.

'Help yourself, Ginger,' said the Controleur as he took his glass.

'I don't think I'll have any, thank you.'

The Controleur put down his glass and looked at Ginger Ted with amazement.

'Why, what's the matter? Aren't you thirsty?'

'I don't mind having a cup of tea.'

'A cup of what?'

'I'm on the wagon. Martha and I are going to be married.'

'Ginger!'

The Controleur's eyes popped out of his head. He scratched his shaven pate.

'You can't marry Miss Jones,' he said. 'No one could marry Miss Jones.'

'Well, I'm going to. That's what I've come to see you about. Owen's going to marry us in chapel, but we want to be married by Dutch law as well.'

'A joke's a joke, Ginger. What's the idea?'

'She wanted it. She fell for me that night we spent on the island when the propeller broke. She's not a bad old girl when you get to know her. It's her last chance, if you understand what I mean, and I'd like to do something to oblige her. And she wants someone to take care of her, there's no doubt about that.'

'Ginger, Ginger, before you can say knife she'll make you into a damned missionary.'

'I don't know that I'd mind that so much if we had a little mission of our own. She says I'm a bloody marvel with the natives. She says I can do more with a native in five minutes than Owen can do in a year. She says she's never known anyone with the magnetism I have. It seems a pity to waste a gift like that.'

The Controleur looked at him without speaking and slowly nodded his head three or four times. She'd nobbled him all right.

'I've converted seventeen already,' said Ginger Ted.

'You? I didn't know you believed in Christianity.'

'Well, I don't know that I did exactly, but when I talked to 'em and they just came into the fold like a lot of blasted sheep, well, it gave me quite a turn. Blimey, I said, I dare say there's something in it after all.'

'You should have raped her, Ginger. I wouldn't have been hard on you. I wouldn't have given you more than three years and three years is soon over.'

'Look here, Controleur, don't you ever let on that the thought never entered my head. Women are touchy, you know, and she'd be as sore as hell if she knew that.'

'I guessed she'd got her eye on you, but I never thought it would come to this.' The Controleur in an agitated manner walked up and down the verandah. 'Listen to me, old boy,' he said after an interval of reflection, 'we've had some grand times together and a friend's a friend. I'll tell you what I'll do, I'll lend you the launch and you can go and hide on one of the islands till the next ship comes along and then I'll get 'em to slow down and take you on board. You've only got one chance now and that's to cut and run.'

Ginger Ted shook his head.

'It's no good, Controleur, I know you mean well, but I'm going to marry the blasted woman, and that's that. You don't know the joy of bringing all them bleeding sinners to repentance, and Christ, that girl can make a treacle pudding. I haven't eaten a better one since I was a kid.'

The Controleur was very much disturbed. The drunken scamp was his only companion on the islands and he did not want to lose him. He discovered that he had even a certain affection for him. Next day he went to see the missionary.

'What's this I hear about your sister marrying

Ginger Ted?' he asked him. 'It's the most extraordinary thing I've ever heard in my life.'

'It's true nevertheless.'

'You must do something about it. It's madness.'

'My sister is of full age and entitled to do as she pleases.'

'But you don't mean to tell me you approve of it. You know Ginger Ted. He's a bum and there are no two ways about it. Have you told her the risk she's running? I mean, bringing sinners to repentance and all that sort of thing's all right, but there are limits. And does the leopard ever change his spots?'

Then for the first time in his life the Controleur saw a twinkle in the missionary's eye.

'My sister is a very determined woman, Mr Gruyter,' he replied. 'From that night they spent on the island he never had a chance.'

The Controleur gasped. He was as surprised as the prophet when the Lord opened the mouth of the ass, and she said unto Balaam, 'What have I done unto thee, that thou hast smitten me these three times?' Perhaps Mr Jones was human after all.

'*Allejesus!*' muttered the Controleur.

Before anything more could be said Miss Jones swept into the room. She was radiant. She looked ten years younger. Her cheeks were flushed and her nose was hardly red at all.

'Have you come to congratulate me, Mr Gruyter?' she cried, and her manner was sprightly and girlish. 'You see, I was right after all. Everyone has some good in them. You don't know how splendid Edward has been all through this terrible time. He's a hero. He's a saint. Even I was surprised.'

'I hope you'll be very happy, Miss Jones.'

'I know I shall. Oh, it would be wicked of me to doubt it, for it is the Lord who has brought us together.'

'Do you think so?'

'I know it. Don't you see? Except for the cholera Edward would never have found himself. Except for the cholera we should never have learnt to know one another. I have never seen the hand of God more plainly manifest.'

The Controleur could not but think that it was rather a clumsy device to bring those two together that necessitated the death of six hundred innocent persons, but not being well versed in the ways of omnipotence he made no remark.

'You'll never guess where we're going for our honeymoon,' said Miss Jones, perhaps a trifle archly.

'Java?'

'No, if you'll lend us the launch, we're going to that island where we were marooned. It has very tender recollections for both of us. It was there that I first guessed how fine and good Edward was. It's there I want him to have his reward.'

The Controleur caught his breath. He left quickly, for he thought that unless he had a bottle of beer at once he would have a fit. He was never so shocked in his life.

The Book-Bag

Some people read for instruction, which is praiseworthy, and some for pleasure, which is innocent, but not a few read from habit, and I suppose that this is neither innocent nor praiseworthy. Of that lamentable company am I. Conversation after a time bores me, games tire me and my own thoughts, which we are told are the unfailing resource of a sensible man, have a tendency to run dry. Then I fly to my book as the opium-smoker to his pipe. I would sooner read the catalogue of the Army and Navy Stores or *Bradshaw's Guide* than nothing at all, and indeed I have spent many delightful hours over both these works. At one time I never went out without a second-hand bookseller's list in my pocket. I know no reading more fruity. Of course to read in this way is as reprehensible as doping, and I never cease to wonder at the impertinence of great readers who, because they are such, look down on the illiterate. From the standpoint of what eternity is it better to have read a thousand books than to have ploughed a million furrows? Let us admit that reading with us is just a drug that we cannot do without – who of this band does not know the restlessness that attacks him when he has been severed from reading too long, the apprehension and irritability, and the sigh of relief which the sight of a printed page extracts from him? – and so let us be no more vainglorious than the poor slaves of the hypodermic needle or the pint-pot.

And like the dope-fiend who cannot move from

place to place without taking with him a plentiful supply of his deadly balm I never venture far without a sufficiency of reading matter. Books are so necessary to me that when in a railway train I have become aware that fellow-travellers have come away without a single one I have been seized with a vertiable dismay. But when I am starting on a long journey the problem is formidable. I have learnt my lesson. Once, imprisoned by illness for three months in a hill-town in Java, I came to the end of all the books I had brought with me, and knowing no Dutch, was obliged to buy the school books from which intelligent Javanese, I suppose, acquired knowledge of French and German. So I read again after five and twenty years the frigid plays of Goethe, the fables of La Fontaine and the tragedies of the tender and exact Racine. I have the greatest admiration for Racine, but I admit that to read his plays one after the other requires a certain effort in a person who is suffering from colitis. Since then I have made a point of travelling with the largest sack made for carrying soiled linen and filling it to the brim with books to suit every possible occasion and every mood. It weighs a ton and strong porters reel under its weight. Custom-house officials look at it askance, but recoil from it with consternation when I give them my word that it contains nothing but books. Its inconvenience is that the particular work I suddenly hanker to read is always at the bottom and it is impossible for me to get it without emptying the book-bag's entire contents upon the floor. Except for this, however, I should perhaps never have heard the singular history of Olive Hardy.

I was wandering about Malaya, staying here and there, a week or two if there was a rest-house or a hotel, and a day or so if I was obliged to inflict myself on a planter or a district officer whose hospitality I had no wish to abuse; and at the moment I happened to be at Penang. It is a pleasant little town, with a hotel that has always seemed to me very agreeable, but the stranger finds little to do there and time hung a trifle heavily on my hands. One morning I received a letter from a man I knew only by name. This was Mark Featherstone. He was Acting Resident, in the absence on leave of the Resident, at a place called Tenggarah. There was a sultan there and it appeared that a water festival of some sort was to take place which Featherstone thought would interest me. He said that he would be glad if I would come and stay with him for a few days. I wired to tell him that I should be delighted and next day took the train to Tenggarah. Featherstone met me at the station. He was a man of about thirty-five, I should think, tall and handsome, with fine eyes and a strong, stern face. He had a wiry black moustache and bushy eyebrows. He looked more like a soldier than a government official. He was very smart in white ducks, with a white topi, and he wore his clothes with elegance. He was a little shy, which seemed odd in a strapping fellow of resolute mien, but I surmised that this was only because he was unused to the society of that strange fish, a writer, and I hoped in a little to put him at his ease.

'My boys'll look after your barang,' he said. 'We'll go down to the club. Give them your keys and they'll unpack before we get back.'

I told him that I had a good deal of luggage and thought it better to leave everything at the station but what I particularly wanted. He would not hear of it.

'It doesn't matter a bit. It'll be safer at my house. It's always better to have one's barang with one.'

'All right.'

I gave my keys and the ticket for my trunk and my book-bag to a Chinese boy who stood at my host's elbow. Outside the station a car was waiting for us and we stepped in.

'Do you play bridge?' asked Featherstone.

'I do.'

'I thought most writers didn't.'

'They don't,' I said. 'It's generally considered among authors a sign of deficient intelligence to play cards.'

The club was a bungalow, pleasing but unpretentious; it had a large reading-room, a billiard-room with one table, and a small card-room. When we arrived it was empty but for one or two persons reading the English weeklies, and we walked through to the tennis courts where a couple of sets were being played. A number of people were sitting on the verandah, looking on, smoking and sipping long drinks. I was introduced to one or two of them. But the light was failing and soon the players could hardly see the ball. Featherstone asked one of the men I had been introduced to if he would like a rubber. He said he would. Featherstone looked about for a fourth. He caught sight of a man sitting a little by himself, paused for a second, and went up to him. The two exchanged a few words and then came towards us. We strolled into the card-room. We had a very nice game. I did not pay much attention to the two men who made up the four. They stood me drinks, and I, a temporary member of the club, returned the compliment. The drinks were very small, quarter whiskies, and in the two hours we played each of us was able to show his open-handedness without an excessive consumption of alcohol. When the advancing hour suggested that the next rubber must be the last we changed from whisky to gin pahits. The rubber came to an end. Featherstone called for the book and the winnings and losings of each one of us were set down. One of the men got up.

'Well, I must be going,' he said.

'Going back to the estate?' asked Featherstone.

'Yes,' he nodded. He turned to me. 'Shall you be here tomorrow?'

'I hope so.'

He went out of the room.

'I'll collect my mem and get along home to dinner,' said the other.

'We might be going too,' said Featherstone.

'I'm ready whenever you are,' I replied.

We got into the car and drove to his house. It was a longish drive. In the darkness I could see nothing much, but presently I realised that we were going up a rather steep hill. We reached the Residency.

It had been an evening like any other, pleasant, but not at all exciting, and I had spent I don't know how many just like it. I did not expect it to leave any sort of impression on me.

Featherstone led me into his sitting-room. It looked comfortable, but it was a trifle ordinary. It had large basket armchairs covered with cretonne and on the walls were a great many framed photographs; the tables were littered with papers, magazines and official reports, with pipes, yellow tins of straight-cut cigarettes and pink tins of tobacco. In a row of shelves were untidily stacked a good many books, their bindings stained with damp and the ravages of white ants. Featherstone showed me my room and left me with the words: 'Shall you be ready for a gin pahit in ten minutes?'

'Easily,' I said.

I had a bath and changed and went downstairs. Featherstone, ready before me, mixed our drink as he heard me clatter down the wooden staircase. We dined. We talked. The festival which I had been invited to see was the next day but one, but Featherstone told me he had arranged for me before that to be received by the sultan.

'He's a jolly old boy,' he said. 'And the palace is a sight for sore eyes.'

After dinner we talked a little more, Featherstone put on the gramophone, and we looked at the latest illustrated papers that had arrived from England. Then we went to bed. Featherstone came to my room to see that I had everything I wanted.

'I suppose you haven't any books with you,' he said. 'I haven't got a thing to read.'

'Books?' I cried.

I pointed to my book-bag. It stood upright, bulging oddly, so that it looked like a humpbacked gnome somewhat the worse for liquor.

'Have you got books in there? I thought that was your dirty linen or a camp-bed or something. Is there anything you can lend me?'

'Look for yourself.'

Featherstone's boys had unlocked the bag, but quailing before the sight that then discovered itself had done no more. I knew from long experience how to unpack it. I threw it over on its side, seized its leather bottom and, walking backwards, dragged the sack away from its contents. A river of books poured on to the floor. A look of stupefaction came upon Featherstone's face.

'You don't mean to say you travel with as many books as that? By George, what a snip.'

He bent down and turning them over rapidly looked at the titles. There were books of all kinds. Volumes of verse, novels, philosophical works, critical studies (they say books about books are profitless, but they certainly make very pleasant reading), biographies, history; there were books to read when you were ill and books to read when your brain, all alert, craved for something to grapple with, there were books that you had always wanted to read, but in the hurry of life at home had never found time to, there were books to read at sea when you were meandering through narrow waters on a tramp steamer, and there were books for bad weather when your whole cabin creaked and you had to wedge yourself in your bunk in order not to fall out; there were books chosen solely for their length, which you took with you when on some expedition you had to travel light, and there were the books you could read when you could read nothing else. Finally Featherstone picked out a life of Byron that had recently appeared.

'Hello, what's this?' he said. 'I read a review of it some time ago.'

'I believe it's very good,' I replied. 'I haven't read it yet.'

'May I take it? It'll do me for tonight at all events.'

'Of course. Take anything you like.'

'No, that's enough. Well, good-night. Breakfast at eight-thirty.'

When I came down next morning the head-boy told me that Featherstone, who had been at work since six, would be in shortly. While I waited for him I glanced at his shelves.

'I see you've got a grand library of books on bridge,' I remarked as we sat down to breakfast.

'Yes, I get every one that comes out. I'm very keen on it.'

'That fellow we were playing with yesterday plays a good game.'

'Which? Hardy?'

'I don't know. Not the one who said he was going to collect his wife. The other.'

'Yes, that was Hardy. That was why I asked him to play. He doesn't come to the club very often.'

'I hope he will tonight.'

'I wouldn't bank on it. He has an estate about thirty miles away. It's a longish ride to come just for a rubber of bridge.'

'Is he married?'

'No. Well, yes. But his wife is in England.'

'It must be awfully lonely for those men who live by themselves on those estates,' I said.

'Oh, he's not so badly off as some. I don't think he much cares about seeing people. I think he'd be just as lonely in London.'

There was something in the way Featherstone spoke that struck me as a little strange. His voice had what I can only describe as a shuttered tone. He seemed suddenly to have moved away from me. It was as though one were passing along a street at night and paused for a second to look in at a lighted window that showed a comfortable room and suddenly an invisible hand pulled down the blind. His eyes, which habitually met those of the person he was talking to with frankness, now avoided mine and I had a notion that it was not only my fancy that read in his face an expression of pain. It was drawn for a moment as it might be by a twinge of neuralgia. I could not think of anything to say and Featherstone did not speak. I was conscious that his thoughts, withdrawn from me and what we were about, were turned upon a subject unknown to me. Presently he gave a little sigh, very slight, but unmistakable, and seemed with a deliberate effort to pull himself together.

'I'm going down to the office immediately after breakfast,' he said. 'What are you going to do with yourself?'

'Oh, don't bother about me. I shall slack around. I'll stroll down and look at the town.'

'There's not much to see.'

'All the better. I'm fed up with sights.'

I found that Featherstone's verandah gave me sufficient entertainment for the morning. It had one of the most enchanting views I had seen in the Federated Malay States. The Residency was built on the top of a hill and the garden was large and well cared for. Great trees gave it almost the look of an English park. It had vast lawns and there Tamils, black and emaciated, were scything with deliberate and beautiful gestures. Beyond and below, the jungle grew thickly to the bank of a broad, winding and swiftly flowing river, and on the other side of this, as far as the eye could reach, stretched the wooded hills of Tenggarah. The contrast between the trim lawns, so strangely English, and the savage growth of the jungle beyond pleasantly titillated the fancy. I sat and read and smoked. It is my business to be curious about people and I asked myself how the peace of this scene, charged nevertheless with a tremulous and dark significance, affected Featherstone who lived with it. He knew it under every aspect: at dawn when the mist rising from the river shrouded it with a ghostly pall; in the splendour of noon; and at last when the shadowy gloaming crept softly out of the jungle, like an army making its way with caution in unknown country, and presently enveloped the green lawns and the great flowering trees and the flaunting cassias in the silent night. I wondered whether, unbeknownst to him, the tender and yet strangely sinister aspect of the scene, acting on his nerves and his loneliness, imbued him with some mystical quality so that the life he led, the life of the capable administrator, the sportsman and the good fellow, on occasion seemed to him not quite real. I smiled at my own fancies, for certainly the conversation we had had the night before had not indicated in him any stirrings of the soul. I had thought him quite nice. He had been at Oxford and was a member of a good London club. He seemed to attach a good deal of importance to social things. He was a gentleman and slightly conscious of the fact that he belonged to a better class than most of the Englishmen his life brought him in contact with. I gathered from the various silver cups that adorned his dining-room that he excelled in games. He played tennis and billiards. When he went on leave he hunted and, anxious to keep his weight down, he dieted carefully. He talked a good deal of what he would do when he retired. He hankered after the life of a country gentleman. A little house in Leicestershire, a couple of hunters and neighbours to play bridge with. He would have his pension and he had a little money of his own. But meanwhile he worked hard and did his job, if not brilliantly, certainly with competence. I have no doubt that he was looked upon by his superiors as a reliable officer. He was cut upon a pattern that I knew too well to find very interesting. He was like a novel that is careful, honest and efficient, yet a little ordinary, so that you seem to have read it all before, and you turn the pages listlessly knowing that it will never afford you a surprise or move you to excitement.

But human beings are incalculable and he is a fool who tells himself that he knows what a man is capable of.

In the afternoon Featherstone took me to see the sultan. We were received by one of his sons, a shy, smiling youth who acted as his ADC. He was dressed in a neat blue suit, but round his waist he wore a sarong, white flowers on a yellow ground, on his head a red fez, and on his feet knobby American shoes. The palace, built in the Moorish style, was like a very big doll's house and it was painted bright yellow, which is the royal colour. We were led into a spacious room, furnished with the sort of furniture you would find in an English lodging-house at the seaside, but the chairs were covered with yellow silk. On the floor was a Brussels carpet and on the walls photographs in very grand gilt frames of the sultan at various state functions. In a cabinet was a large collection of all kinds of fruit done entirely in crochet work. The Sultan came in with several attendants. He was a man of fifty, perhaps, short and stout, dressed in trousers and tunic of a large white and yellow check; round his middle he wore a very beautiful yellow sarong and on his head a white fez. He had large, handsome, friendly eyes. He gave us coffee to drink, sweet cakes to eat and cheroots to smoke. Conversation was not difficult, for he was affable, and he told me that he had never been to a theatre or played cards, for he was very religious, and he had four wives and twenty-four children. The only bar to the happiness of his life seemed to be that common decency obliged him to divide his time equally between his four wives. He said that an hour with one was a month and with another five minutes. I remarked that Professor Einstein – or was it Bergson? – had made similar observations upon time and indeed on this question had given the world much to ponder over. Presently we took our leave and the Sultan presented me with some beautiful white malaccas.

In the evening we went to the club. One of the men we had played with the day before got up from his chair as we entered.

'Ready for a rubber?' he said.

'Where's our fourth?' I asked.

'Oh, there are several fellows here who'll be glad to play.'

'What about that man we played with yesterday?' I had forgotten his name.

'Hardy? He's not here.'

'It's not worth while waiting for him,' said Featherstone.

'He very seldom comes to the club. I was surprised to see him last night.'

I did not know why I had the impression that behind the very ordinary words of these two men there was an odd sense of embarrassment. Hardy had made no impression on me and I did not even remember what he looked like. He was just a fourth at the bridge table. I had a feeling that they had something against him. It was no business of mine and I was quite content to play with a man who at that moment joined us. We certainly had a more cheerful game than before. A good deal of chaff passed from one side of the table to the other. We played less serious bridge. We laughed. I wondered if it was only that they were less shy of the stranger who had happened in upon them or if the presence of Hardy had caused in the other two a certain constraint. At half-past eight we broke up and Featherstone and I went back to dine at his house.

After dinner we lounged in armchairs and smoked cheroots. For some reason our conversation did not flow easily. I tried topic after topic, but could not get Featherstone to interest himself in any of them. I began to think that in the last twenty-four hours he had said all he had to say. I fell somewhat discouraged into silence. It prolonged itself and again, I did not know why, I had a faint sensation that it was charged with a significance that escaped me. I felt slightly uncomfortable. I had that queer feeling that one sometimes has when sitting in an empty room that one is not by oneself. Presently I was conscious that Featherstone was steadily looking at me. I was sitting by a lamp, but he was in shadow so that the play of his features was hidden from me. But he had very large brilliant eyes and in the half-darkness they seemed to shine dimly. They were like new boot-buttons that caught a reflected light. I wondered why he looked at me like that. I gave him a glance and catching his eyes insistently fixed upon me faintly smiled.

'Interesting book that one you lent me last night,' he said suddenly, and I could not help thinking his voice did not sound quite natural. The words issued from his lips as though they were pushed from behind.

'Oh, the *Life of Byron*?' I said breezily. 'Have you read it already?'

'A good deal of it. I read till three.'

'I've heard it's very well done. I'm not sure that Byron interests me so much as all that. There was so much in him that was so frightfully second-rate. It makes one rather uncomfortable.'

'What do you think is the real truth of that story about him and his sister?'

'Augusta Leigh? I don't know very much about it. I've never read Astarte.'

'Do you think they were really in love with one another?'

'I suppose so. Isn't it generally believed that she was the only woman he ever genuinely loved?'

'Can you understand it?'

'I can't really. It doesn't particularly shock me. It just seems to me very unnatural. Perhaps "unnatural" isn't the right word. It's incomprehensible to me. I can't throw myself into the state of feeling in which such a thing seems possible. You know, that's how a writer gets to know the people he writes about, by standing himself in their shoes and feeling with their hearts.'

I knew I did not make myself very clear, but I was trying to describe a sensation, an action of the subconscious, which from experience was perfectly familiar to me, but which no words I knew could precisely indicate. I went on.

'Of course she was only his half-sister, but just as habit kills love I should have thought habit would prevent its arising. When two persons have known one another all their lives and lived together in close contact I can't imagine how or why that sudden spark should flash that results in love. The probabilities are that they would be joined by mutual affection and I don't know anything that is more contrary to love than affection.'

I could just see in the dimness the outline of a smile flicker for a moment on my host's heavy, and it seemed to me then, somewhat saturnine face.

'You only believe in love at first sight?'

'Well, I suppose I do, but with the proviso that people may have met twenty times before seeing one another. "Seeing" has an active side and a passive one. Most people we run across mean so little to us that we never bestir ourselves to look at them. We just suffer the impression they make on us.'

'Oh, but one's often heard of couples who've known one another for years and it's never occurred to one they cared two straws for each other and suddenly they go and get married. How do you explain that?'

'Well, if you're going to bully me into being logical and consistent, I should suggest that their love is of a different kind. After all, passion isn't the only reason for marriage. It may not even be the best one. Two people may marry because they're lonely or because they're good friends or for convenience' sake. Though I said that affection was the greatest enemy of love, I would never deny that it's a very good substitute. I'm not sure that a marriage founded on it isn't the happiest.'

'What did you think of Tim Hardy?'

I was a little surprised at the sudden question, which seemed to have nothing to do with the subject of our conversation.

'I didn't think of him very much. He seemed quite nice. Why?'

'Did he seem to you just like everybody else?'

'Yes. Is there anything peculiar about him? If you'd told me that I'd have paid more attention to him.'

'He's very quiet, isn't he? I suppose one who knew nothing about him would not give him a second thought.'

I tried to remember what he looked like. The only thing that had struck me when we were playing cards was that he had fine hands. It passed idly through my mind that they were not the sort of hands I should have expected a planter to have. But why a planter should have different hands from anybody else I did not trouble to ask myself. His were somewhat large, but very well formed, with peculiarly long fingers, and the nails were of an admirable shape. They were virile and yet oddly sensitive hands. I noticed this and thought no more about it. But if you are a writer, instinct and the habit of years enable you to store up impressions that you are not aware of. Sometimes of course they do not correspond with the facts and a woman for example may remain in your subconsciousness as a dark, massive and ox-eyed creature when she is indeed rather small and of a nondescript colouring. But that is of no consequence. The impression may very well be more exact than the sober truth. And now, seeking to call up from the depths of me a picture of this man, I had a feeling of some ambiguity. He was clean-shaven and his face, oval but not thin, seemed strangely pale under the tan of long exposure to the tropical sun. His features were vague. I did not know whether I remembered it or only imagined now that his rounded chin gave one the impression of a certain weakness. He had thick brown hair, just turning grey, and a long wisp fell down constantly over his forehead. He pushed it back with a gesture that had become habitual. His brown eyes were rather large and gentle, but perhaps a little sad; they had a melting softness which, I could imagine, might be very appealing.

After a pause Featherstone continued: 'It's rather strange that I should run across Tim Hardy here after all these years. But that's the way of the FMS. People move about and you find yourself in the same place as a man you've known years before in another part of the country. I first knew Tim when he had an estate near Sibuku. Have you ever been there?'

'No. Where is it?'

'Oh, it's up north. Towards Siam. It wouldn't be worth your while to go. It's just like every other place in the FMS. But it was rather nice. It had a very jolly little club and there were some quite decent people. There was the schoolmaster and the head of the police, the doctor, the padre and the government engineer. The usual lot, you know. A few planters. Three or four women. I was Assistant District Officer. It was one of my first jobs. Tim Hardy had an estate about twenty-five miles away. He lived there with his sister. They had a bit of money of their own and he'd bought the place. Rubber was pretty good then and he wasn't doing at all badly. We rather cottoned on to one another. Of course it's a toss-up with planters. Some of them are very good fellows, but they're not exactly . . . ' he sought for a word or a phrase that did not sound snobbish. 'Well, they're not the sort of people you'd be likely to meet at home. Tim and

Olive were of one's own class, if you understand what I mean.'

'Olive was the sister?'

'Yes. They'd had a rather unfortunate past. Their parents had separated when they were quite small, seven or eight, and the mother had taken Olive and the father had kept Tim. Tim went to Clifton – they were West Country people – and only came home for the holidays. His father was a retired naval man who lived at Fowey. But Olive went with her mother to Italy. She was educated in Florence; she spoke Italian perfectly and French too. For all those years Tim and Olive never saw one another once, but they used to write to one another regularly. They'd been very much attached when they were children. As far as I could understand, life when their people were living together had been rather stormy with all sorts of scenes and upsets, you know the sort of thing that happens when two people who are married don't get on together, and that had thrown them on their own resources. They were left a good deal to themselves. Then Mrs Hardy died and Olive came home to England and went back to her father. She was eighteen then and Tim was seventeen. A year later the war broke out, Tim joined up and his father, who was over fifty, got some job at Portsmouth. I take it he had been a hard liver and a heavy drinker. He broke down before the end of the war and died after a lingering illness. They don't seem to have had any relations. They were the last of a rather old family; they had a fine old house in Dorsetshire that had belonged to them for a good many generations, but they had never been able to afford to live in it and it was always let. I remember seeing photographs of it.

It was very much a gentleman's house, of grey stone and rather stately, with a coat of arms carved over the front door and mullioned windows. Their great ambition was to make enough money to be able to live in it. They used to talk about it a lot. They never spoke as though either of them would marry, but always as though it were a settled thing that they would remain together. It was rather funny considering how young they were.'

'How old were they then?' I asked.

'Well, I suppose he was twenty-five or twenty-six and she was a year older. They were awfully kind to me when I first went up to Sibuku. They took a fancy to me at once. You see, we had more in common than most of the people there. I think they were glad of my company. They weren't particularly popular.'

'Why not?' I asked.

'They were rather reserved and you couldn't help seeing that they liked their own society better than other people's. I don't know if you've noticed it, but that always seems to put people's backs up. They resent it somehow if they have a feeling that you can get along very well without them.'

'It's tiresome, isn't it?' I said.

'It was rather a grievance to the other planters that Tim was his own master and had private means. They had to put up with an old Ford to get about in, but Tim had a real car. Tim and Olive were very nice when they came to the club and they played in the tennis tournaments and all that sort of thing, but you had an impression that they were always glad to get away again. They'd dine out with people and make themselves very pleasant, but it was pretty obvious that they'd just as soon have stayed at home.

If you had any sense you couldn't blame them. I don't know if you've been much to planters' houses. They're a bit dreary. A lot of gimcrack furniture and silver ornaments and tiger skins. And the food's uneatable. But the Hardys had made their bungalow rather nice. There was nothing very grand in it; it was just easy and homelike and comfortable. Their living-room was like a drawing-room in an English country house. You felt that their things meant something to them and that they had had them a long time. It was a very jolly house to stay at. The bungalow was in the middle of the estate, but it was on the brow of a little hill and you looked right over the rubber trees to the sea in the distance. Olive took a lot of trouble with her garden and it was really topping. I never saw such a show of cannas. I used to go there for weekends. It was only about half an hour's drive to the sea and we'd take our lunch with us and bathe and sail. Tim kept a small boat there. Those days were grand. I never knew one could enjoy oneself so much. It's a beautiful bit of coast and it was really extraordinarily romantic. Then in the evenings we'd play patience and chess or turn on the gramophone. The cooking was damned good too. It was a change from what one generally got. Olive had taught their cook to make all sorts of Italian dishes and we used to have great wallops of macaroni and risotto and gnocchi and things like that. I couldn't help envying them their life, it was so jolly and peaceful, and when they talked of what they'd do when they went back to England for good I used to tell them they'd always regret what they'd left.

' "We've been very happy here," said Olive.

'She had a way of looking at Tim, with a slow, sidelong glance from under her long eyelashes, that was rather engaging.

'In their own house they were quite different from the way they were when they went out. They were so easy and cordial. Everybody admitted that and I'm bound to say that people enjoyed going there. They often asked people over. They had the gift of making you feel at home. It was a very happy house, if you know what I mean. Of course no one could help seeing how attached they were to one another. And whatever people said about their being stand-offish and self-centred, they were bound to be rather touched by the affection they had for one another. People said they couldn't have been more united if they were married, and when you saw how some couples got on you couldn't help thinking they made most marriages look rather like a washout. They seemed to think the same things at the same time. They had little private jokes that made them laugh like children. They were so charming with one another, so gay and happy, that really to stay with them was, well, a spiritual refreshment. I don't know what else you could call it. When you left them, after a couple of days at the bungalow, you felt that you'd absorbed some of their peace and their sober gaiety. It was as though your soul had been sluiced with cool clear water. You felt strangely purified.'

It was singular to hear Featherstone talking in this exalted strain. He looked so spruce in his smart white coat, technically known as a bum-freezer, his moustache was so trim, his thick curly hair so carefully brushed, that his high-flown language made me a trifle uncomfortable. But I realised that he was trying to express in his clumsy way a very sincerely felt emotion.

'What was Olive Hardy like?' I asked.

'I'll show you. I've got quite a lot of snapshots.'

He got up from his chair and going to a shelf brought me a large album. It was the usual thing, indifferent photographs of people in groups and unflattering likenesses of single figures. They were in bathing dress or in shorts or tennis things, generally with their faces all screwed up because the sun blinded them, or puckered by the distortion of laughter. I recognised Hardy, not much changed after ten years, with his wisp of hair hanging across his forehead. I remembered him better now that I saw the snapshots. In them he looked nice and fresh and young. He had an alertness of expression that was attractive and that I certainly had not noticed when I saw him. In his eyes was a sort of eagerness for life that danced and sparkled through the fading print. I glanced at the photographs of his sister. Her bathing dress showed that she had a good figure, well-developed, but slender; and her legs were long and slim.

'They look rather alike,' I said.

'Yes, although she was a year older they might have been twins, they were so much alike. They both had the same oval face and that pale skin without any colour in the cheeks, and they both had those soft brown eyes, very liquid and appealing, so that you felt whatever they did you could never be angry with them. And they both had a sort of careless elegance that made them look charming whatever they wore and however untidy they were. He's lost that now, I suppose, but he certainly had it when I first knew him. They always rather reminded me of the brother and sister in *Twelfth Night*. You know whom I mean.'

'Viola and Sebastian.'

'They never seemed to belong quite to the present. There was something Elizabethan about them. I don't think it was only because I was very young then that I couldn't help feeling they were strangely romantic somehow. I could see them living in Illyria.'

I gave one of the snapshots another glance.

'The girl looks as though she had a good deal more character than her brother,' I remarked.

'She had. I don't know if you'd have called Olive beautiful, but she was awfully attractive. There was something poetic in her, a sort of lyrical quality as it were, that coloured her movements, her acts and everything about her. It seemed to exalt her above common cares. There was something so candid in her expression, so courageous and independent in her bearing, that – oh, I don't know, it made mere beauty just flat and dull.'

'You speak as if you'd been in love with her,' I interrupted.

'Of course I was. I should have thought you'd guessed that at once. I was frightfully in love with her.'

'Was it love at first sight?' I smiled.

'Yes, I think it was, but I didn't know it for a month or so. When it suddenly struck me that what I felt for her – I don't know how to explain it, it was a sort of shattering turmoil that affected every bit of me – that that was love, I knew I'd felt it all along. It was not only her looks, though they were awfully alluring, the smoothness of her pale skin and the way her hair fell over her forehead and the grave sweetness of her brown eyes, it was more than that; you had a sensation of well-being when you were with her, as though you could relax and be quite natural and needn't pretend to be anything you weren't. You felt she was incapable of meanness. It was impossible to think of her as envious of other people or catty. She seemed to have a natural generosity of soul. One could be silent with her for an hour at a time and yet feel that one had had a good time.'

'A rare gift,' I said.

'She was a wonderful companion. If you made a suggestion to do something she was always glad to fall in with it. She was the least exacting girl I ever knew. You could throw her over at the last minute and however disappointed she was it made no difference. Next time you saw her she was just as cordial and serene as ever.'

'Why didn't you marry her?'

Featherstone's cheroot had gone out. He threw the stub away and deliberately lit another. He did not answer for a while. It may seem strange to persons who live in a highly civilised state that he should confide these intimate things to a stranger; it did not seem strange to me. I was used to it. People who live so desperately alone, in the remote places of the earth, find it a relief to tell someone whom in all probability they will never meet again the story that has burdened perhaps for years their waking thoughts and their dreams at night. And I have an inkling that the fact of your being a writer attracts their confidence. They feel that what they tell you will excite your interest in an impersonal way that makes it easier for them to discharge their souls. Besides, as we all know from our own experience, it is never unpleasant to talk about oneself.

'Why didn't you marry her?' I had asked him.

'I wanted to badly enough,' Featherstone answered at length. 'But I hesitated to ask her. Although she was always so nice to me and so easy to get on with, and we were such good friends, I always felt that there was something a little mysterious in her. Although she was so simple, so frank and natural, you never quite got over the feeling of an inner kernel of aloofness, as if deep in her heart she guarded, not a secret, but a sort of privacy of the soul that not a living person would ever be allowed to know. I don't know if I make myself clear.'

'I think so.'

'I put it down to her upbringing. They never talked of their mother, but somehow I got the impression that she was one of those neurotic, emotional women who wreck their own happiness and are a pest to everyone connected with them. I had a suspicion that she'd led rather a hectic life in Florence and it struck me that Olive owed her beautiful serenity to a disciplined effort of her own will and that her aloofness was a sort of citadel she'd built to protect herself from the knowledge of all sorts of shameful things. But of course that aloofness was awfully captivating. It was strangely exciting to think that if she loved you, and you were married to her, you would at last pierce right into the hidden heart of that mystery; and you felt that if you could share that with her it would be as it were a consummation of all you'd ever desired in your life. Heaven wouldn't be in it. You know, I felt about it just like Bluebeard's wife about the forbidden chamber in the castle. Every room was open to me, but I should never rest till I had gone into that last one that was locked against me.'

My eye was caught by a chik-chak, a little brown house lizard with a large head, high up on the wall. It is a friendly little beast and it is good to see it in a house. It watched a fly. It was quite still. On a sudden it made a dart and then as the fly flew away fell back with a sort of jerk into a strange immobility.

'And there was another thing that made me hesitate. I couldn't bear the thought that if I proposed to her and she refused me she wouldn't let me come to the bungalow in the same old way. I should have hated that, I enjoyed going there so awfully. It made me so happy to be with her. But you know, sometimes one can't help oneself. I did ask her at last, but it was almost by accident. One evening, after dinner, when we were sitting on the verandah by ourselves, I took her hand. She withdrew it at once.

' "Why did you do that?" I asked her.

' "I don't very much like being touched," she said. She turned her head a little and smiled. "Are you hurt? You mustn't mind, it's just a funny feeling I have. I can't help it."

' "I wonder if it's ever occurred to you that I'm frightfully fond of you," I said.

'I expect I was terribly awkward about it, but I'd never proposed to anyone before.' Featherstone gave a little sound that was not quite a chuckle and not quite a sigh. 'For the matter of that, I've never proposed to anyone since. She didn't say anything for a minute.

Then she said: ' "I'm very glad, but I don't think I want you to be anything more than that."

' "Why not?" I asked.

' "I could never leave Tim."

' "But supposing he marries?"

' "He never will."

' "I'd gone so far then that I thought I'd better go on. But my throat was so dry that I could hardly speak. I was shaking with nervousness.

' "I'm frightfully in love with you, Olive. I want to marry you more than anything in the world."

'She put her hand very gently on my arm. It was like a flower falling to the ground.

' "No, dear, I can't," she said.

'I was silent. It was difficult for me to say what I wanted to. I'm naturally rather shy. She was a girl. I couldn't very well tell her that it wasn't quite the same thing living with a husband and living with a brother. She was normal and healthy; she must want to have babies; it wasn't reasonable to starve her natural instincts. It was such a waste of her youth. But it was she who spoke first.

' "Don't let's talk about this any more," she said. "D'you mind? It did strike me once or twice that perhaps you cared for me. Tim noticed it. I was sorry because I was afraid it would break up our friendship. I don't want it to do that, Mark. We do get on so well together, the three of us, and we have such jolly times. I don't know what we should do without you now."

' "I thought of that too," I said.

' "D'you think it need?" she asked me.

' "My dear, I don't want it to," I said. "You must know how much I love coming here. I've never been so happy anywhere before!"

' "You're not angry with me?"

' "Why should I be? It's not your fault. It only means that you're not in love with me. If you were you wouldn't care a hang about Tim."

' "You are rather sweet," she said.

'She put her arm round my neck and kissed me lightly on the cheek. I had a notion that in her mind it settled our relation. She adopted me as a second brother.

'A few weeks later Tim went back to England. The tenant of their house in Dorset was leaving and though there was another in the offing, he thought he ought to be on the spot to conduct negotiations. And he wanted some new machinery for the estate. He thought he'd get it at the same time. He didn't expect to be gone more than three months and Olive made up her mind not to go. She knew hardly anyone in England, and it was practically a foreign country to her; she didn't mind being left alone, and she wanted to look after the estate. Of course they could have put a manager in charge, but that wasn't the same thing. Rubber was falling and in case of accidents it was just as well that one or other of them should be there. I promised Tim I'd look after her and if she wanted me she could always call me up. My proposal hadn't changed anything. We carried on as though nothing had happened. I don't know whether she'd told Tim. He made no sign that he knew. Of course I loved her as much as ever, but I kept it to myself. I have a good deal of self-control, you know. I had a sort of feeling I hadn't a chance. I hoped eventually my love would change into something else and we could just be wonderful friends. It's funny, it never has, you know. I suppose I was hit too badly ever to get quite over it.

'She went down to Penang to see Tim off and when she came back I met her at the station and drove her home. I couldn't very well stay at the bungalow while Tim was away, but I went over every Sunday and had tiffin and we'd go down to the sea and have a bathe. People tried to be kind to her and asked her to stay with them, but she wouldn't. She seldom left the estate. She had plenty to do. She read a lot. She was never bored. She seemed quite happy in her own company, and when she had visitors it was only from a sense of duty. She didn't want them to think her ungracious. But it was an effort and she told me she heaved a sigh of relief when she saw the last of them and could again enjoy without disturbance the peaceful loneliness of the bungalow. She was a very curious girl. It was strange that at her age she should be so indifferent to parties and the other small gaieties the station afforded. Spiritually, if you know what I mean, she was entirely self-supporting. I don't know how people found out that I was in love with her; I thought I'd never given myself away in anything, but I had hints here and there that they knew. I gathered they thought Olive hadn't gone home with her brother on my account. One woman, a Mrs Sergison, the policeman's wife, actually asked me when they were going to be able to congratulate me. Of course I pretended I didn't know what she was talking about, but it didn't go down very well. I couldn't help being amused. I meant so little to Olive in that way that I really believe she'd entirely forgotten that I'd asked her to marry me. I can't say she was unkind to me, I don't think she could have been unkind to anyone; but she treated me with just the casualness with which a sister might treat a younger brother. She was two or three years older than I. She was always terribly glad to see me, but it never occurred to her to put herself out for me, she was almost amazingly intimate with me; but unconsciously, you know, as you might be with a person you'd known so well all your life that you never thought of putting on frills with him. I might not have been a man at all, but an old coat that she wore all the time because it was easy and comfortable and she didn't mind what she did in it. I should have been crazy not to see that she was a thousand miles away from loving me.

'Then one day, three or four weeks before Tim was due back, when I went to the bungalow I saw she'd been crying. I was startled. She was always so composed. I'd never seen her upset over anything.

' "Hello, what's the matter?" I said.

' "Nothing."

' "Come off it, darling," I said. "What have you been crying about?"

'She tried to smile.

' "I wish you hadn't got such sharp eyes," she said. "I think I'm being silly. I've just had a cable from Tim to say he's postponed his sailing."

' "Oh, my dear, I am sorry," I said. "You must be awfully disappointed."

' "I've been counting the days. I want him back so badly."

' "Does he say why he's postponing?" I asked.

' "No, he says he's writing. I'll show you the cable."

'I saw that she was very nervous. Her slow quiet eyes were filled with apprehension and there was a little frown of anxiety between her brows. She went into her bedroom and in a moment came back with the cable. I felt that she was watching me anxiously as I read. So far as I remember it ran:

> Darling – I cannot sail on the seventh after all. Please forgive me. Am writing fully. Fondest love. Tim.

' "Well, perhaps the machinery he wanted isn't

ready and he can't bring himself to sail without it," I said.

' "What could it matter if it came by a later ship? Anyhow, it'll be hung up at Penang."

' "It may be something about the house."

' "If it is why doesn't he say so? He must know how frightfully anxious I am."

' "It wouldn't occur to him," I said. "After all, when you're away you don't realise that the people you've left behind don't know something that you take as a matter of course."

'She smiled again, but now more happily.

' "I dare say you're right. In point of fact Tim is a little like that. He's always been rather slack and casual. I dare say I've been making a mountain out of a molehill. I must just wait patiently for his letter."

'Olive was a girl with a lot of self-control and I saw her by an effort of will pull herself together. The little line between her eyebrows vanished and she was once more her serene, smiling and kindly self. She was always gentle: that day she had a mildness so heavenly that it was shattering. But for the rest of the time I could see that she kept her restlessness in check only by the deliberate exercise of her common sense. It was as though she had a foreboding of ill. I was with her the day before the mail was due. Her anxiety was all the more pitiful to see because she took such pains to hide it. I was always busy on mail day, but I promised to go up to the estate later on and hear the news. I was just thinking of starting when Hardy's seis came along in the car with a message from the amah asking me to go at once to her mistress. The amah was a decent, elderly woman to whom I had given a dollar or two and said that if anything went wrong on the estate she was to let me know at once. I jumped into my car. When I arrived I found the amah waiting for me on the steps.

' "A letter came this morning," she said.

'I interrupted her. I ran up the steps. The sitting-room was empty.

' "Olive," I called.

'I went into the passage and suddenly I heard a sound that froze my heart. The amah had followed me and now she opened the door of Olive's room. The sound I had heard was the sound of Olive crying. I went in. She was lying on her bed, on her face, and her sobs shook her from head to foot. I put my hand on her shoulder.

' "Olive, what is it?" I asked.

' "Who's that?" she cried. She sprang to her feet suddenly, as though she were scared out of her wits. And then: "Oh, it's you," she said. She stood in front of me, with her head thrown back and her eyes closed, and the tears streamed from them. It was dreadful. "Tim's married," she gasped, and her face screwed up in a sort of grimace of pain.

'I must admit that for one moment I had a thrill of exultation, it was like a little electric shock tingling through my heart; it struck me that now I had a chance, now she might be willing to marry me; I know it was terribly selfish of me; you see, the news had taken me by surprise; but it was only for a moment, after that I was melted by her awful distress and the only thing I felt was deep sorrow because she was unhappy. I put my arm round her waist.

' "Oh, my dear, I'm so sorry," I said. "Don't stay here. Come into the sitting-room and sit down and we'll talk about it. Let me give you something to drink."

'She let me lead her into the next room and we sat down on the sofa. I told the amah to fetch the whisky and syphon and I mixed her a good strong stengah and made her drink a little. I took her in my arms and rested her head on my shoulder. She let me do what I liked with her. The great tears streamed down her poor face.

' "How could he?" she moaned. "How could he?"

' "My darling," I said, "it was bound to happen sooner or later. He's a young man. How could you expect him never to marry? It's only natural."

' "No, no, no," she gasped.

'Tight-clenched in her hand I saw that she had a letter and I guessed that it was Tim's.

' "What does he say?" I asked.

'She gave a frightened movement and clutched the letter to her heart as though she thought I would take it from her.

' "He says he couldn't help himself. He says he had to. What does it mean?"

' "Well, you know, in his way he's just as attractive as you are. He has so much charm. I suppose he just fell madly in love with some girl and she with him."

' "He's so weak," she moaned.

' "Are they coming out?" I asked.

' "They sailed yesterday. He says it won't make any difference. He's insane. How *can* I stay here?"

'She began to cry hysterically. It was torture to see that girl, usually so calm, utterly shattered by her emotion. I had always felt that her lovely serenity masked a capacity for deep feeling. But the abandon of her distress simply broke me up. I held her in my arms and kissed her, her eyes and her wet cheek and her hair. I don't think she knew what I was doing. I was hardly conscious of it myself. I was so deeply moved.

' "What shall I do?" she wailed.

' "Why won't you marry me?" I said.

'She tried to withdraw herself from me, but I wouldn't let her go.

' "After all, it would be a way out," I said.

' "How can I marry you?" she moaned. "I'm years older than you are."

' "Oh, what nonsense, two or three. What do I care?"

' "No, no."

' "Why not?" I said.

' "I don't love you," she said.

' "What does that matter? I love you."

'I don't know what I said. I told her that I'd try to make her happy. I said I'd never ask anything from her but what she was prepared to give me. I talked and talked. I tried to make her see reason. I felt that she didn't want to stay there, in the same place as Tim, and I told her that I'd be moved soon to some other district. I thought that might tempt her. She couldn't deny that we'd always got on awfully well together. After a time she did seem to grow a little quieter. I had a feeling that she was listening to me. I had even a sort of feeling that she knew that she was lying in my arms and that it comforted her. I made her drink a drop more whisky. I gave her a cigarette. At last I thought I might be just mildly facetious.

'You know, I'm not a bad sort really," I said. "You might do worse."

' "You don't know me," she said. "You know nothing whatever about me."

' "I'm capable of learning," I said.

'She smiled a little. "You're awfully kind, Mark," she said.

' "Say yes, Olive," I begged.

'She gave a deep sigh. For a long time she stared at the ground. But she did not move and I felt the softness of her body in my arms. I waited. I was frightfully nervous and the minutes seemed endless.

' "All right," she said at last, as though she were not conscious that any time had passed between my prayer and her answer.

'I was so moved that I had nothing to say. But when I wanted to kiss her lips, she turned her face away, and wouldn't let me. I wanted us to be married at once, but she was quite firm that she wouldn't. She insisted on waiting till Tim came back. You know how sometimes you see people's thoughts so clearly that you're more certain of them than if they'd spoken them; I saw that she couldn't quite believe that what Tim had written was true and that she had a sort of miserable hope that it was all a mistake and he wasn't married after all. It gave me a pang, but I loved her so much, I just bore it. I was willing to bear anything. I adored her. She wouldn't even let me tell anyone that we were engaged. She made me promise not to say a word till Tim's return. She said she couldn't bear the thought of the congratulations and all that. She wouldn't even let me make any announcement of Tim's marriage. She was obstinate about it. I had a notion that she felt if the fact were spread about it gave it a certainty that she didn't want it to have.

'But the matter was taken out of her hands. News travels mysteriously in the East. I don't know what Olive had said in the amah's hearing when first she received the news of Tim's marriage; anyhow, the Hardys' seis told the Sergisons' and Mrs Sergison attacked me the next time I went into the club.

' "I hear Tim Hardy's married," she said.

' "Oh?' I answered, unwilling to commit myself.

'She smiled at my blank face, and told me that, her amah having told her the rumour, she had rung up Olive and asked her if it was true. Olive's answer had been rather odd. She had not exactly confirmed it, but said that she had received a letter from Tim telling her he was married.

' "She's a strange girl," said Mrs Sergison. "When I asked her for details she said she had none to give and when I said: 'Aren't you thrilled?' she didn't answer."

' "Olive's devoted to Tim, Mrs Sergison," I said. "His marriage has naturally been a shock to her. She knows nothing about Tim's wife. She's nervous about her."

' "And when are you two going to be married?" she asked me abruptly.

' "What an embarrassing question!" I said, trying to laugh it off.

'She looked at me shrewdly.

' "Will you give me your word of honour that you're not engaged to her?"

'I didn't like to tell her a deliberate lie, nor to ask her to mind her own business, and I'd promised Olive faithfully that I would say nothing till Tim got back. I hedged.

' "Mrs Sergison," I said, "when there's anything to tell I promise that you'll be the first person to hear it. All I can say to you now is that I do want to marry Olive more than anything in the world."

' "I'm very glad that Tim's married," she answered.

"And I hope she'll marry you very soon. It was a morbid and unhealthy life that they led up there, those two; they kept far too much to themselves and they were far too much absorbed in one another."

'I saw Olive practically every day. I felt that she didn't want me to make love to her, and I contented myself with kissing her when I came and when I went. She was very nice to me, kindly and thoughtful; I knew she was glad to see me and sorry when it was time for me to go. Ordinarily, she was apt to fall into silence, but during this time she talked more than I had ever heard her talk before. But never of the future and never of Tim and his wife. She told me a lot about her life in Florence with her mother. She had led a strange lonely life, mostly with servants and governesses, while her mother, I suspected, engaged in one affair after another with vague Italian counts and Russian princes. I guessed that by the time she was fourteen there wasn't much she didn't know. It was natural for her to be quite unconventional: in the only world she knew till she was eighteen conventions weren't mentioned because they didn't exist. Gradually, Olive seemed to regain her serenity and I should have thought that she was beginning to accustom herself to the thought of Tim's marriage if it hadn't been that I couldn't but notice how pale and tired she looked. I made up my mind that the moment he arrived I'd press her to marry me at once. I could get short leave whenever I asked for it, and by the time that was up I thought I could manage a transfer to some other post. What she wanted was change of air and fresh scenes.

'We knew, of course, within a day when Tim's ship would reach Penang, but it was a question whether it would get in soon enough for him to catch the train and I wrote to the P&O agent asking him to telegraph as soon as he had definite news. When I got the wire and took it up to Olive I found that she'd just received one from Tim. The ship had docked early and he was arriving next day. The train was supposed to get in at eight o'clock in the morning, but it was liable to be anything from one to six hours late, and I bore with me an invitation from Mrs Sergison asking Olive to come back with me to stay the night with her so that she would be on the spot and need not go to the station till the news came through that the train was coming.

'I was immensely relieved. I thought that when the blow at last fell Olive wouldn't feel it so much. She had worked herself up into such a state that I couldn't help thinking that she must have a reaction now. She might take a fancy to her sister-in-law. There was no reason why they shouldn't all three get on very well together. To my surprise Olive said she wasn't coming down to the station to meet them.

' "They'll be awfully disappointed," I said.

' "I'd rather wait here,' she answered. She smiled a little. "Don't argue with me, Mark, I've quite made up my mind."

' "I've ordered breakfast in my house," I said.

' "That's all right. You meet them and take them to your house and give them breakfast, and then they can come along here afterwards. Of course I'll send the car down."

' "I don't suppose they'll want to breakfast if you're not there," I said.

' "Oh, I'm sure they will. If the train gets in on time they wouldn't have thought of breakfasting before it arrived and they'll be hungry. They won't want to take this long drive without anything to eat."

'I was puzzled. She had been looking forward so intensely to Tim's coming, it seemed strange that she should want to wait all by herself while the rest of us were having a jolly breakfast. I suppose she was nervous and wanted to delay as long as possible meeting the strange woman who had come to take her place. It seemed unreasonable. I couldn't see that an hour sooner or an hour later could make any difference, but I knew women were funny, and anyhow I felt Olive wasn't in the mood for me to press it.

' "Telephone when you're starting so that I shall know when to expect you," she said.

' "All right," I said, "but you know I shan't be able to come with them. It's my day for going to Lahad."

'This was a town that I had to go to once a week to take cases. It was a good way off and one had to ferry across a river, which took some time, so that I never got back till late. There were a few Europeans there and a club. I generally had to go on there for a bit to be sociable and see that things were getting along all right.

' "Besides," I added, "with Tim bringing his wife home for the first time I don't suppose he'll want me about. But if you'd like to ask me to dinner I'll be glad to come to that."

'Olive smiled.

' "I don't think it'll be my place to issue any more invitations, will it?" she said. "You must ask the bride."

'She said this so lightly that my heart leaped. I had a feeling that at last she had made up her mind to accept the altered circumstances and, what was more, was accepting them with cheerfulness. She asked me to stay to dinner. Generally I left about eight and dined at home. She was very sweet, almost tender, and I was happier than I'd been for weeks. I had never been more desperately in love with her. I had a couple of gin pahits and I think I was in rather good form at dinner. I know I made her laugh. I felt that at last she was casting away the load of misery that had oppressed her. That was why I didn't let myself be very much disturbed by what happened at the end.

' "Don't you think it's about time you were leaving a presumably maiden lady?" she said.

'She spoke in a manner that was so quietly gay that I answered without hesitation: "Oh, my dear, if you think you've got a shred of reputation left you deceive yourself. You're surely not under the impression that the ladies of Sibuku don't know that I've been coming to see you every day for a month. The general feeling is that if we're not married it's high time we were. Don't you think it would be just as well if I broke it to them that we're engaged?"

' "Oh, Mark, you mustn't take our engagement very seriously," she said.

'I laughed.

' "How else do you expect me to take it? It is serious."

'She shook her head a little.

' "No. I was upset and hysterical that day. You were being very sweet to me. I said yes because I was too miserable to say no. But now I've had time to collect myself. Don't think me unkind. I made a mistake. I've been very much to blame. You must forgive me."

' "Oh, darling, you're talking nonsense. You've got nothing against me."

'She looked at me steadily. She was quite calm. She had even a little smile at the back of her eyes.

' "I can't marry you. I can't marry anyone. It was absurd of me ever to think I could."

'I didn't answer at once. She was in a queer state and I thought it better not to insist.

' "I suppose I can't drag you to the altar by main force," I said.

'I held out my hand and she gave me hers. I put my arm round her, and she made no attempt to withdraw. She suffered me to kiss her as usual on her cheek.

'Next morning I met the train. For once in a way it was punctual. Tim waved to me as his carriage passed the place where I was standing, and by the time I had walked up he had already jumped out and was handing down his wife. He grasped my hand warmly.

' "Where's Olive?" he said, with a glance along the platform. "This is Sally."

'I shook hands with her and at the same time explained why Olive was not there.

' "It was frightfully early, wasn't it?" said Mrs Hardy.

'I told them that the plan was for them to come and have a bit of breakfast at my house and then drive home.

' "I'd love a bath," said Mrs Hardy.

' "You shall have one," I said.

'She was really an extremely pretty little thing, very fair, with enormous blue eyes and a lovely little straight nose. Her skin, all milk and roses, was exquisite. A little of the chorus-girl type, of course, and you may happen to think that rather namby-pamby, but in that style she was enchanting. We drove to my house, they both had a bath and Tim a shave; I just had two minutes alone with him. He asked me how Olive had taken his marriage. I told him she'd been upset.

' "I was afraid so," he said, frowning a little. He gave a short sigh. "I couldn't do anything else."

'I didn't understand what he meant. At that moment Mrs Hardy joined us and slipped her arm through her husband's. He took her hand in his and gently pressed it. He gave her a look that had in it something pleased and humorously affectionate, as though he didn't take her quite seriously, but enjoyed his sense of proprietorship and was proud of her beauty. She really was lovely. She was not at all shy, she asked me to call her Sally before we'd known one another ten minutes, and she was quick on the uptake. Of course, just then she was excited at arriving. She'd never been East and everything thrilled her. It was quite obvious that she was head over heels in love with Tim. Her eyes never left him and she hung on his words. We had a jolly breakfast and then we parted. They got into their car to go home and I into mine to go to Lahad. I promised to go straight to the estate from there and in point of fact it was out of my way to pass by my house. I took a change with me. I didn't see why Olive shouldn't like Sally very much, she was frank and gay, and ingenuous; she was extremely young, she couldn't have been more than nineteen, and her wonderful prettiness couldn't fail to appeal to Olive. I was just as glad to have had a reasonable excuse to leave the three of them by themselves for the day, but as I started out from Lahad I had a notion that by the time I arrived they would all be pleased to see me. I drove up to the bungalow and blew my horn two or three times, expecting someone to appear. Not a soul. The place was in total darkness. I was surprised. It was absolutely silent. I couldn't make it out. They must be in. Very odd, I thought. I waited a moment, then got out of the car and walked up the steps. At the top of them I stumbled over something. I swore and bent down to see what it was; it had felt like a body. There was a cry and I saw it was the amah. She shrank back cowering as I touched her and broke into loud wails.

' "What the hell's the matter?" I cried, and then I felt a hand on my arm and heard a voice. "Tuan, Tuan." I turned and in the darkness recognised Tim's head-boy. He began to speak in little frightened gasps. I listened to him with horror. What he told me was unspeakable. I pushed him aside and rushed into the house. The sitting-room was dark. I turned on the light. The first thing I saw was Sally huddled up in an armchair. She was startled by my sudden appearance and cried out. I could hardly speak. I asked her if it was true. When she told me it was I felt the room suddenly going round and round me. I had to sit down. As the car that bore Tim and Sally drove up the road that led to the house and Tim sounded the klaxon to announce their arrival and the boys and the amah ran out to greet them there was the sound of a shot. They ran to Olive's room and found her lying in front of the looking-glass in a pool of blood. She had shot herself with Tim's revolver.

' "Is she dead?" I said.

' "No, they sent for the doctor, and he took her to the hospital."

'I hardly knew what I was doing. I didn't even trouble to tell Sally where I was going. I got up and staggered to the door. I got into the car and told my seis to drive like hell to the hospital. I rushed in. I asked where she was. They tried to bar my way, but I pushed them aside. I knew where the private rooms were. Someone clung to my arm, but I shook him off. I vaguely understood that the doctor had given instructions that no one was to go into the room. I didn't care about that. There was an orderly at the door; he put out his arm to prevent me from passing. I swore at him and told him to get out of my way. I suppose I made a row, I was beside myself; the door was opened and the doctor came out.

' "Who's making all this noise?" he said. "Oh, it's you. What do you want?"

' "Is she dead?" I asked.

' "No. But she's unconscious. She never regained consciousness. It's only a matter of an hour or two."

' "I want to see her."

' "You can't."

' "I'm engaged to her."

' "You?" he cried, and even at that moment I was aware that he looked at me strangely. "That's all the more reason."

'I didn't know what he meant. I was stupid with horror.

' "Surely you can do something to save her," I cried.

'He shook his head.

' "If you saw her you wouldn't wish it," he said.

'I stared at him aghast. In the silence I heard a man's convulsive sobbing.

' "Who's that?" I asked.

' "Her brother."

'Then I felt a hand on my arm. I looked round and saw it was Mrs Sergison.

' "My poor boy," she said, "I'm so sorry for you."

' "What on earth made her do it?" I groaned.

' "Come away, my dear," said Mrs Sergison. "You can do no good here."

' "No, I must stay," I said.

' "Well, go and sit in my room," said the doctor.

'I was so broken that I let Mrs Sergison take me by the arm and lead me into the doctor's private room. She made me sit down. I couldn't bring myself to realise that it was true. I thought it was a horrible nightmare from which I must awake. I don't know how long we sat there. Three hours. Four hours. At last the doctor came in.

' "It's all over," he said.

'Then I couldn't help myself, I began to cry. I didn't care what they thought of me. I was so frightfully unhappy.

'We buried her next day.

'Mrs Sergison came back to my house and sat with me for a while. She wanted me to go to the club with her. I hadn't the heart. She was very kind, but I was glad when she left me by myself. I tried to read, but the words meant nothing to me. I felt dead inside. My boy came in and turned on the lights. My head was aching like mad. Then he came back and said that a lady wished to see me. I asked who it was. He wasn't quite sure, but he thought it must be the new wife of the tuan at Putatan. I couldn't imagine what she wanted. I got up and went to the door. He was right. It was Sally. I asked her to come in. I noticed that she was deathly white. I felt sorry for her. It was a frightful experience for a girl of that age and for a bride a miserable homecoming. She sat down. She was very nervous. I tried to put her at her ease by saying conventional things. She made me very uncomfortable because she stared at me with those enormous blue eyes of hers, and they were simply ghastly with horror. She interrupted me suddenly.

' "You're the only person here I know," she said. "I had to come to you. I want you to get me away from here."

'I was dumbfounded.

' "What *do* you mean?" I said.

' "I don't want you to ask me any questions. I just want you to get me away. At once. I want to go back to England!"

' "But you can't leave Tim like that just now," I said. "My dear, you must pull yourself together. I know it's been awful for you. But think of Tim. I mean, he'll be miserable. If you have any love for him the least you can do is to try and make him a little less unhappy."

' "Oh, you don't know," she cried. "I can't tell you. It's too horrible. I beseech you to help me. If there's a train tonight let me get on it. If I can only get to Penang I can get a ship. I can't stay in this place another night. I shall go mad."

'I was absolutely bewildered.

' "Does Tim know?" I asked her.

' "I haven't seen Tim since last night. I'll never see him again. I'd rather die."

'I wanted to gain a little time.

' "But how can you go without your things? Have you got any luggage?"

' "What does that matter?" she cried impatiently. "I've got what I want for the journey."

' "Have you any money?"

' "Enough. Is there a train tonight?"

' "Yes," I said. "It's due just after midnight."

' "Thank God. Will you arrange everything? Can I stay here till then?"

' "You're putting me in a frightful position," I said. "I don't know what to do for the best. You know, it's an awfully serious step you're taking."

' "If you knew everything you'd know it was the only possible thing to do."

' "It'll create an awful scandal here. I don't know what people'll say. Have you thought of the effect on Tim?" I was worried and unhappy. "God knows I don't want to interfere in what isn't my business. But if you want me to help you I ought to know enough to feel justified in doing so. You must tell me what's happened."

' "I can't. I can only tell you that I know everything."

'She hid her face with her hands and shuddered. Then she gave herself a shake as though she were recoiling from some frightful sight.

' "He had no right to marry me. It was monstrous."

'And as she spoke her voice rose shrill and piercing. I was afraid she was going to have an attack of hysterics. Her pretty doll-like face was terrified and her eyes stared as though she could never close them again.

' "Don't you love him any more?" I asked.

' "After that?"

' "What will you do if I refuse to help you?" I said.

' "I suppose there's a clergyman here or a doctor. You can't refuse to take me to one of them."

' "How did you get here?"

' "The head-boy drove me. He got a car from somewhere."

' "Does Tim know you've gone?"

' "I left a letter for him."

' "He'll know you're here."

' "He won't try to stop me. I promise you that. He daren't. For God's sake don't you try either. I tell you I shall go mad if I stay here another night."

'I sighed. After all she was of an age to decide for herself.'

I, the writer of this, hadn't spoken for a long time.

'Did you know what she meant?' I asked Featherstone.

He gave me a long, haggard look.

'There was only one thing she could mean. It was unspeakable. Yes, I knew all right. It explained everything. Poor Olive. Poor sweet. I suppose it was unreasonable of me, but at that moment I only felt a horror of that little pretty fair-haired thing with her terrified eyes. I hated her. I didn't say anything for a while. Then I told her I'd do as she wished. She didn't even say thank you. I think she knew what I felt about her. When it was dinner-time I made her eat something and then she asked me if there was a room she could go and lie down in till it was time to go to the station. I showed her into my spare room and left her. I sat in the sitting-room and waited. My God, I don't think the time has ever passed so slowly for me. I thought twelve would never strike. I rang up the station and was told the train wouldn't be in till nearly two. At midnight she came back to the sitting-room and we sat there for an hour and a half. We had nothing to say to one another and we didn't speak. Then I took her to the station and put her on the train.'

'Was there an awful scandal?'

Featherstone frowned.

'I don't know. I applied for short leave. After that I was moved to another post. I heard that Tim had sold his estate and bought another. But I didn't know where. It was a shock to me at first when I found him here.'

Featherstone, getting up, went over to a table and mixed himself a whisky and soda. In the silence that fell now I heard the monotonous chorus of the croaking frogs. And suddenly the bird that is known as the fever-bird, perched in a tree close to the house, began to call. First, three notes in a descending, chromatic scale, then five, then four. The varying notes of the scale succeeded one another with maddening persistence. One was compelled to listen and to count them, and because one did not know how many there would be it tortured one's nerves.

'Blast that bird,' said Featherstone. 'That means no sleep for me tonight.'

The Round Dozen

I like Elsom. It is a seaside resort in the south of England, not very far from Brighton, and it has something of the late Georgian charm of that agreeable town. But it is neither bustling nor garish. Ten years ago, when I used to go there not infrequently, you might still see here and there an old house, solid and pretentious in no unpleasing fashion (like a decayed gentlewoman of good family whose discreet pride in her ancestry amuses rather than offends you), which was built in the reign of the First Gentleman in Europe and where a courtier of fallen fortunes may well have passed his declining years. The main street had a lackadaisical air and the doctor's motor seemed a trifle out of place. The housewives did their housekeeping in a leisurely manner. They gossiped with the butcher as they watched him cut from his great joint of South Down a piece of the best end of the neck, and they asked amiably after the grocer's wife as he put half a pound of tea and a packet of salt into their string bag. I do not know whether Elsom was ever fashionable: it certainly was not so then; but it was respectable and cheap. Elderly ladies, maiden and widowed, lived there; Indian civilians and retired soldiers: they looked forward with little shudders of dismay to August and September which would bring holiday-makers, but did not disdain to let them their houses and on the proceeds spend a few worldly weeks in a Swiss pension. I never knew Elsom at that hectic time when the lodging-houses were full and young men in blazers sauntered along the front, when Pierrots performed on the beach and in the billiard-room at the Dolphin you heard the click of balls till eleven at night. I only knew it in winter. Then in every house on the seafront, stucco houses with bow-windows built a hundred years ago, there was a sign to inform you that apartments were to let; and the guests of the Dolphin were waited on by a single waiter and the boots. At ten o'clock the porter came into the smoking-room and looked at you in so marked a manner that you got up and went to bed. Then Elsom was a restful place and the Dolphin a very comfortable inn. It was pleasing to think that the Prince Regent drove over with Mrs Fitzherbert more than once to drink a dish of tea in its coffee-room. In the hall was a framed letter from Mr Thackeray ordering a sitting-room and two bedrooms overlooking the sea and giving instructions that a fly should be sent to the station to meet him.

One November, two or three years after the war, having had a bad attack of influenza, I went down to Elsom to regain my strength. I arrived in the afternoon and when I had unpacked my things went for a stroll on the front. The sky was overcast and the calm sea grey and cold. A few seagulls flew close to the shore. Sailing boats, their masts taken down for the winter, were drawn up high on the shingly beach and the bathing huts stood side by side in a long, grey and tattered row. No one was sitting on the benches that the town council had put here and there, but a few people were trudging up and down for exercise. I passed an old colonel with a red nose who stamped along in plus-fours followed by a terrier, two elderly women in short skirts and stout shoes and a plain girl in a tam-o'-shanter. I had never seen the front so deserted. The lodging-houses looked like bedraggled old maids waiting for lovers who would never return, and even the friendly Dolphin seemed wan and desolate. My heart sank. Life on a sudden seemed very drab. I returned to the hotel, drew the curtains of my sitting-room, poked the fire and with a book sought to dispel my melancholy. But I was glad enough when it was time to dress for dinner. I went into the coffee-room and found the guests of the hotel already seated. I gave them a casual glance. There was one lady of middle age by herself and there were two elderly gentlemen, golfers probably, with red faces and baldish heads, who ate their food in moody silence. The only other persons in the room were a group of three who sat in the bow-window, and they immediately attracted my surprised attention. The party consisted of an old gentleman and two ladies, one of whom was old and probably his wife, while the other was younger and possibly his daughter. It was the old lady who first excited my interest. She wore a voluminous dress of black silk and a black lace cap; on her wrists were heavy gold bangles and round her neck a substantial gold chain from which hung a large gold locket; at her neck was a large gold brooch. I did not know that anyone still wore jewellery of that sort. Often, passing second-hand jewellers and pawnbrokers, I had lingered for a moment to look at these strangely old-fashioned articles, so solid, costly and hideous, and thought, with a smile in which there was a tinge of sadness, of the women long since dead who had worn them. They suggested the period when the bustle and the flounce were taking the place of the crinoline and the porkpie hat was ousting the poke-bonnet. The British people liked things solid and good in those days. They went to church on Sunday morning and after church walked in the park. They gave dinner parties of twelve courses where the master of the house carved the beef and the chickens, and after dinner the ladies who could play favoured the company with Mendelssohn's *Songs without Words* and the gentleman with the fine baritone voice sang an old English ballad.

The younger woman had her back turned to me and at first I could see only that she had a slim and youthful figure. She had a great deal of brown hair which seemed to be elaborately arranged. She wore a grey dress. The three of them were chatting in low tones and presently she turned her head so that I saw her profile. It was astonishingly beautiful. The nose was straight and delicate, the line of the cheek exquisitely modelled; I saw then that she wore her hair after the manner of Queen Alexandra. The dinner proceeded to its close and the party got up. The old lady sailed out of the room, looking neither to the right nor to the left, and the young one followed her. Then I saw with a shock that she was old. Her frock was simple enough. The skirt was longer than was at that time worn, and there was something slightly old-fashioned in the cut. I dare say the waist was more clearly indicated than was then usual, but it was a girl's frock. She was tall, like a heroine of Tennyson's, slight, with long legs and a graceful carriage. I had seen the nose before: it was the nose of a Greek goddess; her mouth was beautiful, and her eyes were large and blue. Her skin was of course a little tight on the bones, and there were wrinkles on her forehead and about her eyes, but in youth it must have been lovely. She reminded you of those Roman ladies with features of an exquisite regularity whom Alma-Tadema used to paint, but who, notwithstanding their antique dress, were so stubbornly English. It was a type of cold perfection that one had not seen for five-and-twenty years. Now it is as dead as the epigram. I was like an archaeologist who finds some long-buried statue and I was thrilled in so unexpected a manner to hit upon this survival of a past era. For no day is so dead as the day before yesterday.

The gentleman rose to his feet when the two ladies left, and then resumed his chair. A waiter brought him a glass of heavy port. He smelt it, sipped it, and rolled it round his tongue. I observed him. He was a little man, much shorter than his imposing wife, well-covered without being stout, with a fine head of curling grey hair. His face was much wrinkled and it bore a faintly humorous expression. His lips were tight and his chin was square. He was, according to our present notions, somewhat extravagantly dressed. He wore a black velvet jacket, a frilled shirt with a low collar and a large black tie, and very wide evening trousers. It gave you vaguely the effect of costume. Having drunk his port with deliberation, he got up and sauntered out of the room.

When I passed through the hall, curious to know who these singular people were, I glanced at the visitors' book. I saw, written in an angular feminine hand, the writing that was taught to young ladies in modish schools forty years or so ago, the names: Mr and Mrs Edwin St Clair and Miss Porchester. Their address was given as 68 Leinster Square, Bayswater,

London. These must be the names and this the address of the persons who had so much interested me. I asked the manageress who Mr St Clair was and she told me that she believed he was something in the City. I went into the billiard-room and knocked the balls about for a little while and then on my way upstairs passed through the lounge. The two red-faced gentlemen were reading the evening paper and the middle-aged lady was dozing over a novel. The party of three sat in a corner. Mrs St Clair was knitting, Miss Porchester was busy with embroidery, and Mr St Clair was reading aloud in a discreet but resonant tone. As I passed I discovered that he was reading *Bleak House.*

I read and wrote most of the next day, but in the afternoon I went for a walk and on my way home I sat down for a little on one of those convenient benches on the seafront. It was not quite so cold as the day before and the air was pleasant. For want of anything better to do I watched a figure advancing towards me from a distance. It was a man and as he came nearer I saw that it was rather a shabby little man. He wore a thin black greatcoat and a somewhat battered bowler. He walked with his hands in his pockets and looked cold. He gave me a glance as he passed by, went on a few steps, hesitated, stopped and turned back. When he came up once more to the bench on which I sat he took a hand out of his pocket and touched his hat. I noticed that he wore shabby black gloves, and surmised that he was a widower in straitened circumstances. Or he might have been a mute recovering, like myself, from influenza.

'Excuse me, sir,' he said, 'but could you oblige me with a match?'

'Certainly.'

He sat down beside me and while I put my hand in my pocket for matches he hunted in his for cigarettes. He took out a small packet of Gold Flakes and his face fell.

'Dear, dear, how very annoying! I haven't got a cigarette left.'

'Let me offer you one,' I replied, smiling.

I took out my case and he helped himself.

'Gold?' he asked, giving the case a tap as I closed it. 'Gold? That's a thing I never could keep. I've had three. All stolen.'

His eyes rested in a melancholy way on his boots, which were sadly in need of repair. He was a wizened little man with a long thin nose and pale blue eyes. His skin was sallow and he was much lined. I could not tell what his age was; he might have been five-and-thirty or he might have been sixty. There was nothing remarkable about him except his insignificance. But though evidently poor he was neat and clean. He was respectable and he clung to respectability. No, I did not think he was a mute, I thought he was a solicitor's clerk who had lately buried his wife and been sent to Elsom by an indulgent employer to get over the first shock of his grief.

'Are you making a long stay, sir?' he asked me.

'Ten days or a fortnight.'

'Is this your first visit to Elsom, sir?'

'I have been here before.'

'I know it well, sir. I flatter myself there are very few seaside resorts that I have not been to at one time or another. Elsom is hard to beat, sir. You get a very nice class of people here. There's nothing noisy or vulgar about Elsom if you understand what I mean.

Elsom has very pleasant recollections for me, sir. I knew Elsom well in bygone days. I was married in St Martin's Church, sir.'

'Really,' I said feebly.

'It was a very happy marriage, sir.'

'I'm very glad to hear it,' I returned.

'Nine months, that one lasted,' he said reflectively.

Surely the remark was a trifle singular. I had not looked forward with any enthusiasm to the probability which I so clearly foresaw that he would favour me with an account of his matrimonial experiences, but now I waited if not with eagerness at least with curiosity for a further observation. He made none. He sighed a little. At last I broke the silence.

'There don't seem to be very many people about,' I remarked.

'I like it so. I'm not one for crowds. As I was saying just now I reckon I've spent a good many years at one seaside resort after the other, but I never came in the season. It's the winter I like.'

'Don't you find it a little melancholy?'

He turned towards me and placed his black-gloved hand for an instant on my arm.

'It is melancholy. And because it's melancholy a little ray of sunshine is very welcome.'

The remark seemed to me perfectly idiotic and I did not answer. He withdrew his hand from my arm and got up.

'Well, I mustn't keep you, sir. Pleased to have made your acquaintance.'

He took off his dingy hat very politely and strolled away. It was beginning now to grow chilly and I thought I would return to the Dolphin. As I reached its broad steps a landau drove up, drawn by two scraggy horses, and from it stepped Mr St Clair. He wore a hat that looked like the unhappy result of a union between a bowler and a top-hat. He gave his hand to his wife and then to his niece. The porter carried in after them rugs and cushions. As Mr St Clair paid the driver I heard him tell him to come at the usual time next day, and I understood that the St Clairs took a drive every afternoon in a landau. It would not have surprised me to learn that none of them had ever been in a motor car.

The manageress told me that they kept very much to themselves and sought no acquaintance among the other persons staying at the hotel. I rode my imagination on a loose rein. I watched them eat three meals a day. I watched Mr and Mrs St Clair sit at the top of the hotel steps in the morning. He read *The Times* and she knitted. I supposed Mrs St Clair had never read a paper in her life, for they never took anything but *The Times* and Mr St Clair of course took it with him every day to the City. At about twelve Miss Porchester joined them.

'Have you enjoyed your walk, Eleanor?' asked Mrs St Clair.

'It was very nice, Aunt Gertrude,' answered Miss Porchester.

And I understood that just as Mrs St Clair took 'her drive' every afternoon Miss Porchester took 'her walk' every morning.

'When you have come to the end of your row, my dear,' said Mr St Clair, with a glance at his wife's knitting, 'we might go for a constitutional before luncheon.'

'That will be very nice,' answered Mrs St Clair. She folded up her work and gave it to Miss Porchester.

'If you're going upstairs, Eleanor, will you take my work?'

'Certainly, Aunt Gertrude.'

'I dare say you're a little tired after your walk, my dear.'

'I shall have a little rest before luncheon.'

Miss Porchester went into the hotel and Mr and Mrs St Clair walked slowly along the seafront, side by side, to a certain point, and then walked slowly back.

When I met one of them on the stairs I bowed and received an unsmiling, polite bow in return, and in the morning I ventured upon a good-day, but there the matter ended. It looked as though I should never have a chance to speak to any of them. But presently I thought that Mr St Clair gave me now and then a glance, and thinking he had heard my name I imagined, perhaps vainly, that he looked at me with curiosity. And a day or two after that I was sitting in my room when the porter came in with a message.

'Mr St Clair presents his compliments and could you oblige him with the loan of your *Whitaker's Almanack*.'

I was astonished.

'Why on earth should he think that I have a *Whitaker's Almanack*?'

'Well, sir, the manageress told him you wrote.'

I could not see the connection.

'Tell Mr St Clair that I'm very sorry that I haven't got a *Whitaker's Almanack*, but if I had I would very gladly lend it to him.'

Here was my opportunity. I was by now filled with eagerness to know these fantastic persons more closely. Now and then in the heart of Asia I have come upon a lonely tribe living in a little village among an alien population. No one knows how they came there or why they settled in that spot. They live their own lives, speak their own language, and have no communication with their neighbours. No one knows whether they are the descendants of a band that was left behind when their nation swept in a vast horde across the continent or whether they are the dying remnant of some great people that in that country once held empire. They are a mystery. They have no future and no history. This odd little family seemed to me to have something of the same character. They were of an era that was dead and gone. They reminded me of persons in one of those leisurely, old-fashioned novels that one's father read. They belonged to the eighties and they had not moved since then. How extraordinary it was that they could have lived through the last forty years as though the world stood still! They took me back to my childhood and I recollected people who were long since dead. I wonder if it was only distance that gave me the impression that they were more peculiar than anyone was now. When a person was described then as 'quite a character', by heaven, it meant something.

So that evening after dinner I went into the lounge and boldly addressed Mr St Clair.

'I'm so sorry I haven't got a *Whitaker's Almanack*,' I said, 'but if I have any other book that can be of service to you I shall be delighted to lend it to you.'

Mr St Clair was obviously startled. The two ladies kept their eyes on their work. There was an embarrassed hush.

'It does not matter at all, but I was given to understand by the manageress that you were a novelist.'

I racked my brain. There was evidently some

connection between my profession and *Whitaker's Almanack* that escaped me.

'In days gone by Mr Trollope used often to dine with us in Leinster Square and I remember him saying that the two most useful books to a novelist were the Bible and *Whitaker's Almanack*.'

'I see that Thackeray once stayed in this hotel,' I remarked, anxious not to let the conversation drop.

'I never very much cared for Mr Thackeray, though he dined more than once with my wife's father, the late Mr Sargeant Saunders. He was too cynical for me. My niece has not read *Vanity Fair* to this day.'

Miss Porchester blushed slightly at this reference to herself. A waiter brought in the coffee and Mrs St Clair turned to her husband.

'Perhaps, my dear, this gentleman would do us the pleasure of taking his coffee with us.'

Although not directly addressed, I answered promptly. 'Thank you very much.'

I sat down.

'Mr Trollope was always my favourite novelist,' said Mr St Clair. 'He was so essentially a gentleman. I admire Charles Dickens. But Charles Dickens could never draw a gentleman. I am given to understand that young people nowadays find Mr Trollope a little slow. My niece, Miss Porchester, prefers the novels of Mr William Black.'

'I'm afraid I've never read any,' I said.

'Ah, I see that you are like me; you are not up-to-date. My niece once persuaded me to read a novel by a Miss Rhoda Broughton, but I could not manage more than a hundred pages of it.'

'I did not say I liked it, Uncle Edwin,' said Miss Porchester, defending herself, with another blush. 'I told you it was rather fast, but everybody was talking about it.'

'I'm quite sure it is not the sort of book your Aunt Gertrude would have wished you to read, Eleanor.'

'I remember Miss Broughton telling me once that when she was young people said her books were fast and when she was old they said they were slow, and it was very hard, since she had written exactly the same sort of book for forty years.'

'Oh, did you know Miss Broughton?' asked Miss Porchester, addressing me for the first time. 'How very interesting! And did you know Ouida?'

'My dear Eleanor, what will you say next! I'm quite sure you've never read anything by Ouida.'

'Indeed, I have, Uncle Edwin. I've read *Under Two Flags* and I liked it very much.'

'You amaze and shock me. I don't know what girls are coming to nowadays.'

'You always said that when I was thirty you gave me complete liberty to read anything I liked.'

'There is a difference, my dear Eleanor, between liberty and licence,' said Mr St Clair, smiling a little in order not to make his reproof offensive, but with a certain gravity.

I do not know if in recounting this conversation I have managed to convey the impression it gave me of a charming and old-fashioned air. I could have listened all night to them discussing the depravity of an age that was young in the 1880s. I would have given a good deal for a glimpse of their large and roomy house in Leinster Square. I should have recognised the suite covered in red brocade that stood stiffly about the drawing-room, each piece in its appointed place; and the cabinets filled with Dresden china would have brought me back my childhood. In the dining-room, where they habitually sat, for the drawing-room was used only for parties, there was a Turkey carpet and a vast mahogany sideboard 'groaning' with silver. On the walls were the pictures that had excited the admiration of Mrs Humphry Ward and her uncle Matthew in the Academy of 1880.

Next morning, strolling through a pretty lane at the back of Elsom, I met Miss Porchester, who was taking 'her walk'. I should have liked to go a little way with her, but felt certain that it would embarrass this maiden of fifty to saunter alone with a man even of my respectable years. She bowed as I passed her, and blushed. Oddly enough, a few yards behind her I came upon the funny shabby little man in black gloves with whom I had spoken for a few minutes on the front. He touched his old bowler hat.

'Excuse me, sir, but could you oblige me with a match?' he said.

'Certainly,' I retorted, 'but I'm afraid I have no cigarettes on me.'

'Allow me to offer you one of mine,' he said, taking out the paper case. It was empty. 'Dear, dear, I haven't got one either. What a curious coincidence!'

He went on and I had a notion that he a little hastened his steps. I was beginning to have my doubts about him. I hoped he was not going to bother Miss Porchester. For a moment I thought of walking back, but I did not. He was a civil little man and I did not believe he would make a nuisance of himself to a single lady.

I saw him again that very afternoon. I was sitting

on the front. He walked towards me with little, halting steps. There was something of a wind and he looked like a dried leaf being driven before it. This time he did not hesitate, but sat down beside me.

'We meet again, sir. The world is a small place. If it will not inconvenience you perhaps you will allow me to rest a few minutes. I am a wee bit tired.'

'This is a public bench, and you have just as much right to sit on it as I.'

I did not wait for him to ask me for a match, but at once offered him a cigarette.

'How very kind of you, sir! I have to limit myself to so many cigarettes a day, but I enjoy those I smoke. As one grows older the pleasures of life diminish, but my experience is that one enjoys more those that remain.'

'That is a very consoling thought.'

'Excuse me, sir, but am I right in thinking that you are the well-known author?'

'I am an author,' I replied. 'But what made you think it?'

'I have seen your portrait in the illustrated papers. I suppose you don't recognise me?'

I looked at him again, a weedy little man in neat but shabby black clothes, with a long nose and watery blue eyes.

'I'm afraid I don't.'

'I dare say I've changed,' he sighed. 'There was a time when my photograph was in every paper in the United Kingdom. Of course, those press photographs never do you justice. I give you my word, sir, that if I hadn't seen my name underneath I should never have guessed that some of them were meant for me.'

He was silent for a while. The tide was out, and beyond the shingle of the beach was a strip of yellow mud. The breakwaters were half buried in it like the backbones of prehistoric beasts.

'It must be a wonderfully interesting thing to be an author, sir. I've often thought I had quite a turn for writing myself. At one time and another I've done a rare lot of reading. I haven't kept up with it much lately. For one thing my eyes are not so good as they used to be. I believe I could write a book if I tried.'

'They say anybody can write one,' I answered.

'Not a novel, you know. I'm not much of a one for novels; I prefer histories and that like. But memoirs. If anybody was to make it worth my while I wouldn't mind writing my memoirs.'

'It's very fashionable just now.'

'There are not many people who've had the experiences I've had in one way and another. I did write to one of the Sunday papers about it some little while back, but they never answered my letter.'

He gave me a long, appraising look. He had too respectable an air to be about to ask me for half a crown.

'Of course you don't know who I am, sir, do you?'

'I honestly don't.'

He seemed to ponder for a moment, then he smoothed down his black gloves on his fingers, looked for a moment at a hole in one of them, and then turned to me not without self-consciousness.

'I am the celebrated Mortimer Ellis,' he said.

'Oh?'

I did not know what other ejaculation to make, for to the best of my belief I had never heard the name before. I saw a look of disappointment come over his face, and I was a trifle embarrassed.

'Mortimer Ellis,' he repeated. 'You're not going to tell me you don't know.'

'I'm afraid I must. I'm very often out of England.'

I wondered to what he owed his celebrity. I passed over in my mind various possibilities. He could never have been an athlete, which alone in England gives a man real fame, but he might have been a faith-healer or a champion billiard-player. There is of course no one so obscure as a cabinet minister out of office and he might have been the President of the Board of Trade in a defunct administration. But he had none of the look of a politician.

'That's fame for you,' he said bitterly. 'Why, for weeks I was the most talked-about man in England. Look at me. You must have seen my photograph in the papers. Mortimer Ellis.'

'I'm sorry,' I said, shaking my head.

He paused a moment to give his disclosure effectiveness.

'I am the well-known bigamist.'

Now what are you to reply when a person who is practically a stranger to you informs you that he is a well-known bigamist? I will confess that I have sometimes had the vanity to think that I am not as a rule at a loss for a retort, but here I found myself speechless.

'I've had eleven wives, sir,' he went on.

'Most people find one about as much as they can manage.'

'Ah, that's want of practice. When you've had eleven there's very little you don't know about women.'

'But why did you stop at eleven?'

'There now, I knew you'd say that. The moment I set eyes on you I said to myself, he's got a clever face. You know, sir, that's the thing that always grizzles me. Eleven does seem a funny number, doesn't it? There's something unfinished about it. Now three anyone might have, and seven's all right; they say nine's lucky, and there's nothing wrong with ten. But eleven! That's the one thing I regret. I shouldn't have minded anything if I could have brought it up to the Round Dozen.'

He unbuttoned his coat and from an inside pocket produced a bulging and very greasy pocketbook. From this he took a large bundle of newspaper cuttings; they were worn and creased and dirty. But he spread out two or three.

'Now just you look at those photographs. I ask you, are they like me? It's an outrage. Why, you'd think I was a criminal to look at them.'

The cuttings were of imposing length. In the opinion of sub-editors Mortimer Ellis had obviously been a news item of value. One was headed 'A Much Married Man'; another, 'Heartless Ruffian Brought to Book'; a third, 'Contemptible Scoundrel Meets His Waterloo'.

'Not what you would call a good press,' I murmured.

'I never pay any attention to what the newspapers say,' he answered, with a shrug of his thin shoulders. 'I've known too many journalists myself for that. No, it's the judge I blame. He treated me shocking and it did him no good, mind you; he died within the year.'

I ran my eyes down the report I held.

'I see he gave you five years.'

'Disgraceful, I call it, and see what it says.' He pointed to a place with his forefinger. ' "Three of his victims pleaded for mercy to be shown to him." That shows what they thought of me. And after that he gave me five years. And just look what he called me, a heartless scoundrel – me, the best-hearted man that ever lived – a pest of society and a danger to the public. Said he wished he had the power to give me the cat. I don't so much mind his giving me five years, though you'll never get me to say it wasn't excessive, but I ask you, had he the right to talk to me like that? No, he hadn't, and I'll never forgive him, not if I live to be a hundred.'

The bigamist's cheeks flushed and his watery eyes were filled for a moment with fire. It was a sore subject with him.

'May I read them?' I asked him.

'That's what I gave them you for. I want you to read them, sir. And if you can read them without saying that I'm a much wronged man, well, you're not the man I took you for.'

As I glanced through one cutting after another I saw why Mortimer Ellis had so wide an acquaintance with the seaside resorts of England. They were his hunting-ground. His method was to go to some place when the season was over and take apartments in one of the empty lodging-houses. Apparently it did not take him long to make the acquaintance of some woman or other, widow or spinster, and I noticed that their ages at the time were between thirty-five and fifty. They stated in the witness-box that they had met him first on the seafront. He generally proposed marriage to them within a fortnight of this and they were married shortly after. He induced them in one way or another to entrust him with their savings and in a few months, on the pretext that he had to go to London on business, he left them, never to return. Only one had ever seen him again till, obliged to give evidence, they all saw him in the dock. They were women of a certain respectability: one was the daughter of a doctor and another of a clergyman; there was a lodging-house keeper, there was the widow of a commercial traveller, and there was a retired dressmaker. For the most part, their fortunes ranged from five hundred to a thousand pounds, but whatever the sum the misguided women were stripped of every penny. Some of them told really pitiful stories of the destitution to which they had been reduced. But they all acknowledged that he had been a good husband to them. Not only had three actually pleaded for mercy to be shown him, but one said in the witness-box that, if he was willing to come, she was ready to take him back. He noticed that I was reading this.

'And she'd have worked for me,' he said, 'there's no doubt about that. But I said, better let bygones be bygones. No one likes a cut off the best end of the neck better than I do, but I'm not much of a one for cold roast mutton, I will confess.'

It was only by an accident that Mortimer Ellis did not marry his twelfth wife and so achieve the Round Dozen which I understand appealed to his love of symmetry. It seems he was engaged to be married to a Miss Hubbard – 'two thousand pounds she had, if she had a penny, in a war-loan,' he confided to me – and the banns had been read, when one of his former wives saw him, made enquiries, and communicated with the police. He was arrested on the very day before his twelfth wedding.

'She was a bad one, she was,' he told me. 'She deceived me something cruel.'

'How did she do that?'

'Well, I met her in Eastbourne, one December it

was, on the pier, and she told me in course of conversation that she'd been in the millinery business and had retired. She said she'd made a tidy bit of money. She wouldn't say exactly how much it was, but she gave me to understand it was something like fifteen hundred pounds. And when I married her – would you believe it? – she hadn't got three hundred. And that's the one who gave me away. And mind you, I'd never blamed her. Many a man would have cut up rough when he found out he'd been made a fool of. I never showed her that I was disappointed even, I just went away without a word.'

'But not without the three hundred pounds, I take it.'

'Oh come, sir, you must be reasonable,' he returned in an injured tone. 'You can't expect three hundred pounds to last for ever, and I'd been married to her four months before she confessed the truth.'

'Forgive my asking,' I said, 'and pray don't think my question suggests a disparaging view of your personal attractions, but – why did they marry you?'

'Because I asked them,' he answered, evidently very much surprised at my enquiry.

'But did you never have any refusals?'

'Very seldom. Not more than four or five in the whole course of my career. Of course I didn't propose till I was pretty sure of my ground and I don't say I didn't draw a blank sometimes. You can't expect to click every time, if you know what I mean, and I've often wasted several weeks making up to a woman before I saw there was nothing doing.'

I surrendered myself for a time to my reflections. But I noticed presently that a broad smile had spread over the mobile features of my friend.

'I understand what you mean,' he said. 'It's my appearance that puzzles you. You don't know what it is they see in me. That's what comes of reading novels and going to the pictures. You think what women want is the cowboy type or the romance-of-old-Spain touch, flashing eyes, an olive skin, and a beautiful dancer. You make me laugh.'

'I'm glad,' I said.

'Are you a married man, sir?'

'I am. But I only have one wife.'

'You can't judge by that. You can't generalise from a single instance, if you know what I mean. Now, I ask you, what would you know about dogs if you'd never had anything but one bull-terrier?'

The question was rhetorical and I felt sure did not require an answer. He paused for an effective moment and went on.

'You're wrong, sir. You're quite wrong. They may take a fancy to a good-looking young fellow, but they don't want to marry him. They don't really care about looks.'

'Douglas Jerrold, who was as ugly as he was witty, used to say that if he was given ten minutes' start with a woman he could cut out the handsomest man in the room.'

'They don't want wit. They don't want a man to be funny; they think he's not serious. They don't want a man who's too handsome; they think he's not serious either. That's what they want, they want a man who's serious. Safety first. And then – attention. I may not be handsome and I may not be amusing, but believe me, I've got what every woman wants. Poise. And the proof is, I've made every one of my wives happy.'

'It certainly is much to your credit that three of

them pleaded for mercy to be shown to you and that one was willing to take you back.'

'You don't know what an anxiety that was to me all the time I was in prison. I thought she'd be waiting for me at the gate when I was released, and I said to the governor, "For God's sake, sir, smuggle me out so as no one can see me." '

He smoothed his gloves again over his hands and his eye once more fell upon the hole in the first finger.

'That's what comes of living in lodgings, sir. How's a man to keep himself neat and tidy without a woman to look after him? I've been married too often to be able to get along without a wife. There are men who don't like being married. I can't understand them. The fact is, you can't do a thing really well unless you've got your heart in it, and I like being a married man. It's no difficulty to me to do the little things that women like and that some men can't be bothered with. As I was saying just now, it's attention a woman wants. I never went out of the house without giving my wife a kiss and I never came in without giving her another. And it was very seldom I came in without bringing her some chocolates or a few flowers. I never grudged the expense.'

'After all, it was her money you were spending,' I interposed.

'And what if it was? It's not the money that you've paid for a present that signifies, it's the spirit you give it in. That's what counts with women. No, I'm not one to boast, but I will say this for myself, I am a good husband.'

I looked desultorily at the reports of the trial which I still held.

'I'll tell you what surprises me,' I said. 'All these

women were very respectable, of a certain age, quiet, decent persons. And yet they married you without any enquiry after the shortest possible acquaintance.'

He put his hand impressively on my arm.

'Ah, that's what you don't understand, sir. Women have got a craving to be married. It doesn't matter how young they are or how old they are, if they're short or tall, dark or fair, they've all got one thing in common: they want to be married. And mind you, I married them in church. No woman feels really safe unless she's married in church. You say I'm no beauty. Well, I never thought I was, but if I had one leg and a hump on my back I could find any number of women who'd jump at the chance of marrying me. It's not the man they care about, it's marriage. It's a mania with them. It's a disease. Why, there's hardly one of them who wouldn't have accepted me the second time I saw her only I like to make sure of my ground before I commit myself. When it all came out there was a rare to-do because I'd married eleven times. Eleven times? Why, it's nothing, it's not even a Round Dozen. I could have married thirty times if I'd wanted to. I give you my word, sir, when I consider my opportunities, I'm astounded at my moderation.'

'You told me you were very fond of reading history.'

'Yes, Warren Hastings said that, didn't he? It struck me at the time I read it. It seemed to fit me like a glove.'

'And you never found these constant courtships a trifle monotonous?'

'Well, sir, I think I've got a logical mind, and it always gave me a rare lot of pleasure to see how the same effects followed on the same causes, if you know what I mean. Now, for instance, with a woman who'd never been married before I always passed myself off as a widower. It worked like a charm. You see, a spinster likes a man who knows a thing or two. But with a widow I always said I was a bachelor: a widow's afraid a man who's been married before knows too much.'

I gave him back his cuttings; he folded them up neatly and replaced them in his greasy pocketbook.

'You know, sir, I always think I've been misjudged. Just see what they say about me: a pest of society, unscrupulous villain, contemptible scoundrel. Now just look at me. I ask you, do I look that sort of man? You know me, you're a judge of character, I've told you all about myself; do you think me a bad man?'

'My acquaintance with you is very slight,' I answered with what I thought considerable tact.

'I wonder if the judge, I wonder if the jury, I wonder if the public ever thought about my side of the question. The public booed me when I was taken into court and the police had to protect me from their violence. Did any of them think what I'd done for these women?'

'You took their money.'

'Of course I took their money. I had to live the same as anybody has to live. But what did I give them in exchange for their money?'

This was another rhetorical question, and though he looked at me as though he expected an answer I held my tongue. Indeed I did not know the answer. His voice was raised and he spoke with emphasis. I could see that he was serious.

'I'll tell you what I gave them in exchange for their money. Romance. Look at this place.' He made a wide, circular gesture that embraced the sea and the horizon. 'There are a hundred places in England like this. Look at that sea and that sky; look at these lodging-houses; look at that pier and the front. Doesn't it make your heart sink? It's dead as mutton. It's all very well for you who come down here for a week or two because you're run down. But think of all those women who live here from one year's end to another. They haven't a chance. They hardly know anyone. They've just got enough money to live on and that's all. I wonder if you know how terrible their lives are. Their lives are just like the front, a long, straight, cemented walk that goes on and on from one seaside resort to another. Even in the season there's nothing for them. They're out of it. They might as well be dead. And then I come along. Mind you, I never made advances to a woman who wouldn't have gladly acknowledged to thirty-five. And I give them love. Why, many of them had never known what it was to have a man do them up behind. Many of them had never known what it was to sit on a bench in the dark with a man's arm round their waist. I bring them change and excitement. I give them a new pride in themselves. They were on the shelf and I come along quite quietly and I deliberately take them down. A little ray of sunshine in those drab lives, that's what I was. No wonder they jumped at me, no wonder they wanted me to go back to them. The only one who gave me away was the milliner. She said she was a widow. My private opinion is that she'd never been married at all. You say I did the dirty on them; why, I brought happiness and glamour into eleven lives that never thought they had even a dog's chance of it again. You say I'm a villain and a scoundrel. You're wrong. I'm a philanthropist. Five years, they gave me; they should have given me the medal of the Royal Humane Society.'

He took out his empty packet of Gold Flakes and looked at it with a melancholy shake of the head. When I handed him my cigarette case he helped himself without a word. I watched the spectacle of a good man struggling with his emotion.

'And what did I get out of it, I ask you?' he continued presently. 'Board and lodging and enough to buy cigarettes. But I never was able to save, and the proof is that now, when I'm not so young as I was, I haven't got half a crown in my pocket.' He gave me a sidelong glance. 'It's a great comedown for me to find myself in this position. I've always paid my way and I've never asked a friend for a loan in all my life. I was wondering, sir, if you could oblige me with a trifle. It's humiliating to me to have to suggest it, but the fact is, if you could oblige me with a pound it would mean a great deal to me.'

Well, I had certainly had a pound's worth of entertainment out of the bigamist and I dived for my pocketbook.

'I shall be very glad,' I said.

He looked at the notes I took out.

'I suppose you couldn't make it two, sir?'

'I think I could.'

I handed him a couple of pound notes and he gave a little sigh as he took them.

'You don't know what it means to a man who's used to the comforts of home life not to know where to turn for a night's lodging.'

'But there is one thing I should like you to tell me,' I said. 'I shouldn't like you to think me cynical, but I had a notion that women on the whole take the maxim 'it is more blessed to give than to receive' as applicable exclusively to our sex. How did you persuade these respectable, and no doubt thrifty, women to entrust you so confidently with all their savings?'

An amused smile spread over his undistinguished features.

'Well, sir, you know what Shakespeare said about ambition o'er leaping itself. That's the explanation. Tell a woman you'll double her capital in six months if she'll give it you to handle and she won't be able to give you the money quick enough. Greed, that's what it is. Just greed.'

It was a sharp sensation, stimulating to the appetite (like hot sauce with ice cream), to go from this diverting ruffian to the respectability, all lavender bags and crinolines, of the St Clairs and Miss Porchester. I spent every evening with them now. No sooner had the ladies left him than Mr St Clair sent his compliments to my table and asked me to drink a glass of port with him. When we had finished it we went into the lounge and drank coffee. Mr St Clair enjoyed his glass of old brandy. The hour I thus spent with them was so exquisitely boring that it had for me a singular fascination. They were told by the manageress that I had written plays.

'We used often to go to the theatre when Sir Henry Irving was at the Lyceum,' said Mr St Clair. 'I once had the pleasure of meeting him. I was taken to supper at the Garrick Club by Sir Everard Millais and I was introduced to Mr Irving as he then was.'

'Tell him what he said to you, Edwin,' said Mrs St Clair.

Mr St Clair struck a dramatic attitude and gave not at all a bad imitation of Henry Irving.

' "You have the actor's face, Mr St Clair," he said to me. "If you ever think of going on the stage, come to me and I will give you a part." ' Mr St Clair resumed his natural manner. 'It was enough to turn a young man's head.'

'But it didn't turn yours,' I said.

'I will not deny that if I had been otherwise situated I might have allowed myself to be tempted. But I had my family to think of. It would have broken my father's heart if I had not gone into the business.'

'What is that?' I asked.

'I am a tea-merchant, sir. My firm is the oldest in the City of London. I have spent forty years of my life in combating to the best of my ability the desire of my fellow-countrymen to drink Ceylon tea instead of the China tea which was universally drunk in my youth.'

I thought it charmingly characteristic of him to spend a lifetime in persuading the public to buy something they didn't want rather than something they did.

'But in his younger days my husband did a lot of amateur acting and he was thought very clever,' said Mrs St Clair.

'Shakespeare, you know, and sometimes *The School for Scandal*. I would never consent to act trash. But that is a thing of the past. I had a gift. Perhaps it was a pity to waste it, but it's too late now. When we have a dinner-party I sometimes let the ladies persuade me to recite the great soliloquies of Hamlet. But that is all I do.'

Oh! Oh! Oh! I thought with shuddering fascination of those dinner-parties and wondered whether I should ever be asked to one of them. Mrs St Clair gave me a little smile, half shocked, half prim.

'My husband was very bohemian as a young man,' she said.

'I sowed my wild oats. I knew quite a lot of painters and writers, Wilkie Collins, for instance, and even men who wrote for the papers. Watts painted a portrait of my wife, and I bought a picture of Millais's. I knew a number of the Pre-Raphaelites.'

'Have you a Rossetti?' I asked.

'No. I admired Rossetti's talent, but I could not approve of his private life. I would never buy a picture by an artist whom I should not care to ask to dinner at my house.'

My brain was reeling when Miss Porchester, looking at her watch, said: 'Are you not going to read to us tonight, Uncle Edwin?'

I withdrew.

It was while I was drinking a glass of port with Mr St Clair one evening that he told me the sad story of Miss Porchester. She was engaged to be married to a nephew of Mrs St Clair, a barrister, when it was discovered that he had had an intrigue with the daughter of his laundress.

'It was a terrible thing,' said Mr St Clair. 'A terrible thing. But of course my niece took the only possible course. She returned him his ring, his letters and his photograph, and said that she could never marry him. She implored him to marry the young person he had wronged and said she would be a sister to her. It broke her heart. She has never cared for anyone since.'

'And did he marry the young person?'

Mr St Clair shook his head and sighed.

'No, we were greatly mistaken in him. It has been a

sore grief to my dear wife to think that a nephew of hers should behave in such a dishonourable manner. Some time later we heard that he was engaged to a young lady in a very good position with ten thousand pounds of her own. I considered it my duty to write to her father and put the facts before him. He answered my letter in a most insolent fashion. He said he would much rather his son-in-law had a mistress before marriage than after.'

'What happened then?'

'They were married and now my wife's nephew is one of His Majesty's Judges of the High Court, and his wife is My Lady. But we've never consented to receive them. When my wife's nephew was knighted Eleanor suggested that we should ask them to dinner, but my wife said that he should never darken our doors and I upheld her.'

'And the laundress's daughter?'

'She married in her own class of life and has a public-house at Canterbury. My niece, who has a little money of her own, did everything for her and is godmother to her eldest child.'

Poor Miss Porchester. She had sacrificed herself on the altar of Victorian morality, and I am afraid the consciousness that she had behaved beautifully was the only benefit she had got from it.

'Miss Porchester is a woman of striking appearance,' I said. 'When she was younger she must have been perfectly lovely. I wonder she never married somebody else.'

'Miss Porchester was considered a great beauty. Alma-Tadema admired her so much that he asked her to sit as a model for one of his pictures, but of course we couldn't very well allow that.' Mr St Clair's tone conveyed that the suggestion had deeply outraged his sense of decency. 'No, Miss Porchester never cared for anyone but her cousin. She never speaks of him and it is now thirty years since they parted, but I am convinced that she loves him still. She is a true woman, my dear sir, one life, one love, and though perhaps I regret that she has been deprived of the joys of marriage and motherhood I am bound to admire her fidelity.'

But the heart of woman is incalculable, and rash is the man who thinks she will remain in one stay. Rash, Uncle Edwin. You have known Eleanor for many years, for when, her mother having fallen into a decline and died, you brought the orphan to your comfortable and even luxurious house in Leinster Square, she was but a child; but what, when it comes down to brass tacks, Uncle Edwin, do you really know of Eleanor?

It was but two days after Mr St Clair had confided to me the touching story which explained why Miss Porchester had remained a spinster that, on my return to the hotel in the afternoon after a round of golf, the manageress came up to me in an agitated manner.

'Mr St Clair's compliments and will you go up to number twenty-seven the moment you come in.'

'Certainly. But why?'

'Oh, there's a rare upset. They'll tell you.'

I knocked at the door. I heard a 'Come in, come in' which reminded me that Mr St Clair had played Shakespearean parts in probably the most refined amateur dramatic company in London. I entered and found Mrs St Clair lying on the sofa with a handkerchief soaked in eau-de-Cologne on her brow and a bottle of smelling-salts in her hand. Mr St Clair was standing in front of the fire in such a manner as to prevent anyone else in the room from obtaining any benefit from it.

'I must apologise for asking you to come up in this unceremonious fashion, but we are in great distress, and we thought you might be able to throw some light on what has happened.'

His perturbation was obvious.

'What *has* happened?'

'Our niece, Miss Porchester, has eloped. This morning she sent in a message to my wife that she had one of her sick headaches. When she has one of her sick headaches she likes to be left absolutely alone, and it wasn't till this afternoon that my wife went to see if there was anything she could do for her. The room was empty. Her trunk was packed. Her dressing-case with silver fittings was gone. And on the pillow was a letter telling us of her rash act.'

'I'm very sorry,' I said. 'I don't know exactly what I can do.'

'We were under the impression that you were the only gentleman in Elsom with whom she had any acquaintance.'

His meaning flashed across me.

'I see you haven't eloped with her. At the first moment we thought perhaps . . . but if it isn't you, who is it?'

'I'm sure I don't know.'

'Show him the letter, Edwin,' said Mrs St Clair from the sofa.

'Don't move, Gertrude. It will bring on your lumbago.'

Miss Porchester had 'her' sick headaches and Mrs

St Clair had 'her' lumbago. What had Mr St Clair? I was willing to bet a fiver that Mr St Clair had 'his' gout. He gave me the letter and I read it with an air of decent commiseration.

> DEAREST UNCLE EDWIN AND AUNT GERTRUDE – When you receive this I shall be far away. I am going to be married this morning to a gentleman who is very dear to me. I know I am doing wrong in running away like this, but I was afraid you would endeavour to set obstacles in the way of my marriage, and since nothing would induce me to change my mind I thought it would save us all much unhappiness if I did it without telling you anything about it. My fiancé is a very retiring man, owing to his long residence in tropical countries not in the best of health, and he thought it much better that we should be married quite privately. When you know how radiantly happy I am I hope you will forgive me. Please send my box to the luggage office at Victoria Station,
>
> Your loving niece,
>
> ELEANOR

'I will never forgive her,' said Mr St Clair as I returned him the letter. 'She shall never darken my doors again. Gertrude, I forbid you ever to mention Eleanor's name in my hearing.'

Mrs St Clair began to sob quietly.

'Aren't you rather hard?' I said. 'Is there any reason why Miss Porchester shouldn't marry?'

'At her age?' he answered angrily. 'It's ridiculous. We shall be the laughing-stock of everyone in Leinster Square. Do you know how old she is? She's fifty-one.'

'Fifty-four,' said Mrs St Clair through her sobs.

'She's been the apple of my eye. She's been like a daughter to us. She's been an old maid for years. I think it's positively improper for her to think of marriage.'

'She was always a girl to us, Edwin,' pleaded Mrs St Clair.

'And who is this man she's married? It's the deception that rankles. She must have been carrying on with him under our very noses. She does not even tell us his name. I fear the very worst.'

Suddenly I had an inspiration. That morning after breakfast I had gone out to buy myself some cigarettes and at the tobacconist's I ran across Mortimer Ellis. I had not seen him for some days.

'You're looking very spruce,' I said.

His boots had been repaired and were neatly blacked, his hat was brushed, he was wearing a clean collar and new gloves. I thought he had laid out my two pounds to advantage.

'I have to go to London this morning on business,' he said.

I nodded and left the shop.

I remembered that a fortnight before, walking in the country, I had met Miss Porchester and, a few yards behind, Mortimer Ellis. Was it possible that they had been walking together and he had fallen back as they caught sight of me? By heaven, I saw it all.

'I think you said that Miss Porchester had money of her own,' I said.

'A trifle. She has three thousand pounds.'

Now I was certain. I looked at them blankly. Suddenly Mrs St Clair, with a cry, sprang to her feet.

'Edwin, Edwin, supposing he doesn't marry her?'

Mr St Clair at this put his hand to his head and in a state of collapse sank into a chair.

'The disgrace would kill me,' he groaned.

'Don't be alarmed,' I said. 'He'll marry her all right. He always does. He'll marry her in church.'

They paid no attention to what I said. I suppose they thought I'd suddenly taken leave of my senses. I was quite sure now. Mortimer Ellis had achieved his ambition after all. Miss Porchester completed the Round Dozen.

The Facts of Life

It was Henry Garnet's habit on leaving the City of an afternoon to drop in at his club and play bridge before going home to dinner. He was a pleasant man to play with. He knew the game well and you could be sure that he would make the best of his cards. He was a good loser; and when he won was more inclined to ascribe his success to his luck than to his skill. He was indulgent, and if his partner made a mistake could be trusted to find an excuse for him. It was surprising then on this occasion to hear him telling his partner with unnecessary sharpness that he had never seen a hand worse played; and it was more surprising still to see him not only make a grave error himself, an error of which you would never have thought him capable, but when his partner, not unwilling to get a little of his own back, pointed it out, insist against all reason and with considerable heat that he was perfectly right. But they were all old friends, the men he was playing with, and none of them took his ill-humour very seriously. Henry Garnet was a broker, a partner in a firm of repute, and it occurred to one of them that something had gone wrong with some stock he was interested in.

'How's the market today?' he asked.

'Booming. Even the suckers are making money.'

It was evident that stocks and shares had nothing to do with Henry Garnet's vexation; but something was the matter; that was evident too. He was a hearty fellow, who enjoyed excellent health; he had plenty of money; he was fond of his wife and devoted to his children. As a rule he had high spirits, and he laughed easily at the nonsense they were apt to talk while they played; but today he sat glum and silent. His brows were crossly puckered and there was a sulky look about his mouth. Presently, to ease the tension, one of the others mentioned a subject upon which they all knew Henry Garnet was glad to speak.

'How's your boy, Henry? I see he's done pretty well in the tournament.'

Henry Garnet's frown grew darker.

'He's done no better than I expected him to.'

'When does he come back from Monte?'

'He got back last night.'

'Did he enjoy himself?'

'I suppose so; all I know is that he made a damned fool of himself.'

'Oh. How?'

'I'd rather not talk about it if you don't mind.'

The three men looked at him with curiosity. Henry Garnet scowled at the green baize.

'Sorry, old boy. Your call.'

The game proceeded in a strained silence. Garnet got his bid, and when he played his cards so badly that he went three down not a word was said. Another rubber was begun and in the second game Garnet denied a suit.

'Having none?' his partner asked him.

Garnet's irritability was such that he did not even reply, and when at the end of the hand it appeared that he had revoked, and that his revoke cost the rubber, it was not to be expected that his partner should let his carelessness go without remark.

'What the devil's the matter with you, Henry?' he said. 'You're playing like a fool.'

Garnet was disconcerted. He did not so much mind losing a big rubber himself, but he was sore that his inattention should have made his partner lose too. He pulled himself together.

'I'd better not play any more. I thought a few rubbers would calm me, but the fact is I can't give my mind to the game. To tell you the truth I'm in a hell of a temper.'

They all burst out laughing.

'You don't have to tell us that, old boy. It's obvious.'

Garnet gave them a rueful smile.

'Well, I bet you'd be in a temper if what's happened to me had happened to you. As a matter of fact I'm in a damned awkward situation, and if any of you fellows can give me any advice how to deal with it I'd be grateful.'

'Let's have a drink and you can tell us all about it. You've got a KC, a Home Office official and an eminent surgeon – if we can't tell you how to deal with a situation, nobody can.'

The KC got up and rang the bell for a waiter.

'It's about that damned boy of mine,' said Henry Garnet.

Drinks were ordered and brought. And this is the story that Henry Garnet told them.

The boy of whom he spoke was his only son. His name was Nicholas and of course he was called Nicky. He was eighteen. The Garnets had two daughters besides, one of sixteen and the other of twelve, but however unreasonable it seemed, for a father is generally supposed to like his daughters best, and though he did all he could not to show his preference, there was no doubt that the greater share of Henry Garnet's affection was given to his son. He was kind, in a chaffing, casual way, to his daughters, and gave them handsome presents on their birthdays and at Christmas; but he doted on Nicky. Nothing was too good for him. He thought the world of him. He could hardly take his eyes off him. You could not blame him, for Nicky was a son that any parent might have been proud of. He was six foot two, lithe but muscular, with broad shoulders and a slim waist, and he held himself gallantly erect; he had a charming head, well placed on the shoulders, with pale brown hair that waved slightly, blue eyes with long dark lashes under well-marked eyebrows, a full red mouth and a tanned, clean skin. When he smiled he showed very regular and very white teeth. He was not shy, but there was a modesty in his demeanour that was attractive. In social intercourse he was easy, polite and quietly gay. He was the offspring of nice, healthy, decent parents, he had been well brought up in a good home, he had been sent to a good school, and the general result was as engaging a specimen of young manhood as you were likely to find in a long time. You felt that he was as honest, open and virtuous as he looked. He had never given his parents a moment's uneasiness. As a child he was seldom ill and never naughty. As a boy he did everything that was expected of him. His school reports were excellent. He was wonderfully popular, and he ended his career, with a creditable number of prizes, as head of the school and captain of the football team. But this was not all. At the age of fourteen Nicky had developed an unexpected gift for lawn tennis. This was a game that his father not only was fond of, but played very well, and when he discerned in the boy the promise of a tennis-player he fostered it. During the holidays he had him taught by the best professionals and by the time he was sixteen he had won a number of tournaments for boys of his age. He could beat his father so badly that only parental affection reconciled the older player to the poor show he put up. At eighteen Nicky went to Cambridge and Henry Garnet conceived the ambition that before he was through with the university he should play for it. Nicky had all the qualifications for becoming a great tennis-player. He was tall, he had a long reach, he was quick on his feet and his timing was perfect. He realised instinctively where the ball was coming and, seemingly without hurry, was there to take it. He had a powerful serve, with a nasty break that made it difficult to return, and his forehand drive, low, long and accurate, was deadly. He was not so good on the backhand and his volleying was wild, but all through the summer before he went to Cambridge Henry Garnet made him work on these points under the best teacher in England. At the back of his mind, though he did not even mention it to Nicky, he cherished a further ambition, to see his son play at Wimbledon, and who could tell, perhaps be chosen to represent his country in the Davis Cup. A great lump came into Henry Garnet's throat as he saw in fancy his son leap over the net to shake hands with the American champion whom he had just defeated, and walk off the court to the deafening plaudits of the multitude.

As an assiduous frequenter of Wimbledon Henry Garnet had a good many friends in the tennis world, and one evening he found himself at a City dinner sitting next to one of them, a Colonel Brabazon, and in due course began talking to him of Nicky and what chance there might be of his being chosen to play for his university during the following season.

'Why don't you let him go down to Monte Carlo and play in the spring tournament there?' said the colonel suddenly.

'Oh, I don't think he's good enough for that. He's not nineteen yet, he only went up to Cambridge last October; he wouldn't stand a chance against all those cracks.'

'Of course, Austin and von Cramm and so on would knock spots off him, but he might snatch a game or two; and if he got up against some of the smaller fry there's no reason why he shouldn't win two or three matches. He's never been up against any of the first-rate players and it would be wonderful practice for him. He'd learn a lot more than he'll ever learn in the seaside tournaments you enter him for.'

'I wouldn't dream of it. I'm not going to let him leave Cambridge in the middle of a term. I've always impressed upon him that tennis is only a game and it mustn't interfere with work.'

Colonel Brabazon asked Garnet when the term ended.

'That's all right. He'd only have to cut about three days. Surely that could be arranged. You see, two of the men we were depending on have let us down, and we're in a hole. We want to send as good a team as we can. The Germans are sending their best players and so are the Americans.'

'Nothing doing, old boy. In the first place Nicky's not good enough, and secondly, I don't fancy the idea of sending a kid like that to Monte Carlo without anyone to look after him. If I could get away myself I might think of it, but that's out of the question.'

'I shall be there. I'm going as the non-playing captain of the English team. I'll keep an eye on him.'

'You'll be busy, and besides, it's not a responsibility I'd like to ask you to take. He's never been abroad in his life, and to tell you the truth, I shouldn't have a moment's peace all the time he was there.'

They left it at that and presently Henry Garnet went home. He was so flattered by Colonel Brabazon's suggestion that he could not help telling his wife.

'Fancy his thinking Nicky's as good as that. He told me he'd seen him play and his style was fine. He only wants more practice to get into the first flight. We shall see the kid playing in the semi-finals at Wimbledon yet, old girl.'

To his surprise Mrs Garnet was not so much opposed to the notion as he would have expected.

'After all the boy's eighteen. Nicky's never got into mischief yet and there's no reason to suppose he will now.'

'There's his work to be considered; don't forget that. I think it would be a very bad precedent to let him cut the end of term.'

'But what can three days matter? It seems a shame to rob him of a chance like that. I'm sure he'd jump at it if you asked him.'

'Well, I'm not going to. I haven't sent him to Cambridge just to play tennis. I know he's steady, but it's silly to put temptation in his way. He's much too young to go to Monte Carlo by himself.'

'You say he won't have a chance against these crack players, but you can't tell.'

Henry Garnet sighed a little. On the way home in the car it had struck him that Austin's health was uncertain and that von Cramm had his off-days.

Supposing, just for the sake of argument, that Nicky had a bit of luck like that – then there would be no doubt that he would be chosen to play for Cambridge. But of course that was all nonsense.

'Nothing doing, my dear. I've made up my mind and I'm not going to change it.'

Mrs Garnet held her peace. But next day she wrote to Nicky, telling him what had happened, and suggested to him what she would do in his place if, wanting to go, he wished to get his father's consent. A day or two later Henry Garnet received a letter from his son. He was bubbling over with excitement. He had seen his tutor, who was a tennis-player himself, and the provost of his college, who happened to know Colonel Brabazon, and no objection would be made to his leaving before the end of term; they both thought it an opportunity that shouldn't be missed. He didn't see what harm he could come to, and if only, just this once, his father would stretch a point, well, next term, he promised faithfully, he'd work like blazes. It was a very pretty letter. Mrs Garnet watched her husband read it at the breakfast table; she was undisturbed by the frown on his face. He threw it over to her.

'I don't know why you thought it necessary to tell Nicky something I told you in confidence. It's too bad of you. Now you've thoroughly unsettled him.'

'I'm sorry. I thought it would please him to know that Colonel Brabazon had such a high opinion of him. I don't see why one should only tell people the disagreeable things that are said about them. Of course I made it quite clear that there could be no question of his going.'

'You've put me in an odious position. If there's

anything I hate it's for the boy to look upon me as a spoil-sport and a tyrant.'

'Oh, he'll never do that. He may think you rather silly and unreasonable, but I'm sure he'll understand that it's only for his own good that you're being so unkind.'

'Christ,' said Henry Garnet.

His wife had a great inclination to laugh. She knew the battle was won. Dear, oh dear, how easy it was to get men to do what you wanted. For appearance' sake Henry Garnet held out for forty-eight hours, but then he yielded, and a fortnight later Nicky came to London. He was to start for Monte Carlo next morning, and after dinner, when Mrs Garnet and her elder daughter had left them, Henry took the opportunity to give his son some good advice.

'I don't feel quite comfortable about letting you go off to a place like Monte Carlo at your age practically by yourself,' he finished, 'but there it is and I can only hope you'll be sensible. I don't want to play the heavy father, but there are three things especially that I want to warn you against: one is gambling, don't gamble; the second is money, don't lend anyone money; and the third is women, don't have anything to do with women. If you don't do any of those three things you can't come to much harm, so remember them well.'

'All right, father,' Nicky smiled.

'That's my last word to you. I know the world pretty well and believe me, my advice is sound.'

'I won't forget it. I promise you.'

'That's a good chap. Now let's go up and join the ladies.'

Nicky beat neither Austin nor von Cramm in the Monte Carlo tournament, but he did not disgrace himself. He snatched an unexpected victory over a Spanish player and gave one of the Austrians a closer match than anyone had thought possible. In the mixed doubles he got into the semi-finals. His charm conquered everyone and he vastly enjoyed himself. It was generally allowed that he showed promise, and Colonel Brabazon told him that when he was a little older and had had more practice with first-class players he would be a credit to his father. The tournament came to an end and the day following he was to fly back to London. Anxious to play his best he had lived very carefully, smoking little and drinking nothing, and going to bed early; but on his last evening he thought he would like to see something of the life in Monte Carlo of which he had heard so much. An official dinner was given to the tennis-players and after dinner with the rest of them he went into the Sporting Club. It was the first time he had been there. Monte Carlo was very full and the rooms were crowded. Nicky had never before seen roulette played except in the pictures; in amaze he stopped at the first table he came to; chips of different sizes were scattered over the green cloth in what looked like a hopeless muddle; the croupier gave the wheel a sharp turn and with a flick threw in the little white ball. After what seemed an endless time the ball stopped and another croupier with a broad, indifferent gesture raked in the chips of those who had lost.

Presently Nicky wandered over to where they were playing *trente et quarante*, but he couldn't understand what it was all about and he thought it dull. He saw a crowd in another room and sauntered in. A big game of baccarat was in progress and he was immediately conscious of the tension. The players were protected from the thronging bystanders by a brass rail; they sat round the table, nine on each side, with the dealer in the middle and the croupier facing him. Big money was changing hands. The dealer was a member of the Greek Syndicate. Nicky looked at his impassive face. His eyes were watchful, but his expression never changed whether he won or lost. It was a terrifying, strangely impressive sight. It gave Nicky, who had been thriftily brought up, a peculiar thrill to see someone risk a thousand pounds on the turn of a card and when he lost make a little joke and laugh. It was all terribly exciting. An acquaintance came up to him.

'Been doing any good?' he asked.

'I haven't been playing.'

'Wise of you. Rotten game. Come and have a drink.'

'All right.'

While they were having it Nicky told his friend that this was the first time he had ever been in the rooms.

'Oh, but you must have one little flutter before you go. It's idiotic to leave Monte without having tried your luck. After all it won't hurt you to lose a hundred francs or so.'

'I don't suppose it will, but my father wasn't any too keen on my coming at all and one of the three things he particularly advised me not to do was to gamble.'

But when Nicky left his companion he strolled back to one of the tables where they were playing roulette. He stood for a while looking at the losers' money being raked in by the croupier and the money that was won paid out to the winners. It was impossible to deny that it was thrilling. His friend was right, it did seem silly to leave Monte without putting something on the table just once. It would be an experience, and at his age you had to have all the experience you could get. He reflected that he hadn't promised his father not to gamble, he'd promised him not to forget his advice. It wasn't quite the same, was it? He took a hundred-franc note out of his pocket and rather shyly put it on number eighteen. He chose it because that was his age. With a wildly beating heart he watched the wheel turn; the little white ball whizzed about like a small demon of mischief; the wheel went round more slowly, the little white ball hesitated, it seemed about to stop, it went on again; Nicky could hardly believe his eyes when it fell into number eighteen. A lot of chips were passed over to him and his hands trembled as he took them. It seemed to amount to a lot of money. He was so confused that he never thought of putting anything on the following round; in fact he had no intention of playing any more, once was enough; and he was surprised when eighteen again came up. There was only one chip on it.

'By George, you've won again,' said a man who was standing near to him.

'Me? I hadn't got anything on.'

'Yes, you had. Your original stake. They always leave it on unless you ask for it back. Didn't you know?'

Another packet of chips was handed over to him. Nicky's head reeled. He counted his gains: seven thousand francs. A queer sense of power seized him; he felt wonderfully clever. This was the easiest way of making money that he had ever heard of. His frank, charming face was wreathed in smiles. His bright eyes met those of a woman standing by his side. She smiled.

'You're in luck,' she said.

She spoke English, but with a foreign accent.

'I can hardly believe it. It's the first time I've ever played.'

'That explains it. Lend me a thousand francs, will you? I've lost everything I've got. I'll give it you back in half an hour.'

'All right.'

She took a large red chip from his pile and with a word of thanks disappeared. The man who had spoken to him before grunted.

'You'll never see that again.'

Nicky was dashed. His father had particularly advised him not to lend anyone money. What a silly thing to do! And to somebody he'd never seen in his life. But the fact was, he had felt at that moment such a love for the human race that it had never occurred to him to refuse. And that big red chip, it was almost impossible to realise that it had any value. Oh well, it didn't matter, he still had six thousand francs, he'd just try his luck once or twice more and if he didn't win he'd go home. He put a chip on sixteen, which was his elder sister's age, but it didn't come up; then on twelve, which was his younger sister's, and that didn't come up either; he tried various numbers at random, but without success. It was funny, he seemed to have lost his knack. He thought he would try just once more and then stop; he won. He had made up all his losses and had something over. At the end of an hour, after various ups and downs, having experienced such thrills as he had never known in his life, he found himself with so many chips that they would hardly go in his pockets. He decided to go. He went to the changers' office and he gasped when twenty thousand-franc notes were spread out before him. He had never had so much money in his life. He put it in his pocket and was turning away when the woman to whom he had lent the thousand francs came up to him.

'I've been looking for you everywhere,' she said. 'I was afraid you'd gone. I was in a fever, I didn't know what you'd think of me. Here's your thousand francs and thank you so much for the loan.'

Nicky, blushing scarlet, stared at her in amazement. How he had misjudged her! His father had said, don't gamble; well, he had, and he'd made twenty thousand francs; and his father had said, don't lend anyone money; well, he had, he'd lent quite a lot to a total stranger, and she'd returned it. The fact was that he wasn't nearly such a fool as his father thought: he'd had an instinct that he could lend her the money with safety, and you see, his instinct was right. But he was so obviously taken aback that the little lady was forced to laugh.

'What is the matter with you?' she asked.

'To tell you the truth I never expected to see the money back.'

'What did you take me for? Did you think I was a – cocotte?'

Nicky reddened to the roots of his wavy hair.

'No, of course not.'

'Do I look like one?'

'Not a bit.'

She was dressed very quietly, in black, with a string of gold beads round her neck; her simple frock showed off a neat, slight figure; she had a pretty little face and a trim head. She was made up, but not excessively, and Nicky supposed that she was not more than three or four years older than himself. She gave him a friendly smile.

'My husband is in the administration in Morocco, and I've come to Monte Carlo for a few weeks because he thought I wanted a change.'

'I was just going,' said Nicky because he couldn't think of anything else to say.

'Already!'

'Well, I've got to get up early tomorrow. I'm going back to London by air.'

'Of course. The tournament ended today, didn't it? I saw you play, you know, two or three times.'

'Did you? I don't know why you should have noticed me.'

'You've got a beautiful style. And you looked very sweet in your shorts.'

Nicky was not an immodest youth, but it did cross his mind that perhaps she had borrowed that thousand francs in order to scrape acquaintance with him.

'Do you ever go to the Knickerbocker?' she asked.

'No. I never have.'

'Oh, but you mustn't leave Monte Carlo without having been there. Why don't you come and dance a little? To tell you the truth, I'm starving with hunger and I should adore some bacon and eggs.'

Nicky remembered his father's advice not to have anything to do with women, but this was different; you had only to look at the pretty little thing to know at once that she was perfectly respectable. Her husband was in what corresponded, he supposed, to the Civil Service. His father and mother had friends who were Civil Servants and they and their wives sometimes came to dinner. It was true that the wives were neither so young nor so pretty as this one, but she was just as ladylike as they were. And after winning twenty thousand francs he thought it wouldn't be a bad idea to have a little fun.

'I'd love to go with you,' he said. 'But you won't mind if I don't stay very long. I've left instructions at my hotel that I'm to be called at seven.'

'We'll leave as soon as ever you like.'

Nicky found it very pleasant at the Knickerbocker. He ate his bacon and eggs with appetite. They shared a bottle of champagne. They danced, and the little lady told him he danced beautifully. He knew he danced pretty well, and of course she was easy to dance with. As light as a feather. She laid her cheek against his and when their eyes met there was in hers a smile that made his heart go pit-a-pat. A coloured woman sang in a throaty, sensual voice. The floor was crowded.

'Have you ever been told that you're very good-looking?' she asked.

'I don't think so,' he laughed. 'Gosh,' he thought, 'I believe she's fallen for me.'

Nicky was not such a fool as to be unaware that women often liked him, and when she made that remark he pressed her to him a little more closely. She closed her eyes and a faint sigh escaped her lips.

'I suppose it wouldn't be quite nice if I kissed you before all these people,' he said.

'What do you think they would take me for?'

It began to grow late and Nicky said that really he thought he ought to be going.

'I shall go too,' she said. 'Will you drop me at my hotel on your way?'

Nicky paid the bill. He was rather surprised at its amount, but with all that money he had in his pocket he could afford not to care, and they got into a taxi. She snuggled up to him and he kissed her. She seemed to like it.

'By Jove,' he thought, 'I wonder if there's anything doing.'

It was true that she was a married woman, but her husband was in Morocco, and it certainly did look as if she'd fallen for him. Good and proper. It was true also that his father had warned him to have nothing to do with women, but, he reflected again, he hadn't actually promised he wouldn't, he'd only promised not to forget his advice. Well, he hadn't; he was bearing it in mind that very minute. But circumstances alter cases. She was a sweet little thing; it seemed silly to miss the chance of an adventure when it was handed to you like that on a tray. When they reached the hotel he paid off the taxi.

'I'll walk home,' he said. 'The air will do me good after the stuffy atmosphere of that place.'

'Come up a moment,' she said. 'I'd like to show you the photo of my little boy.'

'Oh, have you got a little boy?' he exclaimed, a trifle dashed.

'Yes, a sweet little boy.'

He walked upstairs after her. He didn't in the least want to see the photograph of her little boy, but he thought it only civil to pretend he did. He was afraid he'd made a fool of himself; it occurred to him that she was taking him up to look at the photograph in order to show him in a nice way that he'd made a mistake. He'd told her he was eighteen.

'I suppose she thinks I'm just a kid.'

He began to wish he hadn't spent all that money on champagne at the nightclub.

But she didn't show him the photograph of her little boy after all. They had no sooner got into her room than she turned to him, flung her arms round his neck, and kissed him full on the lips. He had never in all his life been kissed so passionately.

'Darling,' she said.

For a brief moment his father's advice once more crossed Nicky's mind and then he forgot it.

Nicky was a light sleeper and the least sound was apt to wake him. Two or three hours later he woke and for a moment could not imagine where he was. The room was not quite dark, for the door of the bathroom was ajar, and the light in it had been left on. Suddenly he was conscious that someone was moving about the room. Then he remembered. He saw that it was his little friend, and he was on the point of speaking when something in the way she was behaving stopped him. She was walking very cautiously, as though she were afraid of waking him; she stopped once or twice and looked over at the bed. He wondered what she was after. He soon saw. She went over to the chair on which he had placed his clothes and once more looked in his direction. She waited for what seemed to him an interminable time. The silence was so intense that Nicky thought he could hear his own heart beating. Then, very slowly, very quietly, she took up his coat, slipped her hand into the inside pocket and drew out all those beautiful thousand-franc notes that Nicky had been so proud to win. She put the coat back and placed some other clothes on it so that it should look as though it had not been disturbed, then, with the bundle of notes in her hand, for an appreciable time stood once more stock-still. Nicky had repressed an instinctive impulse to jump up and grab her; it was partly surprise that had kept him quiet, partly the notion that he was in a strange hotel, in a foreign country, and if he made a row he didn't know what might happen. She looked at him. His eyes were partly closed and he was sure that she thought he was asleep. In the silence she could hardly fail to hear his regular breathing. When she had reassured herself that her movements had not disturbed him she stepped, with infinite caution, across the room. On a small table in the window a cineraria was growing in a pot. Nicky watched her now with his eyes wide open. The plant was evidently placed quite loosely in the pot, for taking it by the stalks she lifted it out; she put the banknotes in the bottom of the pot and replaced the plant. It was an excellent hiding-place. No one could have guessed that anything was concealed under that richly-flowering plant. She pressed the earth down with her fingers and then, very slowly, taking care not to make the smallest noise, crept across the room and slipped back into bed.

'Chéri,' she said, in a caressing voice.

Nicky breathed steadily, like a man immersed in deep sleep. The little lady turned over on her side and disposed herself to slumber. But though Nicky lay so still his thoughts worked busily. He was extremely indignant at the scene he had just witnessed, and to himself he spoke his thoughts with vigour.

'She's nothing but a damned tart. She and her dear little boy and her husband in Morocco. My eye! She's a rotten thief, that's what she is. Took me for a mug.

If she thinks she's going to get away with anything like that, she's mistaken.'

He had already made up his mind what he was going to do with the money he had so cleverly won. He had long wanted a car of his own, and had thought it rather mean of his father not to have given him one. After all, a feller doesn't always want to drive about in the family bus. Well, he'd just teach the old man a lesson and buy one himself. For twenty thousand francs, two hundred pounds roughly, he could get a very decent second-hand car. He meant to get the money back, but just then he didn't quite know how. He didn't like the idea of kicking up a row, he was a stranger, in an hotel he knew nothing of; it might very well be that the beastly woman had friends there, he didn't mind facing anyone in a fair fight, but he'd look pretty foolish if someone pulled a gun on him. He reflected besides, very sensibly, that he had no proof the money was his. If it came to a showdown and she swore it was hers, he might very easily find himself hauled off to a police-station. He really didn't know what to do. Presently by her regular breathing he knew that the little lady was asleep. She must have fallen asleep with an easy mind, for she had done her job without a hitch. It infuriated Nicky that she should rest so peacefully while he lay awake worried to death. Suddenly an idea occurred to him. It was such a good one that it was only by the exercise of all his self-control that he prevented himself from jumping out of bed and carrying it out at once. Two could play at her game. She'd stolen his money; well, he'd steal it back again, and they'd be all square. He made up his mind to wait quite quietly until he was sure the deceitful woman was sound asleep. He waited for what seemed to him a very long time. She did not stir. Her breathing was as regular as a child's.

'Darling,' he said at last.

No answer. No movement. She was dead to the world. Very slowly, pausing after every movement, very silently, he slipped out of bed. He stood still for a while, looking at her to see whether he had disturbed her. Her breathing was as regular as before. During the time he was waiting he had taken note carefully of the furniture in the room so that in crossing it he should not knock against a chair or a table and make a noise. He took a couple of steps and waited, he took a couple of steps more; he was very light on his feet and made no sound as he walked; he took fully five minutes to get to the window, and here he waited again. He started, for the bed slightly creaked, but it was only because the sleeper turned in her sleep. He forced himself to wait till he had counted to one hundred. She was sleeping like a log. With infinite care he seized the cineraria by the stalks and gently pulled it out of the pot; he put his other hand in, his heart beat nineteen to the dozen as his fingers touched the notes, his hand closed on them and he slowly drew them out. He replaced the plant and in his turn carefully pressed down the earth. While he was doing all this he had kept one eye on the form lying in the bed. It remained still. After another pause he crept softly to the chair on which his clothes were lying. He first put the bundle of notes in his coat pocket and then proceeded to dress. It took him a good quarter of an hour, because he could afford to make no sound. He had been wearing a soft shirt with his dinner jacket, and he congratulated himself on this, because it was easier to put on silently than a stiff one. He had some difficulty in tying his tie without a looking-glass, but he very wisely reflected that it didn't really matter if it wasn't tied very well. His spirits were rising. The whole thing now began to seem rather a lark. At length he was completely dressed except for his shoes, which he took in his hand; he thought he would put them on when he got into the passage. Now he had to cross the room to get to the door. He reached it so quietly that he could not have disturbed the lightest sleeper. But the door had to be unlocked. He turned the key very slowly; it creaked.

'Who's that?'

The little woman suddenly sat up in bed. Nicky's heart jumped to his mouth. He made a great effort to keep his head.

'It's only me. It's six o'clock and I've got to go. I was trying not to wake you.'

'Oh, I forgot.'

She sank back on to the pillow.

'Now that you're awake I'll put on my shoes.'

He sat down on the edge of the bed and did this.

'Don't make a noise when you go out. The hotel people don't like it. Oh, I'm so sleepy.'

'You go right off to sleep again.'

'Kiss me before you go.' He bent down and kissed her. 'You're a sweet boy and a wonderful lover. *Bon voyage.*'

Nicky did not feel quite safe till he got out of the hotel. The dawn had broken. The sky was unclouded, and in the harbour the yachts and the fishing-boats lay motionless on the still water. On the quay fishermen were getting ready to start on their day's work. The streets were deserted. Nicky took a long breath of the sweet morning air. He felt alert and well. He also felt as pleased as Punch. With a swinging stride, his shoulders well thrown back, he walked up the hill and along the gardens in front of the Casino – the flowers in that clear light had a dewy brilliance that was delicious – till he came to his hotel. Here the day had already begun. In the hall porters with mufflers round their necks and berets on their heads were busy sweeping. Nicky went up to his room and had a hot bath. He lay in it and thought with satisfaction that he was not such a mug as some people might think. After his bath he did his exercises, dressed, packed and went down to breakfast. He had a grand appetite. No continental breakfast for him! He had grapefruit, porridge, bacon and eggs, rolls fresh from the oven, so crisp and delicious they melted in your mouth, marmalade and three cups of coffee. Though feeling perfectly well before, he felt better after that. He lit the pipe he had recently learnt to smoke, paid his bill and stepped into the car that was waiting to take him to the aerodrome on the other side of Cannes. The road as far as Nice ran over the hills and below him was the blue sea and the coastline. He couldn't help thinking it damned pretty. They passed through Nice, so gay and friendly in the early morning, and presently they came to a long stretch of straight road that ran by the sea. Nicky had paid his bill, not with the money he had won the night before, but with the money his father had given him; he had changed a thousand francs to pay for supper at the Knickerbocker, but that deceitful little woman had returned him the thousand francs he had lent her, so that he still had twenty thousand-franc notes in his pocket. He thought he would like to have a look at them. He had so nearly lost them that they had a double value for him. He took them out of his hip-pocket into which for safety's sake he had stuffed them when he put on the suit he was travelling in, and counted them one by one. Something very strange had happened to them. Instead of there being twenty notes as there should have been there were twenty-six. He couldn't understand it at all. He counted them twice more. There was no doubt about it; somehow or other he had twenty-six thousand francs instead of the twenty he should have had. He couldn't make it out. He asked himself if it was possible that he had won more at the Sporting Club than he had realised. But no, that was out of the question; he distinctly remembered the man at the desk laying the notes out in four rows of five, and he had counted them himself. Suddenly the explanation occurred to him; when he had put his hand into the flowerpot, after taking out the cineraria, he had grabbed everything he felt there. The flowerpot was the little hussy's money-box and he had taken out not only his own money, but her savings as well. Nicky leant back in the car and burst into a roar of laughter. It was the funniest thing he had ever heard in his life. And when he thought of her going to the flowerpot some time later in the morning when she awoke, expecting to find the money she had so cleverly got away with, and finding, not only that it wasn't there, but that her own had gone too, he laughed more than ever. And so far as he was concerned there was nothing to do about it; he neither knew her name, nor the name of the hotel to which she had taken him. He couldn't return her money even if he wanted to.

'It serves her damned well right,' he said.

This then was the story that Henry Garnet told his friends over the bridge-table, for the night before, after dinner when his wife and daughter had left them to their port, Nicky had narrated it in full.

'And you know what infuriated me is that he's so damned pleased with himself. Talk of a cat swallowing a canary. And d'you know what he said to me when he'd finished? He looked at me with those innocent eyes of his and said: "You know, father, I can't help thinking there was something wrong about the advice you gave me. You said, don't gamble; well, I did, and I made a packet; you said, don't lend money; well, I did, and I got it back; and you said, don't have anything to do with women; well, I did, and I made six thousand francs on the deal." '

It didn't make it any better for Henry Garnet that his three companions burst out laughing.

'It's all very well for you fellows to laugh, but you know, I'm in a damned awkward position. The boy looked up to me, he respected me, he took whatever I said as gospel truth, and now, I saw it in his eyes, he just looks upon me as a drivelling old fool. It's no good my saying one swallow doesn't make a summer; he doesn't see that it was just a fluke, he thinks the whole thing was due to his own cleverness. It may ruin him.'

'You do look a bit of a damned fool, old man,' said one of the others. 'There's no denying that, is there?'

'I know I do, and I don't like it. It's so dashed unfair. Fate has no right to play one tricks like that. After all, you must admit that my advice was good.'

'Very good.'

'And the wretched boy ought to have burnt his

fingers. Well, he hasn't. You're all men of the world, you tell me how I'm to deal with the situation now.'

But they none of them could.

'Well, Henry, if I were you I wouldn't worry,' said the lawyer. 'My belief is that your boy's born lucky, and in the long run that's better than to be born clever or rich.'

Lord Mountdrago

Dr Audlin looked at the clock on his desk. It was twenty minutes to six. He was surprised that his patient was late, for Lord Mountdrago prided himself on his punctuality; he had a sententious way of expressing himself which gave the air of an epigram to a commonplace remark, and he was in the habit of saying that punctuality is a compliment you pay to the intelligent and a rebuke you administer to the stupid. Lord Mountdrago's appointment was for five-thirty.

There was in Dr Audlin's appearance nothing to attract attention. He was tall and spare, with narrow shoulders and something of a stoop; his hair was grey and thin; his long, sallow face deeply lined. He was not more than fifty, but he looked older. His eyes, pale blue and rather large, were weary. When you had been with him for a while you noticed that they moved very little; they remained fixed on your face, but so empty of expression were they that it was no discomfort. They seldom lit up. They gave no clue to his thoughts nor changed with the words he spoke. If you were of an observant turn it might have struck you that he blinked much less often than most of us. His hands were on the large side, with long, tapering fingers; they were soft, but firm, cool but not clammy. You could never have said what Dr Audlin wore unless you had made a point of looking. His clothes were dark. His tie was black. His dress made his sallow, lined face paler, and his pale eyes more wan. He gave you the impression of being a very sick man.

Dr Audlin was a psychoanalyst. He had adopted the profession by accident and practised it with misgiving. When the war broke out he had not been long qualified and was getting experience at various hospitals; he offered his services to the authorities, and after a time was sent out to France. It was then that he discovered his singular gift. He could allay certain pains by the touch of his cool, firm hands, and by talking to them often induce sleep in men who were suffering from sleeplessness. He spoke slowly. His voice had no particular colour, and its tone did not alter with the words he uttered, but it was musical, soft and lulling. He told the men that they must rest, that they mustn't worry, that they must sleep; and rest stole into their jaded bones, tranquillity pushed their anxieties away, like a man finding a place for himself on a crowded bench, and slumber fell on their tired eyelids like the light rain of spring upon the fresh-turned earth. Dr Audlin found that by speaking to men with that low, monotonous voice of his, by looking at them with his pale, quiet eyes, by stroking their weary foreheads with his long firm hands, he could soothe their perturbations, resolve the conflicts that distracted them and banish the phobias that made their lives a torment. Sometimes he effected cures that seemed miraculous. He restored speech to a man who, after being buried under the earth by a bursting shell, had been struck dumb, and he gave back the use of his limbs to another who had been paralysed after a crash in a plane. He could not understand his powers; he was of a sceptical turn, and though they say that in circumstances of this kind the first thing is to believe in yourself, he never quite succeeded in doing that; and it was only the outcome of his activities, patent to the most incredulous observer, that obliged him to admit that he had some faculty, coming from he knew not where, obscure and uncertain, that enabled him to do things for which he could offer no explanation. When the war was over he went to Vienna and studied there, and afterwards to Zurich; and then settled down in London to practise the art he had so strangely acquired. He had been practising now for fifteen years, and had attained, in the speciality he followed, a distinguished reputation. People told one another of the amazing things he had done, and though his fees were high, he had as many patients as he had time to see. Dr Audlin knew that he had achieved some very extraordinary results; he had saved men from suicide, others from the lunatic asylum, he had assuaged griefs that embittered useful lives, he had turned unhappy marriages into happy ones, he had eradicated abnormal instincts and thus delivered not a few from a hateful bondage, he had given health to the sick in spirit; he had done all this, and yet at the back of his mind remained the suspicion that he was little more than a quack.

It went against his grain to exercise a power that he could not understand, and it offended his honesty to trade on the faith of the people he treated when he had no faith in himself. He was rich enough now to live without working, and the work exhausted him; a dozen times he had been on the point of giving up practice. He knew all that Freud and Jung and the rest of them had written. He was not satisfied; he had an intimate conviction that all their theory was hocus-pocus, and yet there the results were, incomprehensible, but manifest. And what had he not seen of human nature during the fifteen years that patients had been coming to his dingy back room in Wimpole Street? The revelations that had been poured into his ears, sometimes only too willingly, sometimes with shame, with reservations, with anger, had long ceased to surprise him. Nothing could shock him any longer. He knew by now that men were liars, he knew how extravagant was their vanity; he knew far worse than that about them; but he knew that it was not for him to judge or to condemn. But year by year as these terrible confidences were imparted to him his face grew a little greyer, its lines a little more marked and his pale eyes more weary. He seldom laughed, but now and again when for relaxation he read a novel he smiled. Did their authors really think the men and women they wrote of were like that? If they only knew how much more complicated they were, how much more unexpected, what irreconcilable elements co-existed within their souls and what dark and sinister contentions afflicted them!

It was a quarter to six. Of all the strange cases he had been called upon to deal with Dr Audlin could remember none stranger than that of Lord Mountdrago. For one thing the personality of his patient made it singular. Lord Mountdrago was an able and a distinguished man. Appointed Secretary for Foreign Affairs when still under forty, now after three years in office he had seen his policy prevail. It was generally acknowledged that he was the ablest politician in the Conservative Party and only the fact that his father was a peer, on whose death he would no longer be able to sit in the House of Commons, made it impossible for him to aim at the premiership. But if in these democratic times it is out of the question for a Prime Minister of England to be in the House of

Lords, there was nothing to prevent Lord Mountdrago from continuing to be Secretary for Foreign Affairs in successive Conservative administrations and so for long directing the foreign policy of his country.

Lord Mountdrago had many good qualities. He had intelligence and industry. He was widely travelled, and spoke several languages fluently. From early youth he had specialised in foreign affairs, and had conscientiously made himself acquainted with the political and economic circumstances of other countries. He had courage, insight and determination. He was a good speaker, both on the platform and in the House, clear, precise and often witty. He was a brilliant debater and his gift of repartee was celebrated. He had a fine presence: he was a tall, handsome man, rather bald and somewhat too stout, but this gave him solidity and an air of maturity that were of service to him. As a young man he had been something of an athlete and had rowed in the Oxford boat, and he was known to be one of the best shots in England. At twenty-four he had married a girl of eighteen whose father was a duke and her mother a great American heiress, so that she had both position and wealth, and by her he had had two sons. For several years they had lived privately apart, but in public united, so that appearances were saved, and no other attachment on either side had given the gossips occasion to whisper. Lord Mountdrago indeed was too ambitious, too hard-working, and it must be added too patriotic, to be tempted by any pleasures that might interfere with his career. He had, in short, a great deal to make him a popular and successful figure. He had unfortunately great defects.

He was a fearful snob. You would not have been

surprised at this if his father had been the first holder of the title. That the son of an ennobled lawyer, a manufacturer or a distiller should attach an inordinate importance to his rank is understandable. The earldom held by Lord Mountdrago's father was created by Charles II, and the barony held by the first earl dated from the Wars of the Roses. For three hundred years the successive holders of the title had allied themselves with the noblest families of England. But Lord Mountdrago was as conscious of his birth as a *nouveau riche* is conscious of his money. He never missed an opportunity of impressing it upon others. He had beautiful manners when he chose to display them, but this he did only with people whom he regarded as his equals. He was coldly insolent to those whom he looked upon as his social inferiors. He was rude to his servants and insulting to his secretaries. The subordinate officials in the government offices to which he had been successively attached feared and hated him. His arrogance was horrible. He knew that he was a great deal cleverer than most of the persons he had to do with, and never hesitated to apprise them of the fact. He had no patience with the infirmities of human nature. He felt himself born to command and was irritated with people who expected him to listen to their arguments or wished to hear the reasons for his decisions. He was immeasurably selfish. He looked upon any service that was rendered him as a right due to his rank and intelligence and therefore deserving of no gratitude. It never entered his head that he was called upon to do anything for others. He had many enemies: he despised them. He knew no one who merited his assistance, his sympathy or his compassion. He had no friends. He was distrusted by his chiefs, because they doubted his loyalty; he was unpopular with his party, because he was overbearing and discourteous; and yet his merit was so great, his patriotism so evident, his intelligence so solid and his management of affairs so brilliant that they had to put up with him. And what made it possible to do this was that on occasion he could be enchanting: when he was with persons whom he considered his equals, or whom he wished to captivate, in the company of foreign dignitaries or women of distinction, he could be gay, witty and debonair; his manners then reminded you that in his veins ran the same blood as had run in the veins of Lord Chesterfield; he could tell a story with point, he could be natural, sensible and even profound. You were surprised at the extent of his knowledge and the sensitiveness of his taste. You thought him the best company in the world; you forgot that he had insulted you the day before and was quite capable of cutting you dead the next.

Lord Mountdrago almost failed to become Dr Audlin's patient. A secretary rang up the doctor and told him that his lordship, wishing to consult him, would be glad if he would come to his house at ten o'clock on the following morning. Dr Audlin answered that he was unable to go to Lord Mountdrago's house, but would be pleased to give him an appointment at his consulting-room at five o'clock on the next day but one. The secretary took the message and presently rang back to say that Lord Mountdrago insisted on seeing Dr Audlin in his own house and the doctor could fix his own fee. Dr Audlin replied that he only saw patients in his consulting-room and expressed his regret that unless Lord Mountdrago was prepared to come to him he could not give him his attention. In a quarter of an hour a brief message was delivered to him that his lordship would come not next day but one, but next day, at five.

When Lord Mountdrago was then shown in he did not come forward, but stood at the door and insolently looked the doctor up and down. Dr Audlin perceived that he was in a rage; he gazed at him, silently, with still eyes. He saw a big heavy man, with greying hair, receding on the forehead so that it gave nobility to his brow, a puffy face with bold regular features and an expression of haughtiness. He had somewhat the look of one of the Bourbon sovereigns of the eighteenth century.

'It seems that it is as difficult to see you as a Prime Minister, Dr Audlin. I'm an extremely busy man.'

'Won't you sit down?' said the doctor.

His face showed no sign that Lord Mountdrago's speech in any way affected him. Dr Audlin sat in his chair at the desk. Lord Mountdrago still stood and his frown darkened.

'I think I should tell you that I am His Majesty's Secretary for Foreign Affairs,' he said acidly.

'Won't you sit down?' the doctor repeated.

Lord Mountdrago made a gesture, which might have suggested that he was about to turn on his heel and stalk out of the room; but if that was his intention he apparently thought better of it. He seated himself. Dr Audlin opened a large book and took up his pen. He wrote without looking at his patient.

'How old are you?'

'Forty-two.'

'Are you married?'

'Yes.'

'How long have you been married?'

'Eighteen years.'

'Have you any children?'

'I have two sons.'

Dr Audlin noted down the facts as Lord Mountdrago abruptly answered his questions. Then he leaned back in his chair and looked at him. He did not speak; he just looked, gravely, with pale eyes that did not move.

'Why have you come to see me?' he asked at length.

'I've heard about you. Lady Canute is a patient of yours, I understand. She tells me you've done her a certain amount of good.'

Dr Audlin did not reply. His eyes remained fixed on the other's face, but they were so empty of expression that you might have thought he did not even see him.

'I can't do miracles,' he said at length. Not a smile, but the shadow of a smile flickered in his eyes. 'The Royal College of Physicians would not approve of it if I did.'

Lord Mountdrago gave a brief chuckle. It seemed to lessen his hostility. He spoke more amiably.

'You have a very remarkable reputation. People seem to believe in you.'

'Why have you come to me?' repeated Dr Audlin.

Now it was Lord Mountdrago's turn to be silent. It looked as though he found it hard to answer. Dr Audlin waited. At last Lord Mountdrago seemed to make an effort. He spoke.

'I'm in perfect health. Just as a matter of routine I had myself examined by my own doctor the other day, Sir Augustus Fitzherbert, I dare say you've heard of him, and he tells me I have the physique of a man of thirty. I work hard, but I'm never tired, and I enjoy my work. I smoke very little and I'm an extremely moderate drinker. I take a sufficiency of exercise and I lead a regular life. I am a perfectly sound, normal, healthy man. I quite expect you to think it very silly and childish of me to consult you.'

Dr Audlin saw that he must help him.

'I don't know if I can do anything to help you. I'll try. You're distressed?'

Lord Mountdrago frowned.

'The work that I'm engaged in is important. The decisions I am called upon to make can easily affect the welfare of the country and even the peace of the world. It is essential that my judgement should be balanced and my brain clear. I look upon it as my duty to eliminate any cause of worry that may interfere with my usefulness.'

Dr Audlin had never taken his eyes off him. He saw a great deal. He saw behind his patient's pompous manner and arrogant pride an anxiety that he could not dispel.

'I asked you to be good enough to come here because I know by experience that it's easier for someone to speak openly in the dingy surroundings of a doctor's consulting-room than in his accustomed environment.'

'They're certainly dingy,' said Lord Mountdrago acidly. He paused. It was evident that this man who had so much self-assurance, so quick and decided a mind that he was never at a loss, at this moment was embarrassed. He smiled in order to show the doctor that he was at his ease, but his eyes betrayed his disquiet. When he spoke again it was with unnatural heartiness.

'The whole thing's so trivial that I can hardly bring

myself to bother you with it. I'm afraid you'll just tell me not to be a fool and waste your valuable time.'

'Even things that seem very trivial may have their importance. They can be a symptom of a deep-seated derangement. And my time is entirely at your disposal.'

Dr Audlin's voice was low and grave. The monotone in which he spoke was strangely soothing. Lord Mountdrago at length made up his mind to be frank.

'The fact is I've been having some very tiresome dreams lately. I know it's silly to pay any attention to them, but – well, the honest truth is that I'm afraid they've got on my nerves.'

'Can you describe any of them to me?'

Lord Mountdrago smiled, but the smile that tried to be careless was only rueful.

'They're so idiotic, I can hardly bring myself to narrate them.'

'Never mind.'

'Well, the first I had was about a month ago. I dreamt that I was at a party at Connemara House. It was an official party. The King and Queen were to be there and of course decorations were worn. I was wearing my ribbon and my star. I went into a sort of cloakroom they have to take off my coat. There was a little man there called Owen Griffiths, who's a Welsh Member of Parliament, and to tell you the truth, I was surprised to see him. He's very common, and I said to myself: "Really, Lydia Connemara is going too far, whom will she ask next?" I thought he looked at me rather curiously, but I didn't take any notice of him; in fact I cut the little bounder and walked upstairs. I suppose you've never been there?'

'Never.'

'No, it's not the sort of house you'd ever be likely to go to. It's a rather vulgar house, but it's got a very fine marble staircase, and the Connemaras were at the top receiving their guests. Lady Connemara gave me a look of surprise when I shook hands with her, and began to giggle; I didn't pay much attention, she's a very silly, ill-bred woman and her manners are no better than those of her ancestor whom King Charles II made a duchess. I must say the reception rooms at Connemara House are stately. I walked through, nodding to a number of people and shaking hands; then I saw the German Ambassador talking with one of the Austrian archdukes. I particularly wanted to have a word with him, so I went up and held out my hand. The moment the archduke saw me he burst into a roar of laughter. I was deeply affronted. I looked him up and down sternly, but he only laughed the more. I was about to speak to him rather sharply, when there was a sudden hush and I realised that the King and Queen had come. Turning my back on the archduke, I stepped forward, and then, quite suddenly, I noticed that I hadn't got any trousers on. I was in short silk drawers, and I wore scarlet sock-suspenders. No wonder Lady Connemara had giggled; no wonder the archduke had laughed! I can't tell you what that moment was. An agony of shame. I awoke in a cold sweat. Oh, you don't know the relief I felt to find it was only a dream.'

'It's the kind of dream that's not so very uncommon,' said Dr Audlin.

'I dare say not. But an odd thing happened next day. I was in the lobby of the House of Commons, when that fellow Griffiths walked slowly past me. He deliberately looked down at my legs and then he looked me full in the face and I was almost certain he winked. A ridiculous thought came to me. He'd been there the night before and seen me make that ghastly exhibition of myself and was enjoying the joke. But of course I knew that was impossible because it was only a dream. I gave him an icy glare and he walked on. But he was grinning his head off.'

Lord Mountdrago took his handkerchief out of his pocket and wiped the palms of his hands. He was making no attempt now to conceal his perturbation. Dr Audlin never took his eyes off him.

'Tell me another dream.'

'It was the night after, and it was even more absurd than the first one. I dreamt that I was in the House. There was a debate on foreign affairs which not only the country but the world had been looking forward to with the gravest concern. The government had decided on a change in their policy which vitally affected the future of the Empire. The occasion was historic. Of course the House was crowded. All the ambassadors were there. The galleries were packed. It fell to me to make the important speech of the evening. I had prepared it carefully. A man like me has enemies, there are a lot of people who resent my having achieved the position I have at an age when even the cleverest men are content with situations of relative obscurity, and I was determined that my speech should not only be worthy of the occasion, but should silence my detractors. It excited me to think that the whole world was hanging on my lips. I rose to my feet. If you've ever been in the House you'll know how members chat to one another during a debate, rustle papers and turn over reports. The silence was the silence of the grave when I began to speak. Suddenly I caught sight of that odious little bounder on one of the benches opposite, Griffiths the Welsh member; he put out his tongue at me. I don't know if you've ever heard a vulgar music-hall song called *A Bicycle Made For Two*. It was very popular a great many years ago. To show Griffiths how completely I despised him I began to sing it. I sang the first verse right through. There was a moment's surprise, and when I finished they cried "Hear, hear," on the opposite benches. I put up my hand to silence them and sang the second verse. The House listened to me in stony silence and I felt the song wasn't going down very well. I was vexed, for I have a good baritone voice, and I was determined that they should do me justice. When I started the third verse the members began to laugh; in an instant the laughter spread; the ambassadors, the strangers in the Distinguished Strangers' Gallery, the ladies in the Ladies' Gallery, the reporters, they shook, they bellowed, they held their sides, they rolled in their seats; everyone was overcome with laughter except the ministers on the Front Bench immediately behind me. In that incredible, in that unprecedented uproar, they sat petrified. I gave them a glance, and suddenly the enormity of what I had done fell upon me. I had made myself the laughing-stock of the whole world. With misery I realised that I should have to resign. I woke and knew it was only a dream.'

Lord Mountdrago's grand manner had deserted him as he narrated this, and now having finished he was pale and trembling. But with an effort he pulled himself together. He forced a laugh to his shaking lips.

'The whole thing was so fantastic that I couldn't help being amused. I didn't give it another thought, and when I went into the House on the following afternoon I was feeling in very good form. The debate was dull, but I had to be there, and I read some documents that required my attention. For some reason I chanced to look up and I saw that Griffiths was speaking. He has an unpleasant Welsh accent and an unprepossessing appearance. I couldn't imagine that he had anything to say that it was worth my while to listen to, and I was about to return to my papers when he quoted two lines from *A Bicycle Made For Two*. I couldn't help glancing at him and I saw that his eyes were fixed on me with a grin of bitter mockery. I faintly shrugged my shoulders. It was comic that a scrubby little Welsh member should look at me like that. It was an odd coincidence that he should quote two lines from that disastrous song that I'd sung all through in my dream. I began to read my papers again, but I don't mind telling you that I found it difficult to concentrate on them. I was a little puzzled. Owen Griffiths had been in my first dream, the one at Connemara House, and I'd received a very definite impression afterwards that he knew the sorry figure I'd cut. Was it a mere coincidence that he had just quoted those two lines? I asked myself if it was possible that he was dreaming the same dreams as I was. But of course the idea was preposterous and I determined not to give it a second thought.'

There was a silence. Dr Audlin looked at Lord Mountdrago and Lord Mountdrago looked at Dr Audlin.

'Other people's dreams are very boring. My wife used to dream occasionally and insist on telling me her dreams next day with circumstantial detail. I found it maddening.'

Dr Audlin faintly smiled.

'You're not boring me.'

'I'll tell you one more dream I had a few days later. I dreamt that I went into a public house at Limehouse. I've never been to Limehouse in my life and I don't think I've ever been in a public house since I was at Oxford, and yet I saw the street and the place I went into as exactly as if I were at home there. I went into a room, I don't know whether they call it the saloon bar or the private bar; there was a fireplace and a large leather armchair on one side of it, and on the other a small sofa; a bar ran the whole length of the room and over it you could see into the public bar. Near the door was a round marble-topped table and two armchairs beside it. It was a Saturday night and the place was packed. It was brightly lit, but the smoke was so thick that it made my eyes smart. I was dressed like a rough, with a cap on my head and a handkerchief round my neck. It seemed to me that most of the people there were drunk. I thought it rather amusing. There was a gramophone going, or the radio, I don't know which, and in front of the fireplace two women were doing a grotesque dance. There was a little crowd round them, laughing, cheering and singing. I went up to have a look and some man said to me: " 'Ave a drink, Bill?" There were glasses on the table full of a dark liquid which I understand is called brown ale. He gave me a glass and not wishing to be conspicuous I drank it. One of the women who were dancing broke away from the other and took hold of the glass. " 'Ere, what's the idea?" she said. "That's my beer you're putting away." "Oh, I'm so sorry," I said, "this gentleman offered it me and I very naturally thought it was his to offer." "All right, mate," she said, "I don't mind. You come an' 'ave a dance with me." Before I could protest she'd caught hold of me and we were dancing together. And then I found myself sitting in the armchair with the woman on my lap and we were sharing a glass of beer. I should tell you that sex has never played any great part in my life. I married young because in my position it was desirable that I should marry, but also in order to settle once and for all the question of sex. I had the two sons I had made up my mind to have, and then I put the whole matter on one side. I've always been too busy to give much thought to that kind of thing, and living so much in the public eye as I do it would have been madness to do anything that might give rise to scandal. The greatest asset a politician can have is a blameless record as far as women are concerned. I have no patience with the men who smash up their careers for women. I only despise them. The woman I had on my knees was drunk; she wasn't pretty and she wasn't young: in fact, she was just a blowsy old prostitute. She filled me with disgust, and yet when she put her mouth to mine and kissed me, though her breath stank of beer and her teeth were decayed, though I loathed myself, I wanted her – I wanted her with all my soul. Suddenly I heard a voice. "That's right, old boy, have a good time." I looked up and there was Owen Griffiths. I tried to spring out of the chair, but that horrible woman wouldn't let me. "Don't you pay no attention to 'im," she said, " 'e's only one of them nosy parkers." "You go to it," he said. "I know Moll. She'll give you your money's worth all right." You know, I wasn't so much annoyed at his seeing me in that absurd situation as angry that he should address me as "old boy". I pushed the woman aside and stood up and faced him. "I don't know you and I don't want to know you," I said. "I know you all right," he said. "And my advice to you, Molly, is, see that you get your money, he'll bilk you if he can." There was a bottle of beer standing on the table close by. Without a word I seized it by the neck and hit him over the head with it as hard as I could. I made such a violent gesture that it woke me up.'

'A dream of that sort is not incomprehensible,' said Dr Audlin. 'It is the revenge nature takes on persons of unimpeachable character.'

'The story's idiotic. I haven't told it you for its own sake. I've told it you for what happened next day. I wanted to look up something in a hurry and I went into the library of the House. I got the book and began reading. I hadn't noticed when I sat down that Griffiths was sitting in a chair close by me. Another of the Labour members came in and went up to him. "Hello, Owen," he said to him, "you're looking pretty dicky today." "I've got an awful headache," he answered. "I feel as if I'd been cracked over the head with a bottle." '

Now Lord Mountdrago's face was grey with anguish.

'I knew then that the idea I'd had and dismissed as preposterous was true. I knew that Griffiths was dreaming my dreams and that he remembered them as well as I did.'

'It may also have been a coincidence.'

'When he spoke he didn't speak to his friend, he deliberately spoke to me. He looked at me with sullen resentment.'

'Can you offer any suggestion why this same man should come into your dreams?'

'None.'

Dr Audlin's eyes had not left his patient's face and he saw that he lied. He had a pencil in his hand and he drew a straggling line or two on his blotting-paper. It often took a long time to get people to tell the truth, and yet they knew that unless they told it he could do nothing for them.

'The dream you've just described to me took place just over three weeks ago. Have you had any since?'

'Every night.'

'And does this man Griffiths come into them all?'

'Yes.'

The doctor drew more lines on his blotting-paper. He wanted the silence, the drabness, the dull light of that little room to have its effect on Lord Mountdrago's sensibility. Lord Mountdrago threw himself back in his chair and turned his head away so that he should not see the other's grave eyes.

'Dr Audlin, you must do something for me. I'm at the end of my tether. I shall go mad if this goes on. I'm afraid to go to sleep. Two or three nights I haven't. I've sat up reading and when I felt drowsy put on my coat and walked till I was exhausted. But I must have sleep. With all the work I have to do I must be at concert pitch; I must be in complete control of all my faculties. I need rest; sleep brings me none. I no sooner fall asleep than my dreams begin, and he's always there, that vulgar little cad, grinning at me, mocking me, despising me. It's a monstrous persecution. I tell you, doctor, I'm not the man of my dreams; it's not fair to judge me by them. Ask anyone you like. I'm an honest, upright, decent man. No one can say anything against my moral character, either private or public. My whole ambition is to serve my country and maintain its greatness. I have money, I have rank, I'm not exposed to many of the temptations of lesser men, so that it's no credit to me to be incorruptible; but this I can claim, that no honour, no personal advantage, no thought of self would induce me to swerve by a hair's breadth from my duty. I've sacrificed everything to become the man I am. Greatness is my aim. Greatness is within my reach and I'm losing my nerve. I'm not that mean, despicable, cowardly, lewd creature that horrible little man sees. I've told you three of my dreams; they're nothing; that man has seen me do things that are so beastly, so horrible, so shameful, that even if my life depended on it I wouldn't tell them. And he remembers them. I can hardly meet the derision and disgust I see in his eyes and I even hesitate to speak because I know my words can seem to him nothing but utter humbug. He's seen me do things that no man with any self-respect would do, things for which men are driven out of the society of their fellows and sentenced to long terms of imprisonment; he's heard the foulness of my speech; he's seen me not only ridiculous, but revolting. He despises me and he no longer pretends to conceal it. I tell you that if you can't do something to help me I shall either kill myself or kill him.'

'I wouldn't kill him if I were you,' said Dr Audlin, coolly, in that soothing voice of his. 'In this country the consequences of killing a fellow-creature are awkward.'

'I shouldn't be hanged for it, if that's what you mean. Who would know that I'd killed him? That dream of mine has shown me how. I told you, the day after I'd hit him over the head with a beer-bottle he had such a headache that he couldn't see straight. He said so himself. That shows that he can feel with his waking body what happens to his body asleep. It's not with a bottle I shall hit him next time. One night, when I'm dreaming, I shall find myself with a knife in my hand or a revolver in my pocket, I must because I want to so intensely, and then I shall seize my opportunity. I'll stick him like a pig; I'll shoot him like a dog. In the heart. And then I shall be free of this fiendish persecution.'

Some people might have thought that Lord Mountdrago was mad; after all the years during which Dr Audlin had been treating the diseased souls of men he knew how thin a line divides those whom we call sane from those whom we call insane. He knew how often in men who to all appearance were healthy and normal, who were seemingly devoid of imagination, and who fulfilled the duties of common life with credit to themselves and with benefit to their fellows, when you gained their confidence, when you tore away the mask they wore to the world, you found not only hideous abnormality, but kinks so strange, mental extravagances so fantastic, that in that respect you could only call them lunatic. If you put them in asylums not all the asylums in the world would be numerous enough. Anyhow, a man was not certifiable because he had strange dreams and they had shattered his nerve. The case was singular, but it was only an exaggeration of others that had come under Dr Audlin's observation; he was doubtful, however, whether the methods of treatment that he had so often found efficacious would here avail.

'Have you consulted any other member of my profession?' he asked.

'Only Sir Augustus. I merely told him that I suffered from nightmares. He said I was overworked and recommended me to go for a cruise. That's absurd. I can't leave the Foreign Office just now when the international situation needs constant attention. I'm indispensable, and I know it. On my conduct at the present juncture my whole future depends. He gave me sedatives. They had no effect. He gave me tonics. They were worse than useless. He's an old fool.'

'Can you give any reason why it should be this particular man who persists in coming into your dreams?'

'You asked me that question before. I answered it.'

That was true. But Dr Audlin had not been satisfied with the answer.

'Just now you talked of persecution. Why should Owen Griffiths want to persecute you?'

'I don't know.'

Lord Mountdrago's eyes shifted a little. Dr Audlin was sure that he was not speaking the truth.

'Have you ever done him an injury?'

'Never.'

Lord Mountdrago made no movement, but Dr Audlin had a queer feeling that he shrank into his skin. He saw before him a large, proud man who gave the impression that the questions put to him were an insolence, and yet for all that, behind that façade, was something shifting and startled that made you think of a frightened animal in a trap. Dr Audlin leaned forward and by the power of his eyes forced Lord Mountdrago to meet them.

'Are you quite sure?'

'Quite sure. You don't seem to understand that our ways lead along different paths. I don't wish to harp on it, but I must remind you that I am a Minister of the Crown and Griffiths is an obscure member of the Labour Party. Naturally there's no social connection between us; he's a man of very humble origin, he's not the sort of person I should be likely to meet at any of the houses I go to; and politically our respective stations are so far separated that we could not possibly have anything in common.'

'I can do nothing for you unless you tell me the complete truth.'

Lord Mountdrago raised his eyebrows. His voice was rasping.

'I'm not accustomed to having my word doubted, Dr Audlin. If you're going to do that I think to take up any more of your time can only be a waste of mine. If you will kindly let my secretary know what your fee is he will see that a cheque is sent to you.'

For all the expression that was to be seen on Dr Audlin's face you might have thought that he simply had not heard what Lord Mountdrago said. He continued to look steadily into his eyes and his voice was grave and low.

'Have you done anything to this man that *he* might look upon as an injury?'

Lord Mountdrago hesitated. He looked away, and then, as though there were in Dr Audlin's eyes a compelling force that he could not resist, looked back. He answered sulkily: 'Only if he was a dirty, second-rate little cad.'

'But that is exactly what you've described him to be.'

Lord Mountdrago sighed. He was beaten. Dr Audlin knew that the sigh meant he was going at last to say what he had till then held back. Now he had no longer to insist. He dropped his eyes and began again drawing vague geometrical figures on his blotting-paper. The silence lasted two or three minutes.

'I'm anxious to tell you everything that can be of any use to you. If I didn't mention this before, it's only because it was so unimportant that I didn't see how it could possibly have anything to do with the case. Griffiths won a seat at the last election and he began to make a nuisance of himself almost at once. His father's a miner, and he worked in a mine himself when he was a boy; he's been a schoolmaster in the board schools and a journalist. He's that half-baked, conceited intellectual, with inadequate knowledge, ill-considered ideas and impracticable plans, that compulsory education has brought forth from the working-classes. He's a scrawny, grey-faced man, who looks half-starved, and he's always very slovenly in appearance; heaven knows members nowadays don't bother much about their dress, but his clothes are an outrage to the dignity of the House. They're ostentatiously shabby, his collar's never clean and his tie's never tied properly; he looks as if he hadn't had a bath for a month and his hands are filthy. The Labour Party have two or three fellows on the Front Bench who've got a certain ability, but the rest of them don't amount to much. In the kingdom of the blind the one-eyed man is king: because Griffiths is glib and has a lot of superficial information on a number of subjects, the Whips on his side began to put him up to speak whenever there was a chance. It appeared that he fancied himself on foreign affairs, and he was continually asking me silly, tiresome questions. I don't mind telling you that I made a point of snubbing him as soundly as I thought he deserved. From the beginning I hated the way he talked, his whining voice and his vulgar accent; he had nervous mannerisms that intensely irritated me. He talked rather shyly, hesitatingly, as though it were torture to him to speak and yet he was forced to by some inner passion, and often he used to say some very disconcerting things. I'll admit that now and again he had a sort of tub-thumping eloquence. It had a certain influence over the ill-regulated minds of the members of his party. They were impressed by his earnestness and they weren't, as I was, nauseated by his sentimentality. A certain sentimentality is the common coin of political debate. Nations are governed by self-interest, but they prefer to believe that their aims are altruistic, and the politician is justified if with fair words and fine phrases he can persuade the electorate that the hard bargain he is driving for his country's advantage tends to the good of humanity. The mistake people like Griffiths make is to take these fair words and fine phrases at their face value. He's a crank, and a noxious crank. He calls himself an idealist. He has at his tongue's end all the tedious blather that the intelligentsia have been boring us with for years. Non-resistance. The brotherhood of man. You know the hopeless rubbish. The worst of it was that it impressed not only his own party, it even shook some of the sillier, more sloppy-minded members of ours. I heard rumours that Griffiths was likely to get office when a Labour government came in; I even heard it suggested that he might get the Foreign Office. The notion was grotesque but not impossible. One day I had occasion to wind up a debate on foreign affairs which Griffiths had opened. He'd spoken for an hour. I thought it a very good opportunity to cook his goose, and by God, sir, I cooked it. I tore his speech to pieces. I pointed out the faultiness of his reasoning and emphasised the deficiency of his knowledge. In the House of Commons the most devastating weapon is ridicule: I mocked him; I bantered him; I was in good form that day and the House rocked with laughter. Their laughter excited me and I excelled myself. The Opposition sat glum and silent, but even some of them couldn't help laughing once or twice; it's not intolerable, you know, to see a colleague, perhaps a rival, made a fool of. And if ever a man was made a fool of I made a fool of Griffiths. He shrank down in a seat, I saw his face go white, and presently he buried it in his hands. When I sat down I'd killed him. I'd destroyed his prestige for ever; he had no more chance of getting office when a Labour government came in than the policeman at the door. I heard afterwards that his father, the old miner, and his mother had come up from Wales, with various supporters of his in the constituency, to watch the triumph they expected him to have. They had seen only his utter humiliation. He'd won the constituency by the narrowest margin. An incident like that might very easily lose him his seat. But that was no business of mine.'

'Should I be putting it too strongly if I said you had ruined his career?' asked Dr Audlin.

'I don't suppose you would.'

'That is a very serious injury you've done him.'

'He brought it on himself.'

'Have you never felt any qualms about it?'

'I think perhaps if I'd known that his father and mother were there I might have let him down a little more gently.'

There was nothing further for Dr Audlin to say, and he set about treating his patient in such a manner as he thought might avail. He sought by suggestion to make him forget his dreams when he awoke; he sought to make him sleep so deeply that he would not dream. He found Lord Mountdrago's resistance impossible to break down. At the end of an hour he dismissed him. Since then he had seen Lord Mountdrago half a dozen times. He had done him no good. The frightful dreams continued every night to harass the unfortunate man, and it was clear that his general condition was growing rapidly worse. He was worn out. His irritability was uncontrollable. Lord Mountdrago was angry because he received no benefit from his treatment, and yet continued it, not only because it seemed his only hope, but because it was a relief to him to have someone with whom he could talk openly. Dr Audlin came to the conclusion at last that there was only one way in which Lord Mountdrago could achieve deliverance, but he knew him well enough to be assured that of his own free will he would never, never take it. If Lord Mountdrago was to be saved from the breakdown that was threatening he must be induced to take a step that must be abhorrent to his pride of birth and his self-complacency. Dr Audlin was convinced that to delay was impossible. He was treating his patient by suggestion, and after several visits found him more susceptible to it. At length he managed to get him into a condition of somnolence. With his low, soft, monotonous voice he soothed his tortured nerves. He repeated the same words over and over again. Lord Mountdrago lay quite still, his eyes closed; his breathing was regular, and his limbs were relaxed. Then Dr Audlin in the same quiet tone spoke the words he had prepared.

'You will go to Owen Griffiths and say that you are sorry that you caused him that great injury. You will say that you will do whatever lies in your power to undo the harm that you have done him.'

The words acted on Lord Mountdrago like the blow of a whip across his face. He shook himself out of his hypnotic state and sprang to his feet. His eyes blazed with passion and he poured forth upon Dr Audlin a stream of angry vituperation such as even he had never heard. He swore at him. He cursed him. He used language of such obscenity that Dr Audlin, who had heard every sort of foul word, sometimes from the lips of chaste and distinguished women, was surprised that he knew it.

'Apologise to that filthy little Welshman? I'd rather kill myself.'

'I believe it to be the only way in which you can regain your balance.'

Dr Audlin had not often seen a man presumably sane in such a condition of uncontrollable fury. He grew red in the face and his eyes bulged out of his head. He did really foam at the mouth. Dr Audlin watched him coolly, waiting for the storm to wear itself out, and presently he saw that Lord Mountdrago, weakened by the strain to which he had been subjected for so many weeks, was exhausted.

'Sit down,' he said then, sharply.

Lord Mountdrago crumpled up into a chair.

'Christ, I feel all in. I must rest a minute and then I'll go.'

For five minutes perhaps they sat in complete silence. Lord Mountdrago was a gross, blustering bully, but he was also a gentleman. When he broke the silence he had recovered his self-control.

'I'm afraid I've been very rude to you. I'm ashamed of the things I've said to you and I can only say you'd be justified if you refused to have anything more to do with me. I hope you won't do that. I feel that my visits to you do help me. I think you're my only chance.'

'You mustn't give another thought to what you said. It was of no consequence.'

'But there's one thing you mustn't ask me to do, and that is to make excuses to Griffiths.'

'I've thought a great deal about your case. I don't pretend to understand it, but I believe that your only chance of release is to do what I proposed. I have a notion that we're none of us one self, but many, and one of the selves in you has risen up against the injury you did Griffiths and has taken on the form of Griffiths in your mind and is punishing you for what you cruelly did. If I were a priest I should tell you that it is your conscience that has adopted the shape and lineaments of this man to scourge you to repentance and persuade you to reparation.'

'My conscience is clear. It's not my fault if I smashed the man's career. I crushed him like a slug in my garden. I regret nothing.'

It was on these words that Lord Mountdrago had left him. Reading through his notes, while he waited, Dr Audlin considered how best he could bring his patient to the state of mind that, now that his usual methods of treatment had failed, he thought alone could help him. He glanced at his clock. It was six. It was strange that Lord Mountdrago did not come. He knew he had intended to because a secretary had rung up that morning to say that he would be with him at the usual hour. He must have been detained by pressing work. This notion gave Dr Audlin something else to think of: Lord Mountdrago was quite unfit to work and in no condition to deal with important matters of state. Dr Audlin wondered whether it behooved him to get in touch with someone in authority, the Prime Minister or the Permanent Under-Secretary for Foreign Affairs, and impart to him his conviction that Lord Mountdrago's mind was so unbalanced that it was dangerous to leave affairs of moment in his hands. It was a ticklish thing to do. He might cause needless trouble and get roundly snubbed for his pains. He shrugged his shoulders.

'After all,' he reflected, 'the politicians have made such a mess of the world during the last five-and-twenty years, I don't suppose it makes much odds if they're mad or sane.'

He rang the bell.

'If Lord Mountdrago comes now will you tell him that I have another appointment at six-fifteen and so I'm afraid I can't see him.'

'Very good, sir.'

'Has the evening paper come yet?'

'I'll go and see.'

In a moment the servant brought it in. A huge headline ran across the front page: Tragic Death of Foreign Minister.

'My God!' cried Dr Audlin.

For once he was wrenched out of his wonted calm.

He was shocked, horribly shocked, and yet he was not altogether surprised. The possibility that Lord Mountdrago might commit suicide had occurred to him several times – for that it was suicide he could not doubt. The paper said that Lord Mountdrago had been waiting in a tube station, standing on the edge of the platform, and as the train came in was seen to fall on the rail. It was supposed that he had had a sudden attack of faintness. The paper went on to say that Lord Mountdrago had been suffering for some weeks from the effects of overwork, but had felt it impossible to absent himself while the foreign situation demanded his unremitting attention. Lord Mountdrago was another victim of the strain that modern politics placed upon those who played the more important parts in it. There was a neat little piece about the talents and industry, the patriotism and vision, of the deceased statesman, followed by various surmises upon the Prime Minister's choice of his successor. Dr Audlin read all this. He had not liked Lord Mountdrago. The chief emotion that his death caused in him was dissatisfaction with himself because he had been able to do nothing for him.

Perhaps he had done wrong in not getting into touch with Lord Mountdrago's doctor. He was discouraged, as always when failure frustrated his conscientious efforts, and repulsion seized him for the theory and practice of this empiric doctrine by which he earned his living. He was dealing with dark and mysterious forces that it was perhaps beyond the powers of the human mind to understand. He was like a man blindfold trying to feel his way he knew not whither. Listlessly he turned the pages of the paper. Suddenly he gave a great start, and an exclamation once more was forced from his lips. His eyes had fallen on a small paragraph near the bottom of a column. Sudden Death of an MP, he read. Mr Owen Griffiths, member for so-and-so, had been taken ill in Fleet Street that afternoon and when he was brought to Charing Cross Hospital life was found to be extinct. It was supposed that death was due to natural causes, but an inquest would be held. Dr Audlin could hardly believe his eyes. Was it possible that the night before Lord Mountdrago had at last in his dream found himself possessed of the weapon, knife or gun, that he had wanted, and had killed his tormentor, and had that ghostly act, in the same way as the blow with the bottle had given him a racking headache on the following day, taken effect a certain number of hours later on the waking man? Or was it, more mysterious and more frightful, that when Lord Mountdrago sought relief in death, the enemy he had so cruelly wronged, unappeased, escaping from his own mortality, had pursued him to some other sphere there to torment him still? It was strange. The sensible thing was to look upon it merely as an odd coincidence. Dr Audlin rang the bell.

'Tell Mrs Milton that I'm sorry I can't see her this evening. I'm not well.'

It was true; he shivered as though of an ague. With some kind of spiritual sense he seemed to envisage a bleak, a horrible void. The dark night of the soul engulfed him, and he felt a strange, primeval terror of he knew not what.

The Colonel's Lady

All this happened two or three years before the outbreak of the war.

The Peregrines were having breakfast. Though they were alone and the table was long they sat at opposite ends of it. From the walls George Peregrine's ancestors, painted by the fashionable painters of the day, looked down upon them. The butler brought in the morning post. There were several letters for the colonel, business letters, *The Times* and a small parcel for his wife Evie. He looked at his letters and then, opening *The Times*, began to read it. They finished breakfast and rose from the table. He noticed that his wife hadn't opened the parcel.

'What's that?' he asked.

'Only some books.'

'Shall I open it for you?'

'If you like.'

He hated to cut string and so with some difficulty untied the knots.

'But they're all the same,' he said when he had unwrapped the parcel. 'What on earth d'you want six copies of the same book for?' He opened one of them. Poetry. Then he looked at the title page. *When Pyramids Decay*, he read, by E. K. Hamilton. Eva Katherine Hamilton: that was his wife's maiden name. He looked at her with smiling surprise. 'Have you written a book, Evie? You are a sly-boots.'

'I didn't think it would interest you very much. Would you like a copy?'

'Well, you know poetry isn't much in my line, but – yes, I'd like a copy; I'll read it. I'll take it along to my study. I've got a lot to do this morning.'

He gathered up *The Times*, his letters and the book, and went out. His study was a large and comfortable room, with a big desk, leather armchairs and what he called 'trophies of the chase' on the walls. On the bookshelves were works of reference, books on farming, gardening, fishing and shooting, and books on the last war, in which he had won an MC and a DSO, for before his marriage he had been in the Welsh Guards. At the end of the war he retired and settled down to the life of a country gentleman in the spacious house, some twenty miles from Sheffield, which one of his forebears had built in the reign of George III. George Peregrine had an estate of some fifteen hundred acres which he managed with ability; he was a Justice of the Peace and performed his duties conscientiously. During the season he rode to hounds two days a week. He was a good shot, a golfer and though now a little over fifty could still play a hard game of tennis. He could describe himself with propriety as an all-round sportsman.

He had been putting on weight lately, but was still a fine figure of a man; tall, with grey curly hair, only just beginning to grow thin on the crown, frank blue eyes, good features and a high colour. He was a public-spirited man, chairman of any number of local organisations and, as became his class and station, a loyal member of the Conservative Party. He looked upon it as his duty to see to the welfare of the people on his estate and it was a satisfaction to him to know that Evie could be trusted to tend the sick and succour the poor. He had built a cottage hospital on the outskirts of the village and paid the wages of a nurse out of his own pocket. All he asked of the recipients of his bounty was that at elections, county or general, they should vote for his candidate. He was a friendly man, affable to his inferiors, considerate with his tenants and popular with the neighbouring gentry. He would have been pleased and at the same time slightly embarrassed if someone had told him he was a jolly good fellow. That was what he wanted to be. He desired no higher praise.

It was hard luck that he had no children. He would have been an excellent father, kindly but strict, and would have brought up his sons as gentlemen's sons should be brought up, sent them to Eton, you know, taught them to fish, shoot and ride. As it was, his heir was a nephew, son of his brother killed in a motor accident, not a bad boy, but not a chip off the old block, no, sir, far from it; and would you believe it, his fool of a mother was sending him to a co-educational school. Evie had been a sad disappointment to him. Of course she was a lady, and she had a bit of money of her own; she managed the house uncommonly well and she was a good hostess. The village people adored her. She had been a pretty little thing when he married her, with a creamy skin, light brown hair and a trim figure, healthy too and not a bad tennis player; he couldn't understand why she'd had no children; of course she was faded now, she must be getting on for five-and-forty; her skin was drab, her hair had lost its sheen and she was as thin as a rail. She was always neat and suitably dressed, but she didn't seem to bother how she looked, she wore no make-up and didn't even use lipstick; sometimes at night when she dolled herself up for a party you could tell that once she'd been quite attractive, but ordinarily she was – well, the sort of woman you simply didn't notice. A nice woman, of course, a good wife, and it wasn't her fault if she was barren, but it was tough on a fellow who wanted an heir of his own loins; she hadn't any vitality, that's what was the matter with her. He supposed he'd been in love with her when he asked her to marry him, as least sufficiently in love for a man who wanted to marry and settle down, but with time he discovered that they had nothing much in common. She didn't care about hunting, and fishing bored her. Naturally they'd drifted apart. He had to do her the justice to admit that she'd never bothered him. There'd been no scenes. They had no quarrels. She seemed to take it for granted that he should go his own way. When he went up to London now and then she never wanted to come with him. He had a girl there, well, she wasn't exactly a girl, she was thirty-five if she was a day, but she was blonde and luscious and he only had to wire ahead of time and they'd dine, do a show and spend the night together. Well, a man, a healthy normal man had to have some fun in his life. The thought crossed his mind that if Evie hadn't been such a good woman she'd have been a better wife; but it was not the sort of thought that he welcomed and he put it away from him.

George Peregrine finished his *Times* and being a considerate fellow rang the bell and told the butler to take it to Evie. Then he looked at his watch. It was half-past ten and at eleven he had an appointment with one of his tenants. He had half an hour to spare.

'I'd better have a look at Evie's book,' he said to himself.

He took it up with a smile. Evie had a lot of highbrow books in her sitting-room, not the sort of books that interested him, but if they amused her he had no objection to her reading them. He noticed that the volume he now held in his hand contained no more than ninety pages. That was all to the good. He shared Edgar Allan Poe's opinion that poems should be short. But as he turned the pages he noticed that several of Evie's had long lines of irregular length and didn't rhyme. He didn't like that. At his first school, when he was a little boy, he remembered learning a poem that began: *The boy stood on the burning deck*, and later, at Eton, one that started: *Ruin seize thee, ruthless king*; and then there was Henry V; they'd had to take that, one half. He stared at Evie's pages with consternation.

'That's not what I call poetry,' he said.

Fortunately it wasn't all like that. Interspersed with the pieces that looked so odd, lines of three or four words and then a line of ten or fifteen, there were little poems, quite short, that rhymed, thank God, with the lines all the same length. Several of the pages were just headed with the word *Sonnet*, and out of curiosity he counted the lines; there were fourteen of them. He read them. They seemed all right, but he didn't quite know what they were all about. He repeated to himself: *Ruin seize thee, ruthless king.*

'Poor Evie,' he sighed.

At that moment the farmer he was expecting was ushered into the study, and putting the book down he made him welcome. They embarked on their business.

'I read your book, Evie,' he said as they sat down

to lunch. 'Jolly good. Did it cost you a packet to have it printed?'

'No, I was lucky. I sent it to a publisher and he took it.'

'Not much money in poetry, my dear,' he said in his good-natured, hearty way.

'No, I don't suppose there is. What did Bannock want to see you about this morning?'

Bannock was the tenant who had interrupted his reading of Evie's poems.

'He's asked me to advance the money for a pedigree bull he wants to buy. He's a good man and I've half a mind to do it.'

George Peregrine saw that Evie didn't want to talk about her book and he was not sorry to change the subject. He was glad she had used her maiden name on the title page; he didn't suppose anyone would ever hear about the book, but he was proud of his own unusual name and he wouldn't have liked it if some damned penny-a-liner had made fun of Evie's effort in one of the papers.

During the few weeks that followed he thought it tactful not to ask Evie any questions about her venture into verse, and she never referred to it. It might have been a discreditable incident that they had silently agreed not to mention. But then a strange thing happened. He had to go to London on business and he took Daphne out to dinner. That was the name of the girl with whom he was in the habit of passing a few agreeable hours whenever he went to town.

'Oh, George,' she said, 'is that your wife who's written a book they're all talking about?'

'What on earth d'you mean?'

'Well, there's a fellow I know who's a critic. He

took me out to dinner the other night and he had a book with him. "Got anything for me to read?" I said. "What's that?" "Oh, I don't think that's your cup of tea," he said. "It's poetry. I've just been reviewing it." "No poetry for me," I said. "It's about the hottest stuff I ever read," he said. "Selling like hot cakes. And it's damned good." '

'Who's the book by?' asked George.

'A woman called Hamilton. My friend told me that wasn't her real name. He said her real name was Peregrine. "Funny," I said, "I know a fellow called Peregrine." "Colonel in the army," he said. "Lives near Sheffield." '

'I'd just as soon you didn't talk about me to your friends,' said George with a frown of vexation.

'Keep your shirt on, dearie. Who d'you take me for? I just said: "It's not the same one." ' Daphne giggled. 'My friend said: "They say he's a regular Colonel Blimp." '

George had a keen sense of humour.

'You could tell them better than that,' he laughed. 'If my wife had written a book I'd be the first to know about it, wouldn't I?'

'I suppose you would.'

Anyhow the matter didn't interest her and when the colonel began to talk of other things she forgot about it. He put it out of his mind too. There was nothing to it, he decided, and that silly fool of a critic had just been pulling Daphne's leg. He was amused at the thought of her tackling that book because she had been told it was hot stuff and then finding it just a lot of bosh cut up into unequal lines.

He was a member of several clubs and next day he thought he'd lunch at one in St James's Street. He was catching a train back to Sheffield early in the afternoon. He was sitting in a comfortable armchair having a glass of sherry before going into the dining-room when an old friend came up to him.

'Well, old boy, how's life?' he said. 'How d'you like being the husband of a celebrity?'

George Peregrine looked at his friend. He thought he saw an amused twinkle in his eyes.

'I don't know what you're talking about,' he answered.

'Come off it, George. Everyone knows E. K. Hamilton is your wife. Not often a book of verse has a success like that. Look here, Henry Dashwood is lunching with me. He'd like to meet you.'

'Who the devil is Henry Dashwood and why should he want to meet me?'

'Oh, my dear fellow, what do you do with yourself all the time in the country? Henry's about the best critic we've got. He wrote a wonderful review of Evie's book. D'you mean to say she didn't show it you?'

Before George could answer his friend had called a man over. A tall, thin man, with a high forehead, a beard, a long nose and a stoop, just the sort of man whom George was prepared to dislike at first sight. Introductions were effected. Henry Dashwood sat down.

'Is Mrs Peregrine in London by any chance? I should very much like to meet her,' he said.

'No, my wife doesn't like London. She prefers the country,' said George stiffly.

'She wrote me a very nice letter about my review. I was pleased. You know, we critics get more kicks than halfpence. I was simply bowled over by her book. It's so fresh and original, very modern without being obscure. She seems to be as much at her ease in free verse as in the classical metres.' Then because he was a critic he thought he should criticise. 'Sometimes her ear is a trifle at fault, but you can say the same of Emily Dickinson. There are several of those short lyrics of hers that might have been written by Landor.'

All this was gibberish to George Peregrine. The man was nothing but a disgusting highbrow. But the colonel had good manners and he answered with proper civility.

Henry Dashwood went on as though he hadn't spoken. 'But what makes the book so outstanding is the passion that throbs in every line. So many of these young poets are so anaemic, cold, bloodless, dully intellectual, but here you have real, naked, earthy passion; of course deep, sincere emotion like that is tragic – ah, my dear Colonel, how right Heine was when he said that the poet makes little songs out of his great sorrows. You know, now and then, as I read and reread those heart-rending pages I thought of Sappho.'

This was too much for George Peregrine and he got up.

'Well, it's jolly nice of you to say such nice things about my wife's little book. I'm sure she'll be delighted. But I must bolt, I've got to catch a train and I want to get a bite of lunch.'

'Damned fool,' he said irritably to himself as he walked upstairs to the dining-room.

He got home in time for dinner and after Evie had gone to bed he went into his study and looked for her book. He thought he'd just glance through it again to see for himself what they were making such a fuss about, but he couldn't find it. Evie must have taken it away.

'Silly,' he muttered.

He'd told her he thought it jolly good. What more could a fellow be expected to say? Well, it didn't matter. He lit his pipe and read the *Field* till he felt sleepy. But a week or so later it happened that he had to go into Sheffield for the day. He lunched there at his club. He had nearly finished when the Duke of Haverel came in. This was the great local magnate and of course the colonel knew him, but only to say how d'you do to; and he was surprised when the duke stopped at his table.

'We're so sorry your wife couldn't come to us for the weekend,' he said, with a sort of shy cordiality. 'We're expecting rather a nice lot of people.'

George was taken aback. He guessed that the Haverels had asked him and Evie over for the weekend and Evie, without saying a word to him about it, had refused. He had the presence of mind to say he was sorry too.

'Better luck next time,' said the duke pleasantly and moved on.

Colonel Peregrine was very angry and when he got home he said to his wife: 'Look here, what's this about our being asked over to Haverel? Why on earth did you say we couldn't go? We've never been asked before and it's the best shooting in the county.'

'I didn't think of that. I thought it would only bore you.'

'Damn it all, you might at least have asked me if I wanted to go.'

'I'm sorry.'

He looked at her closely. There was something in

her expression that he didn't quite understand. He frowned.

'I suppose *I* was asked?' he barked.

Evie flushed a little.

'Well, in point of fact you weren't.'

'I call it damned rude of them to ask you without asking me.'

'I suppose they thought it wasn't your sort of party. The duchess is rather fond of writers and people like that, you know. She's having Henry Dashwood, the critic, and for some reason he wants to meet me.'

'It was damned nice of you to refuse, Evie.'

'It's the least I could do,' she smiled. She hesitated a moment. 'George, my publishers want to give a little dinner party for me one day towards the end of the month and of course they want you to come too.'

'Oh, I don't think that's quite my mark. I'll come up to London with you if you like. I'll find someone to dine with.'

Daphne.

'I expect it'll be very dull, but they're making rather a point of it. And the day after, the American publisher who's taken my book is giving a cocktail party at Claridge's. I'd like you to come to that if you wouldn't mind.'

'Sounds like a crashing bore, but if you really want me to come I'll come.'

'It would be sweet of you.'

George Peregrine was dazed by the cocktail party. There were a lot of people. Some of them didn't look so bad, a few of the women were decently turned out, but the men seemed to him pretty awful. He was introduced to everyone as Colonel Peregrine, E. K. Hamilton's husband, you know. The men didn't seem to have anything to say to him, but the women gushed.

'You *must* be proud of your wife. Isn't it *wonderful*? You know, I read it right through at a sitting, I simply couldn't put it down, and when I'd finished I started again at the beginning and read it right through a second time. I was simply *thrilled*.'

The English publisher said to him: 'We've not had a success like this with a book of verse for twenty years. I've never seen such reviews.'

The American publisher said to him: 'It's swell. It'll be a smash hit in America. You wait and see.'

The American publisher had sent Evie a great spray of orchids. Damned ridiculous, thought George. As they came in, people were taken up to Evie, and it was evident that they said flattering things to her, which she took with a pleasant smile and a word or two of thanks. She was a trifle flushed with the excitement, but seemed quite at her ease. Though he thought the whole thing a lot of stuff and nonsense George noted with approval that his wife was carrying it off in just the right way.

'Well, there's one thing,' he said to himself, 'you can see she's a lady and that's a damned sight more than you can say of anyone else here.'

He drank a good many cocktails. But there was one thing that bothered him. He had a notion that some of the people he was introduced to looked at him in rather a funny sort of way, he couldn't quite make out what it meant, and once when he strolled by two women who were sitting together on a sofa he had the impression that they were talking about him and after he passed he was almost certain they tittered. He was very glad when the party came to an end.

In the taxi on their way back to their hotel Evie said to him: 'You were wonderful, dear. You made quite a hit. The girls simply raved about you: they thought you so handsome.'

'Girls,' he said bitterly. 'Old hags.'

'Were you bored, dear?'

'Stiff.'

She pressed his hand in a gesture of sympathy.

'I hope you won't mind if we wait and go down by the afternoon train. I've got some things to do in the morning.'

'No, that's all right. Shopping?'

'I do want to buy one or two things, but I've got to go and be photographed. I hate the idea, but they think I ought to be. For America, you know.'

He said nothing. But he thought. He thought it would be a shock to the American public when they saw the portrait of the homely, desiccated little woman who was his wife. He'd always been under the impression that they liked glamour in America.

He went on thinking, and next morning when Evie had gone out he went to his club and up to the library. There he looked up recent numbers of *The Times Literary Supplement,* the *New Statesman* and the *Spectator.* Presently he found reviews of Evie's book. He didn't read them very carefully, but enough to see that they were extremely favourable. Then he went to the bookseller's in Piccadilly where he occasionally bought books. He'd made up his mind that he had to read this damned thing of Evie's properly, but he didn't want to ask her what she'd done with the copy she'd given him. He'd buy one for himself. Before going in he looked in the window and the first thing he saw was a display of *When*

Pyramids Decay. Damned silly title! He went in. A young man came forward and asked if he could help him.

'No, I'm just having a look round.' It embarrassed him to ask for Evie's book and he thought he'd find it for himself and then take it to the salesman. But he couldn't see it anywhere and at last, finding the young man near him, he said in a carefully casual tone: 'By the way, have you got a book called *When Pyramids Decay*?'

'The new edition came in this morning. I'll get a copy.'

In a moment the young man returned with it. He was a short, rather stout young man, with a shock of untidy carroty hair and spectacles. George Peregrine, tall, upstanding, very military, towered over him.

'Is this a new edition then?' he asked.

'Yes, sir. The fifth. It might be a novel the way it's selling.'

George Peregrine hesitated a moment.

'Why d'you suppose it's such a success? I've always been told no one reads poetry.'

'Well, it's good, you know. I've read it meself.' The young man, though obviously cultured, had a slight Cockney accent, and George quite instinctively adopted a patronising attitude. 'It's the story they like. Sexy, you know, but tragic.'

George frowned a little. He was coming to the conclusion that the young man was rather impertinent. No one had told him anything about there being a story in the damned book and he had not gathered that from reading the reviews. The young man went on: 'Of course it's only a flash in the pan, if you know what I mean. The way I look at it, she was sort of inspired like by a personal experience, like Housman was with *The Shropshire Lad*. She'll never write anything else.'

'How much is the book?' said George coldly to stop his chatter. 'You needn't wrap it up, I'll just slip it into my pocket.'

The November morning was raw and he was wearing a greatcoat.

At the station he bought the evening papers and magazines and he and Evie settled themselves comfortably in opposite corners of a first-class carriage and read. At five o'clock they went along to the restaurant car to have tea and chatted a little. They arrived. They drove home in the car which was waiting for them. They bathed, dressed for dinner, and after dinner Evie, saying she was tired out, went to bed. She kissed him, as was her habit, on the forehead. Then he went into the hall, took Evie's book out of his greatcoat pocket and going into the study began to read it. He didn't read verse very easily and though he read with attention, every word of it, the impression he received was far from clear. Then he began at the beginning again and read it a second time. He read with increasing malaise, but he was not a stupid man and when he had finished he had a distinct understanding of what it was all about. Part of the book was in free verse, part in conventional metres, but the story it related was coherent and plain to the meanest intelligence. It was the story of a passionate love affair between an older woman, married, and a young man. George Peregrine made out the steps of it as easily as if he had been doing a sum in simple addition.

Written in the first person, it began with the

tremulous surprise of the woman, past her youth, when it dawned upon her that the young man was in love with her. She hesitated to believe it. She thought she must be deceiving herself. And she was terrified when on a sudden she discovered that she was passionately in love with him. She told herself it was absurd; with the disparity of age between them nothing but unhappiness could come to her if she yielded to her emotion. She tried to prevent him from speaking but the day came when he told her that he loved her and forced her to tell him that she loved him too. He begged her to run away with him. She couldn't leave her husband, her home; and what life could they look forward to, she an ageing woman, he so young? How could she expect his love to last? She begged him to have mercy on her. But his love was impetuous. He wanted her, he wanted her with all his heart, and at last trembling, afraid, desirous, she yielded to him. Then there was a period of ecstatic happiness. The world, the dull, humdrum world of every day, blazed with glory. Love songs flowed from her pen. The woman worshipped the young, virile body of her lover. George flushed darkly when she praised his broad chest and slim flanks, the beauty of his legs and the flatness of his belly.

Hot stuff, Daphne's friend had said. It was that all right. Disgusting.

There were sad little pieces in which she lamented the emptiness of her life when as must happen he left her, but they ended with a cry that all she had to suffer would be worth it for the bliss that for a while had been hers. She wrote of the long, tremulous nights they passed together and the languor that lulled them to sleep in one another's arms. She wrote of the rapture of brief stolen moments when, braving all danger, their passion overwhelmed them and they surrendered to its call.

She thought it would be an affair of a few weeks, but miraculously it lasted. One of the poems referred to three years having gone by without lessening the love that filled their hearts. It looked as though he continued to press her to go away with him, far away, to a hill town in Italy, a Greek island, a walled city in Tunisia, so that they could be together always, for in another of the poems she besought him to let things be as they were. Their happiness was precarious. Perhaps it was owing to the difficulties they had to encounter and the rarity of their meetings that their love had retained for so long its first enchanting ardour. Then on a sudden the young man died. How, when or where George could not discover. There followed a long, heartbroken cry of bitter grief, grief she could not indulge in, grief that had to be hidden. She had to be cheerful, give dinner-parties and go out to dinner, behave as she had always behaved, though the light had gone out of her life and she was bowed down with anguish. The last poem of all was a set of four short stanzas in which the writer, sadly resigned to her loss, thanked the dark powers that rule man's destiny that she had been privileged at least for a while to enjoy the greatest happiness that we poor human beings can ever hope to know.

It was three o'clock in the morning when George Peregrine finally put the book down. It had seemed to him that he heard Evie's voice in every line, over and over again he came upon turns of phrase he had heard her use, there were details that were as familiar to him as to her: there was no doubt about it; it was her own story she had told, and it was as plain as anything could be that she had had a lover and her lover had died. It was not anger so much that he felt, nor horror or dismay, though he was dismayed and he was horrified, but amazement. It was as inconceivable that Evie should have had a love affair, and a wildly passionate one at that, as that the trout in a glass case over the chimney piece in his study, the finest he had ever caught, should suddenly wag its tail. He understood now the meaning of the amused look he had seen in the eyes of that man he had spoken to at the club, he understood why Daphne when she was talking about the book had seemed to be enjoying a private joke, and why those two women at the cocktail party had tittered when he strolled past them.

He broke out into a sweat. Then on a sudden he was seized with fury and he jumped up to go and awake Evie and ask her sternly for an explanation. But he stopped at the door. After all, what proof had he? A book. He remembered that he'd told Evie he thought it jolly good. True, he hadn't read it, but he'd pretended he had. He would look a perfect fool if he had to admit that.

'I must watch my step,' he muttered.

He made up his mind to wait for two or three days and think it all over. Then he'd decide what to do. He went to bed, but he couldn't sleep for a long time.

'Evie,' he kept on saying to himself. 'Evie, of all people.'

They met at breakfast next morning as usual. Evie was as she always was, quiet, demure and self-possessed, a middle-aged woman who made no effort to look younger than she was, a woman who had nothing of what he still called It. He looked at her as he hadn't looked at her for years. She had her usual placid serenity. Her pale blue eyes were untroubled. There was no sign of guilt on her candid brow. She made the same little casual remarks she always made.

'It's nice to get back to the country again after those two hectic days in London. What are you going to do this morning?'

It was incomprehensible.

Three days later he went to see his solicitor. Henry Blane was an old friend of George's as well as his lawyer. He had a place not far from Peregrine's and for years they had shot over one another's preserves. For two days a week he was a country gentleman and for the other five a busy lawyer in Sheffield. He was a tall, robust fellow, with a boisterous manner and a jovial laugh, which suggested that he liked to be looked upon essentially as a sportsman and a good fellow and only incidentally as a lawyer. But he was shrewd and worldly-wise.

'Well, George, what's brought you here today?' he boomed as the colonel was shown into his office. 'Have a good time in London? I'm taking my missus up for a few days next week. How's Evie?'

'It's about Evie I've come to see you,' said Peregrine, giving him a suspicious look. 'Have you read her book?'

His sensitivity had been sharpened during those last days of troubled thought and he was conscious of a faint change in the lawyer's expression. It was as though he were suddenly on his guard.

'Yes, I've read it. Great success, isn't it? Fancy Evie breaking out into poetry. Wonders will never cease.'

George Peregrine was inclined to lose his temper.

'It's made me look a perfect damned fool.'

'Oh, what nonsense, George! There's no harm in Evie's writing a book. You ought to be jolly proud of her.'

'Don't talk such rot. It's her own story. You know it and everyone else knows it. I suppose I'm the only one who doesn't know who her lover was.'

'There is such a thing as imagination, old boy. There's no reason to suppose the whole thing isn't made up.'

'Look here, Henry, we've known one another all our lives. We've had all sorts of good times together. Be honest with me. Can you look me in the face and tell me you believe it's a made-up story?'

Harry Blane moved uneasily in his chair. He was disturbed by the distress in old George's voice.

'You've got no right to ask me a question like that. Ask Evie.'

'I daren't,' George answered after an anguished pause. 'I'm afraid she'd tell me the truth.'

There was an uncomfortable silence.

'Who was the chap?'

Harry Blane looked at him straight in the eye.

'I don't know, and if I did I wouldn't tell you.'

'You swine. Don't you see what a position I'm in? Do you think it's very pleasant to be made absolutely ridiculous?'

The lawyer lit a cigarette and for some moments silently puffed it.

'I don't see what I can do for you,' he said at last.

'You've got private detectives you employ, I suppose. I want you to put them on the job and let them find everything out.'

'It's not very pretty to put detectives on one's wife, old boy; and besides, taking for granted for a moment that Evie had an affair, it was a good many years ago and I don't suppose it would be possible to find out a thing. They seem to have covered their tracks pretty carefully.'

'I don't care. You put the detectives on. I want to know the truth.'

'I won't, George. If you're determined to do that you'd better consult someone else. And look here, even if you got evidence that Evie had been unfaithful to you what would you do with it? You'd look rather silly divorcing your wife because she'd committed adultery ten years ago.'

'At all events I could have it out with her.'

'You can do that now, but you know just as well as I do that if you do she'll leave you. D'you want her to do that?'

George gave him an unhappy look.

'I don't know. I always thought she'd been a damned good wife to me. She runs the house perfectly, we never have any servant trouble; she's done wonders with the garden and she's splendid with all the village people. But damn it, I have my self-respect to think of. How can I go on living with her when I know that she was grossly unfaithful to me?'

'Have you always been faithful to her?'

'More or less, you know. After all, we've been married for nearly twenty-four years and Evie was never much for bed.'

The solicitor slightly raised his eyebrows, but George was too intent on what he was saying to notice.

'I don't deny that I've had a bit of fun now and then. A man wants it. Women are different.'

'We only have men's word for that,' said Harry Blane, with a faint smile.

'Evie's absolutely the last woman I'd have suspected of kicking over the traces. I mean, she's a very fastidious, reticent woman. What on earth made her write the damned book?'

'I suppose it was a very poignant experience and perhaps it was a relief to her to get it off her chest like that.'

'Well, if she had to write it why the devil didn't she write it under an assumed name?'

'She used her maiden name. I suppose she thought that was enough, and it would have been if the book hadn't had this amazing boom.'

George Peregrine and the lawyer were sitting opposite one another with a desk between them. George, his elbow on the desk, his cheek on his hand, frowned at his thought.

'It's so rotten not to know what sort of a chap he was. One can't even tell if he was by way of being a gentleman. I mean, for all I know he may have been a farmhand or a clerk in a lawyer's office.'

Harry Blane did not permit himself to smile and when he answered there was in his eyes a kindly, tolerant look.

'Knowing Evie so well I think the probabilities are that he was all right. Anyhow I'm sure he wasn't a clerk in my office.'

'It's been a shock to me,' the colonel sighed. 'I thought she was fond of me. She couldn't have written that book unless she hated me.'

'Oh, I don't believe that. I don't think she's capable of hatred.'

'You're not going to pretend that she loves me.'

'No.'

'Well, what does she feel for me?'

Harry Blane leaned back in his swivel chair and looked at George reflectively.

'Indifference, I should say.'

The colonel gave a little shudder and reddened.

'After all, you're not in love with her, are you?'

George Peregrine did not answer directly.

'It's been a great blow to me not to have any children, but I've never let her see that I think she's let me down. I've always been kind to her. Within reasonable limits I've tried to do my duty by her.'

The lawyer passed a large hand over his mouth to conceal the smile that trembled on his lips.

'It's been such an awful shock to me,' Peregrine went on. 'Damn it all, even ten years ago Evie was no chicken and God knows, she wasn't much to look at. It's so ugly.' He sighed deeply. 'What would *you* do in my place?'

'Nothing.'

George Peregrine drew himself bolt upright in his chair and he looked at Harry with the stern set face that he must have worn when he inspected his regiment.

'I can't overlook a thing like this. I've been made a laughing-stock. I can never hold up my head again.'

'Nonsense,' said the lawyer sharply, and then, in a pleasant, kindly manner, 'Listen, old boy: the man's dead; it all happened a long while back. Forget it. Talk to people about Evie's book, rave about it, tell 'em how proud you are of her. Behave as though you had so much confidence in her, you *knew* she could never have been unfaithful to you. The world moves so quickly and people's memories are so short. They'll forget.'

'I shan't forget.'

'You're both middle-aged people. She probably does a great deal more for you than you think and you'd be awfully lonely without her. I don't think it matters if you don't forget. It'll be all to the good if you can get it into that thick head of yours that there's a lot more in Evie than you ever had the gumption to see.'

'Damn it all, you talk as if *I* was to blame.'

'No, I don't think you were to blame, but I'm not so sure that Evie was either. I don't suppose she wanted to fall in love with this boy. D'you remember those verses right at the end? The impression they gave me was that though she was shattered by his death, in a strange sort of way she welcomed it. All through she'd been aware of the fragility of the tie that bound them. He died in the full flush of his first love and had never known that love so seldom endures; he'd only known its bliss and beauty. In her own bitter grief she found solace in the thought that he'd been spared all sorrow.'

'All that's a bit above my head, old boy. I see more or less what you mean.'

George Peregrine stared unhappily at the inkstand on the desk. He was silent and the lawyer looked at him with curious, yet sympathetic, eyes.

'Do you realise what courage she must have had never by a sign to show how dreadfully unhappy she was?' he said gently.

Colonel Peregrine sighed.

'I'm broken. I suppose you're right; it's no good crying over spilt milk and it would only make things worse if I made a fuss.'

'Well?'

George Peregrine gave him a pitiful little smile.

'I'll take your advice. I'll do nothing. Let them think me a damned fool and to hell with them. The truth is, I don't know what I'd do without Evie. But I'll tell you what, there's one thing I shall never understand till my dying day: What in the name of heaven did the fellow ever see in her?'

The Treasure

Richard Harenger was a happy man. Notwithstanding what the pessimists, from Ecclesiastes onwards, have said, this is not so rare a thing to find in this unhappy world, but Richard Harenger knew it, and that is a very rare thing indeed. The golden mean which the ancients so highly prized is out of fashion, and those who follow it must put up with polite derision from those who see no merit in self-restraint and no virtue in common sense. Richard Harenger shrugged a polite and amused shoulder. Let others live dangerously, let others burn with a hard gemlike flame, let others stake their fortunes on the turn of a card, walk the tightrope that leads to glory or the grave, or hazard their lives for a cause, a passion or an adventure. He neither envied the fame their exploits brought them nor wasted his pity on them when their efforts ended in disaster.

But it must not be inferred from this that Richard Harenger was a selfish or a callous man. He was neither. He was considerate and of a generous disposition. He was always ready to oblige a friend and he was sufficiently well off to be able to indulge himself in the pleasure of helping others. He had some money of his own and he occupied in the Home Office a position that brought him an adequate stipend. The work suited him. It was regular, responsible and pleasant. Every day when he left the office he went to his club to play bridge for a couple of hours, and on Saturdays and Sundays he played golf. He went abroad for his holidays, staying at good hotels, and visited churches, galleries and museums. He was a regular first-nighter. He dined out a good deal. His friends liked him. He was easy to talk to. He was well-read, knowledgeable and amusing. He was besides of a personable exterior, not remarkably handsome, but tall, slim and erect of carriage, with a lean, intelligent face; his hair was growing thin, for he was now approaching the age of fifty, but his brown eyes retained their smile and his teeth were all his own. He had from nature a good constitution and he had always taken care of himself. There was no reason in the world why he should not be a happy man, and if there had been in him a trace of self-complacency he might have claimed that he deserved to be.

He had the good fortune even to sail safely through those perilous, unquiet straits of marriage in which so many wise and good men have made shipwreck. Married for love in the early twenties, his wife and he, after some years of almost perfect felicity, had drifted gradually apart. Neither of them wished to marry anyone else, so there was no question of divorce (which indeed Richard Harenger's situation in the government service made undesirable), but for convenience's sake, with the help of the family lawyer, they arranged a separation which left them free to lead their lives as each one wished without interference from the other. They parted with mutual expressions of respect and goodwill.

Richard Harenger sold his house in St John's Wood and took a flat within convenient walking distance of Whitehall. It had a sitting-room which he lined with his books, a dining-room into which his Chippendale furniture just fitted, a nice-sized bedroom for himself, and beyond the kitchen a couple of maids' rooms. He brought his cook, whom he had had for many years, from St John's Wood, but needing no longer so large a staff dismissed the rest of the servants and applied at a registry office for a house-parlourmaid. He knew exactly what he wanted and he explained his needs to the superintendent of the agency with precision. He wanted a maid who was not too young, first because young women are flighty and secondly because, though he was of mature age and a man of principle, people would talk, the porter and the tradesmen if nobody else, and both for the sake of his own reputation and that of the young person he considered that the applicant should have reached years of discretion. Besides that he wanted a maid who could clean silver well. He had always had a fancy for old silver, and it was reasonable to demand that the forks and spoons that had been used by a woman of quality under the reign of Queen Anne should be treated with tenderness and respect. He was of a hospitable nature and liked to give at least once a week little dinners of not less than four people and not more than eight. He could trust his cook to send in a meal that his guests would take pleasure in eating and he desired his parlourmaid to wait with neatness and dispatch. Then he needed a perfect valet. He dressed well, in a manner that suited his age and condition, and he liked his clothes to be properly looked after. The parlourmaid he was looking for must be able to press trousers and iron a tie, and he was very particular that his shoes should be well shone. He had small feet and he took a good deal of trouble to have well-cut shoes. He had a large supply and he insisted that they should be treed up the moment he took them off. Finally the flat must be kept clean and tidy. It was of course understood that any applicant for the post must be of irreproachable character, sober, honest, reliable and of a pleasing exterior. In return for this he was prepared to offer good wages, reasonable liberty and ample holidays. The superintendent listened without batting an eyelash and, telling him that she was quite sure she could suit him, sent him a string of candidates which proved that she had not paid the smallest attention to a word he said. He saw them all personally. Some were obviously inefficient, some looked fast, some were too old, others too young, some lacked the presence he thought essential; there was not one to whom he was inclined even to give a trial. He was a kindly, polite man and he declined their services with a smile and a pleasant expression of regret. He did not lose patience. He was prepared to interview house-parlourmaids till he found one who was suitable.

Now it is a funny thing about life, if you refuse to accept anything but the best you very often get it: if you utterly decline to make do with what you can get, then somehow or other you are very likely to get what you want. It is as though Fate said, 'This man's a perfect fool, he's asking for perfection,' and then just out of her feminine wilfulness flung it in his lap. One day the porter of the flats said to Richard Harenger out of a blue sky: 'I hear you're lookin' for a house-parlourmaid, sir. There's someone I know lookin' for a situation as might do.'

'Can you recommend her personally?'

Richard Harenger had the sound opinion that one servant's recommendation of another was worth much more than that of an employer.

'I can vouch for her respectability. She's been in some very good situations.'

'I shall be coming in to dress about seven. If that's convenient to her I could see her then.'

'Very good, sir. I'll see that she's told.'

He had not been in more than five minutes when the cook, having answered a ring at the front door, came in and told him that the person the porter had spoken to him about had called.

'Show her in,' he said.

He turned on some more light so that he could see what the applicant looked like and, getting up, stood with his back to the fireplace. A woman came in and stood just inside the door in a respectful attitude.

'Good-evening,' he said. 'What is your name?'

'Pritchard, sir.'

'How old are you?'

'Thirty-five, sir.'

'Well, that's a reasonable age.'

He gave his cigarette a puff and looked at her reflectively. She was on the tall side, nearly as tall as he, but he guessed that she wore high heels. Her black dress fitted her station. She held herself well. She had good features and a rather high colour.

'Will you take off your hat?' he asked.

She did so and he saw that she had pale brown hair. It was neatly and becomingly dressed. She looked strong and healthy. She was neither fat nor thin. In a proper uniform she would look very presentable. She was not inconveniently handsome, but she was certainly a comely, in another class of life you might almost have said a handsome, woman. He proceeded to ask her a number of questions. Her answers were satisfactory. She had left her last place for an adequate reason. She had been trained under a butler and appeared to be well acquainted with her duties. In her last place she had been head parlourmaid of three, but she did not mind undertaking the work of the flat single-handed. She had valeted a gentleman before who had sent her to a tailor's to learn how to press clothes. She was a little shy, but neither timid nor ill-at-ease. Richard asked her his questions in his amiable, leisurely way and she answered them with modest composure. He was considerably impressed. He asked her what references she could give. They seemed extremely satisfactory.

'Now look here,' he said, 'I'm very much inclined to engage you. But I hate changes, I've had my cook for twelve years: if you suit me and the place suits you I hope you'll stay. I mean, I don't want you to come to me in three or four months and say that you're leaving to get married.'

'There's not much fear of that, sir. I'm a widow. I don't believe marriage is much catch for anyone in my position, sir. My husband never did a stroke of work from the day I married him to the day he died, and I had to keep him. What I want now is a good home.'

'I'm inclined to agree with you,' he smiled. 'Marriage is a very good thing, but I think it's a mistake to make a habit of it.'

She very properly made no reply to this, but waited for him to announce his decision. She did not seem anxious about it. He reflected that if she was as competent as she appeared she must be well aware that she would have no difficulty in finding a place. He told her what wages he was offering and these seemed to be satisfactory to her. He gave her the necessary information about the place, but she gave him to understand that she was already apprised of this, and he received the impression, which amused rather than disconcerted him, that she had made certain enquiries about him before applying for the situation. It showed prudence on her part and good sense.

'When would you be able to come in if I engaged you? I haven't got anybody at the moment. The cook's managing as best she can with a char, but I should like to get settled as soon as possible.'

'Well, sir, I was going to give myself a week's holiday, but if it's a matter of obliging a gentleman I don't mind giving that up. I could come in tomorrow if it was convenient.'

Richard Harenger gave her his attractive smile.

'I shouldn't like you to do without a holiday that I dare say you've been looking forward to. I can very well go on like this for another week. Go and have your holiday and come to me when it's over.'

'Thank you very much, sir. Would it do if I came in tomorrow week?'

'Quite well.'

When she left, Richard Harenger felt he had done a good day's work. It looked as though he had found exactly what he was after. He rang for the cook and told her he had engaged a house-parlourmaid at last.

'I think you'll like her, sir,' she said. 'She came in and 'ad a talk with me this afternoon. I could see at once she knew her duties. And she's not one of them flighty ones.'

'We can but try, Mrs Jeddy. I hope you gave me a good character.'

'Well, I said you was particular, sir. I said you was a gentleman as liked things just so.'

'I admit that.'

'She said she didn't mind that. She said she liked a gentleman as knew what was what. She said there's no satisfaction in doing things proper if nobody notices. I expect you'll find she'll take a rare lot of pride in her work.'

'That's what I want her to do. I think we might go farther and fare worse.'

'Well, sir, there is that to it, of course. And the proof of the pudding's the eating. But if you ask my opinion I think she's going to be a real treasure.'

And that is precisely what Pritchard turned out. No man was ever better served. The way she shone shoes was marvellous, and he set out of a fine morning for his walk to the office with a more jaunty step because you could almost see yourself reflected in them. She looked after his clothes with such attention that his colleagues began to chaff him about being the best-dressed man in the Civil Service. One day, coming home unexpectedly, he found a line of socks and handkerchiefs hung up to dry in the bathroom. He called Prichard.

'D'you wash my socks and handkerchiefs yourself, Pritchard? I should have thought you had enough to do without that.'

'They do ruin them so at the laundry, sir. I prefer to do them at home if you have no objection.'

She knew exactly what he should wear on every occasion, and without asking him was aware whether she should put out a dinner-jacket and a black tie in the evening or a dress coat and a white one. When he was going to a party where decorations were to be worn he found his neat little row of medals automatically affixed to the lapel if his coat. He soon ceased to choose every morning from his wardrobe the tie he wanted, for he found that she put out for him without fail the one he would have himself selected. Her taste was perfect. He supposed she read his letters, for she always knew what his movements were, and if he had forgotten at what hour he had an engagement he had no need to look in his book, for Pritchard could tell him. She knew exactly what tone to use with persons with whom she conversed on the telephone. Except with tradesmen, with whom she was apt to be peremptory, she was always polite, but there was a distinct difference in her manner if she was addressing one of Mr Harenger's literary friends or the wife of a Cabinet Minister. She knew by instinct with whom he wished to speak and with whom he didn't. From his sitting-room he sometimes heard her with placid sincerity assuring a caller that he was out, and then she would come in and tell him that So-and-So had rung up, but she thought he wouldn't wish to be disturbed.

'Quite right, Pritchard,' he smiled.

'I knew she only wanted to bother you about that concert,' said Pritchard.

His friends made appointments with him through her, and she would tell him what she had done on his return in the evening.

'Mrs Soames rang up, sir, and asked if you would lunch with her on Thursday, the eighth, but I said you were very sorry but you were lunching with Lady Versinder. Mr Oakley rang up and asked if you'd go to a cocktail party at the Savoy next Tuesday at six. I said you would if you possibly could, but you might have to go to the dentist's.'

'Quite right.'

'I thought you could see when the time came, sir.'

She kept the flat like a new pin. On one occasion soon after she entered his service, Richard coming back from a holiday took out a book from his shelves and at once noticed that it had been dusted. He rang the bell.

'I forgot to tell you when I went away under no circumstances ever to touch my books. When books are taken out to be dusted they're never put back in the right place. I don't mind my books being dirty, but I hate not being able to find them.'

'I'm very sorry, sir,' said Pritchard. 'I know some gentlemen are very particular and I took care to put back every book exactly where I took it from.'

Richard Harenger gave his books a glance. So far as he could see every one was in its accustomed place. He smiled.

'I apologise, Pritchard.'

'They were in a muck, sir. I mean, you couldn't open one without getting your hands black with dust.'

She certainly kept his silver as he had never had it kept before. He felt called upon to give her a special word of praise.

'Most of it's Queen Anne and George I, you know,' he explained.

'Yes, I know, sir. When you've got something good like that to look after it's a pleasure to keep it like it should be.'

'You certainly have a knack for it. I never knew a butler who kept his silver as well as you do.'

'Men haven't the patience women have,' she replied modestly.

As soon as he thought Pritchard had settled down in the place he resumed the little dinners he was fond of giving once a week. He had already discovered that she knew how to wait at table, but it was with a warm sense of complacency that he realised then how competently she could manage a party. She was quick, silent and watchful. A guest had hardly felt the need of something before Pritchard was at his elbow offering him what he wanted. She soon learned the tastes of his more intimate friends and remembered that one liked water instead of soda with his whisky and that another particularly fancied the knuckle end of a leg of lamb. She knew exactly how cold a hock should be not to ruin its taste and how long claret should have stood in the room to bring out its bouquet. It was a pleasure to see her pour out a bottle of burgundy in such a fashion as not to disturb the grounds. On one occasion she did not serve the wine Richard had ordered. He somewhat sharply pointed this out to her.

'I opened the bottle, sir, and it was slightly corked. So I got the Chambertin, as I thought it was safer.'

'Quite right, Pritchard.'

Presently he left this matter entirely in her hands, for he discovered that she knew perfectly what wines his guests would like. Without orders from him she would provide the best in his cellar and his oldest brandy if she thought they were the sort of people who knew what they were drinking. She had no belief in the palate of women, and when they were of the party was apt to serve the champagne which had to be drunk before it went off. She had the English servant's instinctive knowledge of social differences and neither rank nor money blinded her to the fact that someone was not a gentleman, but she had favourites among his friends, and when someone she particularly liked was dining, with the air of a cat that has swallowed a canary she would decant for him a bottle of a wine that Harenger kept for very special occasions. It amused him.

'You've got on the right side of Pritchard, old boy,' he exclaimed. 'There aren't many people she gives this wine to.'

Pritchard became an institution. She was known very soon to be the perfect parlourmaid. People envied Harenger the possession of her as they envied nothing else that he had. She was worth her weight in gold. Her price was above rubies. Richard Harenger beamed with self-complacency when they praised her.

'Good masters make good servants,' he said gaily.

One evening, when they were sitting over their port and she had left the room, they were talking about her.

'It'll be an awful blow when she leaves you.'

'Why should she leave me? One or two people have tried to get her away from me, but she turned them down. She knows where she's well off.'

'She'll get married one of these days.'

'I don't think she's that sort.'

'She's a good-looking woman.'

'Yes, she has quite a decent presence.'

'What are you talking about? She's a very handsome creature. In another class of life she'd be a well-known society beauty with her photograph in all the papers.'

At that moment Pritchard came in with the coffee. Richard Harenger looked at her. After seeing her every day, off and on, for four years it was now – my word, how time flies – he had really forgotten what she looked like. She did not seem to have changed much since he had first seen her. She was no stouter than then, she still had the high colour, and her regular features bore the same expression which was at once intent and vacuous. The black uniform suited her. She left the room.

'She's a paragon and there's no doubt about it.'

'I know she is,' answered Harenger. 'She's perfection. I should be lost without her. And the strange thing is that I don't very much like her.'

'Why not?'

'I think she bores me a little. You see, she has no conversation. I've often tried to talk to her. She answers when I speak to her, but that's all. In four years she's never volunteered a remark of her own. I know absolutely nothing about her. I don't know if she likes me or if she's completely indifferent to me. She's an automaton. I respect her, I appreciate her, I trust her. She has every quality in the world and I've often wondered why it is that with all that I'm so completely indifferent to her. I think it must be that she is entirely devoid of charm.'

They left it at that.

Two or three days after this, since it was Pritchard's night out and he had no engagement, Richard Harenger dined by himself at his club. A pageboy came to him and told him that they had just rung up from his flat to say that he had gone out without his keys and should they be brought along to him in a taxi? He put his hand to his pocket. It was a fact. By a singular chance he had forgotten to replace them when he had changed into a blue serge suit before coming out to dinner. His intention had been to play bridge, but it was an off-night at the club and there seemed little chance of a decent game; it occurred to him that it would be a good opportunity to see a picture that he had heard talked about, so he sent back the message by the page that he would call for the keys himself in half an hour.

He rang at the door of his flat and it was opened by Pritchard. She had the keys in her hand.

'What are you doing here, Pritchard?' he asked. 'It's your night out, isn't it?'

'Yes, sir. But I didn't care about going, so I told Mrs Jeddy she could go instead.'

'You ought to get out when you have the chance,' he said, with his usual thoughtfulness. 'It's not good for you to be cooped up here all the time.'

'I get out now and then on an errand, but I haven't been out in the evening for the last month.'

'Why on earth not?'

'Well, it's not very cheerful going out by yourself, and somehow I don't know anyone just now I'm particularly keen on going out with.'

'You ought to have a bit of fun now and then. It's good for you.'

'I've got out of the habit of it somehow.'

'Look here, I'm just going to the cinema. Would you like to come along with me?'

He spoke in kindliness, on the spur of the moment, and the moment he had said the words half regretted them.

'Yes, sir, I'd like to,' said Pritchard.

'Run along then and put on a hat.'

'I shan't be a minute.'

She disappeared and he went into the sitting-room and lit a cigarette. He was a little amused at what he was doing, and pleased too; it was nice to be able to make someone happy with so little trouble to himself.

It was characteristic of Pritchard that she had shown neither surprise nor hesitation. She kept him waiting about five minutes, and when she came back he noticed that she had changed her dress. She wore a blue frock in what he supposed was artificial silk, a small black hat with a blue brooch on it, and a silver fox round her neck. He was a trifle relieved to see that she looked neither shabby nor showy. It would never occur to anyone who happened to see them that this was a distinguished official in the Home Office taking his housemaid to the pictures.

'I'm sorry to have kept you waiting, sir.'

'It doesn't matter at all,' he said graciously.

He opened the front door for her and she went out before him. He remembered the familiar anecdote of Louis XIV and the courtier and appreciated the fact that she had not hesitated to precede him. The cinema for which they were bound was at no great distance from Mr Harenger's flat and they walked there. He talked about the weather and the state of the roads and Adolf Hitler. Pritchard made suitable replies. They arrived just as *Mickey Mouse* was starting and this put them in a good humour. During the four years she had been in his service Richard Harenger had hardly ever seen Pritchard even smile, and now it diverted him vastly to hear peal upon peal of her joyous laughter. He enjoyed her pleasure. Then the principal attraction was thrown on the screen. It was a good picture and they both watched it with breathless excitement. Taking his cigarette-case out to help himself he automatically offered it to Pritchard.

'Thank you, sir,' she said, taking one.

He lit it for her. Her eyes were on the screen and she was almost unconscious of his action. When the picture was finished they streamed out with the crowd into the street. They walked back towards the flat. It was a fine starry night.

'Did you like it?' he said.

'Like anything, sir. It was a real treat.'

A thought occurred to him.

'By the way, did you have any supper tonight?'

'No, sir, I didn't have time.'

'Aren't you starving?'

'I'll have a bit of bread and cheese when I get in and I'll make meself a cup of cocoa.'

'That sounds rather grim.' There was a feeling of gaiety in the air, and the people who poured past them, one way and another, seemed filled with a pleasant elation. In for a penny, in for a pound, he said to himself. 'Look here, would you like to come and have a bit of supper with me somewhere?'

'If you'd like to, sir.'

'Come on.'

He hailed a cab. He was feeling very philanthropic and it was not a feeling that he disliked at all. He told the driver to go to a restaurant in Oxford Street which was gay, but at which he was confident there was no chance of meeting anyone he knew. There was an orchestra and people danced. It would amuse Pritchard to see them. When they sat down a waiter came up to them.

'They've got a set supper here,' he said, thinking that was what she would like. 'I suggest we have that. What would you like to drink? A little white wine?'

'What I really fancy is a glass of ginger beer,' she said.

Richard Harenger ordered himself a whisky and soda. She ate the supper with hearty appetite, and though Harenger was not hungry, to put her at her ease he ate too. The picture they had just seen gave them something to talk about. It was quite true what they had said the other night, Pritchard was not a bad-looking woman, and even if someone had seen them together he would not have minded. It would make rather a good story for his friends when he told them how he had taken the incomparable Pritchard to the cinema and then afterwards to supper. Pritchard was looking at the dancers with a faint smile on her lips.

'Do you like dancing?' he said.

'I used to be a rare one for it when I was a girl. I never danced much after I was married. My husband was a bit shorter than me and somehow I never think it looks well unless the gentleman's taller, if you know what I mean. I suppose I shall be getting too old for it soon.'

Richard was certainly taller than his parlourmaid. They would look all right. He was fond of dancing and he danced well. But he hesitated. He did not want to embarrass Pritchard by asking her to dance with him. It was better not to go too far perhaps. And yet what did it matter? It was a drab life she led. She was so sensible, if she thought it a mistake he was pretty sure she would find a decent excuse.

'Would you like to take a turn, Pritchard?' he said, as the band struck up again.

'I'm terribly out of practice, sir.'

'What does that matter?'

'If you don't mind, sir,' she answered coolly, rising from her seat.

She was not in the least shy. She was only afraid that she would not be able to follow his step. They moved on to the floor. He found she danced very well.

'Why, you dance perfectly, Pritchard,' he said.

'It's coming back to me.'

Although she was a big woman she was light on her feet and she had a natural sense of rhythm. She was very pleasant to dance with. He gave a glance at the mirrors that lined the walls and he could not help reflecting that they looked very well together. Their eyes met in the mirror; he wondered whether she was thinking that too. They had two more dances and then Richard Harenger suggested that they should go. He paid the bill and they walked out. He noticed that she threaded her way through the crowd without a trace of self-consciousness. They got into a taxi and in ten minutes were at home.

'I'll go up the back way, sir,' said Pritchard.

'There's no need to do that. Come up in the lift with me.'

He took her up, giving the night-porter an icy glance, so that he should not think it strange that he came back at that somewhat late hour with his parlourmaid, and with his latchkey let her into the flat.

'Well, good-night, sir,' she said. 'Thank you very much. It's been a real treat for me.'

'Thank *you*, Pritchard. I should have had a very dull evening by myself. I hope you've enjoyed your outing.'

'That I have, sir, more than I can say.'

It had been a success. Richard Harenger was satisfied with himself. It was a kindly thing for him to have done. It was a very agreeable sensation to give anyone so much real pleasure. His benevolence warmed him and for a moment he felt a great love in his heart for the whole human race.

'Good-night, Pritchard,' he said, and because he felt happy and good he put his arm round her waist and kissed her on the lips.

Her lips were very soft. They lingered on his and she returned his kiss. It was the warm, hearty embrace of a healthy woman in the prime of life. He found it very pleasant and he held her to him a little more closely. She put her arms round his neck.

As a general rule he did not wake till Pritchard came in with his letters, but next morning he woke at half-past seven. He had a curious sensation that he did not recognise. He was accustomed to sleep with two pillows under his head and he suddenly grew aware of the fact that he had only one. Then he remembered and with a start looked round. The other pillow was beside his own. Thank God, no sleeping head rested there, but it was plain that one had. His heart sank. He broke out into a cold sweat.

'My God, what a fool I've been!' he cried out loud.

How could he have done anything so stupid? What on earth had come over him? He was the last man to play about with servant girls. What a disgraceful thing to do! At his age and in his position. He had not heard Pritchard slip away. He must have been asleep. It wasn't even as if he'd liked her very much. She wasn't his type. And, as he had said the other night, she rather bored him. Even now he only knew her as Pritchard. He had no notion what her first name was. What madness! And what was to happen now? The position was impossible. It was obvious he couldn't keep her, and yet to send her away for what was his fault as much as hers seemed shockingly unfair. How idiotic to lose the best parlourmaid a man ever had just for an hour's folly!

'It's that damned kindness of heart of mine,' he groaned.

He would never find anyone else to look after his clothes so admirably or clean the silver so well. She knew all his friends' telephone numbers and she understood wine. But of course she must go. She must see for herself that after what had happened things could never be the same. He would make her a handsome present and give her an excellent reference. At any minute she would be coming in now. Would she be arch, would she be familiar? Or would she put on airs? Perhaps even she wouldn't trouble to come in with his letters. It would be awful if he had to ring the bell and Mrs Jeddy came in and said: Pritchard's not up yet, sir, she's having a lie in after last night.

'What a fool I've been! What a contemptible cad!'

There was a knock at the door. He was sick with anxiety.

'Come in.'

Richard Harenger was a very unhappy man.

Pritchard came in as the clock struck. She wore the print dress she was in the habit of wearing during the early part of the day.

'Good-morning, sir,' she said.

'Good-morning.'

She drew the curtains and handed him his letters and the papers. Her face was impassive. She looked exactly as she always looked. Her movements had the same competent deliberation that they always had. She neither avoided Richard's glance nor sought it.

'Will you wear your grey, sir? It came back from the tailor's yesterday.'

'Yes.'

He pretended to read his letters, but he watched her from under his eyelashes. Her back was turned to him. She took his vest and drawers and folded them over a chair. She took the studs out of the shirt he had worn the day before and studded a clean one. She put out some clean socks for him and placed them on the seat of a chair with the suspenders to match by the side. Then she put out his grey suit and attached the braces to the back buttons of the trousers. She opened his wardrobe and after a moment's reflection chose a tie to go with the suit. She collected on her arm the suit of the day before and picked up the shoes.

'Will you have breakfast now, sir, or will you have your bath first?'

'I'll have breakfast now,' he said.

'Very good, sir.'

With her slow quiet movements, unruffled, she left the room. Her face bore that rather serious, deferential, vacuous look it always bore. What had happened might have been a dream. Nothing in Pritchard's demeanour suggested that she had the smallest recollection of the night before. He gave a sigh of relief. It was going to be all right. She need not go, she need not go. Pritchard was the perfect parlourmaid. He knew that never by word nor gesture would she ever refer to the fact that for a moment their relations had been other than those of master and servant. Richard Harenger was a very happy man.

'Will you wear your grey suit for [illegible] the [illegible] yesterday?'

[illegible] went [illegible] her [illegible] back was turned [illegible] the [illegible] and [illegible] the [illegible] on [illegible] Then [illegible] put on the grey suit and [illegible] trousers [illegible] collected [illegible]

'Will you have [illegible] breakfast now [illegible]'

'[illegible] have breakfast now,' he said.

[illegible] good.'

[illegible] the [illegible] had rather [illegible] been [illegible] What had happened [illegible] a dream. Nothing [illegible] she [illegible] before [illegible] now [illegible] with [illegible] not [illegible] for a minute [illegible] had been [illegible] Richard [illegible]

Rain

It was nearly bedtime and when they awoke next morning land would be in sight. Dr Macphail lit his pipe and, leaning over the rail, searched the heavens for the Southern Cross. After two years at the front and a wound that had taken longer to heal than it should, he was glad to settle down quietly at Apia for twelve months at least, and he felt already better for the journey. Since some of the passengers were leaving the ship next day at Pago-Pago they had had a little dance that evening and in his ears hammered still the harsh notes of the mechanical piano. But the deck was quiet at last. A little way off he saw his wife in a long chair talking with the Davidsons, and he strolled over to her. When he sat down under the light and took off his hat you saw that he had very red hair, with a bald patch on the crown, and the red, freckled skin which accompanies red hair; he was a man of forty, thin, with a pinched face, precise and rather pedantic; and he spoke with a Scots accent in a very low, quiet voice.

Between the Macphails and the Davidsons, who were missionaries, there had arisen the intimacy of shipboard, which is due to propinquity rather than to any community of taste. Their chief tie was the disapproval they shared of the men who spent their days and nights in the smoking-room playing poker or bridge and drinking. Mrs Macphail was not a little flattered to think that she and her husband were the only people on board with whom the Davidsons were willing to associate, and even the doctor, shy but no fool, half unconsciously acknowledged the compliment. It was only because he was of an argumentative mind that in their cabin at night he permitted himself to carp.

'Mrs Davidson was saying she didn't know how they'd have got through the journey if it hadn't been for us,' said Mrs Macphail, as she neatly brushed out her transformation. 'She said we were really the only people on the ship they cared to know.'

'I shouldn't have thought a missionary was such a big bug that he could afford to put on frills.'

'It's not frills. I quite understand what she means. It wouldn't have been very nice for the Davidsons to have to mix with all that rough lot in the smoking-room.'

'The founder of their religion wasn't so exclusive,' said Dr Macphail with a chuckle.

'I've asked you over and over again not to joke about religion,' answered his wife. 'I shouldn't like to have a nature like yours, Alec. You never look for the best in people.'

He gave her a sidelong glance with his pale, blue eyes, but did not reply. After many years of married life he had learned that it was more conducive to peace to leave his wife with the last word. He was undressed before she was, and climbing into the upper bunk he settled down to read himself to sleep.

When he came on deck next morning they were close to land. He looked at it with greedy eyes. There was a thin strip of silver beach rising quickly to hills covered to the top with luxuriant vegetation. The coconut trees, thick and green, came nearly to the water's edge, and among them you saw the grass houses of the Samoans; and here and there, gleaming white, a little church. Mrs Davidson came and stood beside him. She was dressed in black and wore round her neck a gold chain, from which dangled a small cross. She was a little woman, with brown, dull hair very elaborately arranged, and she had prominent blue eyes behind invisible pince-nez. Her face was long, like a sheep's, but she gave no impression of foolishness, rather of extreme alertness; she had the quick movements of a bird. The most remarkable thing about her was her voice, high, metallic, and without inflection; it fell on the ear with a hard monotony, irritating to the nerves like the pitiless clamour of the pneumatic drill.

'This must seem like home to you,' said Dr Macphail, with his thin, difficult smile.

'Ours are low islands, you know, not like these. Coral. These are volcanic. We've got another ten days' journey to reach them.'

'In these parts that's almost like being in the next street at home,' said Dr Macphail facetiously.

'Well, that's rather an exaggerated way of putting it, but one does look at distances differently in the South Seas. So far you're right.'

Dr Macphail sighed faintly.

'I'm glad we're not stationed here,' she went on. 'They say this is a terribly difficult place to work in. The steamers' touching makes the people unsettled; and then there's the naval station; that's bad for the natives. In our district we don't have difficulties like that to contend with. There are one or two traders, of course, but we take care to make them behave, and if they don't we make the place so hot for them they're glad to go.'

Fixing the glasses on her nose she looked at the green island with a ruthless stare.

'It's almost a hopeless task for the missionaries here. I can never be sufficiently thankful to God that we are at least spared that.'

Davidson's district consisted of a group of islands to the north of Samoa; they were widely separated and he had frequently to go long distances by canoe. At these times his wife remained at their headquarters and managed the mission. Dr Macphail felt his heart sink when he considered the efficiency with which she certainly managed it. She spoke of the depravity of the natives in a voice which nothing could hush, but with a vehemently unctuous horror. Her sense of delicacy was singular. Early in their acquaintance she had said to him: 'You know, their marriage customs when we first settled in the islands were so shocking that I couldn't possibly describe them to you. But I'll tell Mrs Macphail and she'll tell you.'

Then he had seen his wife and Mrs Davidson, their deckchairs close together, in earnest conversation for about two hours. As he walked past them backwards and forwards for the sake of exercise, he had heard Mrs Davidson's agitated whisper, like the distant flow of a mountain torrent, and he saw by his wife's open mouth and pale face that she was enjoying an alarming experience. At night in their cabin she repeated to him with bated breath all she had heard.

'Well, what did I say to you?' cried Mrs Davidson, exultant, next morning. 'Did you ever hear anything more dreadful? You don't wonder that I couldn't tell you myself, do you? Even though you are a doctor.'

Mrs Davidson scanned his face. She had a dramatic

eagerness to see that she had achieved the desired effect.

'Can you wonder that when we first went there our hearts sank? You'll hardly believe me when I tell you it was impossible to find a single good girl in any of the villages.'

She used the word *good* in a severely technical manner.

'Mr Davidson and I talked it over, and we made up our minds the first thing to do was to put down the dancing. The natives were crazy about dancing.'

'I was not averse to it myself when I was a young man,' said Dr Macphail.

'I guessed as much when I heard you ask Mrs Macphail to have a turn with you last night. I don't think there's any real harm if a man dances with his wife, but I was relieved that she wouldn't. Under the circumstances I thought it better that we should keep ourselves to ourselves.'

'Under what circumstances?'

Mrs Davidson gave him a quick look through the pince-nez, but did not answer his question.

'But among white people it's not quite the same,' she went on, 'though I must say I agree with Mr Davidson, who says he can't understand how a husband can stand by and see his wife in another man's arms, and as far as I'm concerned I've never danced a step since I married. But the native dancing is quite another matter. It's not only immoral in itself, but it distinctly leads to immorality. However, I'm thankful to God that we stamped it out, and I don't think I'm wrong in saying that no one has danced in our district for eight years.'

But now they came to the mouth of the harbour

and Mrs Macphail joined them. The ship turned sharply and steamed slowly in. It was a great land-locked harbour big enough to hold a fleet of battle-ships; and all around it rose, high and steep, the green hills. Near the entrance, getting such breeze as blew from the sea, stood the governor's house in a garden. The Stars and Stripes dangled languidly from a flag-staff. They passed two or three trim bungalows, and a tennis court, and then they came to the quay with its warehouses. Mrs Davidson pointed out the schooner, moored two or three hundred yards from the side, which was to take them to Apia. There was a crowd of eager, noisy and good-humoured natives come from all parts of the island, some from curiosity, others to barter with the travellers on their way to Sydney; and they brought pineapples and huge bunches of bananas, *tapa* cloths, necklaces of shells or sharks' teeth, *kava*-bowls and models of war canoes. American sailors, neat and trim, clean-shaven and frank of face, sauntered among them, and there was a little group of officials. While their luggage was being landed the Macphails and Mrs Davidson watched the crowd. Dr Macphail looked at the yaws from which most of the children and the young boys seemed to suffer, dis-figuring sores like torpid ulcers, and his professional eyes glistened when he saw for the first time in his experience cases of elephantiasis, men going about with a huge, heavy arm or dragging along a grossly disfigured leg. Men and women wore the *lava-lava*.

'It's a very indecent costume,' said Mrs Davidson. 'Mr Davidson thinks it should be prohibited by law. How can you expect people to be moral when they wear nothing but a strip of red cotton round their loins?'

'It's suitable enough to the climate,' said the doctor, wiping the sweat off his head.

Now that they were on land the heat, though it was so early in the morning, was already oppressive. Closed in by its hills, not a breath of air came in to Pago-Pago.

'In our islands,' Mrs Davidson went on in her high-pitched tones, 'we've practically eradicated the *lava-lava*. A few old men still continue to wear it, but that's all. The women have all taken to the Mother Hubbard, and the men wear trousers and singlets. At the very beginning of our stay Mr Davidson said in one of his reports: the inhabitants of these islands will never be thoroughly Christianised till every boy of more than ten years is made to wear a pair of trousers.'

But Mrs Davidson had given two or three of her birdlike glances at heavy grey clouds that came floating over the mouth of the harbour. A few drops began to fall.

'We'd better take shelter,' she said.

They made their way with all the crowd to a great shed of corrugated iron, and the rain began to fall in torrents. They stood there for some time and then were joined by Mr Davidson. He had been polite enough to the Macphails during the journey, but he had not his wife's sociability, and had spent much of his time reading. He was a silent, rather sullen man, and you felt that his affability was a duty that he imposed on himself Christianly; he was by nature reserved, even morose. His appearance was singular. He was very tall and thin, with long limbs loosely jointed; hollow cheeks and curiously high cheek-bones; he had so cadaverous an air that it surprised you to notice how full and sensual were his lips. He wore his hair very long. His dark eyes, set deep in their sockets, were large and tragic; and his hands with their big, long fingers, were finely shaped; they gave him a look of great strength. But the most striking thing about him was the feeling he gave you of suppressed fire. It was impressive and vaguely troubling. He was not a man with whom any intimacy was possible.

He brought now unwelcome news. There was an epidemic of measles, a serious and often fatal disease among the Kanakas, on the island, and a case had developed among the crew of the schooner which was to take them on their journey. The sick man had been brought ashore and put in hospital on the quarantine station, but telegraphic instructions had been sent from Apia to say that the schooner would not be allowed to enter the harbour till it was certain no other member of the crew was affected.

'It means we shall have to stay here for ten days at least.'

'But I'm urgently needed at Apia,' said Dr Macphail.

'That can't be helped. If no more cases develop on board, the schooner will be allowed to sail with white passengers, but all native traffic is prohibited for three months.'

'Is there a hotel here?' asked Mrs Macphail.

Davidson gave a low chuckle.

'There's not.'

'What shall we do then?'

'I've been talking to the governor. There's a trader along the front who has rooms that he rents, and my proposition is that as soon as the rain lets up we should go along there and see what we can do. Don't expect comfort. You've just got to be thankful if we get a bed to sleep on and a roof over our heads.'

But the rain showed no sign of stopping, and at length with umbrellas and waterproofs they set out. There was no town, but merely a group of official buildings, a store or two, and at the back, among the coconut trees and plantains, a few native dwellings. The house they sought was about five minutes' walk from the wharf. It was a frame house of two storeys, with broad verandahs on both floors and a roof of corrugated iron. The owner was a half-caste named Horn, with a native wife surrounded by little brown children, and on the ground floor he had a store where he sold canned goods and cottons. The rooms he showed them were almost bare of furniture. In the Macphails' there was nothing but a poor, worn bed with a ragged mosquito net, a rickety chair and a washstand. They looked round with dismay. The rain poured down without ceasing.

'I'm not going to unpack more than we actually need,' said Mrs Macphail.

Mrs Davidson came into the room as she was unlocking a portmanteau. She was very brisk and alert. The cheerless surroundings had no effect on her.

'If you'll take my advice you'll get a needle and cotton and start right in to mend the mosquito net,' she said, 'or you'll not be able to get a wink of sleep tonight.'

'Will they be very bad?' asked Dr Macphail.

'This is the season for them. When you're asked to a party at Government House at Apia you'll notice that all the ladies are given a pillowslip to put their – their lower extremities in.'

'I wish the rain would stop for a moment,' said Mrs

Macphail. 'I could try to make the place comfortable with more heart if the sun were shining.'

'Oh, if you wait for that, you'll wait a long time. Pago-Pago is about the rainiest place in the Pacific. You see, the hills, and that bay, they attract the water, and one expects rain at this time of year anyway.'

She looked from Macphail to his wife, standing helplessly in different parts of the room, like lost souls, and she pursed her lips. She saw that she must take them in hand. Feckless people like that made her impatient, but her hands itched to put everything in order which came so naturally to her.

'Here, you give me a needle and cotton and I'll mend that net of yours, while you go on with your unpacking. Dinner's at one. Dr Macphail, you'd better go down to the wharf and see that your heavy luggage has been put in a dry place. You know what these natives are, they're quite capable of storing it where the rain will beat in on it all the time.'

The doctor put on his waterproof again and went downstairs. At the door Mr Horn was standing in conversation with the quartermaster of the ship they had just arrived on and a second-class passenger whom Dr Macphail had seen several times on board. The quartermaster, a little, shrivelled man, extremely dirty, nodded to him as he passed.

'This is a bad job about the measles, doc,' he said. 'I see you've fixed yourself up already.'

Dr Macphail thought he was rather familiar, but he was a timid man and he did not take offence easily.

'Yes, we've got a room upstairs.'

'Miss Thompson was sailing with you to Apia, so I've brought her along here.'

The quartermaster pointed with his thumb to the

woman standing by his side. She was twenty-seven perhaps, plump, and in a coarse fashion pretty. She wore a white dress and a large white hat. Her fat calves in white cotton stockings bulged over the tops of long white boots in glacé kid. She gave Macphail an ingratiating smile.

'The feller's tryin' to soak me a dollar and a half a day for the meanest-sized room,' she said in a hoarse voice.

'I tell you she's a friend of mine, Jo,' said the quartermaster. 'She can't pay more than a dollar, and you've sure got to take her for that.'

The trader was fat and smooth and quietly smiling.

'Well, if you put it like that, Mr Swan, I'll see what I can do about it. I'll talk to Mrs Horn and if we think we can make a reduction we will.'

'Don't try to pull that stuff with me,' said Miss Thompson. 'We'll settle this right now. You get a dollar a day for the room and not one bean more.'

Dr Macphail smiled. He admired the effrontery with which she bargained. He was the sort of man who always paid what he was asked. He preferred to be over-charged than to haggle.

The trader sighed. 'Well, to oblige Mr Swan I'll take it.'

'That's the goods,' said Miss Thompson. 'Come right in and have a shot of hooch. I've got some real good rye in that grip if you'll bring it along, Mr Swan. You come along too, doctor.'

'Oh, I don't think I will, thank you,' he answered. 'I'm just going down to see that our luggage is all right.'

He stepped out into the rain. It swept in from the opening of the harbour in sheets and the opposite shore was all blurred. He passed two or three natives clad in nothing but the *lava-lava*, with huge umbrellas over them. They walked finely, with leisurely movements, very upright; and they smiled and greeted him in a strange tongue as they went by.

It was nearly dinner-time when he got back, and their meal was laid in the trader's parlour. It was a room designed not to live in but for purposes of prestige, and it had a musty, melancholy air. A suite of stamped plush was arranged neatly round the walls, and from the middle of the ceiling, protected from the flies by yellow tissue paper, hung a gilt chandelier. Davidson did not come.

'I know he went to call on the governor,' said Mrs Davidson, 'and I guess he's kept him to dinner.'

A little native girl brought them a dish of hamburger steak, and after a while the trader came up to see that they had everything they wanted.

'I see we have a fellow lodger, Mr Horn,' said Dr Macphail.

'She's taken a room, that's all,' answered the trader. 'She's getting her own board.'

He looked at the two ladies with an obsequious air.

'I put her downstairs so she shouldn't be in the way. She won't be any trouble to you.'

'Is it someone who was on the boat?' asked Mrs Macphail.

'Yes, ma'am, she was in the second cabin. She was going to Apia. She has a position as cashier waiting for her.'

'Oh!'

When the trader was gone Macphail said: 'I shouldn't think she'd find it exactly cheerful having her meals in her room.'

'If she was in the second cabin I guess she'd rather,' answered Mrs Davidson. 'I don't exactly know who it can be.'

'I happened to be there when the quartermaster brought her along. Her name's Thompson.'

'It's not the woman who was dancing with the quartermaster last night?' asked Mrs Davidson.

'That's who it must be,' said Mrs Macphail. 'I wondered at the time what she was. She looked rather fast to me.'

'Not good style at all,' said Mrs Davidson.

They began to talk of other things, and after dinner, tired with their early rise, they separated and slept. When they awoke, though the sky was still grey and the clouds hung low, it was not raining and they went for a walk on the high road which the Americans had built along the bay.

On their return they found that Davidson had just come in.

'We may be here for a fortnight,' he said irritably. 'I've argued it out with the governor, but he says there is nothing to be done.'

'Mr Davidson's just longing to get back to his work,' said his wife, with an anxious glance at him.

'We've been away for a year,' he said, walking up and down the verandah. 'The mission has been in the charge of native missionaries and I'm terribly nervous that they've let things slide. They're good men, I'm not saying a word against them, God-fearing, devout, and truly Christian men – their Christianity would put many so-called Christians at home to the blush – but they're pitifully lacking in energy. They can make a stand once, they can make a stand twice, but they can't make a stand all the time. If you leave a mission in the charge of a native missionary, no matter how trustworthy he seems, in course of time you'll find he's let abuses creep in.'

Mr Davidson stood still. With his tall, spare form, and his great eyes flashing out of his pale face, he was an impressive figure. His sincerity was obvious in the fire of his gestures and in his deep, ringing voice.

'I expect to have my work cut out for me. I shall act and I shall act promptly. If the tree is rotten it shall be cut down and cast into the flames.'

And in the evening after the high tea which was their last meal, while they sat in the stiff parlour, the ladies working and Dr Macphail smoking his pipe, the missionary told them of his work in the islands.

'When we went there they had no sense of sin at all,' he said. 'They broke the Commandments one after the other and never knew they were doing wrong. And I think that was the most difficult part of my work, to instil into the natives the sense of sin.'

The Macphails knew already that Davidson had worked in the Solomons for five years before he met his wife. She had been a missionary in China, and they had become acquainted in Boston, where they were both spending part of their leave to attend a missionary congress. On their marriage they had been appointed to the islands in which they had laboured ever since.

In the course of all the conversations they had had with Mr Davidson one thing had shone out clearly and that was the man's unflinching courage. He was a medical missionary, and he was liable to be called at any time to one or other of the islands in the group. Even the whaleboat is not so very safe a conveyance in the stormy Pacific of the wet season, but often he would be sent for in a canoe, and then the danger was great. In cases of illness or accident he never hesitated. A dozen times he had spent the whole night baling for his life, and more than once Mrs Davidson had given him up for lost.

'I'd beg him not to go sometimes,' she said, 'or at least to wait till the weather was more settled, but he'd never listen. He's obstinate, and when he's once made up his mind, nothing can move him.'

'How can I ask the natives to put their trust in the Lord if I am afraid to do so myself?' cried Davidson. 'And I'm not, I'm not. They know that if they send for me in their trouble I'll come if it's humanly possible. And do you think the Lord is going to abandon me when I am on his business? The wind blows at his bidding and the waves toss and rage at his word.'

Dr Macphail was a timid man. He had never been able to get used to the hurtling of the shells over the trenches, and when he was operating in an advanced dressing-station the sweat poured from his brow and dimmed his spectacles with the effort he made to control his unsteady hand. He shuddered a little as he looked at the missionary.

'I wish I could say that I've never been afraid,' he said.

'I wish you could say that you believed in God,' retorted the other.

But for some reason, that evening the missionary's thoughts travelled back to the early days he and his wife had spent on the islands.

'Sometimes Mrs Davidson and I would look at one another and the tears would stream down our cheeks. We worked without ceasing, day and night, and we seemed to make no progress. I don't know what I should have done without her then. When I felt my heart sink, when I was very near despair, she gave me courage and hope.'

Mrs Davidson looked down at her work, and a slight colour rose to her thin cheeks. Her hands trembled a little. She did not trust herself to speak.

'We had no one to help us. We were alone, thousands of miles from any of our own people, surrounded by darkness. When I was broken and weary she would put her work aside and take the Bible and read to me till peace came and settled upon me like sleep upon the eyelids of a child, and when at last she closed the book she'd say: "We'll save them in spite of themselves." And I felt strong again in the Lord, and I answered: "Yes, with God's help I'll save them. I must save them." '

He came over to the table and stood in front of it as though it were a lectern.

'You see, they were so naturally depraved that they couldn't be brought to see their wickedness. We had to make sins out of what they thought were natural actions. We had to make it a sin, not only to commit adultery and to lie and thieve, but to expose their bodies, and to dance and not to come to church. I made it a sin for a girl to show her bosom and a sin for a man not to wear trousers.'

'How?' asked Dr Macphail, not without surprise.

'I instituted fines. Obviously the only way to make people realise that an action is sinful is to punish them if they commit it. I fined them if they didn't come to church, and I fined them if they danced. I fined them if they were improperly dressed. I had a tariff, and every sin had to be paid for either in money or work. And at last I made them understand.'

'But did they never refuse to pay?'

'How could they?' asked the missionary.

'It would be a brave man who tried to stand up against Mr Davidson,' said his wife, tightening her lips.

Dr Macphail looked at Davidson with troubled eyes. What he heard shocked him, but he hesitated to express his disapproval.

'You must remember that in the last resort I could expel them from their church membership.'

'Did they mind that?'

Davidson smiled a little and gently rubbed his hands.

'They couldn't sell their copra. When the men fished they got no share of the catch. It meant something very like starvation. Yes, they minded quite a lot.'

'Tell him about Fred Ohlson,' said Mrs Davidson.

The missionary fixed his fiery eyes on Dr Macphail.

'Fred Ohlson was a Danish trader who had been in the islands a good many years. He was a pretty rich man as traders go, and he wasn't very pleased when we came. You see, he'd had things very much his own way. He paid the natives what he liked for their copra, and he paid in goods and whisky. He had a native wife, but he was flagrantly unfaithful to her. He was a drunkard. I gave him a chance to mend his ways, but he wouldn't take it. He laughed at me.'

Davidson's voice fell to a deep bass as he said the last words, and he was silent for a minute or two. The silence was heavy with menace.

'In two years he was a ruined man. He'd lost everything he'd saved in a quarter of a century. I broke him, and at last he was forced to come to me like a beggar and beseech me to give him a passage back to Sydney.'

'I wish you could have seen him when he came to see Mr Davidson,' said the missionary's wife. 'He had been a fine, powerful man, with a lot of fat on him, and he had a great big voice, but now he was half the size, and he was shaking all over. He'd suddenly become an old man.'

With abstracted gaze Davidson looked out into the night. The rain was falling again.

Suddenly from below came a sound, and Davidson turned and looked questioningly at his wife. It was the sound of a gramophone, harsh and loud, wheezing out a syncopated tune.

'What's that?' he asked.

Mrs Davidson fixed her pince-nez more firmly on her nose.

'One of the second-class passengers has a room in the house. I guess it comes from there.'

They listened in silence, and presently they heard the sound of dancing. Then the music stopped, and they heard the popping of corks and voices raised in animated conversation.

'I dare say she's giving a farewell party to her friends on board,' said Dr Macphail. 'The ship sails at twelve, doesn't it?'

Davidson made no remark, but he looked at his watch.

'Are you ready?' he asked his wife.

She got up and folded her work.

'Yes, I guess I am,' she answered.

'It's early to go to bed yet, isn't it?' said the doctor.

'We have a good deal of reading to do,' explained

Mrs Davidson. 'Wherever we are, we read a chapter of the Bible before retiring for the night and we study it with the commentaries, you know, and discuss it thoroughly. It's a wonderful training for the mind.'

The two couples bade one another good-night. Dr and Mrs Macphail were left alone. For two or three minutes they did not speak.

'I think I'll go and fetch the cards,' the doctor said at last.

Mrs Macphail looked at him doubtfully. Her conversation with the Davidsons had left her a little uneasy, but she did not like to say that she thought they had better not play cards when the Davidsons might come in at any moment. Dr Macphail brought them and she watched him, though with a vague sense of guilt, while he laid out his patience. Below the sound of revelry continued.

It was fine enough next day, and the Macphails, condemned to spend a fortnight of idleness at Pago-Pago, set about making the best of things. They went down to the quay and got out of their boxes a number of books. The doctor called on the chief surgeon of the naval hospital and went round the beds with him. They left cards on the governor. They passed Miss Thompson on the road. The doctor took off his hat, and she gave him a, 'Good-morning, doc,' in a loud, cheerful voice. She was dressed as on the day before, in a white frock, and her shiny white boots with their high heels, her fat legs bulging over the tops of them, were strange things in that exotic scene.

'I don't think she's very suitably dressed, I must say,' said Mrs Macphail. 'She looks extremely common to me.'

When they got back to their house, she was on the verandah playing with one of the trader's dark children.

'Say a word to her,' Dr Macphail whispered to his wife. 'She's all alone here, and it seems rather unkind to ignore her.'

Mrs Macphail was shy, but she was in the habit of doing what her husband bade her.

'I think we're fellow lodgers here,' she said, rather foolishly.

'Terrible, ain't it, bein' cooped up in a one-horse burg like this?' answered Miss Thompson. 'And they tell me I'm lucky to have gotten a room. I don't see myself livin' in a native house, and that's what some have to do. I don't know why they don't have a hotel.'

They exchanged a few more words. Miss Thompson, loud-voiced and garrulous, was evidently quite willing to gossip, but Mrs Macphail had a poor stock of small talk and presently she said: 'Well, I think we must go upstairs.'

In the evening when they sat down to their high-tea Davidson on coming in said: 'I see that woman downstairs has a couple of sailors sitting there. I wonder how she's gotten acquainted with them.'

'She can't be very particular,' said Mrs Davidson.

They were all rather tired after the idle, aimless day.

'If there's going to be a fortnight of this I don't know what we shall feel like at the end of it,' said Dr Macphail.

'The only thing to do is to portion out the day to different activities,' answered the missionary. 'I shall set aside a certain number of hours to study and a certain number to exercise, rain or fine – in the wet season you can't afford to pay any attention to the rain – and a certain number to recreation.'

Dr Macphail looked at his companion with misgiving. Davidson's programme oppressed him. They were eating hamburger steak again. It seemed the only dish the cook knew how to make. Then below the gramophone began. Davidson started nervously when he heard it, but said nothing. Men's voices floated up. Miss Thompson's guests were joining in a well-known song and presently they heard her voice too, hoarse and loud. There was a good deal of shouting and laughing. The four people upstairs, trying to make conversation, listened despite themselves to the clink of glasses and the scrape of chairs. More people had evidently come. Miss Thompson was giving a party.

'I wonder how she gets them all in,' said Mrs Macphail, suddenly breaking into a medical conversation between the missionary and her husband.

It showed whither her thoughts were wandering. The twitch of Davidson's face proved that, though he spoke of scientific things, his mind was busy in the same direction. Suddenly, while the doctor was giving some experience of practice on the Flanders front, rather prosily, he sprang to his feet with a cry.

'What's the matter, Alfred?' asked Mrs Davidson.

'Of course! It never occurred to me. She's out of Iwelei.'

'She can't be.'

'She came on board at Honolulu. It's obvious. And she's carrying on her trade here. Here.'

He uttered the last word with a passion of indignation.

'What's Iwelei?' asked Mrs Macphail.

He turned his gloomy eyes on her and his voice trembled with horror.

'The plague spot of Honolulu. The red-light district. It was a blot on our civilisation.'

Iwelei was on the edge of the city. You went down side streets by the harbour, in the darkness, across a rickety bridge, till you came to a deserted road, all ruts and holes, and then suddenly you came out into the light. There was parking room for motors on each side of the road, and there were saloons, tawdry and bright, each one noisy with its mechanical piano, and there were barbers' shops and tobacconists. There was a stir in the air and a sense of expectant gaiety. You turned down a narrow alley, either to the right or to the left, for the road divided Iwelei into two parts, and you found yourself in the district. There were rows of little bungalows, trim and neatly painted in green, and the pathway between them was broad and straight. It was laid out like a garden-city. In its respectable regularity, its order and spruceness, it gave an impression of sardonic horror; for never can the search for love have been so systematised and ordered. The pathways were lit by a rare lamp, but they would have been dark except for the lights that came from the open windows of the bungalows. Men wandered about, looking at the women who sat at their windows, reading or sewing, for the most part taking no notice of the passers-by; and like the women they were of all nationalities. There were Americans, sailors from the ships in port, enlisted men off the gunboats, sombrely drunk, and soldiers from the regiments, white and black, quartered on the island; there were Japanese, walking in twos and threes; Hawaiians, Chinese in long robes, and Filipinos in preposterous hats. They were silent and as it were oppressed. Desire is sad.

'It was the most crying scandal of the Pacific,'

exclaimed Davidson vehemently. 'The missionaries had been agitating against it for years, and at last the local press took it up. The police refused to stir. You know their argument. They say that vice is inevitable and consequently the best thing is to localise and control it. The truth is, they were paid. Paid. They were paid by the saloon-keepers, paid by the bullies, paid by the women themselves. At last they were forced to move.'

'I read about it in the papers that came on board at Honolulu,' said Dr Macphail.

'Iwelei, with its sin and shame, ceased to exist on the very day we arrived. The whole population was brought before the justices. I don't know why I didn't understand at once what that woman was.'

'Now you come to speak of it,' said Mrs Macphail, 'I remember seeing her come on board only a few minutes before the boat sailed. I remember thinking at the time she was cutting it rather fine.'

'How dare she come here!' cried Davidson indignantly. 'I'm not going to allow it.'

He strode towards the door.

'What are you going to do?' asked Macphail.

'What do you expect me to do? I'm going to stop it. I'm not going to have this house turned into – into . . . '

He sought for a word that should not offend the ladies' ears. His eyes were flashing and his pale face was paler still in his emotion.

'It sounds as though there were three or four men down there,' said the doctor. 'Don't you think it's rather rash to go in just now?'

The missionary gave him a contemptuous look and without a word flung out of the room.

'You know Mr Davidson very little if you think the fear of personal danger can stop him in the performance of his duty,' said his wife.

She sat with her hands nervously clasped, a spot of colour on her high cheekbones, listening to what was about to happen below. They all listened. They heard him clatter down the wooden stairs and throw open the door. The singing stopped suddenly, but the gramophone continued to bray out its vulgar tune. They heard Davidson's voice and then the noise of something heavy falling. The music stopped. He had hurled the gramophone on the floor. Then again they heard Davidson's voice, they could not make out the words, then Miss Thompson's, loud and shrill, then a confused clamour as though several people were shouting together at the top of their lungs. Mrs Davidson gave a little gasp, and she clenched her hands more tightly. Dr Macphail looked uncertainly from her to his wife. He did not want to go down, but he wondered if they expected him to. Then there was something that sounded like a scuffle. The noise now was more distinct. It might be that Davidson was being thrown out of the room. The door was slammed. There was a moment's silence and they heard Davidson come up the stairs again. He went to his room.

'I think I'll go to him,' said Mrs Davidson.

She got up and went out.

'If you want me, just call,' said Mrs Macphail, and then when the other was gone: 'I hope he isn't hurt.'

'Why couldn't he mind his own business?' said Dr Macphail.

They sat in silence for a minute or two and then

they both started, for the gramophone began to play once more, defiantly, and mocking voices shouted hoarsely the words of an obscene song.

Next day Mrs Davidson was pale and tired. She complained of headache, and she looked old and wizened. She told Mrs Macphail that the missionary had not slept at all; he had passed the night in a state of frightful agitation and at five had got up and gone out. A glass of beer had been thrown over him and his clothes were stained and stinking. But a sombre fire glowed in Mrs Davidson's eyes when she spoke of Miss Thompson.

'She'll bitterly rue the day she flouted Mr Davidson,' she said. 'Mr Davidson has a wonderful heart and no one who is in trouble has ever gone to him without being comforted, but he has no mercy for sin, and when his righteous wrath is excited he's terrible.'

'Why, what will he do?' asked Mrs Macphail.

'I don't know, but I wouldn't stand in that creature's shoes for anything in the world.'

Mrs Macphail shuddered. There was something positively alarming in the triumphant assurance of the little woman's manner. They were going out together that morning, and they went down the stairs side by side. Miss Thompson's door was open, and they saw her in a bedraggled dressing-gown, cooking something in a chafing-dish.

'Good-morning,' she called. 'Is Mr Davidson better this morning?'

They passed her in silence, with their noses in the air, as if she did not exist. They flushed, however, when she burst into a shout of derisive laughter. Mrs Davidson turned on her suddenly.

'Don't you dare to speak to me,' she screamed. 'If you insult me I shall have you turned out of here.'

'Say, did I ask Mr Davidson to visit with me?'

'Don't answer her,' whispered Mrs Macphail hurriedly.

They walked on till they were out of earshot.

'She's brazen, brazen,' burst from Mrs Davidson. Her anger almost suffocated her.

And on their way home they met her strolling towards the quay. She had all her finery on. Her great white hat with its vulgar, showy flowers was an affront. She called out cheerily to them as she went by, and a couple of American sailors who were standing there grinned as the ladies set their faces to an icy stare. They got in just before the rain began to fall again.

'I guess she'll get her fine clothes spoilt,' said Mrs Davidson with a bitter sneer.

Davidson did not come in till they were halfway through dinner. He was wet through, but he would not change. He sat, morose and silent, refusing to eat more than a mouthful, and he stared at the slanting rain. When Mrs Davidson told him of their two encounters with Miss Thompson he did not answer. His deepening frown alone showed that he had heard.

'Don't you think we ought to make Mr Horn turn her out of here?' asked Mrs Davidson. 'We can't allow her to insult us.'

'There doesn't seem to be any other place for her to go,' said Macphail.

'She can live with one of the natives.'

'In weather like this a native hut must be a rather uncomfortable place to live in.'

'I lived in one for years,' said the missionary.

When the little native girl brought in the fried bananas which formed the sweet they had every day, Davidson turned to her.

'Ask Miss Thompson when it would be convenient for me to see her,' he said.

The girl nodded shyly and went out.

'What do you want to see her for, Alfred?' asked his wife.

'It's my duty to see her. I won't act till I've given her every chance.'

'You don't know what she is. She'll insult you.'

'Let her insult me. Let her spit on me. She has an immortal soul, and I must do all that is in my power to save it.'

Mrs Davidson's ears rang still with the harlot's mocking laughter.

'She's gone too far.'

'Too far for the mercy of God?' His eyes lit up suddenly and his voice grew mellow and soft. 'Never. The sinner may be deeper in sin than the depth of hell itself, but the love of the Lord Jesus can reach him still.'

The girl came back with the message.

'Miss Thompson's compliments and as long as Reverend Davidson don't come in business hours she'll be glad to see him any time.'

The party received it in stony silence, and Dr Macphail quickly effaced from his lips the smile which had come upon them. He knew his wife would be vexed with him if he found Miss Thompson's effrontery amusing.

They finished the meal in silence. When it was over the two ladies rose and took up their work. Mrs

Macphail was making another of the innumerable comforters which she had turned out since the beginning of the war, and the doctor lit his pipe. But Davidson remained in his chair and with abstracted eyes stared at the table. At last he got up and without a word went out of the room. They heard him go down and they heard Miss Thompson's defiant 'Come in' when he knocked at the door. He remained with her for an hour. And Dr Macphail watched the rain. It was beginning to get on his nerves. It was not like our soft English rain that drops gently on the earth; it was unmerciful and somehow terrible; you felt in it the malignancy of the primitive powers of nature. It did not pour, it flowed. It was like a deluge from heaven, and it rattled on the roof of corrugated iron with a steady persistence that was maddening. It seemed to have a fury of its own. And sometimes you felt that you must scream if it did not stop, and then suddenly you felt powerless, as though your bones had suddenly become soft; and you were miserable and hopeless.

Macphail turned his head when the missionary came back. The two women looked up.

'I've given her every chance. I have exhorted her to repent. She is an evil woman.'

He paused, and Dr Macphail saw his eyes darken and his pale face grow hard and stern.

'Now I shall take the whips with which the Lord Jesus drove the usurers and the money changers out of the Temple of the Most High.'

He walked up and down the room. His mouth was close set, and his black brows were frowning.

'If she fled to the uttermost parts of the earth I should pursue her.'

With a sudden movement he turned round and strode out of the room. They heard him go downstairs again.

'What is he going to do?' asked Mrs Macphail.

'I don't know.' Mrs Davidson took off her pince-nez and wiped them. 'When he is on the Lord's work I never ask him questions.'

She sighed a little.

'What is the matter?'

'He'll wear himself out. He doesn't know what it is to spare himself.'

Dr Macphail learnt the first results of the missionary's activity from the half-caste trader in whose house they lodged. He stopped the doctor when he passed the store and came out to speak to him on the stoop. His fat face was worried.

'The Reverend Davidson has been at me for letting Miss Thompson have a room here,' he said, 'but I didn't know what she was when I rented it to her. When people come and ask if I can rent them a room all I want to know is if they've the money to pay for it. And she paid me for hers a week in advance.'

Dr Macphail did not want to commit himself.

'When all's said and done it's your house. We're very much obliged to you for taking us in at all.'

Horn looked at him doubtfully. He was not certain yet how definitely Macphail stood on the missionary's side.

'The missionaries are in with one another,' he said, hesitatingly. 'If they get it in for a trader he may just as well shut up his store and quit.'

'Did he want you to turn her out?'

'No, he said so long as she behaved herself he couldn't ask me to do that. He said he wanted to be just to me. I promised she wouldn't have no more visitors. I've just been and told her.'

'How did she take it?'

'She gave me hell.'

The trader squirmed in his old ducks. He had found Miss Thompson a rough customer.

'Oh, well, I dare say she'll get out. I don't suppose she wants to stay here if she can't have anyone in.'

'There's nowhere she can go, only a native house, and no native'll take her now, not now that the missionaries have got their knife in her.'

Dr Macphail looked at the falling rain.

'Well, I don't suppose it's any good waiting for it to clear up.'

In the evening when they sat in the parlour Davidson talked to them of his early days at college. He had had no means and had worked his way through by doing odd jobs during the vacations. There was silence downstairs. Miss Thompson was sitting in her little room alone. But suddenly the gramophone began to play. She had set it on in defiance, to cheat her loneliness, but there was no one to sing, and it had a melancholy note. It was like a cry for help. Davidson took no notice. He was in the middle of a long anecdote and without change of expression went on. The gramophone continued. Miss Thompson put on one reel after another. It looked as though the silence of the night were getting on her nerves. It was breathless and sultry. When the Macphails went to bed they could not sleep. They lay side by side with their eyes wide open, listening to the cruel singing of the mosquitoes outside their curtain.

'What's that?' whispered Mrs Macphail at last.

They heard a voice, Davidson's voice, through the

wooden partition. It went on with a monotonous, earnest insistence. He was praying aloud. He was praying for the soul of Miss Thompson.

Two or three days went by. Now when they passed Miss Thompson on the road she did not greet them with ironic cordiality or smile; she passed with her nose in the air, a sulky look on her painted face, frowning, as though she did not see them. The trader told Macphail that she had tried to get lodging elsewhere, but had failed. In the evening she played through the various reels of her gramophone, but the pretence of mirth was obvious now. The ragtime had a cracked, heartbroken rhythm as though it were a one-step of despair. When she began to play on Sunday, Davidson sent Horn to beg her to stop at once since it was the Lord's day. The reel was taken off and the house was silent except for the steady pattering of the rain on the iron roof.

'I think she's getting a bit worked up,' said the trader next day to Macphail. 'She don't know what Mr Davidson's up to and it makes her scared.'

Macphail had caught a glimpse of her that morning and it struck him that her arrogant expression had changed. There was in her face a hunted look. The half-caste gave him a sidelong glance.

'I suppose you don't know what Mr Davidson is doing about it?' he hazarded.

'No, I don't.'

It was singular that Horn should ask him that question, for he also had the idea that the missionary was mysteriously at work. He had an impression that he was weaving a net around the woman, carefully, systematically, and suddenly, when everything was ready, would pull the strings tight.

'He told me to tell her,' said the trader, 'that if at any time she wanted him she only had to send and he'd come.'

'What did she say when you told her that?'

'She didn't say nothing. I didn't stop. I just said what he said I was to and then I beat it. I thought she might be going to start weepin'.'

'I have no doubt the loneliness is getting on her nerves,' said the doctor. 'And the rain – that's enough to make anyone jumpy,' he continued irritably. 'Doesn't it ever stop in this confounded place?'

'It goes on pretty steady in the rainy season. We have three hundred inches in the year. You see, it's the shape of the bay. It seems to attract the rain from all over the Pacific.'

'Damn the shape of the bay,' said the doctor.

He scratched his mosquito bites. He felt very short-tempered. When the rain stopped and the sun shone, it was like a hot-house, seething, humid, sultry, breathless, and you had a strange feeling that everything was growing with a savage violence. The natives, blithe and childlike by reputation, seemed then, with their tattooing and their dyed hair, to have something sinister in their appearance; and when they pattered along at your heels with their naked feet you looked back instinctively. You felt they might at any moment come behind you swiftly and thrust a long knife between your shoulder blades. You could not tell what dark thoughts lurked behind their wide-set eyes. They had a little the look of ancient Egyptians painted on a temple wall, and there was about them the terror of what is immeasurably old.

The missionary came and went. He was busy, but the Macphails did not know what he was doing. Horn told the doctor that he saw the governor every day, and once Davidson mentioned him.

'He looks as if he had plenty of determination,' he said, 'but when you come down to brass tacks he has no backbone.'

'I suppose that means he won't do exactly what you want,' suggested the doctor facetiously.

The missionary did not smile.

'I want him to do what's right. It shouldn't be necessary to persuade a man to do that.'

'But there may be differences of opinion about what is right.'

'If a man had a gangrenous foot would you have patience with anyone who hesitated to amputate it?'

'Gangrene is a matter of fact.'

'And Evil?'

What Davidson had done soon appeared. The four of them had just finished their midday meal, and they had not yet separated for the siesta which the heat imposed on the ladies and on the doctor. Davidson had little patience with the slothful habit. The door was suddenly flung open and Miss Thompson came in. She looked round the room and then went up to Davidson.

'You low-down skunk, what have you been saying about me to the governor?'

She was spluttering with rage. There was a moment's pause. Then the missionary drew forward a chair.

'Won't you be seated, Miss Thompson? I've been hoping to have another talk with you.'

'You poor low-life bastard.'

She burst into a torrent of insult, foul and insolent. Davidson kept his grave eyes on her.

'I'm indifferent to the abuse you think fit to heap

on me, Miss Thompson,' he said, 'but I must beg you to remember that ladies are present.'

Tears by now were struggling with her anger. Her face was red and swollen as though she were choking.

'What has happened?' asked Dr Macphail.

'A feller's just been in here and he says I gotter beat it on the next boat.'

Was there a gleam in the missionary's eyes? His face remained impassive.

'You could hardly expect the governor to let you stay here under the circumstances.'

'You done it,' she shrieked. 'You can't kid me. You done it.'

'I don't want to deceive you. I urged the governor to take the only possible step consistent with his obligations.'

'Why couldn't you leave me be? I wasn't doin' you no harm.'

'You may be sure that if you had I should be the last man to resent it.'

'Do you think I want to stay on in this poor imitation of a burg? I don't look no busher, do I?'

'In that case I don't see what cause of complaint you have,' he answered.

She gave an inarticulate cry of rage and flung out of the room. There was a short silence.

'It's a relief to know that the governor has acted at last,' said Davidson finally. 'He's a weak man and he shilly-shallied. He said she was only here for a fortnight anyway, and if she went on to Apia that was under British jurisdiction and had nothing to do with him.'

The missionary sprang to his feet and strode across the room.

'It's terrible the way the men who are in authority seek to evade their responsibility. They speak as though evil that was out of sight ceased to be evil. The very existence of that woman is a scandal and it does not help matters to shift it to another of the islands. In the end I had to speak straight from the shoulder.'

Davidson's brow lowered, and he protruded his firm chin. He looked fierce and determined.

'What do you mean by that?'

'Our mission is not entirely without influence at Washington. I pointed out to the governor that it wouldn't do him any good if there was a complaint about the way he managed things here.'

'When has she got to go?' asked the doctor, after a pause.

'The San Francisco boat is due here from Sydney next Tuesday. She's to sail on that.'

That was in five days' time. It was next day, when he was coming back from the hospital where for want of something better to do Macphail spent most of his mornings, that the half-caste stopped him as he was going upstairs.

'Excuse me, Dr Macphail, Miss Thompson's sick. Will you have a look at her?'

'Certainly.'

Horn led him to her room. She was sitting in a chair idly, neither reading nor sewing, staring in front of her. She wore her white dress and the large hat with the flowers on it. Macphail noticed that her skin was yellow and muddy under her powder, and her eyes were heavy.

'I'm sorry to hear you're not well,' he said.

'Oh, I ain't sick really. I just said that, because I

just had to see you. I've got to clear on a boat that's going to 'Frisco.'

She looked at him and he saw that her eyes were suddenly startled. She opened and clenched her hands spasmodically. The trader stood at the door, listening.

'So I understand,' said the doctor.

She gave a little gulp.

'I guess it ain't very convenient for me to go to 'Frisco just now. I went to see the governor yesterday afternoon, but I couldn't get to him. I saw the secretary, and he told me I'd got to take that boat and that was all there was to it. I just had to see the governor, so I waited outside his house this morning, and when he come out I spoke to him. He didn't want to speak to me, I'll say, but I wouldn't let him shake me off, and at last he said he hadn't no objection to my staying here till the next boat to Sydney if the Reverend Davidson will stand for it.'

She stopped and looked at Dr Macphail anxiously.

'I don't know exactly what I can do,' he said.

'Well, I thought maybe you wouldn't mind asking him. I swear to God I won't start anything here if he'll just only let me stay. I won't go out of the house if that'll suit him. It's no more'n a fortnight.'

'I'll ask him.'

'He won't stand for it,' said Horn. 'He'll have you out on Tuesday, so you may as well make up your mind to it.'

'Tell him I can get work in Sydney, straight stuff, I mean. 'Tain't asking very much.'

'I'll do what I can.'

'And come and tell me right away, will you? I can't set down to a thing till I get the dope one way or the other.'

It was not an errand that much pleased the doctor, and, characteristically perhaps, he went about it indirectly. He told his wife what Miss Thompson had said to him and asked her to speak to Mrs Davidson. The missionary's attitude seemed rather arbitrary and it could do no harm if the girl were allowed to stay in Pago-Pago another fortnight. But he was not prepared for the result of his diplomacy. The missionary came to him straightway.

'Mrs Davidson tells me that Thompson has been speaking to you.'

Dr Macphail, thus directly tackled, had the shy man's resentment at being forced out into the open. He felt his temper rising, and he flushed.

'I don't see that it can make any difference if she goes to Sydney rather than to San Francisco, and so long as she promises to behave while she's here it's dashed hard to persecute her.'

The missionary fixed him with his stern eyes.

'Why is she unwilling to go back to San Francisco?'

'I didn't enquire,' answered the doctor with some asperity. 'And I think one does better to mind one's own business.'

Perhaps it was not a very tactful answer.

'The governor has ordered her to be deported by the first boat that leaves the island. He's only done his duty and I will not interfere. Her presence is a peril here.'

'I think you're very harsh and tyrannical.'

The two ladies looked up at the doctor with some alarm, but they need not have feared a quarrel, for the missionary smiled gently.

'I'm terribly sorry you should think that of me, Dr Macphail. Believe me, my heart bleeds for that unfortunate woman, but I'm only trying to do my duty.'

The doctor made no answer. He looked out of the window sullenly. For once it was not raining and across the bay you saw nestling among the trees the huts of a native village.

'I think I'll take advantage of the rain stopping to go out,' he said.

'Please don't bear me malice because I can't accede to your wish,' said Davidson, with a melancholy smile. 'I respect you very much, doctor, and I should be sorry if you thought ill of me.'

'I have no doubt you have a sufficiently good opinion of yourself to bear mine with equanimity,' he retorted.

'That's one on me,' chuckled Davidson.

When Dr Macphail, vexed with himself because he had been uncivil to no purpose, went downstairs, Miss Thompson was waiting for him with her door ajar.

'Well,' she said, 'have you spoken to him?'

'Yes, I'm sorry, he won't do anything,' he answered, not looking at her in his embarrassment.

But then he gave her a quick glance, for a sob broke from her. He saw that her face was white with fear. It gave him a shock of dismay. And suddenly he had an idea.

'But don't give up hope yet. I think it's a shame the way they're treating you and I'm going to see the governor myself.'

'Now?'

He nodded.

Her face brightened. 'Say, that's real good of you. I'm sure he'll let me stay if you speak for me. I just won't do a thing I didn't ought all the time I'm here.'

Dr Macphail hardly knew why he had made up his mind to appeal to the governor. He was perfectly indifferent to Miss Thompson's affairs, but the missionary had irritated him, and with him temper was a smouldering thing. He found the governor at home. He was a large, handsome man, a sailor, with a grey toothbrush moustache; and he wore a spotless uniform of white drill.

'I've come to see you about a woman who's lodging in the same house as we are,' he said. 'Her name's Thompson.'

'I guess I've heard nearly enough about her, Dr Macphail,' said the governor, smiling. 'I've given her the order to get out next Tuesday and that's all I can do.'

'I wanted to ask you if you couldn't stretch a point and let her stay here till the boat comes in from San Francisco so that she can go to Sydney. I will guarantee her good behaviour.'

The governor continued to smile, but his eyes grew small and serious.

'I'd be very glad to oblige you, Dr Macphail, but I've given the order and it must stand.'

The doctor put the case as reasonably as he could, but now the governor ceased to smile at all. He listened sullenly, with averted gaze. Macphail saw that he was making no impression.

'I'm sorry to cause any lady inconvenience, but she'll have to sail on Tuesday and that's all there is to it.'

'But what difference can it make?'

'Pardon me, doctor, but I don't feel called upon to explain my official actions except to the proper authorities.'

Macphail looked at him shrewdly. He remembered Davidson's hint that he had used threats, and in the governor's attitude he read a singular embarrassment.

'Davidson's a damned busybody,' he said hotly.

'Between ourselves, Dr Macphail, I don't say that I have formed a very favourable opinion of Mr Davidson, but I am bound to confess that he was within his rights in pointing out to me the danger that the presence of a woman of Miss Thompson's character was to a place like this where a number of enlisted men are stationed among a native population.' He got up and Dr Macphail was obliged to do so too. 'I must ask you to excuse me. I have an engagement. Please give my respects to Mrs Macphail.'

The doctor left him crestfallen. He knew that Miss Thompson would be waiting for him, and unwilling to tell her himself that he had failed, he went into the house by the back door and sneaked up the stairs as though he had something to hide.

At supper he was silent and ill-at-ease, but the missionary was jovial and animated. Dr Macphail thought his eyes rested on him now and then with triumphant good-humour. It struck him suddenly that Davidson knew of his visit to the governor and of its ill success. But how on earth could he have heard of it? There was something sinister about the power of that man. After supper he saw Horn on the verandah and, as though to have a casual word with him, went out.

'She wants to know if you've seen the governor,' the trader whispered.

'Yes. He wouldn't do anything. I'm awfully sorry, I can't do anything more.'

'I knew he wouldn't. They daren't go against the missionaries.'

'What are you talking about?' said Davidson affably, coming out to join them.

'I was just saying there was no chance of your getting over to Apia for at least another week,' said the trader glibly.

He left them, and the two men returned to the parlour. Mr Davidson devoted one hour after each meal to recreation. Presently a timid knock was heard at the door.

'Come in,' said Mrs Davidson, in her sharp voice.

The door was not opened. She got up and opened it. They saw Miss Thompson standing at the threshold. But the change in her appearance was extraordinary. This was no longer the flaunting hussy who had jeered at them in the road, but a broken, frightened woman. Her hair, as a rule so elaborately arranged, was tumbling untidily over her neck. She wore bedroom slippers and a skirt and blouse. They were unfresh and bedraggled. She stood at the door with the tears streaming down her face and did not dare to enter.

'What do you want?' said Mrs Davidson harshly.

'May I speak to Mr Davidson?' she said in a choking voice.

The missionary rose and went towards her.

'Come right in, Miss Thompson,' he said in cordial tones. 'What can I do for you?'

She entered the room.

'Say, I'm sorry for what I said to you the other day an' for – for everythin' else. I guess I was a bit lit up. I beg pardon.'

'Oh, it was nothing. I guess my back's broad enough to bear a few hard words.'

She stepped towards him with a movement that was horribly cringing.

'You've got me beat. I'm all in. You won't make me go back to 'Frisco?'

His genial manner vanished and his voice grew on a sudden hard and stern.

'Why don't you want to go back there?'

She cowered before him.

'I guess my people live there. I don't want them to see me like this. I'll go anywhere else you say.'

'Why don't you want to go back to San Francisco?'

'I've told you.'

He leaned forward, staring at her, and his great, shining eyes seemed to try to bore into her soul. He gave a sudden gasp.

'The penitentiary.'

She screamed, and then she fell at his feet, clasping his legs.

'Don't send me back there. I swear to you before God I'll be a good woman. I'll give all this up.'

She burst into a torrent of confused supplication and the tears coursed down her painted cheeks. He leaned over her and, lifting her face, forced her to look at him.

'Is that it, the penitentiary?'

'I beat it before they could get me,' she gasped. 'If the bulls grab me it's three years for mine.'

He let go his hold of her and she fell in a heap on the floor, sobbing bitterly.

Dr Macphail stood up. 'This alters the whole thing,' he said. 'You can't make her go back when you know this. Give her another chance. She wants to turn over a new leaf.'

'I'm going to give her the finest chance she's ever had. If she repents let her accept her punishment.'

She misunderstood the words and looked up. There was a gleam of hope in her heavy eyes.

'You'll let me go?'

'No. You shall sail for San Francisco on Tuesday.'

She gave a groan of horror and then burst into low, hoarse shrieks which sounded hardly human, and she beat her head passionately on the ground. Dr Macphail sprang to her and lifted her up. 'Come on, you mustn't do that. You'd better go to your room and lie down. I'll get you something.'

He raised her to her feet and partly dragging her, partly carrying her, got her downstairs. He was furious with Mrs Davidson and with his wife because they made no effort to help. The half-caste was standing on the landing and with his assistance he managed to get her on the bed. She was moaning and crying. She was almost insensible. He gave her a hypodermic injection. He was hot and exhausted when he went upstairs again.

'I've got her to lie down.'

The two women and Davidson were in the same positions as when he had left them. They could not have moved or spoken since he went.

'I was waiting for you,' said Davidson, in a strange, distant voice. 'I want you all to pray with me for the soul of our erring sister.'

He took the Bible off a shelf, and sat down at the table at which they had supped. It had not been cleared, and he pushed the teapot out of the way. In a powerful voice, resonant and deep, he read to them the chapter in which is narrated the meeting of Jesus Christ with the woman taken in adultery.

'Now kneel with me and let us pray for the soul of our dear sister, Sadie Thompson.'

He burst into a long, passionate prayer in which he implored God to have mercy on the sinful woman.

Mrs Macphail and Mrs Davidson knelt with covered eyes. The doctor, taken by surprise, awkward and sheepish, knelt too. The missionary's prayer had a savage eloquence. He was extraordinarily moved, and as he spoke the tears ran down his cheeks. Outside, the pitiless rain fell, fell steadily, with a fierce malignity that was all too human.

At last he stopped. He paused for a moment and said: 'We will now repeat the Lord's prayer.'

They said it and then, following him, they rose from their knees. Mrs Davidson's face was pale and restful. She was comforted and at peace, but the Macphails felt suddenly bashful. They did not know which way to look.

'I'll just go down and see how she is now,' said Dr Macphail.

When he knocked at her door it was opened for him by Horn. Miss Thompson was in a rocking-chair, sobbing quietly.

'What are you doing there?' exclaimed Macphail. 'I told you to lie down.'

'I can't lie down. I want to see Mr Davidson.'

'My poor child, what do you think is the good of it? You'll never move him.'

'He said he'd come if I sent for him.'

Macphail motioned to the trader.

'Go and fetch him.'

He waited with her in silence while the trader went upstairs.

Davidson came in.

'Excuse me for asking you to come here,' she said, looking at him sombrely.

'I was expecting you to send for me. I knew the Lord would answer my prayer.'

They stared at one another for a moment and then she looked away. She kept her eyes averted when she spoke.

'I've been a bad woman. I wanted to repent.'

'Thank God! thank God! He has heard our prayers.'

He turned to the two men.

'Leave me alone with her. Tell Mrs Davidson that our prayers have been answered.'

They went out and closed the door behind them.

'Gee whizz,' said the trader.

That night Dr Macphail could not get to sleep till late, and when he heard the missionary come upstairs he looked at his watch. It was two o'clock. But even then he did not go to bed at once, for through the wooden partition that separated their rooms he heard him praying aloud, till he himself, exhausted, fell asleep.

When he saw him next morning he was surprised at his appearance. He was paler than ever, tired, but his eyes shone with an inhuman fire. It looked as though he were filled with an overwhelming joy.

'I want you to go down presently and see Sadie,' he said. 'I can't hope that her body is better, but her soul – her soul is transformed.'

The doctor was feeling wan and nervous.

'You were with her very late last night,' he said.

'Yes, she couldn't bear to have me leave her.'

'You look as pleased as Punch,' the doctor said irritably.

Davidson's eyes shone with ecstasy.

'A great mercy has been vouchsafed me. Last night I was privileged to bring a lost soul to the loving arms of Jesus.'

Miss Thompson was again in the rocking-chair.

The bed had not been made. The room was in disorder. She had not troubled to dress herself, but wore a dirty dressing-gown, and her hair was tied in a sluttish knot. She had given her face a dab with a wet towel, but it was all swollen and creased with crying. She looked a drab.

She raised her eyes dully when the doctor came in. She was cowed and broken.

'Where's Mr Davidson?' she asked.

'He'll come presently if you want him,' answered Macphail acidly. 'I came here to see how you were.'

'Oh, I guess I'm OK. You needn't worry about that.'

'Have you had anything to eat?'

'Horn brought me some coffee.'

She looked anxiously at the door.

'D'you think he'll come down soon? I feel as if it wasn't so terrible when he's with me.'

'Are you still going on Tuesday?'

'Yes, he says I've got to go. Please tell him to come right along. You can't do me any good. He's the only one as can help me now.'

'Very well,' said Dr Macphail.

During the next three days the missionary spent almost all his time with Sadie Thompson. He joined the others only to have his meals. Dr Macphail noticed that he hardly ate.

'He's wearing himself out,' said Mrs Davidson pitifully. 'He'll have a breakdown if he doesn't take care, but he won't spare himself.'

She herself was white and pale. She told Mrs Macphail that she had had no sleep. When the missionary came upstairs from Miss Thompson he prayed till he was exhausted, but even then he did not sleep for long. After an hour or two he got up and dressed himself, and went for a tramp along the bay. He had strange dreams.

'This morning he told me that he'd been dreaming about the mountains of Nebraska,' said Mrs Davidson.

'That's curious,' said Dr Macphail.

He remembered seeing them from the windows of the train when he crossed America. They were like huge molehills, rounded and smooth, and they rose from the plain abruptly. Dr Macphail remembered how it struck him that they were like a woman's breasts.

Davidson's restlessness was intolerable even to himself. But he was buoyed up by a wonderful exhilaration. He was tearing out by the roots the last vestiges of sin that lurked in the hidden corners of that poor woman's heart. He read with her and prayed with her.

'It's wonderful,' he said to them one day at supper. 'It's a true rebirth. Her soul, which was black as night, is now pure and white like the new-fallen snow. I am humble and afraid. Her remorse for all her sins is beautiful. I am not worthy to touch the hem of her garment.'

'Have you the heart to send her back to San Francisco?' said the doctor. 'Three years in an American prison. I should have thought you might have saved her from that.'

'Ah, but don't you see? It's necessary. Do you think my heart doesn't bleed for her? I love her as I love my wife and my sister. All the time that she is in prison I shall suffer all the pain that she suffers.'

'Bunkum,' cried the doctor impatiently.

'You don't understand because you're blind. She's sinned, and she must suffer. I know what she'll endure. She'll be starved and tortured and humiliated. I want her to accept the punishment of man as a sacrifice to God. I want her to accept it joyfully. She has an opportunity which is offered to very few of us. God is very good and very merciful.'

Davidson's voice trembled with excitement. He could hardly articulate the words that tumbled passionately from his lips.

'All day I pray with her and when I leave her I pray again, I pray with all my might and main, so that Jesus may grant her this great mercy. I want to put in her heart the passionate desire to be punished so that at the end, even if I offered to let her go, she would refuse. I want her to feel that the bitter punishment of prison is the thank-offering that she places at the feet of our Blessed Lord, who gave his life for her.'

The days passed slowly. The whole household, intent on the wretched, tortured woman downstairs, lived in a state of unnatural excitement. She was like a victim that was being prepared for the savage rites of a bloody idolatry. Her terror numbed her. She could not bear to let Davidson out of her sight; it was only when he was with her that she had courage, and she hung upon him with a slavish dependence. She cried a great deal, and she read the Bible, and prayed. Sometimes she was exhausted and apathetic. Then she did indeed look forward to her ordeal, for it seemed to offer an escape, direct and concrete, from the anguish she was enduring. She could not bear much longer the vague terrors which now assailed her. With her sins she had put aside all personal vanity, and she slopped about her room, unkempt and dishevelled, in her tawdry dressing-gown. She had not taken off her nightdress for four days, nor put on stockings. Her room was littered and untidy.

Meanwhile the rain fell with a cruel persistence. You felt that the heavens must at last be empty of water, but still it poured down, straight and heavy, with a maddening iteration, on the iron roof. Everything was damp and clammy. There was mildew on the walls and on the boots that stood on the floor. Through the sleepless nights the mosquitoes droned their angry chant.

'If it would only stop raining for a single day it wouldn't be so bad,' said Dr Macphail.

They all looked forward to the Tuesday when the boat for San Francisco was to arrive from Sydney. The strain was intolerable. So far as Dr Macphail was concerned, his pity and his resentment were alike extinguished by his desire to be rid of the unfortunate woman. The inevitable must be accepted. He felt he would breathe more freely when the ship had sailed. Sadie Thompson was to be escorted on board by a clerk in the governor's office. This person called on the Monday evening and told Miss Thompson to be prepared at eleven in the morning. Davidson was with her.

'I'll see that everything is ready. I mean to come on board with her myself.'

Miss Thompson did not speak.

When Dr Macphail blew out his candle and crawled cautiously under his mosquito curtains, he gave a sigh of relief.

'Well, thank God that's over. By this time tomorrow she'll be gone.'

'Mrs Davidson will be glad too. She says he's wearing himself to a shadow,' said Mrs Macphail. 'She's a different woman.'

'Who?'

'Sadie. I should never have thought it possible. It makes one humble.'

Dr Macphail did not answer, and presently he fell asleep. He was tired out, and he slept more soundly than usual.

He was awakened in the morning by a hand placed on his arm, and, starting up, saw Horn by the side of his bed. The trader put his finger on his mouth to prevent any exclamation from Dr Macphail and beckoned to him to come. As a rule he wore shabby ducks, but now he was barefoot and wore only the *lava-lava* of the natives. He looked suddenly savage, and Dr Macphail, getting out of bed, saw that he was heavily tattooed. Horn made him a sign to come on to the verandah. Dr Macphail got out of bed and followed the trader out.

'Don't make a noise,' he whispered. 'You're wanted. Put on a coat and some shoes. Quick.'

Dr Macphail's first thought was that something had happened to Miss Thompson.

'What is it? Shall I bring my instruments?'

'Hurry, please, hurry.'

Dr Macphail crept back into the bedroom, put on a waterproof over his pyjamas, and a pair of rubber-soled shoes. He rejoined the trader, and together they tiptoed down the stairs. The door leading out to the road was open and at it were standing half a dozen natives.

'What is it?' repeated the doctor.

'Come along with me,' said Horn.

He walked out and the doctor followed him. The natives came after them in a little bunch. They crossed the road and came on to the beach. The doctor saw a group of natives standing round some object at the water's edge. They hurried along, a couple of dozen yards perhaps, and the natives opened out as the doctor came up. The trader pushed him forwards. Then he saw, lying half in the water and half out, a dreadful object, the body of Davidson. Dr Macphail bent down – he was not a man to lose his head in an emergency – and turned the body over. The throat was cut from ear to ear, and in the right hand was still the razor with which the deed was done.

'He's quite cold,' said the doctor. 'He must have been dead some time.'

'One of the boys saw him lying there on his way to work just now and came and told me. Do you think he did it himself?'

'Yes. Someone ought to go for the police.'

Horn said something in the native tongue, and two youths started off.

'We must leave him here till they come,' said the doctor.

'They mustn't take him into my house. I won't have him in my house.'

'You'll do what the authorities say,' replied the doctor sharply. 'In point of fact I expect they'll take him to the mortuary.'

They stood waiting where they were. The trader took a cigarette from a fold in his *lava-lava* and gave one to Dr Macphail. They smoked while they stared at the corpse. Dr Macphail could not understand.

'Why do you think he did it?' asked Horn.

The doctor shrugged his shoulders. In a little while native police came along, under the charge of a marine, with a stretcher, and immediately afterwards a couple of naval officers and a naval doctor. They managed everything in a businesslike manner.

'What about the wife?' said one of the officers.

'Now that you've come I'll go back to the house and get some things on. I'll see that it's broken to her. She'd better not see him till he's been fixed up a little.'

'I guess that's right,' said the naval doctor.

When Dr Macphail went back he found his wife nearly dressed.

'Mrs Davidson's in a dreadful state about her husband,' she said to him as soon as he appeared. 'He hasn't been to bed all night. She heard him leave Miss Thompson's room at two, but he went out. If he's been walking about since then he'll be absolutely dead.'

Dr Macphail told her what had happened and asked her to break the news to Mrs Davidson.

'But why did he do it?' she asked, horror-stricken.

'I don't know.'

'But I can't. I can't.'

'You must.'

She gave him a frightened look and went out. He heard her go into Mrs Davidson's room. He waited a minute to gather himself together and then began to shave and wash. When he was dressed he sat down on the bed and waited for his wife. At last she came.

'She wants to see him,' she said.

'They've taken him to the mortuary. We'd better go down with her. How did she take it?'

'I think she's stunned. She didn't cry. But she's trembling like a leaf.'

'We'd better go at once.'

When they knocked at her door Mrs Davidson came out. She was very pale, but dry-eyed. To the doctor she seemed unnaturally composed. No word was exchanged, and they set out in silence down the road. When they arrived at the mortuary Mrs Davidson spoke.

'Let me go in and see him alone.'

They stood aside. A native opened a door for her and closed it behind her. They sat down and waited. One or two white men came and talked to them in undertones. Dr Macphail told them again what he knew of the tragedy. At last the door was quietly opened and Mrs Davidson came out. Silence fell upon them.

'I'm ready to go back now,' she said.

Her voice was hard and steady. Dr Macphail could not understand the look in her eyes. Her pale face was very stern. They walked back slowly, never saying a word, and at last they came round the bend on the other side of which stood their house. Mrs Davidson gave a gasp, and for a moment they stopped still. An incredible sound assaulted their ears. The gramophone which had been silent for so long was playing, playing ragtime loud and harsh.

'What's that?' cried Mrs Macphail with horror.

'Let's go on,' said Mrs Davidson.

They walked up the steps and entered the hall. Miss Thompson was standing at her door, chatting with a sailor. A sudden change had taken place in her. She was no longer the cowed drudge of the last days. She was dressed in all her finery, in her white dress, with the high shiny boots over which her fat legs bulged in their cotton stockings; her hair was elaborately arranged; and she wore that enormous hat covered with gaudy flowers. Her face was painted, her eyebrows were boldly black, and her lips were scarlet. She held herself erect. She was the flaunting queen that they had known at first. As they came in she broke into a loud, jeering laugh; and then, when Mrs Davidson involuntarily stopped, she collected the spittle in her mouth and spat. Mrs Davidson cowered back, and two red spots rose suddenly to her cheeks. Then, covering her face with her hands, she broke away and ran quickly up the stairs. Dr Macphail was outraged. He pushed past the woman into her room.

'What the devil are you doing?' he cried. 'Stop that damned machine.'

He went up to it and tore the record off. She turned on him.

'Say, doc, you can that stuff with me. What the hell are you doin' in my room?'

'What do you mean?' he cried. 'What d'you mean?'

She gathered herself together. No one could describe the scorn of her expression or the contemptuous hatred she put into her answer.

'You men! You filthy, dirty pigs! You're all the same, all of you. Pigs! Pigs!'

Dr Macphail gasped. He understood.

P&O

Mrs Hamlyn lay on her long chair and lazily watched the passengers come along the gangway. The ship had reached Singapore in the night and since dawn had been taking on cargo; the winches had been grinding away all day, but by now her ears were accustomed to their insistent clamour. She had lunched at the Europe and for lack of anything better to do had driven in a rickshaw through the gay, multitudinous streets of the city. Singapore is the meeting-place of many races. The Malays, though natives of the soil, dwell uneasily in towns, and are few; and it is the Chinese, supple, alert and industrious, who throng the streets, the dark-skinned Tamils walk on their silent, naked feet as though they were but brief sojourners in a strange land, but the Bengalis, sleek and prosperous, are easy in their surroundings and self-assured; the sly and obsequious Japanese seem busy with pressing and secret affairs; and the English in their topis and white ducks, speeding past in motor cars or at leisure in their rickshaws, wear a nonchalant and careless air. The rulers of these teeming peoples take their authority with a smiling unconcern. And now, tired and hot, Mrs Hamlyn waited for the ship to set out again on its long journey across the Indian Ocean.

She waved a rather large hand, for she was a big woman, to the doctor and Mrs Linsell as they came on board. She had been on the ship since it left Yokohama, and had watched with acid amusement the intimacy which had sprung up between the two.

Linsell was a naval officer who had been attached to the British Embassy in Tokyo, and she had wondered at the indifference with which he took the attentions that the doctor paid his wife. Two men came along the gangway, new passengers, and she amused herself by trying to discover from their demeanour whether they were married or single. Close by, a group of men were sitting together on rattan chairs, planters she judged by their khaki suits and wide-brimmed double felt hats, and they kept the deck-steward busy with their orders. They were talking loudly and laughing, for they had all drunk enough to make them somewhat foolishly hilarious, and they were evidently giving one of their number a send-off; but Mrs Hamlyn could not tell which it was that was to be a fellow-passenger. The time was growing short. More passengers arrived, and then Mr Jephson with dignity strolled up the gangway. He was a consul and was going home on leave. He had joined the ship at Shanghai and had immediately set about making himself agreeable to Mrs Hamlyn. But just then she was disinclined for anything in the nature of a flirtation. She frowned as she thought of the reason which was taking her back to England. She would be spending Christmas at sea, far from anyone who cared two straws for her, and for a moment she felt a little twist at her heart-strings; it vexed her that a subject which she was so resolute to put away from her should so constantly intrude on her unwilling mind.

But a warning bell clanged loudly and there was a general movement among the men who sat beside her.

'Well, if we don't want to be taken on we'd better be toddling,' said one of them.

They rose and walked towards the gangway. Now that they were all shaking hands she saw who it was that they had come to see the last of. There was nothing very interesting about the man on whom Mrs Hamlyn's eyes rested, but because she had nothing better to do she gave him more than a casual glance. He was a big fellow, well over six feet high, broad and stout; he was dressed in a bedraggled suit of khaki drill and his hat was battered and shabby. His friends left him, but they bandied chaff from the quay, and Mrs Hamlyn noticed that he had a strong Irish brogue; his voice was full, loud and hearty.

Mrs Linsell had gone below and the doctor came and sat down beside Mrs Hamlyn. They told one another their small adventures of the day. The bell sounded again and presently the ship slid away from the wharf. The Irishman waved a last farewell to his friends and then sauntered towards the chair on which he had left papers and magazines. He nodded to the doctor.

'Is that someone you know?' asked Mrs Hamlyn.

'I was introduced to him at the club before tiffin. His name is Gallagher. He's a planter.'

After the hubbub of the port and the noisy bustle of departure, the silence of the ship was marked and grateful. They steamed slowly past green-clad, rocky cliffs (the P&O anchorage was in a charming and secluded cove), and came out into the main harbour. Ships of all nations lay at anchor, a great multitude, passenger boats, tugs, lighters, tramps; and beyond, behind the breakwater, you saw the crowded masts, a bare straight forest, of the native junks. In the soft light of the evening the busy scene was strangely touched with mystery, and you felt that all those vessels, their activity for the moment suspended, waited for some event of a peculiar significance.

Mrs Hamlyn was a bad sleeper and when the dawn broke she was in the habit of going on deck. It rested her troubled heart to watch the last faint stars fade before the encroaching day and at that early hour the glassy sea had often an immobility which seemed to make all earthly sorrows of little consequence. The light was wan, and there was a pleasant shiver in the air. But next morning when she went to the end of the promenade deck, she found that some one was up before her. It was Gallagher. He was watching the low coast of Sumatra which the sunrise like a magician seemed to call forth from the dark sea. She was startled and a little vexed, but before she could turn away he had seen her and nodded.

'Up early,' he said. 'Have a cigarette?'

He was in pyjamas and slippers. He took his case from his coat pocket and handed it to her. She hesitated. She had on nothing but a dressing-gown and a little lace cap which she had put over her tousled hair, and she knew that she must look a sight; but she had her reasons for scourging her soul.

'I suppose a woman of forty has no right to mind how she looks,' she smiled, as though he must know what vain thoughts occupied her. She took the cigarette. 'But you're up early too.'

'I'm a planter. I've had to get up at five in the morning for so many years that I don't know how I'm going to get out of the habit.'

'You'll not find it will make you very popular at home.'

She saw his face better now that it was not shadowed by a hat. It was agreeable without being handsome. He was of course much too fat, and his features which must have been good enough when he was a young man were thickened. His skin was red and bloated. But his dark eyes were merry; and though he could not have been less than five and forty his hair was black and thick. He gave you an impression of great strength. He was a heavy, ungraceful, commonplace man, and Mrs Hamlyn, except for the promiscuity of shipboard, would never have thought it worth while to talk to him.

'Are you going home on leave?' she hazarded.

'No, I'm going home for good.'

His black eyes twinkled. He was of a communicative turn, and before it was time for Mrs Hamlyn to go below in order to have her bath he had told her a good deal about himself. He had been in the Federated Malay States for twenty-five years, and for the last ten had managed an estate in Selantan. It was a hundred miles from anything that could be described as civilisation and the life had been lonely; but he had made money; during the rubber boom he had done very well and with an astuteness which was unexpected in a man who looked so happy-go-lucky he had invested his savings in government stock. Now that the slump had come he was prepared to retire.

'What part of Ireland do you come from?' asked Mrs Hamlyn.

'Galway.'

Mrs Hamlyn had once motored through Ireland and she had a vague recollection of a sad and moody town with great stone warehouses, deserted and crumbling, which faced the melancholy sea. She had a sensation of greenness and of soft rain, of silence and of resignation. Was it here that Mr Gallagher meant to spend the rest of his life? He spoke of it with boyish eagerness. The thought of his vitality in that grey world of shadows was so incongruous that Mrs Hamlyn was intrigued.

'Does your family live there?' she asked.

'I've got no family. My mother and father are dead. So far as I know I haven't a relation in the world.'

He had made all his plans, he had been making them for twenty-five years, and he was pleased to have someone to talk to of all these things that he had been obliged for so long only to talk to himself about. He meant to buy a house and he would keep a motor car. He was going to breed horses. He didn't much care about shooting; he had shot a lot of big game during his first years in the FMS; but now he had lost his zest. He didn't see why the beasts of the jungle should be killed; he had lived in the jungle so long. But he could hunt.

'Do you think I'm too heavy?' he asked.

Mrs Hamlyn, smiling, looked him up and down with appraising eyes.

'You must weigh a ton,' she said.

He laughed. The Irish horses were the best in the world, and he'd always kept pretty fit. You had a devil of a lot of walking exercise on a rubber estate and he'd played a good deal of tennis. He'd soon get thin in Ireland. Then he'd marry. Mrs Hamlyn looked silently at the sea, coloured now with the tenderness of the sunrise. She sighed.

'Was it easy to drag up all your roots? Is there no one you regret leaving behind? I should have thought after so many years, however much you'd looked forward to going home, when the time came at last to go it must have given you a pang.'

'I was glad to get out. I was fed up. I never want to see the country again or anyone in it.'

One or two early passengers now began to walk round the deck and Mrs Hamlyn, remembering that she was scantily clad, went below.

During the next day or two she saw little of Mr Gallagher who passed his time in the smoking-room. Owing to a strike the ship was not touching at Colombo and the passengers settled down to a pleasant voyage across the Indian Ocean. They played deck games, they gossiped about one another, they flirted. The approach of Christmas gave them an occupation, for someone had suggested that there should be a fancy-dress dance on Christmas Day, and the ladies set about making their dresses. A meeting was held of the first-class passengers to decide whether the second-class passengers should be invited, and notwithstanding the heat the discussion was animated. The ladies said that the second-class passengers would only feel ill-at-ease. On Christmas Day it was to be expected that they would drink more than was good for them and unpleasantness might ensue. Everyone who spoke insisted that there was in his (or her) mind no idea of class distinction, no one would be so snobbish as to think there was any difference between first- and second-class passengers as far as that went, but it would really be kinder to the second-class passengers not to put them in a false position. They would enjoy themselves much more if they had a party of their own in the second-class cabin. On the other hand, no one wanted to hurt their feelings, and of course one had to be more democratic nowadays (this was in reply to the wife of a missionary in China who said she had travelled on the P&O for thirty-five years and she had never heard of the second-class passengers being invited to a dance in the first-class saloon) and even though they wouldn't enjoy it, they might like to come. Mr Gallagher, dragged unwillingly from the card-table, because it had been foreseen that the voting would be close, was asked his opinion by the consul. He was taking home in the second-class a man who had been employed on his estate. He raised his massive bulk from the couch on which he sat.

'As far as I'm concerned I've only got this to say: I've got the man who was looking after our engines with me. He's a rattling good fellow and he's just as fit to come to your party as I am. But he won't come because I'm going to make him so drunk on Christmas Day that by six o'clock he'll be fit for nothing but to be put to bed.'

Mr Jephson, the consul, gave a distorted smile. On account of his official position he had been chosen to preside at the meeting and he wished the matter to be taken seriously. He was a man who often said that if a thing was worth doing it was worth doing well.

'I gather from your observations,' he said, not without acidity, 'that the question before the meeting does not seem to you of great importance.'

'I don't think it matters a tinker's curse,' said Gallagher, with twinkling eyes.

Mrs Hamlyn laughed. The scheme was at last devised to invite the second-class passengers, but to go to the captain privily and point out to him the advisability of withholding his consent to their coming into the first-class saloon. It was on the evening of the day on which this happened that Mrs Hamlyn, having dressed for dinner, came on deck at the same time as Mr Gallagher.

'Just in time for a cocktail, Mrs Hamlyn,' he said jovially.

'I'd like one. To tell you the truth I need cheering up.'

'Why?' he smiled.

Mrs Hamlyn thought his smile attractive, but she did not want to answer his question.

'I told you the other morning,' she answered cheerfully. 'I'm forty.'

'I never met a woman who insisted on the fact so much.'

They went into the lounge and the Irishman ordered a dry Martini for her and a gin pahit for himself. He had lived too long in the East to drink anything else.

'You've got hiccups,' said Mrs Hamlyn.

'Yes, I've had them all the afternoon,' he answered carelessly. 'It's rather funny, they came on just as we got out of sight of land.'

'I dare say they'll pass off after dinner.'

They drank, the second bell rang, and they went into the dining-saloon.

'You don't play bridge?' he said, as they parted.

'No.'

Mrs Hamlyn did not notice that she saw nothing of Gallagher for two or three days. She was occupied with her own thoughts. They crowded upon her when she was sewing; they came between her and the novel with which she sought to cheat their insistence. She had hoped that as the ship took her farther away from the scene of her unhappiness the torment of her mind would be eased; but contrariwise, each day that brought her nearer England increased her distress. She looked forward with dismay to the bleak emptiness of the life that awaited her; and then, turning her exhausted wits from a prospect that made her flinch, she considered, as she had done she knew not how many times before, the situation from which she had fled.

She had been married for twenty years. It was a long time and of course she could not expect her husband to be still madly in love with her; she was not madly in love with him; but they were good friends and they understood one another. Their marriage, as marriages go, might very well have been looked upon as a success. Suddenly she discovered that he had fallen in love. She would not have objected to a flirtation, he had had those before, and she had chaffed him about them; he had not minded that, it somewhat flattered him, and they had laughed together at an inclination which was neither deep nor serious. But this was different. He was in love as passionately as a boy of eighteen. He was fifty-two. It was ridiculous. It was indecent. And he loved without sense or prudence: by the time the hideous fact was forced upon her all the foreigners in Yokohama knew it. After the first shock of astonished anger, for he was the last man from whom such a folly might have been expected, she tried to persuade herself that she could have understood, and so have forgiven, if he had fallen in love with a girl. Middle-aged men often make fools of themselves with flappers, and after twenty years in the Far East she knew that the fifties were the dangerous age for men. But he had no excuse. He was in love with a woman eight years older than herself. It was grotesque, and it made her, his wife, perfectly absurd. Dorothy Lacom was hard on fifty. He had known her for eighteen years, for Lacom, like her own husband, was a silk merchant in Yokohama. Year in, year out, they had seen one another three or four times a week, and once, when they happened to be in England together, had shared a house at the seaside. But nothing! Not till a year ago had there been anything between them but a chaffing friendship. It was incredible. Of course Dorothy was a handsome woman; she had a good figure, overdeveloped, perhaps, but still comely; with bold black eyes and a red mouth and lovely hair; but all that she had had years before. She was forty-eight. Forty-eight!

Mrs Hamlyn tackled her husband at once. At first he swore that there was not a word of truth in what she accused him of, but she had her proofs; he grew sulky; and at last he admitted what he could no longer deny. Then he said an astonishing thing.

'Why should you care?' he asked.

It maddened her. She answered him with angry scorn. She was voluble, finding in the bitterness of her heart wounding things to say. He listened to her quietly.

'I've not been such a bad husband to you for the twenty years we've been married. For a long time now we've only been friends. I have a great affection for you and this hasn't altered it in the very smallest degree. I'm giving Dorothy nothing that I take away from you.'

'But what have you to complain of in me?'

'Nothing. No man could want a better wife.'

'How can you say that when you have the heart to treat me so cruelly?'

'I don't want to be cruel to you. I can't help myself.'

'But what on earth made you fall in love with her?'

'How can I tell? You don't think I wanted to, do you?'

'Couldn't you have resisted?'

'I tried. I think we both tried.'

'You talk as though you were twenty. Why, you're both middle-aged people. She's eight years older than I am. It makes me look such a perfect fool.'

He did not answer. She did not know what emotions seethed in her heart. Was it jealousy that seemed to clutch at her throat, anger, or was it merely wounded pride?

'I'm not going to let it go on. If only you and she were concerned I would divorce you, but there's her husband and then there are the children. Good heavens, does it occur to you that if they were girls instead of boys she might be a grandmother by now?'

'Easily.'

'What a mercy that we have no children!'

He put out an affectionate hand as though to caress her, but she drew back in horror.

'You've made me the laughing-stock of all my friends. For all our sakes I'm willing to hold my tongue, but only on the condition that everything stops now, at once, and for ever.'

He looked down and played reflectively with a Japanese knick-knack that was on the table.

'I'll tell Dorothy what you say,' he replied at last.

She gave him a little bow, silently, and walked past him out of the room. She was too angry to observe that she was somewhat melodramatic.

She waited for him to tell her the result of his interview with Dorothy Lacom, but he made no further reference to the scene. He was quiet, polite, and silent; and at last she was obliged to ask him.

'Have you forgotten what I said to you the other day?' she enquired frigidly.

'No. I talked to Dorothy. She wishes me to tell you that she is desperately sorry that she has caused you so much pain. She would like to come and see you, but she is afraid you wouldn't like it.'

'What decision have you come to?'

He hesitated. He was very grave, but his voice trembled a little.

'I'm afraid there's no use in our making a promise we shouldn't be able to keep.'

'That settles it then,' she answered.

'I think I should tell you that if you brought an action for divorce we should have to contest it. You would find it impossible to get the necessary evidence and you would lose your case.'

'I wasn't thinking of doing that. I shall go back to England and consult a lawyer. Nowadays these things can be managed fairly easily and I shall throw myself on your generosity. I dare say you will enable me to get my freedom without bringing Dorothy Lacom into the matter.'

He sighed.

'It's an awful muddle, isn't it? I don't want you to divorce me, but of course I'll do anything I can to meet your wishes.'

'What on earth do you expect me to do?' she cried, her anger rising again. 'Do you expect me to sit still and be made a damned fool of?'

'I'm awfully sorry to put you in a humiliating position.' He looked at her with harassed eyes. 'I'm quite sure we didn't want to fall in love with one another. We're both of us very conscious of our age. Dorothy, as you say, is old enough to be a grandmother and I'm a baldish, stoutish gentleman of fifty-two. When you fall in love at twenty you think your love will last for ever, but at fifty you know so much, about life and about love, and you know that it will last so short a time.' His voice was low and rueful. It was as though before his mind's eye he saw the sadness of autumn and the leaves falling from the trees. He looked at her gravely. 'And at that age you feel that you can't afford to throw away the chance of happiness which a freakish destiny has given you. In five years it will certainly be over, and perhaps in six months. Life is rather drab and grey, and happiness is so rare. We shall be dead so long.'

It gave Mrs Hamlyn a bitter sensation of pain to hear her husband, a matter-of-fact and practical man, speak in a strain which was quite new to her. He had gained on a sudden a wistful and tragic personality of which she knew nothing. The twenty years during which they had lived together had no power over him and she was helpless in face of his determination. She could do nothing but go, and now, resentfully determined to get the divorce with which she had threatened him, she was on her way to England.

The smooth sea, upon which the sun beat down so that it shone like a sheet of glass, was as empty and hostile as the life in which there was no place for her. For three days no other craft had broken in upon the solitariness of that expanse. Now and again its even surface was scattered for the twinkling of an eye by the scurry of flying fish. The heat was so great that even the most energetic of passengers had given up deck games and now (it was after luncheon) such as were not resting in their cabins lay about on chairs. Linsell strolled towards her and sat down.

'Where's Mrs Linsell?' asked Mrs Hamlyn.

'Oh, I don't know. She's about somewhere.'

His indifference exasperated her. Was it possible that he did not see that his wife and the surgeon were falling in love with one another? Yet, not so very long ago, he must have cared. Their marriage had been romantic. They had become engaged when Mrs Linsell was still at school and he little more than a boy. They must have been a charming, handsome pair, and their youth and their mutual love must have been touching. And now, after so short a time, they were tired of one another. It was heartbreaking. What had her husband said?

'I suppose you're going to live in London when you get home?' asked Linsell lazily, for something to say.

'I suppose so,' said Mrs Hamlyn.

It was hard to reconcile herself to the fact that she had nowhere to go and where she lived mattered not in the least to anyone alive. Some association of ideas made her think of Gallagher. She envied the eagerness with which he was returning to his native land, and she was touched, and at the same time amused, when she remembered the exuberant imagination he showed in describing the house he meant to live in and the wife he meant to marry. Her friends in Yokohama, apprised in confidence of her determination to divorce her husband, had assured her that she would marry again. She did not much want to enter a second time upon a state which had once so disappointed her, and besides, most men would think twice before they suggested marriage to a woman of forty. Mr Gallagher wanted a buxom young person.

'Where is Mr Gallagher?' she asked the submissive Linsell. 'I haven't seen him for the last day or two.'

'Didn't you know? He's ill.'

'Poor thing. What's the matter with him?'

'He's got hiccups.'

Mrs Hamlyn laughed. 'Hiccups don't make one ill, do they?'

'The surgeon is rather worried. He's tried all sorts of things, but he can't stop them.'

'How very odd.'

She thought no more about it, but next morning, chancing upon the surgeon, she asked him how Mr Gallagher was. She was surprised to see his boyish, cheerful face darken and grow perplexed.

'I'm afraid he's very bad, poor chap.'

'With hiccups?' she cried in amazement. It was a disorder that really it was impossible to take seriously.

'You see, he can't keep any food down. He can't sleep. He's fearfully exhausted. I've tried everything I can think of.' He hesitated. 'Unless I can stop them soon – I don't quite know what'll happen.'

Mrs Hamlyn was startled. 'But he's so strong. He seemed so full of vitality.'

'I wish you could see him now.'

'Would he like me to go and see him?'

'Come along.'

Gallagher had been moved from his cabin into the ship's hospital, and as they approached it they heard a loud hiccup. The sound, perhaps owing to its connection with insobriety, had in it something ludicrous. But Gallagher's appearance gave Mrs Hamlyn a shock. He had lost flesh and the skin hung about his neck in loose folds; under the sunburn his face was pale. His eyes, before full of fun and laughter, were haggard and tormented. His great body was shaken incessantly by the hiccups, and now there was nothing ludicrous in the sound; to Mrs Hamlyn, for no reason that she knew, it seemed strangely terrifying. He smiled when she came in.

'I'm sorry to see you like this,' she said.

'I shan't die of it, you know,' he gasped. 'I shall reach the green shores of Erin all right.'

There was a man sitting beside him and he rose as they entered.

'This is Mr Pryce,' said the surgeon. 'He was in charge of the machinery on Mr Gallagher's estate.'

Mrs Hamlyn nodded. This was the second-class passenger to whom Gallagher had referred when they had discussed the party which was to be given on Christmas Day. He was a very small man, but sturdy, with a pleasantly impudent countenance and an air of self-assurance.

'Are you glad to be going home?' asked Mrs Hamlyn.

'You bet I am, lady,' he answered.

The intonation of the few words told Mrs Hamlyn that he was a cockney and, recognising the cheerful, sensible, good-humoured and careless type, her heart warmed to him.

'You're not Irish?' she smiled.

'Not me, miss. London's my 'ome and I shan't be sorry to see it again, I can tell you.'

Mrs Hamlyn never thought it offensive to be called miss.

'Well, sir, I'll be getting along,' he said to Gallagher, with the beginning of a gesture as though he were going to touch a cap which he hadn't got on.

Mrs Hamlyn asked the sick man whether she could do anything for him and in a minute or two left him with the doctor. The little cockney was waiting outside the door.

'Can I speak to you a minute or two, miss?' he asked.

'Of course.'

The hospital cabin was aft and they stood, leaning against the rail, and looked down on the well-deck where lascars and stewards off duty were lounging about on the covered hatches.

'I don't know exactly 'ow to begin,' said Pryce, uncertainly, a serious look strangely changing his lively, puckered face. 'I've been with Mr Gallagher for four years now and a better gentleman you wouldn't find in a week of Sundays.'

He hesitated again.

'I don't like it and that's the truth.'

'What don't you like?'

'Well, if you ask me 'e's for it, and the doctor don't know it. I told 'im, but 'e won't listen to a word I say.'

'You mustn't be too depressed, Mr Pryce. Of course the doctor's young, but I think he's quite clever, and people don't die of hiccups, you know. I'm sure Mr Gallagher will be all right in a day or two.'

'You know when it come on? Just as we was out of sight of land. She said 'e'd never see 'is 'ome.'

Mrs Hamlyn turned and faced him. She stood a good three inches taller than he.

'What do you mean?'

'My belief is, it's a spell that's been put on 'im, if you understand what I mean. Medicine's going to do 'im no good. You don't know them Malay women like what I do.'

For a moment Mrs Hamlyn was startled, and

because she was startled she shrugged her shoulders and laughed.

'Oh, Mr Pryce, that's nonsense.'

'That's what the doctor said when I told 'im. But you mark my words, 'e'll die before we see land again.

The man was so serious that Mrs Hamlyn, vaguely uneasy, was against her will impressed.

'Why should anyone cast a spell on Mr Gallagher?' she asked.

'Well, it's a bit awkward speakin' of it to a lady.'

'Please tell me.'

Pryce was so embarrassed that at another time Mrs Hamlyn would have had difficulty in concealing her amusement.

'Mr Gallagher's lived a long time up-country, if you understand what I mean, and of course it's lonely, and you know what men are, miss.'

'I've been married for twenty years,' she replied, smiling.

'I beg your pardon, ma'am. The fact is he had a Malay girl living with him. I don't know 'ow long, ten or twelve years, I think. Well, when he made up 'is mind to come 'ome for good she didn't say nothing. She just sat there. He thought she'd carry on no end, but she didn't. Of course 'e provided for 'er all right, 'e gave 'er a little 'ouse for herself, an' 'e fixed it up so as so much should be paid 'er every month; 'e wasn't mean, I will say that for 'im, an' she knew all along as 'e'd be going sometime. She didn't cry or anything. When 'e packed up all 'is things and sent them off she just sat there an' watched 'em go. And when 'e sold 'is furniture to the Chinks she never said a word. He'd give 'er all she wanted. And when it was time for 'im to go so as to catch the boat she just kep' on sitting, on the steps of the bungalow, you know, and she just looked an' said nothing. He wanted to say goodbye to 'er, same as anyone would, 'an, would you believe it? she never even moved. "Aren't you going to say goodbye to me?" he says. A rare funny look came over 'er face. And do you know what she says? "You go," she says; they 'ave a funny way of talking, them natives, not like we 'ave, "you go," she says, "but I tell you that you will never come to your own country. When the land sinks into the sea death will come upon you, an' before them as goes with you sees the land again, death will have took you." It gave me quite a turn.'

'What did Mr Gallagher say?' asked Mrs Hamlyn.

'Oh, well, you know what 'e is. He just laughed. "Always merry an' bright," he says and he jumps into the motor, an' off we go.'

Mrs Hamlyn saw the bright and sunny road that ran through the rubber estates, with their trim green trees, carefully spaced, and their silence, and then wound its way uphill and down through the tangled jungle. The car raced on, driven by a reckless Malay, with its white passengers, past Malay houses that stood away from the road among the coconut trees, sequestered and taciturn, and through busy villages where the marketplace was crowded with dark-skinned little people in gay sarongs. Then towards evening it reached the trim, modern town, with its clubs and its golf links, its well-ordered rest-house, its white people, and its railway station, from which the two men could take the train to Singapore. And the woman sat on the steps of the bungalow, empty till the new manager moved in, and watched the road down which the car had panted, watched the car as it sped on, and watched till at last it was lost in the shadow of the night.

'What was she like?' Mrs Hamlyn asked.

'Oh, well, to my way of thinking them Malay women are all very much alike, you know,' Pryce answered. 'Of course she wasn't so young any more and you know what they are, them natives, they run to fat something terrible.'

'Fat?'

The thought, absurdly enough, filled Mrs Hamlyn with dismay.

'Mr Gallagher was always one to do himself well, if you understand what I mean.'

The idea of corpulence at once brought Mrs Hamlyn back to common sense. She was impatient with herself because for an instant she had seemed to accept the little cockney's suggestion.

'It's perfectly absurd, Mr Pryce. Fat women can't throw spells on people at a distance of a thousand miles. In fact life is very difficult for a fat woman anyway.'

'You can laugh, miss, but unless something's done, you mark my words, the governor's for it. And medicine ain't goin' to save him, not white man's medicine.'

'Pull yourself together, Mr Pryce. This fat lady had no particular grievance against Mr Gallagher. As these things are done in the East he seems to have treated her very well. Why should she wish him any harm?'

'We don't know 'ow they look at things. Why, a man can live there for twenty years with one of them natives, and d'you think 'e knows what's goin' on in that black heart of hers? Not 'im!'

She could not smile at his melodramatic language,

for his intensity was impressive. And she knew, if any one did, that the hearts of men, whether their skins are yellow or white or brown, are incalculable.

'But even if she felt angry with him, even if she hated him and wanted to kill him, what could she do?' It was strange that Mrs Hamlyn with her questions was trying now, unconsciously, to reassure herself. 'There's no poison that could start working after six or seven days.'

'I never said it was poison.'

'I'm sorry, Mr Pryce,' she smiled, 'but I'm not going to believe in a magic spell, you know.'

'You've lived in the East.'

'Off and on for twenty years.'

'Well, if you can say what they can do and what they can't, it's more than I can.' He clenched his fist and beat it on the rail with sudden, angry violence. 'I'm fed up with the bloody country. It's got on my nerves, that's what it is. We're no match for them, us white men, and that's a fact. If you'll excuse me I think I'll go an' 'ave a tiddley. I've got the jumps.'

He nodded abruptly and left her. Mrs Hamlyn watched him, a sturdy, shuffling little man in shabby khaki, slither down the companion into the waist of the ship, walk across it with bent head, and disappear into the second-class saloon. She did not know why he left with her a vague uneasiness. She could not get out of her mind that picture of a stout woman, no longer young, in a sarong, a coloured jacket and gold ornaments, who sat on the steps of a bungalow looking at an empty road. Her heavy face was painted, but in her large, tearless eyes there was no expression. The men who drove in the car were like schoolboys going home for the holidays. Gallagher gave a sigh of relief. In the early morning, under the bright sky, his spirits bubbled. The future was like a sunny road that wandered through a wide-flung, wooded plain.

Later in the day Mrs Hamlyn asked the doctor how his patient did. The doctor shook his head.

'I'm done. I'm at the end of my tether.' He frowned unhappily. 'It's rotten luck, striking a case like this. It would be bad enough at home, but on board ship . . .'

He was an Edinburgh man, but recently qualified, and he was taking this voyage as a holiday before settling down to practice. He felt himself aggrieved. He wanted to have a good time and, faced with this mysterious illness, he was worried to death. Of course he was inexperienced, but he was doing everything that could be done and it exasperated him to suspect that the passengers thought him an ignorant fool.

'Have you heard what Mr Pryce thinks?' asked Mrs Hamlyn.

'I never heard such rot. I told the captain and he's right up in the air. He doesn't want it talked about. He thinks it'll upset the passengers.'

'I'll be as silent as the grave.'

The surgeon looked at her sharply.

'Of course you don't believe that there can be any truth in nonsense of that sort?' he asked.

'Of course not.' She looked out at the sea which shone, blue and oily and still, all round them. 'I've lived in the East a long time,' she added. 'Strange things happen there.'

'This is getting on my nerves,' said the doctor.

Near them two little Japanese gentlemen were playing deck quoits. They were trim and neat in their tennis shirts, white trousers and buckram shoes. They looked very European, they even called the score to one another in English, and yet somehow to look at them filled Mrs Hamlyn at that moment with a vague disquiet. Because they seemed to wear so easily a disguise there was about them something sinister. Her nerves too were on edge.

And presently, no one quite knew how, the notion spread through the ship that Gallagher was bewitched. While the ladies sat about on their deckchairs, stitching away at the costumes they were making for the fancy-dress party on Christmas Day, they gossiped about it in undertones, and the men in the smoking-room talked of it over their cocktails. A good many of the passengers had lived long in the East and from the recesses of their memory they produced strange and inexplicable stories. Of course it was absurd to think seriously that Gallagher was suffering from a malignant spell, such things were impossible, and yet this and that was a fact and no one had been able to explain it. The doctor had to confess that he could suggest no cause for Gallagher's condition; he was able to give a physiological explanation, but why these terrible spasms should have suddenly assailed him he could not say. Feeling vaguely to blame, he tried to defend himself.

'Why, it's the sort of case you might never come across in the whole of your practice,' he said. 'It's rotten luck.'

He was in wireless communication with passing ships and suggestions for treatment came from here and there.

'I've tried everything they tell me,' he said irritably. 'The doctor of the Japanese boat advised adrenalin.

How the devil does he expect me to have adrenalin in the middle of the Indian Ocean?'

There was something impressive in the thought of this ship speeding through a deserted sea while to her from all parts came unseen messages. She seemed at that moment strangely alone and yet the centre of the world. In the lazaret the sick man, shaken by the cruel spasms, gasped for life. Then the passengers became conscious that the ship's course was altered and they heard that the captain had made up his mind to put in at Aden. Gallagher was to be landed there and taken to the hospital where he could have attention which on board was impossible. The chief engineer received orders to force his engines. The ship was an old one and she throbbed with the greater effort. The passengers had grown used to the sound and feel of her engines and now the greater vibration shook their nerves with a new sensation. It would not pass into each one's unconsciousness, but beat on their sensibilities so that each felt a personal concern. And still the wide sea was empty of traffic so that they seemed to traverse an empty world. And now the uneasiness which had descended upon the ship, but which no one had been willing to acknowledge, became a definite malaise. The passengers grew irritable, and people quarrelled over trifles which at another time would have seemed insignificant. Mr Jephson made his hackneyed jokes, but no one any longer repaid him with a smile. The Linsells had an altercation and Mrs Linsell was heard late at night walking round the deck with her husband, and uttering in a low, tense voice a stream of vehement reproaches. There was a violent scene in the smoking-room one night over a game of bridge, and the reconciliation which followed it was attended with general intoxication. People talked little of Gallagher, but he was seldom absent from their thoughts. They examined the route map. The doctor said now that Gallagher could not live more than three or four days and they discussed acrimoniously what was the shortest time in which Aden could be reached. What happened to him after he was landed was no affair of theirs; they did not want him to die on board.

Mrs Hamlyn saw Gallagher every day. With the suddenness with which after tropical rain in the spring you seem to see the herbage grow before your very eyes, she saw him go to pieces. Already his skin hung loosely on his bones and his double chin was like the wrinkled wattle of a turkey-cock. His cheeks were sunken. You saw now how large his frame was and through the sheet under which he lay his bony structure was like the skeleton of a prehistoric giant. For the most part he lay with his eyes closed, torpid with morphia, but shaken still with terrible spasms, and when now and again he opened his eyes they were preternaturally large; they looked at you vaguely, perplexed and troubled, from the depths of their bony sockets. But when, emerging from his stupor, he recognised Mrs Hamlyn he forced a gallant smile to his lips.

'How are you, Mr Gallagher?' she said.

'Getting along, getting along. I shall be all right when we get out of this confounded heat. Lord, how I look forward to a dip in the Atlantic. I'd give anything for a good long swim. I want to feel the cold grey sea of Galway beating against my chest.'

Then the hiccup shook him from the crown of his head to the sole of his foot. Mr Pryce and the stewardess shared the care of him. The little cockney's face wore no longer its look of impudent gaiety, but instead was sullen.

'The captain sent for me yesterday,' he told Mrs Hamlyn when they were alone. 'He gave me a rare talking to.'

'What about?'

'He said 'e wouldn't 'ave all this hoodoo stuff. He said it was frightening the passengers and I'd better keep a watch on me tongue or I'd 'ave 'im to reckon with. It's not my doing. I never said a word except to you and the doctor.'

'It's all over the ship.'

'I know it is. D'you think it's only me that's saying it? All them lascars and the Chinese, they all know what's the matter with him. You don't think you can teach them much, do you? They know it ain't a natural illness.'

Mrs Hamlyn was silent. She knew through the amahs of some of the passengers that there was no one on the ship, except the whites, who doubted that the woman whom Gallagher had left in distant Selantan was killing him with her magic. All were convinced that as they sighted the barren rocks of Arabia his soul would be parted from his body.

'The captain says if he hears of me trying any hanky-panky he'll confine me to my cabin for the rest of the voyage,' said Pryce suddenly, a surly frown on his puckered face.

'What do you mean by hanky-panky?'

He looked at her for a moment fiercely as though she too were an object of the anger he felt against the captain.

'The doctor's tried every damned thing he knows,

and he's wirelessed all over the place, and what good 'as 'e done? Tell me that. Can't 'e see the man's dying? There's only one way to save him now.'

'What do you mean?'

'It's magic what's killing 'im, and it's only magic what'll save him. Oh, don't you say it can't be done. I've seen it with me own eyes.' His voice rose, irritable and shrill. 'I've seen a man dragged from the jaws of death, as you might say, when they got in a *pawang*, what we call a witch-doctor, an' 'e did 'is little tricks. I seen it with me own eyes, I tell you.'

Mrs Hamlyn did not speak. Pryce gave her a searching look.

'One of them lascars on board, he's a witch-doctor, same as the *pawang* that we 'ave in the FMS. An' 'e says he'll do it. Only he must 'ave a live animal. A cock would do.'

'What do you want a live animal for?' Mrs Hamlyn asked, frowning a little.

The cockney looked at her with quick suspicion.

'If you take my advice you won't know anything about it. But I tell you what, I'm going to leave no stone unturned to save my governor. An' if the captain 'ears of it and shuts me up in me cabin, well, let 'im.'

At that moment Mrs Linsell came up and Pryce with his quaint gesture of salute left them. Mrs Linsell wanted Mrs Hamlyn to fit the dress she had been making herself for the fancy-dress ball, and on the way down to the cabin she spoke to her anxiously about the possibility that Mr Gallagher might die on Christmas Day. They could not possibly have the dance if he did. She had told the doctor that she would never speak to him again if this happened, and the doctor promised her faithfully that he would keep the man alive over Christmas Day somehow.

'It would be nice for him, too,' said Mrs Linsell.

'For whom?' asked Mrs Hamlyn.

'For poor Mr Gallagher. Naturally no one likes to die on Christmas Day. Do they?'

'I don't really know,' said Mrs Hamlyn.

That night, after she had been asleep a little while, she awoke weeping. It dismayed her that she should cry in her sleep. It was as though then the weakness of the flesh mastered her, and her will broken, she was defenceless against a natural sorrow. She turned over in her mind, as so often before, the details of the disaster which had so profoundly affected her; she repeated the conversations with her husband, wishing she had said this and blaming herself because she had said the other. She wished with all her heart that she had remained in comfortable ignorance of her husband's infatuation, and asked herself whether she would not have been wiser to pocket her pride and shut her eyes to the unwelcome truth. She was a woman of the world and she knew too well how much more she lost in separating herself from her husband than his love; she lost the settled establishment and the assured position, the ample means and the support of a recognised background. She had known of many separated wives, living equivocally on smallish incomes, and knew how quickly their friends found them tiresome. And she was lonely. She was as lonely as the ship that throbbed its hasting way through an unpeopled sea, and lonely as the friendless man who lay dying in the ship's lazaret. Mrs Hamlyn knew that her thoughts had got the better of her now and that she would not easily sleep again. It was very hot in her cabin. She looked at the time; it was between four and half-past; she must pass two mortal hours before broke the reassuring day.

She slipped into a kimono and went on deck. The night was sombre and although the sky was unclouded no stars were visible. Panting and shaking, the old ship under full steam lumbered through the darkness. The silence was uncanny. Mrs Hamlyn with bare feet groped her way slowly along the deserted deck. It was so black that she could see nothing. She came to the end of the promenade deck and leaned against the rail. Suddenly she started and her attention was fixed, for on the lower deck she caught a fitful glow. She leaned forward cautiously. It was a little fire, and she saw only the glow because the naked backs of men, crouched round, hid the flame. At the edge of the circle she divined, rather than saw, a stocky figure in pyjamas. The rest were natives, but this was a European. It must be Pryce and she guessed immediately that some dark ceremony of exorcism was in progress. Straining her ears she heard a low voice muttering a string of secret words. She began to tremble. She was aware that they were too intent upon their business to think that anyone was watching them, but she dared not move. Suddenly, rending the sultry silence of the night like a piece of silk violently torn in two, came the crowing of a cock. Mrs Hamlyn almost shrieked. Mr Pryce was trying to save the life of his friend and master by a sacrifice to the strange gods of the East. The voice went on, low and insistent. Then in the dark circle there was a movement, something was happening, she knew not what; there was a cluck-cluck from the cock, angry and frightened, and then a strange, indescribable sound: the magician was cutting the cock's throat; then silence; there were vague doings that she could not follow, and in a little while it looked as though someone was stamping out the fire. The figures she had dimly seen were dissolved in the night and all once more was still. She heard again the regular throbbing of the engines.

Mrs Hamlyn stood still for a little while, strangely shaken, and then walked slowly along the deck. She found a chair and lay down in it. She was trembling still. She could only guess what had happened. She did not know how long she lay there, but at last she felt that the dawn was approaching. It was not yet day, but it was no longer night. Against the darkness of the sky she could now see the ship's rail. Then she saw a figure come towards her. It was a man in pyjamas.

'Who's that?' she cried nervously.

'Only the doctor,' came a friendly voice.

'Oh! What are you doing here at this time of night?'

'I've been with Gallagher.' He sat down beside her and lit a cigarette. 'I've given him a good strong hypodermic and he's quiet now.'

'Has he been very ill?'

'I thought he was going to pass out. I was watching him, and suddenly he started up on his bed and began to talk Malay. Of course I couldn't understand a thing. He kept on saying one word over and over again.'

'Perhaps it was a name, a woman's name.'

'He wanted to get out of bed. He's a damned powerful man even now. By George, I had a struggle with him. I was afraid he'd throw himself overboard. He seemed to think someone was calling him.'

'When was that?' asked Mrs Hamlyn slowly.

'Between four and half-past. Why?'

'Nothing.'

She shuddered.

Later in the morning when the ship's life was set upon its daily round, Mrs Hamlyn passed Pryce on the deck, but he gave her a brief greeting and walked on with quickly averted gaze. He looked tired and overwrought. Mrs Hamlyn thought again of that fat woman, with golden ornaments in her thick, black hair, who sat on the steps of the deserted bungalow and looked at the road which ran through the trim lines of the rubber trees.

It was fearfully hot. She knew now why the night had been so dark. The sky was no longer blue, but a dead, level white; its surface was too even to give the effect of cloud; it was as though in the upper air the heat hung like a pall. There was no breeze and the sea, as colourless as the sky, was smooth and shining like the dye in a dyer's vat. The passengers were listeless; when they walked round the deck they panted and beads of sweat broke out on their foreheads. They spoke in undertones. Something uncanny and disquieting brooded over the ship, and they could not bring themselves to laugh. A feeling of resentment arose in their hearts; they were alive and well, and it exasperated them that, so near, a man should be dying and by the fact (which was after all no concern of theirs) so mysteriously affect them. A planter in the smoking-room over a gin sling said brutally what most of them felt, though none had confessed.

'Well, if he's going to peg out,' he said, 'I wish he'd hurry up and get it over. It gives me the creeps.'

The day was interminable. Mrs Hamlyn was

thankful when the dinner hour arrived. So much time, at all events, was passed. She sat at the doctor's table.

'When do we reach Aden?' she asked.

'Some time tomorrow. The captain says we shall sight land between five and six in the morning.'

She gave him a sharp look. He stared at her for a moment, then dropped his eyes and reddened. He remembered that the woman, the fat woman sitting on the bungalow steps, had said that Gallagher would never see the land. Mrs Hamlyn wondered whether he, the sceptical, matter-of-fact young doctor, was wavering at last. He frowned a little, and then, as though he sought to pull himself together, looked at her once more.

'I shan't be sorry to hand over my patient to the hospital people at Aden, I can tell you,' he said.

Next day was Christmas Eve. When Mrs Hamlyn awoke from a troubled sleep the dawn was breaking. She looked out of her porthole and saw that the sky was clear and silvery; during the night the haze had melted, and the morning was brilliant. With a lighter heart she went on deck. She walked as far forward as she could go. A late star twinkled palely close to the horizon. There was a shimmer on the sea as though a loitering breeze passed playful fingers over its surface. The light was exquisitely soft, tenuous like a budding wood in spring, and crystalline so that it reminded you of the bubbling of water in a mountain brook. She turned to look at the sun rising rosy in the east, and saw coming towards her the doctor. He wore his uniform; he had not been to bed all night; he was dishevelled and he walked, with bowed shoulders, as though he were dog-tired. She knew at once that Gallagher was dead. When he came up to her she saw that he was crying. He looked so young then that her heart went out to him. She took his hand.

'You poor dear,' she said. 'You're tired out.'

'I did all I could,' he said. 'I wanted so awfully to save him.'

His voice shook and she saw that he was almost hysterical.

'When did he die?' she asked.

He closed his eyes, trying to control himself, and his lips trembled. 'A few minutes ago.'

Mrs Hamlyn sighed. She found nothing to say. Her gaze wandered across the calm, dispassionate and ageless sea. It stretched on all sides of them as infinite as human sorrow. But on a sudden her eyes were held, for there, ahead of them on the horizon, was something which looked like a precipitous and massy cloud. But its outline was too sharp to be a cloud's. She touched the doctor on the arm.

'What's that?'

He looked at it for a moment and under his sunburn she saw him grow white.

'Land.'

Once more Mrs Hamlyn thought of the fat Malay woman who sat silent on the steps of Gallagher's bungalow. Did she know?

They buried him when the sun was high in the heavens. They stood on the lower deck and on the hatches, the first- and second-class passengers, the white stewards and the European officers. The missionary read the burial service.

'Man that is born of woman hath but a short time to live, and is full of misery. He cometh up, and is cut down, like a flower; he fleeth as it were a shadow, and never continueth in one stay.'

Pryce looked down at the deck with knit brows. His teeth were tightly clenched. He did not grieve, for his heart was hot with anger. The doctor and the consul stood side by side. The consul bore to a nicety the expression of an official regret, but the doctor, clean-shaven now, in his neat fresh uniform and his gold braid, was pale and harassed. From him Mrs Hamlyn's eyes wandered to Mrs Linsell. She was pressed against her husband, weeping, and he was holding her hand tenderly. Mrs Hamlyn did not know why this sight singularly affected her. At that moment of grief, her nerves distraught, the little woman went by instinct to the protection and support of her husband. But then Mrs Hamlyn felt a little shudder pass through her and she fixed her eyes on the seams in the deck, for she did not want to see what was untoward. There was a pause in the reading. There were various movements. One of the officers gave an order. The missionary's voice continued.

'Forasmuch as it has pleased Almighty God of his great mercy to take unto himself the soul of our dear brother here departed, we therefore commit his body to the deep, to be turned into corruption, looking for the resurrection of the body when the sea shall give up its dead.'

Mrs Hamlyn felt the hot tears flow down her cheeks. There was a dull splash. The missionary's voice went on.

When the service was finished the passengers scattered; the second-class passengers returned to their quarters and a bell rang to summon them to luncheon. But the first-class passengers sauntered aimlessly about the promenade deck. Most of the men made for the smoking-room and sought to cheer themselves with whiskies and sodas and with gin slings. But the consul put up a notice on the board outside the dining-saloon summoning the passengers to a meeting. Most of them had an idea for what purpose it was called and at the appointed hour they assembled. They were more cheerful than they had been for a week and they chattered with a gaiety which was only subdued by a mannerly reserve. The consul, an eye-glass in his eye, said that he had gathered them together to discuss the question of the fancy-dress ball on the following day. He knew they all had the deepest sympathy for Mr Gallagher and he would have proposed that they should combine to send an appropriate message to the deceased's relatives; but his papers had been examined by the purser and no trace could be found of any relative or friend with whom it was possible to communicate. The late Mr Gallagher appeared to be quite alone in the world. Meanwhile he (the consul) ventured to offer his sincere sympathy to the doctor who, he was quite sure, had done everything that was possible in the circumstances.

'Hear, hear,' said the passengers.

They had all passed through a very trying time, proceeded the consul, and to some it might seem that it would be more respectful to the deceased's memory if the fancy-dress ball were postponed till New Year's Eve. This, however, he told them frankly was not his view, and he was convinced that Mr Gallagher himself would not have wished it. Of course it was a question for the majority to decide. The doctor got up and thanked the consul and the passengers for the kind things that had been said of him, it had of course been a very trying time, but he was authorised by the captain to say that the captain expressly wished all the festivities to be carried out on Christmas Day as though nothing had happened. He (the doctor) told them in confidence that the captain felt the passengers had got into a rather morbid state and thought it would do them all good if they had a jolly good time on Christmas Day. Then the missionary's wife rose and said they mustn't think only of themselves; it had been arranged by the Entertainment Committee that there should be a Christmas tree for the children immediately after the first-class passengers' dinner, and the children had been looking forward to seeing everyone in fancy dress; it would be too bad to disappoint them; she yielded to no one in her respect for the dead and she sympathised with anyone who felt too sad to think of dancing just then. Her own heart was very heavy, but she did feel it would be merely selfish to give way to a feeling which could do no good to anyone. Let them think of the little ones. This very much impressed the passengers. They wanted to forget the brooding terror which had hung over the boat for so many days, they were alive and they wanted to enjoy themselves; but they had an uneasy notion that it would be decent to exhibit a certain grief. It was quite another matter if they could do as they wished from altruistic motives. When the consul called for a show of hands everyone but Mrs Hamlyn and one old lady who was rheumatic held up an eager arm.

'The ayes have it,' said the consul. 'And I venture to congratulate the meeting on a very sensible decision.'

It was just going to break up when one of the planters got on his feet and said he wished to offer a suggestion. In the circumstances didn't they all think it would be as well to invite the second-class passengers? They had all come to the funeral that morning. The missionary jumped up and seconded the motion. The events of the last few days had drawn them all together, he said, and in the presence of death all men were equal. The consul again addressed them. This matter had been discussed at a previous meeting and the conclusion had been reached that it would be pleasanter for the second-class passengers to have their own party, but circumstances alter cases, and he was distinctly of the opinion that their previous decision should be reversed.

'Hear, hear,' said the passengers.

A wave of democratic feeling swept over them and the motion was carried by acclamation. They separated light-heartedly, they felt charitable and kindly. Everyone stood everyone else drinks in the smoking-room.

And so, on the following evening, Mrs Hamlyn put on her fancy-dress. She had no heart for the gaiety before her, and for a moment had thought of feigning illness, but she knew no one would believe her, and was afraid to be thought affected. She was dressed as Carmen and she could not resist the vanity of making herself as attractive as possible. She darkened her eyelashes and rouged her cheeks. The costume suited her. When the bugle sounded and she went into the saloon she was received with flattering surprise. The consul (always a humorist) was dressed as a ballet-girl and was greeted with shouts of delighted laughter. The missionary and his wife, self-conscious but pleased with themselves, were very grand as Manchus. Mrs Linsell, as Columbine, showed all that was possible of her very pretty legs.

Her husband was an Arab sheikh and the doctor was a Malay sultan.

A subscription had been collected to provide champagne at dinner and the meal was hilarious. The company had provided crackers in which were paper hats of various shapes and these the passengers put on. There were paper streamers too which they threw at one another and little balloons which they beat from one to the other across the room. They laughed and shouted. They were very gay. No one could say that they were not having a good time. As soon as dinner was finished they went into the saloon where the Christmas tree, with candles lit, was ready, and the children were brought in, shrieking with delight, and given presents. Then the dance began. The second-class passengers stood about shyly round the part of the deck reserved for dancing and occasionally danced with one another.

'I'm glad we had them,' said the consul, dancing with Mrs Hamlyn. 'I'm all for democracy, and I think they're very sensible to keep themselves to themselves.'

But he noticed that Pryce was not to be seen, and when an opportunity presented asked one of the second-class passengers where he was.

'Blind to the world,' was the answer. 'We put him to bed in the afternoon and locked him up in his cabin.'

The consul claimed her for another dance. He was very facetious. Suddenly Mrs Hamlyn felt that she could not bear it any more, the noise of the amateur band, the consul's jokes, the gaiety of the dancers. She knew not why, but the merriment of those people passing on their ship through the night and the solitary sea affected her on a sudden with horror. When the consul released her she slipped away and, with a look to see that no one had noticed her, ascended the companion to the boat-deck. Here everything was in darkness. She walked softly to a spot where she knew she would be safe from all intrusion. But she heard a faint laugh and she caught sight in a hidden corner of a Columbine and a Malay sultan. Mrs Linsell and the doctor had resumed already the flirtation which the death of Gallagher had interrupted.

Already all those people had put out of their minds with a kind of ferocity the thought of that poor lonely man who had so strangely died in their midst. They felt no compassion for him, but resentment rather, because on his account they had been ill-at-ease. They seized upon life avidly. They made their jokes, they flirted, they gossiped. Mrs Hamlyn remembered what the consul had said, that among Mr Gallagher's papers no letter could be found, not the name of a single friend to whom the news of his death might be sent, and she knew not why this seemed to her unbearably tragic. There was something mysterious in a man who could pass through the world in such solitariness. When she remembered how he had come on deck in Singapore, so short a while since, in such rude health, full of vitality, and his arrogant plans for the future, she was seized with dismay. Those words of the burial service filled her with a solemn awe: 'Man that is born of woman hath but a short time to live, and is full of misery. He cometh up, and is cut down, like a flower. . . ' Year in, year out, he had made his plans for the future, he wanted to live so much and he had so much to live for, and then just when he stretched out his hand – oh, it was pitiful; it made all the other distresses of the world of small account. Death with its mystery was the only thing that really mattered. Mrs Hamlyn leaned over the rail and looked at the starry sky. Why did people make themselves unhappy? Let them weep for the death of those they loved, death was terrible always, but for the rest, was it worth while to be wretched, to harbour malice, to be vain and uncharitable? She thought again of herself and her husband and the woman he so strangely loved. He too had said that we live to be happy so short a time and we are so long dead. She pondered long and intently, and suddenly, as summer lightning flashes across the darkness of the night, she made a discovery which filled her with tremulous surprise; for she found that in her heart was no longer anger with her husband nor jealousy of her rival. A notion dawned on some remote horizon of her consciousness and like the morning sun suffused her soul with a tender, blissful glow. Out of the tragedy of that unknown Irishman's death she gathered elatedly the courage for a desperate resolution. Her heart beat quickly, she was impatient to carry it into effect. A passion for self-sacrifice seized her.

The music had stopped, the ball was over; most of the passengers would have gone to bed and the rest would be in the smoking-room. She went down to her cabin and met no one on the way. She took her writing-pad and wrote a letter to her husband.

My dear – It is Christmas Day and I want to tell you that my heart is filled with kindly thoughts towards both of you. I have been foolish and unreasonable. I think we should allow those we care for to be happy in their own way, and we should care for them enough not to let it make us unhappy. I want you to know that I grudge you none of the joy that has so strangely come into your life. I am no longer jealous, nor hurt, nor vindictive. Do not think I shall be unhappy or lonely. If ever you feel that you need me, come to me, and I will welcome you with a cheerful spirit and without reproach or ill-will. I am most grateful for all the years of happiness and of tenderness that you gave me, and in return I wish to offer you an affection which makes no claim on you and is, I hope, utterly disinterested. Think kindly of me and be happy, happy, happy.

She signed her name and put the letter into an envelope. Though it would not go till they reached Port Said she wanted to place it at once in the letter-box. When she had done this, beginning to undress, she looked at herself in the glass. Her eyes were shining and under her rouge her colour was bright. The future was no longer desolate, but bright with a fair hope. She slipped into bed and fell at once into a sound and dreamless sleep.